Love
&
Madness

Rev. Date 8/28/2016

Published By

RockHill Publishing LLC
PO Box 62241
Virginia Beach, VA 23466-2241
www.rockhillpublishing.com

Love
&
Madness

By Athina Paris

PART ONE

CHAPTER ONE

1975

'Sofia,' a little concern seeped into Sister Margareta's voice. 'Are you sure you want to be doing this? It's such a beautiful day,' she pointed to the heavens. 'Shouldn't you be outside doing something more appropriate to your age?'

Sofia smiled. 'But I love marking the little ones' books,' she held the basket up, where about twenty exercise books sat in a neat pile.

'And I am so thankful that you find the time to help me. I am inundated with all these problems... Mother Superior is under immense pressure. We are not doing as well as we should, and there is even talk of possible closure.'

Sofia's brown eyes widened in surprise. 'Oh, I'm so sorry to hear it, I didn't realise.'

'Well,' Sister Margareta gave her a reassuring smile. 'Whatever happens, it will only be by year's end as we are committed to all our girls until then. So, at least you will be able to finish your school career in peace.'

'I thank you for that.' Sofia gazed at the high convent walls where a creeper tumbled indolently over the thick wall, the cobbled path she had walked thousands of times wound gently round the bend, and the cypress trees stood guard. She felt sad at the possibility that it could all simply end.

'You know, it is true,' Sister Margareta continued. 'When doors close in one place others open elsewhere.' Reaching the gate, she swung its wide mouth open and with a caress, let her hand run along its weather-beaten wood and metal studs.

'I had a good time here,' Sofia sighed. 'And I always thought that after I qualified I would teach here.'

'Yes, that was something I was also looking forward to. But those children who will eventually get you have no idea what a blessing you will be to them.'

Sofia dropped her gaze shyly. 'Thank you Sister Margareta, you have always been encouraging.'

'I still think you should be swimming or doing something fun,' Sister Margareta pointed to the basket.

'This is fun.' A gorgeous smile spread across Sofia's face. 'And it's hardly hard work.'

'Okay then, go enjoy your afternoon.' Sister Margareta held the gate open. 'And don't forget to write all those positive little messages. The children love it when you mark their books.' She laughed. 'And they are all doing better in English because they want to impress you so hard.'

'That is sweet.' Sofia lifted a hand in greeting. 'Goodbye Sister Margareta, see you tomorrow.'

Turning left, Sofia stopped then walked to the end of the block. Unexpectedly, a boy on a bicycle flipped around the corner, clearly out of control. She screamed, he screamed, and his three friends, all on bicycles, screamed. She threw herself against the wall, dropping everything she was carrying, and within seconds, the exhibitionists disappeared. She sat there a moment, a hand on her chest, feeling her pounding heart. About to get to her feet, she saw a hand outstretched to her.

Glancing up, she recognised the young man she had noticed a couple of times during the last few months in the park across the convent.

'Are you all right?' Pulling her to her feet, he gave her a quick appraisal. She was almost certainly from one of the Mediterranean countries. Not what one would call exotic but pretty, with beautiful dark hair and kind brown eyes.

'Friends of yours?'

'No, just school kids. Robert Thomas Powell.' He liked to say his entire name when introducing himself. It made him feel important to carry his two grandfathers' names.

She watched the blue gaze intently, light hair blowing in the wind, and a nice smile. She placed her hand in his. 'Sofia Andriotti.'

'Pleased to meet you,' he quickly gathered the pile of exercise books into the basket again, grabbed her discarded school bag, and handed them to her. Then sauntering across the street, he got onto his motorcycle and rode away.

Robert leaned against the tree, stretched his lithe legs over the motorcycle seat, and gazed upward. Gnarled branches swayed and nodded in the breeze, revealing intricate web-like patterns against the pale blue sky, as if it were a living puzzle. Quite possibly, this was the last season the oak would stand here. Ancient and decayed, exposed roots gave it a crab-like appearance. Feeling pity for the wasted giant, he pulled a drawing pad from the saddlebag and captured some of its last moments of glory.

A noise across the street interrupted his concentration. Amused, he watched as the same four boys arrived. Five minutes later, the convent's metal-studded gate swung open, pouring out dozens of schoolgirls. Seeing the boys, they did what girls do to valiant heroes, pretend to ignore them. Robert smiled, understanding the game rules well.

Laughter and giggling floated towards him as some threw him furtive glances. Over the months he had been coming here, a few had been bold enough to start conversations but he had quickly and politely let them know that he had neither the time nor the inclination to support teenage fantasies. As the street became vacant, the boys started spinning and flipping again.

Hearing the gate swing its wide mouth almost shut, Robert glimpsed Sofia slip through the gap and grinned when the boys disappeared at the sight of her. Beyond sight, a woman's voice said something and both laughed, then, closing the gate, she went about her duties behind its comforting protection. He watched Sofia with interest. Every day, she did exactly the same thing. She stood there a moment, as if she went through her walk home plan mentally, before she tackled it physically.

'Sofia,' He greeted days later, as he turned the corner on foot.

'Hello. Where's your bike?' She tried to balance a pile of books under one arm.

'Hopefully still in the park. May I carry some of those?'

She gave him part of the load.

'Where's your basket?'

'Sister Margareta needed it for something.' She dismissed with a hand. 'Robert, right?'

He nodded and fell into step beside her. 'I've never seen you walk home with friends, don't you have any?'

'I stay behind to help Sister Margareta. She says it's part of my training.'

'Don't tell me...'

A hint of a smile crossed her lips. 'I want to be a teacher.'

He sighed visibly. 'I thought you were about to say nun.'

'Strangely,' she told him conspirationally.'It never crossed my mind.'

They chatted about nothing in particular and he noticed that she was curious and smart.

'Do you have brothers or sisters?' She asked.

'Two younger brothers, and you?'

'I have one older brother, Andrea. He and his wife Sarah live in England. But right now,' she told him brightly. 'I want to hear about yours.'

'Charles,' Robert took a deep breath. 'There's a crazy for you. Will try anything at least once and is afraid of absolutely nothing. Before mom died she used to say that he would be the death of her.'

'I'm sorry.' She commiserated and placed a finger on his arm.

It felt as if a ladybird had made a pit stop. 'One gets used to it.'

'So, was Charles the death of her?'

'No, she had cancer. Now William... William is a sensitive boy and tragedies affect him deeply; maybe because he lost her so young. He is also very talented, an exquisite poet.'

'I live here.'

Glancing at the freshly painted house and manicured garden, Robert nodded approval.

'After helping me carry these books I feel awful that I can't invite you in, papa's rules.' She told him apologetically.

'Not to worry, my lady.' He bowed.

She giggled. 'Thank you, Robert.'

'Have a nice day and I'll see you tomorrow.' Waiting until she was in the house, he returned to the park.

'Mama is not too bad but papa is strict.' Sofia said as they sat on the grass.

They had taken to spending time in the park, as it was mostly safe from prying eyes. She had never had cause to dislike her neighbours but one might innocently mention seeing them together. Michael Andriotti was not one for allowing anything he imagined out of his control.

Robert was curious about her family, so she explained how they had immigrated from Greece ten years previously and owned the local grocery store. 'But,' she added with a smile. 'Must be a Greek thing because what he is really interested in is hotels. So he's saving for his perfect place.'

'Is that what he calls it?'

'Yes, but mama doesn't really want to hear about it because he has a heart condition. She believes pursuit of this reckless idea might kill him.'

'She might have a point; then again, it's not as if he would run the place singlehandedly.'

Sofia nodded. 'Oh but he complains endlessly at her unfairness, and only calms down when Andrea is here.' Sofia continued. 'Though, it wasn't always like that. When Andrea met Sarah – she was holidaying here from England – there were constant fights. Papa wanted to know nothing about her; she wasn't Greek, couldn't cook, blonde, too thin, too this and that, the list was endless. Andrea completely ignored him and followed her to London.'

'How did he take that?'

'Not well, but we weren't aware of his problem then. Although, he seems to feel worse when he is not getting his way.'

'It's called the martyr syndrome. I ignore it. What do they do?'

She smiled. 'They run an inn. It's the Andriotti thing, we love to serve.'

'Then that also explains why you want to teach.'

'Sorry I haven't asked before, but what do you do?'

Robert shifted on the grass. 'Right now, I'm pretending to be an architect.'

'Pretending,'

'I went to University but gave it up last June. That did not go down well with my father. So it's eighteen months down the drain.' He announced sarcastically. 'And he does not approve of what I really want to do.'

'Which is what?' She asked curiously.

'Photography. According to him, it's not a career, and definitely not worthy of a Powell.'

'Yes, fathers are very hard to please.'

'Anyway, let's just leave it because I usually get upset. So, are you an aunty yet?' He teased.

'No. Quite unfairly, papa tells whoever wants to listen that they will remain childless because they refused to follow good advice – his, naturally.' She looked thoughtful. 'If they suddenly announced that she was expecting, he would probably have cardiac arrest. I don't know which is worse, to die of disappointment or happiness. Either way you are still dead.'

'For sure,' he pushed the drawing pad aside and regarded her. Unable to control himself any longer, he reached for her face and very softly let his lips brush hers. She didn't move, her eyes merely following his. As his pulse raced and urged him on, he stroked the soft cheek and let her go. 'I think it's time you went home.'

Sitting behind his desk, Robert swivelled the chair around to stare at the wall. Dozens of girls had crossed his path but none had affected him the way Sofia did. She was innocent, straightforward, and often aroused feelings of guilt as he remembered she was barely eighteen. Nevertheless, she was like a fever, occupying his mind like no one else, almost driving him insane as he longed to touch her.

'Robert,' Benjamin broke into his daydream. 'Go get me Louw's plans. Broken leg or not this drawing from home is causing unnecessary upheaval. I want those blueprints here, today.'

'Sorry father,' Robert glanced at the time. 'Wild horses would not drag me from what I have planned.'

Benjamin looked as if he were about to explode; however, he asked calmly. 'Yes, tell me about what it is you do that Powells – where you owe your undivided attention – cannot keep you away from.'

Robert grabbed his leather jacket. 'Ask someone else. Besides, I had mother's car taken to the garage and have to pick it up.'

Benjamin acquired an expression of displeasure that would have intimidated anyone else. 'You dare say no to me?'

'Why not, it's the seventies, the age of selfishness, debauchery, and disobedience. Didn't you know that all kids have gone mad?' Robert grinned, and waving, disappeared down the corridor.

'Where are we?' Sofia stared in awe at the large house.

'My backyard. We have a guest-house by the pool and Munro prepared something special.'

'Your butler... what will he tell your father?'

'Nothing. He was loyal to mother and now is to my brothers and me.' Accelerating up the driveway, Robert parked the red MG under a tree.

She gasped as she saw the beautifully decorated interior. 'Should we even be here?'

'If father can have slobs traipsing all over the place, why not us?' Opening a drawer, he took out a camera and started clicking.

She touched the back of a chair and sat down. 'Yours?' She pointed to the walls covered in black and white photographs. 'They're wonderful.'

'Glad I impress someone.' He gave her a lopsided smile. 'Which is why they are here and not at the house. It's my double-edged sword.'

Turning in the chair, she hooked a leg over the side. 'Explain,'

'Design is design, right? not where father is concerned. So half my talent is commended and the other half is reviled. I'm so tired of counting discussions, disagreements, and disputes I've had since my mother's death.'

'So he wants you to design but not with a camera.' She pointed at the walls again. 'Pity, you're excellent. Of course I've never seen your other designs.'

'The problem is that I'm not bad at those either. But this is my dream, the reason why I quit architecture school, but somehow, he bamboozled me into joining Powells Inc., where I draw every day. And I feel like an animal caught in a trap. But let's leave all the complaining for another day. Today, we are going to have a grand time.' Offering her a hand, he led her to the table Munro had prepared.

Sofia smiled.

Noticing, he asked curiously. 'What are you smiling about?'

'Is this a date?'

He returned the smile. 'Well, I didn't want to label it, but it sort of is.'

The meal was exceptional, and she told him to thank Munro for taking such care to please them.

Robert nodded, and she had no idea how much better everything tasted as he gazed at her. Innocently, she couldn't hide how breathless she felt when their eyes locked and he was finding the exercise quite the aphrodisiac.

Suddenly, she announced, 'Mother Superior finally told us today that the convent is closing at the end of the year.'

'Why?' He gathered a few juice bottles and started mixing two drinks.

'Financially viable, upkeep, expensive, and public schools.' She arched her brows. 'The words I remember from her long speech during assembly.'

'It's not really going to affect you, is it?'

Sofia accepted the drink offered. 'No, I'll be off to teacher's college. It's still sad; I wanted to teach there.'

Holding her hand, he led her to the sofa.

Sipping the drinks in silence, their eyes met with anticipation and promises not yet made. Nervously, she swallowed the glass's contents and stared at its emptiness.

He couldn't understand how such a simple reaction could turn him on. Taking the glass away, he pulled her up with him, leaned over, and kissed her. Just short of twenty-one, he was Valentino in comparison. Dating since seventeen, he had a few years in the art of lovemaking, Sofia… At eighteen, he wondered if she had ever held a boy's hand, but her eager responses were enough to drive any numb male heart crazy. Her eyes so beautiful filled with desire that he couldn't have stopped had a truck crashed through the wall. Leading her to the bedroom, he kept asking if she was okay, if she liked what he did, if he should stop…

'Never stop,' her breath was warm and sweet between kisses. 'Teach me.'

So he guided her into a world where only sensations existed, where neither was in control, where everything became a blur of wondrous delight. He had always speculated why the comparison of girls and flowers but as he gazed into her eyes as she gave herself to him, he thought of orchids. Beautiful white orchids that seemed fragile but could withstand the strongest blizzard. He swore under his breath as he held her tightly in his arms. 'I'm sorry— No, I'm not, I just wasn't thinking.'

She closed her eyes, letting the tears escape.

He was startled to hear a sob. 'Sofia, look at me.'

She turned slowly.

In feather-like gestures, he kissed the tears away. 'Did you think I brought you here only for this?'

She nodded.

'I admit; it has been on my mind ever since I laid eyes on you, but it's not the only reason. Don't you know that I love you, that only you can make me this happy?'

Her voice came unsteadily. 'I'm not a mere conquest?'

'You have got it all wrong.' He put gentle hands to her face. 'You are the conqueror for you have vanquished me.'

Robert pushed the motorcycle into the garage and began driving the MG permanently. Benjamin watched with nervous interest and wondered if he was not about to regret having given his first-born the chance he often doubted he deserved. Instead, Robert surprised him, having a commitment to work seldom seen in anyone young. Reluctantly, Benjamin nodded approval, congratulating himself for having exercised patience.

Born to dirt-poor parents in London, Benjamin had left at age fifteen after losing both to some disease he could barely recall, promising to return only after making his first million.

Just able to scrape enough money together to pay for a voyage that took him away from the dreary existence, he found himself on the shores of South Africa. There, he realised that one could make a fortune, if one knew how; Benjamin Powell did. As he first walked the streets of Cape Town and later those of Johannesburg, he noticed everywhere he went new buildings darting up. Wasting no time, he joined a construction company as a bricklayer, attended night classes, and read every scrap of information possible.

Never spending an unnecessary penny, he had accumulated a small fortune by his twenty-second birthday, with which he started Powells.

A man of power needs a certain kind of woman and he made certain he found the best. Miss Elaine Nichols was not only a beautiful only child but also extremely wealthy – her family having made their fortune in diamonds.

They were married within months and Robert soon made his appearance in the world. Two more sons followed; Charles and William, and Benjamin knew that he had started an empire. Many tried to emulate him, few succeeded, and countless envious at how easy everything seemed for him. Money, power, position; he had them all.

Then tragedy struck. Elaine began complaining of a pain in her stomach but instead of going to the doctor for diagnosis and treatment, she took to consuming large amounts of alcohol to numb it. When she finally collapsed into a coma and died, no one knew if the cancer or the alcohol had killed her.

Subsequently, women came and went through Benjamin's life and he discovered that his freedom had become a target for nubile socialites, the last being more determined than the previous. Stubbornly, he hardened his heart. His sons and their futures mattered, especially Robert's. He needed no woman's interference.

Now, Benjamin watched his eldest son proudly, aware that Robert had over the months become happier and more dashing. Just a pity he had dropped out of Architect School. A Powell with talent and formal education – something Benjamin regretted not possessing – was exactly what Powells needed.

Curiosity growing, Benjamin questioned Robert about his interests, but the more he tried to discover, the more secretive the boy became. "Where the hell does he go?" He wondered until he could contain himself no longer. 'Get me Hamilton.' He demanded from his secretary.

Hamilton was in his mid-thirties, with a talent for getting things done in mysterious ways. He snooped around sites, men's working areas, and didn't shy away from a few dirty tricks to get the boss a contract or two, and he always had papers, files, or folders. 'You sent for me, Mr Powell?'

'Yes.' Benjamin motioned him in. 'From Monday, you will follow my son, Robert.'

'Sir?' Even Hamilton was surprised.

'I have no idea what he does, where he goes, who he sees.'

'Just follow?'

'Take pictures, get names, the usual.' A wave of the hand dismissed Hamilton, his blue eyes glinting displeasure.

Two weeks later, Hamilton had a pile of photographs, a report of intensely researched information, and a giant headache. 'Here, Mr Powell,' he handed over the large envelope.

Benjamin poured the contents onto the desk and picked a photograph. A smile spread on his lips. 'At least he has taste.' Then he picked another. 'What's this?'

'A grocery—'

'I can see that!' Benjamin grabbed the file. 'What's this child's name?'

'Andriotti. When I first heard it I thought it might be Italian, it's Greek.'

'Is there a difference? Is this serious?' Benjamin thundered.

Hamilton pointed to a picture where the young lovers lay in each other's arms. In the guesthouse's bed!

Benjamin was livid. Paging through the photographs, he stopped on the neat white house. 'I doubt the Taj Mahal would impress me right now. I slaved to get out of the gutter, travelled an ocean to make a new life, and now I'm going to let my son drag me back there? Not bloody likely!'

'Just as you succeeded, so have they, Mr Powell. In fact, Mr Andriotti is considering some excellent opportunities in hotels—'

'Hotels?' He ground the word out. 'Leave me, I need to think.'

'So, who is doing what these school holidays?' Robert queried over dinner one evening in March.

'Father wants to drag us to England.' The eighteen-year-old Charles told him. 'I'd rather go to Durban with my friends. The water is still warm.'

'Me too,' William nodded.

Everyone knew Benjamin was a workaholic, who went nowhere during the year, unless it involved Powells. The only time he condescended on himself was three weeks over Christmas and only because the construction fraternity closed. However, in the last ten years, he had taken to making trips back to England and developed a friendship with James Dawes, who was quickly becoming one of Europe's most sought-after architects.

'Work?' Robert queried.

'Not quite.' Benjamin said, his mind trying to formulate the plan that still eluded him.

'I'd rather go to Greece. The cost is the same and to be honest, I have no wish to see Janet so soon after

Christmas.' Janet was James' daughter, who, somehow, tested everyone's sanity. When younger, her attitude had amused him, now, he found it annoying.

Dreamily, Robert recalled that afternoon. They had spent a crazy time in the guesthouse and he had given Sofia an engraved ring with his personal design of two entwined letters, R and S.

'So,' he asked as they tumbled onto the bed. 'When can I ask your father to start dating you in public?'

'I will have to be out of school, but I'm not sure about college.' She knew her father's views on dating non-Greeks, whom he considered akin to heathens. She was too young and inexperienced to win a battle of wills and there was no way she was going to bring his wrath down on her, because she would never survive not seeing Robert. Then, there was also his heart. She often suspected him of blatantly using it as an excuse to get his way. But whether he did or not, she couldn't tempt fate.

'It's not exactly forever.' Robert kissed her. He would marry her tomorrow if he could. 'What are you doing this Easter?'

'My mom and I are going to visit my sick grandmother. Know where Lindos is now?' She teased.

'Looked it up; it's on an island called Rhodes, near Turkey. I expect there is a hotel?'

'More than one, why?'

'Mustn't forget to give me your address, I'll make sure I find you.'

She threw her arms around his neck, pulling him down to her. 'Oh, Robert.'

Gazing at his father now, Robert hoped Benjamin wasn't about to become difficult. It had been a happy day; he absolutely didn't want it to end on a sour note.

Making an extraordinary effort, Benjamin hid his rage. 'What is wrong with Janet? We have known her forever and her father is undoubtedly the best architect.' He gave Robert an accusing look. 'Something you should be considering. She is also very beautiful and—'

'Loaded.' Charles finished. 'Father, if you heard a donkey had a penny you would find him attractive.'

'Are you implying money is all I care about?' Benjamin blustered. 'But you can't deny she is lovely.'

'And she would be lovelier if she married Robert.' William joined in. 'Father, can't you see he couldn't care less if she were the queen of Sheba?'

'Yes.' Irritation showing, Benjamin waved a hand dismissively. 'Do whatever you wish.' In fact, that was probably advisable so he could formulate the plan that would get rid of Miss Andriotti for good.

'Impressive.' Benjamin flipped through the designs. 'I didn't expect you to draw while on holiday.'

A smile appeared on Robert's face. 'I had some free time.'

'Talent like yours should be encouraged and that is what I am constantly trying to do. Why don't you go back to school?' Seeing Robert's face, Benjamin added quickly. 'Actually, it's not school I had in mind. The idea came to me while I was in London. You should go over. Having talent alone is not enough, it needs to be honed, and who better to do that than James Dawes? You should want to be, not good but excellent. Powells is yours but you have to improve it with a formal education, something I never acquired, and James would guide you. Do you know what that means?'

'Had you suggested it in January, I'd have jumped at the idea, now... sorry father, I can't.'

'If your mother were here, she would agree with me.' Benjamin knew that mentioning Elaine always touched a chord.

'Perhaps,' Robert said and left the office.

Benjamin watched his son's retreating figure, his mouth set in a straight line, the icy blue eyes blazing. Opening a drawer, he took out a photograph and stared at it for a second. Throwing it back into the drawer, he banged it shut.

Robert discovered that having an idea put into one's head effectively made it impossible to ignore. Just as he saw the benefits of going, he also knew that leaving Sofia was unthinkable, however tempting the offer might sound, or for however short a time. She meant more to him than any job or money. After they married, it would be different. As he could already see their idyllic life.

'You're not paying attention.' She noticed days later.

'Just thinking about something my father is driving me crazy about.'

Reaching for his hand on the grass, she held it tight. 'Can I help?'

He told her.

'England! When?' An instant sadness appeared in her drowning eyes.

Lifting her face, he wiped the tears tenderly. 'I can't go without you.'

'But it's your future, Robert.'

'You are my future.' Pulling her into an embrace, he held her close. 'Besides, I'm not saying no, just postponing.'

Busy with homework that afternoon, she recalled Robert's news. Guilt filled her presently. She wanted him to grab the opportunity, yet she hoped he kept saying no. A black car stopped in front of the house and she watched it for a moment as it was half-hidden behind a bush. Imagining the man was visiting one of her neighbours, she was startled when the doorbell rang.

'Good afternoon, may I help you?' She wondered what he would try sell her.

The well-dressed man surprised her. 'I hope so, Miss Andriotti. I'm Benjamin Powell, Robert's father.'

'Oh! Please, come in.' She told him in confusion. 'Is something the matter?'

'It depends. I would also appreciate it if you didn't mention that I have been to see you. Robert is a trifle emotional lately and I don't want to upset him any further.'

She had often heard that secrecy was the devil's playground, which meant that she often felt contrite about hiding her relationship with Robert. As she looked at Benjamin now, she had no doubt that he was about to suggest something she would like even less. 'Would you like to sit down, perhaps have a drink?' Whatever her feelings, he was Robert's father.

'Nothing, thanks.' Benjamin made himself comfortable in an armchair. 'Robert is very talented, but right now he is being stubborn and making an awful mistake. Let me be brutally honest so neither of us has delusions as to what is being discussed. You are holding him back.'

She gasped and opened her mouth to retort.

Benjamin waved her still. 'I am a man who aspires for distinction and when it comes to my family, I am exacting.' He rose. 'Powells belongs to Robert and to one day run it successfully, he needs to broaden his horizons, to learn and grow. He's doing nothing of the sort here. However, it seems he won't go anywhere unless you give him permission to do so. You have a hold on him I never imagined possible, something I don't like but obviously have to accept.

'He didn't listen to me before he met you, came and went as he pleased, but at least spent eighteen months in Architect School. Now, he won't budge. Is it fair to expect him to give up his future?' He fixed his cold gaze on her. 'You think you know Robert but I have been his father far longer and let me tell you what I do know. One day, this exciting romance will become old news. I've seen it happen before and it's never pleasant. What will you do then, when he can no longer stand the sight of you? When recriminations and accusations fly? How can you destroy the best chance he will ever have?'

'Mr Powel,' she began as calmly as she could. 'I never asked and I definitely never told him not to go. He made the decision on his own, even before I knew.' She announced, highly stung by his insinuation.

'Come, Miss Andriotti. Women know perfectly well words don't have to be spoken for men to understand the message. So my question remains, is it fair?'

Neither was what he was doing but that was not going to stop him. 'Mr Powell,' she said as she battled with her furious heart. 'What is it you want me to do?'

'Tell him to grab this opportunity, for another might not come along. It's true I have money to do almost anything, but not everyone can receive training under one of the world's best architects, and that is what he's refusing. Therefore, do I have your word on this matter?'

He did not offer his hand and she knew that she had no wish to touch him in any way.

After seeing him to the door, she wandered through the house as if dazed. She cried, talked to herself, and although disliking it intensely, agreed with him.

Once she convinced Robert of the advantages, possibilities, and opportunities, there was no turning back. She cried night and day, stopped eating, and became a nervous wreck, but never did she let him see the deep hurt, or that the idea hadn't been hers. Often, she imagined that her heart had exploded for it felt as if it was having trouble fitting in her chest. But now, there was nothing to do but bear it.

'I faithfully promise to write and send photographs often. It will be good practice. I'll try my best to come home after three months, but Christmas is definitely on.' He gazed at her longingly and saw the brimming eyes. 'Why do you push me when I have no inclination? I love you so much, it's breaking my heart.'

'Just promise that you won't forget me.'

'You say the craziest things sometimes, I love you forever.' He whispered against her face, touching the silky hair and kissing the mouth that could give him so much pleasure.

She waved as he climbed into the car and drove away. How would she survive?

Standing in the elevator, self-consciousness filled her, and tightening the jersey about her, she stared at the pattern on her shoes.

'Yes?' The secretary looked at her as she stopped in front of the desk.

'Is it possible—?'

'Hello.' Benjamin greeted surprised as he appeared in his office's doorway, then motioned for her to follow him quickly. Sinking into the leather chair, he grinned. 'So, how may I be of assistance?'

'Now that I'm here, I feel silly.'

'No, no, go ahead. What do you need?'

'Robert's address. I know he didn't have one when he left but I expect you might know where he is staying.' Then it occurred to her. "Robert didn't know because then I would know."

His next words confirmed her sense of foreboding. 'I'm afraid he is not going to be in London for a while. Anything else I can help you with, perhaps some money?'

She saw how utterly phoney everything about him was, seeing the smile of a high priest about to sacrifice a victim at the altar. A blank expression plastered itself on her face as he began to ramble. And had he just offered her money? One thing she knew, this man had no intention of helping her or of bringing Robert back, not even giving her a simple address, for this had been his plan from the beginning. What a fool she had been!

But however smart he was, they were not complete idiots either; Robert had her address. Glancing around the room, she noticed how screamingly expensive everything was. Wide mahogany desk, dark shelves filled with leather-bound volumes, blue silk drapes on the windows and a large painting behind his desk. She would forever associate the artist with this man; she didn't like either.

Patting his breast pocket, he eyed her with interest, as he was almost certain she had come for a pay-out, and he had already written the cheque, a handsome amount in anyone's language. He studied her for a second. 'Robert may not think so, but he has lost interest. There is a young woman in London, Janet; and that is the only union I will support.' Benjamin's face became hard. 'You may not have known it then but the deal is that there will be no further contact. Should you endeavour to do so, this envelope will find its way to your father.' Opening it, he spread photographs before her.

She stared in disbelief. There they walked, laughed, kissed, and… Her head shot up. 'What about…' she said with difficulty.

'Perhaps you should discuss that with your father.' He frowned, thinking her the most infuriating person he had ever had the misfortune to encounter. There was something that he intensely disliked about her, and it wasn't just that she was foreign. People who cowered and begged were easy to control, Sofia although young, was not one of them. He would never control her, much less Robert if he married her.

CHAPTER TWO

Sitting at her desk, Sofia felt as if she were on a tightrope, one that threatened to snap without warning. Lately, she only stared out of windows, and when she wasn't doing that, she was crying, wondering how she was going to extricate herself from this plight.

'Sofia,' Sister Margareta jolted her out of her distraction, and quietly led her to the Mother Superior's office.

The old lady sat in deep concentration at her desk, a frown creasing her brow. Only when Sofia approached and made a noise did she look up, and studied the girl before rising. With a grace that was as much part of her as the habit she wore, she walked over to the window, touched the curtain, and then turned. 'Sofia, it has come to my attention that you are not performing at your usual best. I realise that you have always been different from the others, having an inner strength seldom seen in your peers and previously, I took it as a blessing, but as I look at you trying to deal with something that is so much bigger than you are, I see it threatening to overtake your very soul. It is exceedingly clear that you are in dire need of help and that is why we are here. Please Sofia, share your burden, or it will engulf you in despair.'

Sofia couldn't answer. Her head dropped as the tears of pain did likewise.

'Tell me, whatever happened to that young man you were seeing? Does this dramatic change concern him?'

Sofia looked up. 'How do you know about Robert?'

A faint smile passed over Mother Superior's lips. 'We do have some idea of what goes on outside these walls. Did you have a falling out?'

'He left.' Sofia sniffed as tears poured. 'He promised that he would write. That he wouldn't forget. It has been weeks.'

'Men have been known to promise the unattainable so they may get what one is unwilling to give freely. You would not be the first to be lied to.'

'No, Robert loves me!' However, she knew who would stop at nothing to annihilate the relationship. 'He would never abandon me, especially now.'

'Sweet innocent child, don't ever be surprised by anything you hear. Men have their own way of doing things and it is not always the right one.' She studied the girl before her. 'Sofia, was your relationship of a more intimate nature?'

Sofia fell onto her knees, thrusting herself against the black robes. 'Oh, Mother Superior, I've done something terrible...' She couldn't continue, an uncontrollable shaking raking her body.

Bending, Mother Superior pulled the girl to her feet and with immense gentleness sat her back in the chair. Taking the other, she leaned forward. 'If what I suspect is true then no amount of crying will solve it. The solution is to send you away.' She arose and took a few steps.

Sofia looked up through her tears. 'How, and what possible explanation do I give my parents? I'm in such trouble.'

'I will have your father come see me.' She saw total fear appear on the young face. 'I do not intend to mention your condition. I expect this has been confirmed by a doctor?' Seeing the girl nod, she became pensive. 'Fortunately, fate is on your side. As you are one of our top pupils and we are closing by year's end, he won't make much of it. We will send you to our sisters in Grahamstown to complete your schooling. And Rhodes University is literally on their front step...' Her kind old hand smoothed the girl's hair. 'No one should carry loads of this magnitude alone. Now, get your books and go home to rest. I will let you know what arrangements have been made.'

Things became confusing in the ensuing days. Sofia recalled her parents congratulating her but she knew she deserved none of it for she hadn't done anything right in months. Then when her father announced that it was probably for the best anyway as he had also found his dream hotel, she was no longer stunned but in shock. How was it possible that events could happen with such precision, as if orchestrated by hidden hands? Was it possible that Benjamin would go to such lengths to protect her from her father? If he had anything to do with it, it was not for her sake, or even Robert's. But for once, she didn't want to reason why.

'Mr Powell,' Mother Superior greeted in surprise. 'I wasn't expecting to see you again.'

'I have been preoccupied and it is at times like these that I am thankful I have no daughters, as the vultures never stop circling. Unhappily, right now, that very vulture just happens to be my son, which is why I have to do as much as I can.'

'Yes, I would hate to imagine what would surely happen if her father discovered the truth. As is, I informed him that she received a bursary to complete her schooling, which thankfully, is true.' She gazed at him, as if trying to decipher his motives. Unfortunately, she had seen this scenario far too many times. The only difference here was the size of the purse. 'I know that people such as yourself often endow large sums to charities, but your contribution is extraordinary, Mr Powell.'

'And I am glad to give every cent. It was part of my late wife's estate and I see no better use than to help those in need.' "And if it keeps Miss Andriotti out of my life all the better."

'As grateful as I am, I am also disappointed that it could not have been offered to save us in Johannesburg, where the need is immense...' she felt guilty at the hint, and then realised that it would have taken twenty times the amount to save this crumbling ruin.

'Well, you see, my wife grew up in Grahamstown and she always spoke of helping the community there, it was in fact, her death wish.' Not true but how would this woman know? He had sent Hamilton digging again and discovered that the Order possessed a second convent there. But best of all and most convenient, it was discreet, with tall walls and turrets.

'Of course, and Our Lord always knows best. Now I recall,' Mother Superior made a gesture. 'Sofia left a letter. Seems convinced that your son will come looking for her.'

The brat sure had guts. 'Perhaps it's best she is not told the truth. Were her father to know, would he send the law?'

'I doubt Sofia wants that. She loves him very much.'

'Do you suppose that if I sent him the letter, that he would realise how serious the situation is?'

Opening the drawer, she removed a white envelope. 'As I have been recalled to Germany sooner than I expected, I would not want it to be misplaced or lost.' If only he had given the money months ago to save this place. Now, it was beyond salvation. Mortified, she knew she was being worldly. 'If he were to change his mind, it would be a blessing.' She placed the white envelope inside a brown one, wrote Sofia's name, and handed it to him.

'Any letters, Mr Hayden?'

'One from your father; but that is not the one you are waiting for.' Every day the same question, every day the same answer, and every day Mr Hayden saw the anxious face.

"I'm going mad," Robert thought. After six letters, she had not yet replied. The last three had come back with "RETURN TO SENDER" scrawled across and he thought he must have made a mistake. Looking in the address book, he read her handwriting. "What if papa found out?" He called the house. Incredulously, the number sounded disconnected. If only someone had the sense to do something about these international lines. Glancing up, he knew he was supposed to be enjoying himself, and during the first few weeks, he had.

Arriving in London, he found he was not staying. James Dawes sent him directly to Liverpool, where he was from and still kept the original office. A furnished apartment – Benjamin's compliments – awaited, overlooking a park. There, he spent a lot of time, as it was reminiscent of the one back home. Going for long walks, he fed the ever-hungry ducks and snapped his camera continuously.

'Dreaming again?' A female voice interrupted.

Looking up, he saw Janet. Robert recalled playing with her when they were younger, but in the last two years, she had begun working on his nerves, which was nothing compared to the irritation he felt every time he saw her now.

Whether because of her name or money, she imagined everything her property, men included. During the few weeks he had been here he had already heard enough stories concerning just about every man who had had the misfortune of working for James Dawes and a few others, for him to know to give her a wide berth. Especially exasperating was that she not only displayed undisguised interest, but also managed to follow him almost everywhere he went.

'Just in the neighbourhood', she batted her lashes innocently. As far as he knew, she had not been that since her fifteenth birthday. Yet, that was hardly comparable to the vexation he felt when he saw the hordes of photographers, who followed her constantly. He had hardly settled in and the gossip columns already assumed they were an item.

He watched the strange green eyes. She was striking in her fashionable blonde hairdo and clothes, somehow reminiscent of a modern Marilyn Monroe; and a complete contrast to Sofia.

'If I were your father, I would ban you from setting foot in the office. And, Martin's is that way.' He pointed, feeling sorry for her latest conquest. Who knew? Perhaps in another time and under different circumstances the bad girl aura would have intrigued him.

'Already checked, he's not in. Besides, I prefer your company.'

'The feeling isn't mutual. You're always up to no good and I don't like it. And stop following me, one would swear Liverpool has run dry in the man department. Have anyone, do anything, just leave me out of your jaunts.'

'Ah, you had someone back home. But guess what,' she opened her eyes, made a face she imagined alluring, and passed a hand over her hips. 'She's not here, I am.'

'And a very irritating little girl you are.'

'I'm not.' She snapped crossly. 'I'm all grown-up and desirable, every man tells me so.' She stormed out of the office.

Stepping into his apartment that evening, the strange odour reached Robert instantly. 'What the hell!' Flicking switches on as he went, he walked into the bedroom where the stench was strongest. He came to a sudden halt. 'Out,' bending over, he picked some of the strewn clothes and threw them at her, then reaching the window, opened it. 'Get dressed and extinguish all this crap.' He waved his arms at the flickering candles and drifting whorls. 'What is it?'

Rolling over, Janet exposed her voluptuous naked curves. 'Lavender incense, isn't it romantic?'

'When are you going to get it? I don't want you here, woman.'

'Ah-ha, so you have noticed.' Running her hands up her body, she stopped at the breasts, licked her red lips, and pouted.

'I'm merely stating a biological fact. Now, put your clothes on and depart.' He waved his arms again to rid the room of the intoxicating smell.

Janet Dawes was not used to the word no, or to see a man turn his back on her. 'Come to bed, Robert.' She called huskily.

Turning on his heels, he went to the kitchen.

Raging, she jumped out of bed, grabbed a shoe, threw it in his general direction, and then followed him. 'Whoever she is I doubt she's better than me.'

'At what?' He searched for something in the refrigerator.

'Everything. Who is she?' Her eyes filled with curiosity.

'None of your business. And did it ever cross your vain little mind that not every male finds you attractive?' Chopping vegetables into a bowl, he ignored the fact that she was starkers.

'Your faithfulness is commendable but totally unnecessary because she would never know. Besides,' she picked a carrot from the bowl and took a bite. 'You're lying. All men I meet want to make love to me. I'm young, free, beautiful, desirable, and rich.'

'But we're feeling conceited today.'

'Well then,' her blonde mane swung round her shoulders. 'Since I'm not welcome, I'll get dressed and go home.'

'Thanks.' He didn't even look up.

Sofia glanced around the sparseness she was obviously going to become accustomed to, the narrow bed, beige carpet, desk, chair, and the closet in the corner, much what she had imagined as standard convent furniture.

The last few days had been quiet. After the state she had gotten herself into in Johannesburg, she was thankful, especially after she had made enquiries at the post office. Perhaps she wasn't aware of some disruption. No, they told her, all post to and from England, was coming, and going, as it should. That could only mean two things; either Benjamin was interfering or Robert had given up. The first was the most logical but when she thought about the second. Benjamin was so eager for Robert and Janet to form an alliance. Jealous rage filled her, her mind seeing pictures of pornographic explicitness. She felt sick.

Instantly, her mind drifted to the train trip she and Sister Margareta had undertaken. The rocking motion made her curl-up in the corner and wish she were dead. Instead, she survived the dreadful ride with Sister Margareta sitting beside her, an immense concern on her face.

'What everyone must think,' Sofia whispered in the faintly lit compartment.

Sister Margareta wiped the ashen face with a mildly cooling cloth. 'Only Mother Superior and I know. All the other Sisters are going to Kenya or Malawi, so I doubt they'll ever hear of it.'

'Do you think my mother would have understood?'

'It's hard to guess how people will react, but perhaps it is best we don't dwell on it. Let us take small steps, and they will be exceptionally arduous ones.' Sister Margareta became pensive. Why was Mother Superior sending them to Grahamstown? Then again, Johannesburg was beyond repair, and if anyone tried, it would take an absolute fortune. She had seen the derelict walkways, decaying ceilings, rusted pipes, faulty wiring, and disintegrating walls. The list was so long, it didn't surprise her in the least that the solution lay in tearing down the place. She sighed and returned her thoughts to the present. A shroud of mystery surrounded the girl's circumstances and perhaps it was prudent to begin afresh elsewhere.

'If I weren't such a coward to face my father...' Sofia broke down then, with Sister Margareta comforting her as if she were a child.

In the present, Sofia got out of bed, and went exploring. A dozen or so doors just like hers lined both sides of the long passage. She wondered how many had inmates, because what else were they? She turned into another passage at the end of which was a bright light. It was a sitting room with a large window. Looking over the parking lot, she saw the building across the street, "St Matthew's Orphanage."

Turning, she became aware of another girl. 'I'm Sofia.' She offered a hand.

The girl ignored it. 'If it makes you feel better, I'm Denise.'

Watching the lifeless eyes, Sofia sat opposite her. 'Been here long?'

'A fortnight but let me tell you something, Sofia. Don't try to make friends.' Getting to her feet, Denise left the room.

Her brutal detachment stunned Sofia. But as D-wing began receiving its tragedies, she understood. This was a time of trauma and seclusion and few wanted to make attachments that would continue beyond the duration, for they might divulge fiercely guarded secrets.

Unless spoken to, Denise kept to herself, but when endeavouring to partake in conversations, it was to make people wonder where she had come from. Her warped caustic venom was one that hurt deeply. Yet, she was the voice of reason, but so mean, that no one wanted to hear it.

School progressed at a leisurely pace, as at times, one of the teaching Sisters had to interrupt English, History, or Mathematics to console a broken heart. After seven weeks, four babies had been born and Sofia watched the inmates leave empty-handed, as most, revelled in their regained freedom.

Apart from classes, Sofia tried to fill her days with as much as she could, be it some mindless activity. This particular afternoon she was in the sitting room flicking through a magazine. She stopped suddenly, feeling as she did that ten thousand volts had struck her. She got to her feet, but the floor rushed up, and she gladly met it halfway.

'Are you all right?' Denise asked.

'What happened?'

'How should I know? You were paging through the book and then, wham!'

Gulping dryly, Sofia grabbed the magazine and went to her room. "It can't be." She thought as she read the caption, 'SOUTH AFRICAN HOOKED BY HEIRESS'

Returning to the sitting room that evening, she systematically paged through every magazine. And there he was once more with the same blonde, Janet Dawes. The girl with Benjamin's blessing!

As she spiralled towards despair, Denise was the only one who got a word edgewise, somehow keeping her sane and contrary to character, even telling her that perhaps everything would turn out all right. Sofia knew that it wouldn't. Without Robert, it couldn't.

'You have to consider adoption.' Seeing Sofia's furious glance, Denise raised her voice. 'Dream all you like but if no one minded, you wouldn't be here. You're angry, with him, yourself, and looking at the baby will only make it worse. It'll be a fresh start, just like the rest of us. And no one need ever know-'

'I would.' Sofia bolted for her room and cried for hours.

Emerging the next day, she had dark rings under her eyes. Nevertheless, she agreed, time was running out and a decision had to be made, not one where only she but also her child benefited, as there would be no Robert to bail them out.

Within days, Denise went into labour and had a stillbirth. There were no tears and no mourning, just silent acceptance, and then she was gone.

Robert found it increasingly harder to concentrate. He dreamt almost constantly of Sofia, rested little, worried a great deal, and now, knew that he had to ascertain what was happening, for something surely was. She could even be ill. Doggedly, he went about work, but flair was waning and mindless mistakes were creeping into the once inspired designs. Unable to continue, he reached for the phone and asked the operator to make the connection.

'Powell residence.'

'Charles! I'm glad I got you. How are you?'

'Okay. But why is it I know this call has nothing to do with my health?'

'Pay attention. This is what I want you to do, today!'

Hours later, they were speaking to each other again.

'So?' Robert urged.

'I don't know where she's gone because the nun I spoke to says she doesn't know who Sofia is. She's just arrived to help the others move, and she couldn't find the transfer card.'

'Crap!' Now, he understood nothing. He had written James' address in her book! No, wait, he had written the London address... So if his letters weren't getting to her, hers would definitely never get to him. He had to call the London office and check if they had kept those letters.

'Look, the place is closing down. I snooped around a bit, asked other girls. All they know is that Sofia was the first to leave. So I asked to see the Mother Superior,   she's in Germany finalising business about schools in Kenya, Malawi, or something. Running out of ideas I went to the shop.'

'Good! I hope you were discreet and polite to her parents.'

'They moved away too, so maybe it's a family thing. A Mr Eksteen bought the shop and the house. He did mention that they bought a hotel. Before you ask, he doesn't know where. What's with this girl, anyway? Under the circumstances, it's the best I could do. If you want to know more, come find out for yourself!'

'I will. Tell father I'll be there in a few days.' Robert stared at the wall. Where was she? Why hadn't she at least received and answered the first letter? Had she planned this? Angrily, he punched the desk, rattling everything on it. He had known that leaving was a bad idea. Oh, how he missed her!

That evening, Charles was making the usual spectacle of himself at dinner. Benjamin glared at him. 'Can't you at least make the effort to be more like your brothers?'

'Mentioning brothers, Robert called. Don't get excited, father, he didn't want to know about us. He's trying to find some girl and sent me on a merry chase. When I told him that I can't find her, he freaked out and said that he'll be here in a few days.'

'Does she have a name?' William asked curiously.

'Sofia, must be his girlfriend because he's climbing walls.'

'What do you mean you can't find her?' William went on.

'She moved away with her parents or something. I don't know.'

Staring at the sketch, Robert wondered why James wrote across it, "not paying attention." Mistakes were worrying, but nothing compared to the constant apprehension he felt over Sofia's unexplained disappearance. Fortunately, James didn't let any design leave his office unless he checked it personally and so saved everyone embarrassments and potential disasters.

He had called the London office and checked with whoever was in charge of the mail that no letters from Sofia had ever arrived there. No, no one knew anything.

Pushing ruler and pencil aside, Robert stood up, grabbed his jacket, and went home. He had barely closed the door when there was a knock. 'What do you want?' He asked tiredly as he saw Janet in the doorway.

'On occasion, I have been known to actually care. You haven't been eating or sleeping properly so I hope this helps.' She showed him the basket on her arm.

'I eat when necessary.'

'I didn't come to fight either, so I'll just leave it and go.' She urged him to take it.

He felt like an eel. 'I apologise and thank you. But you'll have to excuse me; I desperately need a good night's sleep.'

'I'll just set everything out.' Walking in, she went straight to the coffee table, pulled the tablecloth from the basket, and took out the contents. When done, she smiled. 'I'll collect it another day.'

'Stay and share it with me.' It was the least he could do.

'I don't mind to stay a while but I don't want anything.' She patted her stomach. 'I already had dinner.'

'Wine?' Taking the bottle in his hands, he reached for two glasses.

'Ta. May I watch the telly while you eat?'

'Sure.' He poured two glasses, handed her one and sitting down began on the dishes she had taken care to put together even if not having cooked personally. There was a delicious cottage pie, a salad and a plate of cheese. Then leaning back on the sofa with satisfaction, he slowly drifted off to sleep.

In the velvety darkness, a pair of hands ran up his body. Instinctively, he reached out. 'Sofia,' pulling her up to the sofa, he made love to her, fast and hungry, as it was the first time in many months, and later, slow and tender, the way he could truly express his love for her. Subconsciously, he imagined that her body felt, tasted, and smelled different, but his need for her was such that he pushed all doubt aside.

Snapping his eyes open, he saw the table leg. His gaze travelled up. One full wine glass glared back at him. Turning his head, he saw a figure curled a short distance away. Jumping to his feet, he pulled his pants on, grabbed the blanket with a wild gesture, and saw Janet's naked body. 'Up,' he prodded her with a foot. 'I must be bloody demented to have fallen for this Good Samaritan crap!'

'Robert,'

'Don't open your mouth, witch!' He raged. 'You drugged the wine, or everything else. You are not a woman, you're a piranha, worse than, a sex-fiend that lies in wait for the unsuspecting victim.'

'It was so beautiful.' She stretched lazily on the carpet.

'File it under memories. Now, get out!'

'So, Sofia, lucky girl.' She sat up gingerly. 'You said some strange words, what language-'

'Go now! Before I change my mind and do you an injury.' He told her and walking to the bedroom, banged the door shut.

Time passed at a snail's pace, insomnia was ever-present, and everything felt like a wound that refused to heal. Sofia took to studying at night, discovering that she could easily replace any teacher where the younger girls' education was concerned. She made the suggestion, thinking that this might be overstepping the boundaries, perhaps becoming too familiar in a world that was renowned for secrecy. Instead, not only Sister Margareta but also their new Mother Superior reacted with confident pleasure. Both stressing how perfect Sofia's gentle nature was. So with great enthusiasm, Sofia taught English, having so much to do that she almost had enough to make her forget.

A letter arrived from Johannesburg mid-November. Turning it over, she recognised old Mother Superior's handwriting. Her brows lifted. It wasn't as if this Order had taken a vow of silence or letter writing, but hadn't Mother Superior left for Germany? Tearing the brown envelope open, she found newspaper clippings, magazine pages, and a note with three words,

"I always win"

Flicking the papers in her hand, they felt like hot coals, as if just having them in her possession transported her to an unreal world, one she had to escape, or it might destroy her. Rolling everything into a ball, she dropped it in the dustbin.

So, Robert would never forget. Lies! Had everything he told her been lies? No, he had loved her, just not enough!

And with Benjamin pulling the strings, she had never stood a chance. She wished Miss Janet Dawes good luck!

Slumping onto the garden bench, tears gathered. How could she return home with a fatherless child? Papa would never sit still, keep quiet, or accept the situation. He would demand to know who was responsible for the violation of his daughter's honour and the family name. Michael Andriotti was a man of integrity and responsibility and he would expect Robert to think likewise, if not voluntarily then by force. Greeks were famous for unreasonable and irresponsible behaviour and although sorely tempted to see Robert's reaction, she refused to cheapen herself by causing a twentieth-century Greek tragedy. Let him be happy with Janet, for her and her child there was… Unable to control the tears any longer, she let them fall as she ran to the safety of her room.

Never had there been pleasant times, but now it had become unbearable, and days later, she went into labour. To her dismay, it was a particularly long and difficult delivery, and she was almost glad when sister Margareta carried the screaming baby boy away. Afterwards, she lay sedated in her lonely bed wondering why she felt as if she'd been sucked into a vacuum, where feelings were born and died in the same instant. 'My son,' she said softly. 'What can I give you? Nothing, no future, not even your father's name.' Her sobs travelled down D-wing for hours; leading everyone to believe that she would never be able to stop again.

'Sofia,' Sister Margareta called and offered a hand. 'Don't torment yourself. Although difficult, you made the right decision. Please come back to classes.' She knew these were mere words but perhaps she would eventually reach the girl in the pit. 'Someone's pain is always someone else's gain, and here, three people benefit. It is that that you must think about.'

'Should I meet them?' Sofia began tentatively.

'Oh no, the less you know about each other the better. This baby is going to start a new life; all ties with the past must be severed. You could change your mind in three, five, even ten years, and the harm you could inflict! Most of these children never know they are adopted, it would cause unspeakable distress for all involved.' Sister Margareta wiped the unstoppable tears with a kind hand.

'Did you meet them?'

'There is only a lawyer and a nurse. Which tells you these people have some means. The nurse took your ring, so perhaps they will tell him about you one day.'

Sofia nodded absent-mindedly. What she was doing was unnatural because they should be together; instead, she was changing the rhythm of life. Slowly getting to her feet, she faced Sister Margareta. 'I so wanted to name him, after my father.'

'I mentioned it but it's not up to them.' Sister Margareta held her close in her arms lovingly. 'It doesn't seem possible now but you will eventually lead a normal life again.'

"What is normal?" Sofia thought, she certainly didn't remember it.

'We must get you out of here; perhaps into a hostel.' Sister Margareta announced.

'I would prefer it if Mother Superior let me stay- there's comfort here. And if my parents heard, they would ask me home. I can't go, not yet.'

'You're right. I'll speak to Mother Superior and have you moved to our wing. It's different there, a haven of peace, prayer, and song.'

'Thank you, Sister Margareta.' Sofia told her, deeply touched by the generosity that continuously flowed from this kindly woman.

'Yes, tomorrow we move, not just your room, but on with life. Things will go better, you'll see.'

Christmas crept closer and Sofia knew that unless she was at death's door she had to go home. She almost wished she were dying. Six months was a long time for anyone who had never been away from home for longer than a few weeks, and always in the company of one of her parents, but predictably, there was no wish to return. But never would they settle for reasons or excuses, no matter how convincing and the feeling of dread grew like a tornado as she grappled with the guilt that they could guess at her secrets.

Returning from Johannesburg, Sofia enrolled at Rhodes University for a degree in English, and began spending most of her free time at the orphanage, getting as many rewards as she had her heart broken. Many nights crying and praying over the innocents whose lives she saw being decided in lawyers' and obscure brokers' offices, sometimes instinctively knowing that it was a disaster in the making and yet having no authority to intervene.

She also prayed that she might never go home again. A charade such as that put over Christmas as she pretended a gayety she was far from feeling was not good acting; it was more a silent torture that took place in her very soul. If nothing else, the knowledge of papa's deteriorating heart had half-taken her mind off the nightmarish situation, but one day, he would succumb and then she would have no choice but to return.

Exploration had become her one passion, as she particularly enjoyed visiting the old buildings. She knew most priests, pastors, and preachers in the area, and made good use of their knowledge where and when needed. In return, she had their utmost respect and willing participation in most activities concerning the orphanage.

Papa's dreaded heart attack finally happened in March, so what could she do but go support mama? Who, Sofia had noticed, was never good at confronting difficulties on her own. Papa's hospitalisation and running of the hotel were not hurdles but major obstacles and Sofia knew that her mother was ill equipped to deal with either.

She caught the train the same day, wondering how long she would be gone and if Andrea and Sarah were on their way,

After a vigil of six days, papa gave up on life. As expected, mama was devastated and suddenly became old.

'As soon as the estate is finalised I'm selling this.' Andrea pointed to the walls as they sat in the private lounge. 'Papa knew this could happen so he left everything in order. As for mama, we're taking her home. We're doing well, expanding in fact, and there's more than enough room. What about you, will you come too?'

'No, I have to finish my studies.'

'So grown-up,' Andrea smiled and leaning over, kissed his sister. 'Yes, nothing need change.'

As she travelled by train again, Sofia realised how untrue those words were. Everything had already changed. How could she imagine this time last year that so many heartaches would come her way? She had lost Robert and their son, now papa, and in a sense mama, Andrea, and Sarah too. It felt odd to know that she was alone in South Africa, but for her it had been impossible to leave. She couldn't bury everything yet, and she couldn't think of herself in England, near Robert, and yet, an infinity between them.

CHAPTER THREE

It was April and Robert had been trying to get home since November. Since then, nothing had gone right. First, there was that stupid episode with Janet. Secondly, someone broke into his apartment and stole a few items, hardly worth anything but with them had gone his passport and he discovered that it was excruciatingly difficult to replace outside South Africa. Third, Benjamin appeared with his brothers as soon as their school holidays had begun before Christmas and was extremely keen to take them on sightseeing tours. After they left, Robert tried to find Andrea, to no avail. Lastly, James requested a design for one of their celebrity clients. Now, he was sick and tired of depending on others to do what he must. Grabbing his newly acquired passport, he filled one suitcase and flew back home.

'Master Robert!' Munro greeted surprised. 'It's good to see you again, but you've lost weight. Don't the English know how to cook?'

'They cook fine, Munro. The problem is my appetite. Where's father?'

'He's in the study.'

Walking down the passage, he knocked and entered. 'Hello father.'

'What the hell are you doing here?'

Robert flopped into a chair. 'May I borrow Hamilton?'

Benjamin was clearly shaken. 'This wouldn't be about that girl-'

'Yes it is, because how can someone just disappear?'

'Fine, but there's a time limit.' Studying Robert, Benjamin realised how persistent the boy was. If only he dedicated himself to Powells that earnestly.

Three fruitless weeks followed, Robert thinking that there would never be any results because half the people involved in the search didn't care and the other half were incompetent.

'Janet!' Robert exclaimed when he walked into the living room. 'What are you doing here?'

'I could ask the same thing, but I can guess.'

'So, what brings you to Africa?'

'You,'

'Look here Janet, I told you before-'

Her green eyes flashed. 'Damn it Robert, I'm pregnant.'

'So? You're not suggesting... But, I never... not willingly that is. You drugged and raped me.'

Her expression changed at his words. 'Which court is going to believe that?'

'And what is it you expect me to do?' He passed an angry hand over his hair.

'Marry me.'

'I want to marry someone else.'

'Ah yes, the famous Sofia. Where is she?'

'I can't find her. Do you have proof of this?' He waved disdainfully towards her stomach.

'I asked my doctor to write a note.' She searched in her handbag.

'And I'm supposed to accept that as proof?'

'Do whatever you wish but tomorrow I'm seeing your family doctor and then he'll tell you all you want to know.'

'Can he tell me it's mine?'

Robert was numb with disbelief, imagining that she was pulling a fast one, but with both their fathers in the midst of the cataclysm, he had no doubt that things could only get worse. He wasn't certain what James was doing in London but Benjamin started celebrating as if a king were about to be born, and before Robert had time to recover, the engagement was announced and wedding date set.

It was the picture of a radiant Janet and a dazed Robert that Sofia had the misfortune of seeing in the newspaper, her worst fears confirmed; he'd never return to her. She was nineteen and trying to hold onto what she no longer had.

Arriving at the convent, she saw sister Margareta waiting for her.

'Is something the matter?'

'I hope not.' Sister Margareta gave her an envelope. 'It's from your brother.'

Sofia tore it open with trepidation. 'Everyone is in good health, doing very well, but selling the inn, because… They're buying something else. Oh, my goodness,' she looked at Sister Margareta. 'They are having- two babies! If they're boys, Michael, my father's name, and Andrew, my brother's English name,' tears filled her eyes, as if she needed an excuse to cry.

When Robert finally protested and rebelled against everyone who had pushed him into a situation he had no wish for, he vaguely recalled spending some time in Janet's presence. Never did he believe the child was his and when he saw the mop of jet-black hair, he knew with certainty that he hadn't fathered the helpless creature; but who had. He knew she was a witch. Deciding the farce had continued far too long, he cornered her and threatened with a scandal so awful that neither their name nor their money would save her. When she admitted that Martin was the father, Robert felt like putting her in front of a firing squad and immediately filed for divorce.

As another dreadful Christmas arrived, Robert returned to South Africa, determined to find Sofia. To Benjamin's chagrin, he hired a private investigator.

'Don't you think you've wasted enough time and money?' Benjamin asked one day.

'Why? I love her; she loves me. Don't you understand? I need to do this; even if just to hear that she doesn't want me anymore.'

'Who did you get to investigate?'

'Eric Simmons.' Robert told him tiredly. 'See you later.'

Two weeks later, the investigator had some news.

Robert stared at the report as they sat at a restaurant. 'There's no mistake?'

'None, Mr Andriotti died.' The investigator showed him an obituary and then pointed to a photograph. 'This was their hotel. The son came from England and sold everything. Where anyone is...' he shrugged his shoulders.

'She had a grandmother in Greece,' Robert wrote the name and address on a piece of paper. 'Can you find out?'

Weeks later, Robert heard it was a lost cause, the old lady was dead.

'What's wrong with you?' Benjamin asked that evening as he found Robert sitting in darkness.

'It's as if she never existed.'

'Are we talking about the girl again? Can't you just leave the damn thing alone?' Benjamin was so close to losing his temper that he knew he'd soon give himself away.

Robert sold his mother's car, removed the motorcycle from the garage, and packing some personal belongings into a rucksack, rode away.

William, the eternal poet, although not saying it, was deeply hurt, wondering why a girl none had ever met could change his brother so dramatically, being inspired to write ream upon ream on the devastation of thwarted love. Charles wondered. How could Robert become so frustrated, almost reaching a level of derangement?

Benjamin used the situation to prove to his younger sons that women were capricious and that Robert merely needed time to come to the realisation that there was no woman, dead or alive, who should be trusted. Robert would return, he assured, and then their lives would go back to normal.

It was during one of her many explorations, that Sofia met Christopher. He had suddenly appeared on his bicycle from behind a tree and trying to avoid crashing into her, collided with a rose bush. Falling on her knees to help him, she saw to her horror that he had received the worst of it; there were thorns everywhere. Apologising profusely, she immediately assisted him to the convent, as it was closest.

Christopher Watson took one look at her and fell hopelessly in love. She on the other hand was a careful if not frightened participant in the friendship that developed, often discouraging him from paying her too much attention. He paid no heed and kept appearing wherever she happened to be, even going as far as volunteering to work at the orphanage.

His curiosity about her past increased and the mere fact that she lived where she did aroused suspicion that she too had been a victim. However, she never divulged information and made it clear that unless she shared something voluntarily there were no questions to answer. One thing he knew, she had erected insurmountable obstacles around her heart, and he wondered if he would ever be able to scale them.

Christopher was also a student at the University but had changed his major so many times that even he was having trouble remembering what it was he did there, although, his latest interest was music. It was on that subject and English Literature that they concentrated most of their conversations.

Sofia still yearned for Robert's return, and with it, she fanned the burning desire of bringing their son home. Often, she watched Christopher with genuine interest and then knew that only their outwardly appearance was alike. Nothing he did was like Robert, and perhaps that was better, otherwise she might never get out of the past.

Acutely aware of his feelings, she seesawed between flattered and frightened. Occasionally, when she saw him walking towards her with that mischievous grin on his face, she wished she would love him as she did Robert, but knew she couldn't. Then to her own surprise, she discovered that she did have feelings towards him, not a passionate love, but a kind and tender love nevertheless.

Courage growing, he eventually asked her to marry him. She reacted without surprise, then walked back to the convent and confided in Sister Margareta. The news was hardly that to her, she too had been expecting this development.

'What should I do, what do I tell him?'

'Tell him as much as makes you comfortable.' Sister Margareta said gently. 'If he loves you, none of it will matter. Just remember that marriage is a serious commitment. If you're still hoping that Robert returns, it's best you take your time. But we both know that he married so what future is there?'

She told him about Robert, but not about the baby. The hurt there was still raw.

'You know how I feel. When you're ready, tell me.'

Christopher finally gave up on his studies, bought a house, started teaching music and repairing pianos, which he did extremely well and earned himself a good reputation in the region.

Sofia wanted to fight, or run somewhere where her past didn't exist, where she couldn't dream and remember. Then one day, she knew that including Christopher in her life would make it richer.

As Christopher gazed at his beautiful bride, he knew that he couldn't possibly love her more, but he was no fool. There was a chasm in his wife's heart, and he couldn't mend it. At those times, he hated Robert; for he had left her like a broken puzzle. Silently, he tried to repair, but the pieces could never again fit together for those she had lost were the most important ones.

Robert's nomadic life eventually led him to the Northern Transvaal. Encountering yet another farming community, he checked his finances. As usual, these were running low. Glancing at the squat building, which he found at the end of the dusty road, he noticed that what it lacked in height it more than compensated in length. It was a business centre, where everyone from the surrounding area bought, sold, or traded for whatever they didn't have.

There was a general store, post office, bar, hardware store, pharmacy, and butchery.

Not seeing the compulsory garage and petrol-pump, he dismounted the motorcycle, walked to the end of the building and peered around the corner. There it was. Turning, he saw a girl come out of the store. 'Excuse me, Miss, where might I find a place to stay?' She reminded him of a porcelain doll his mother had possessed. Almost transparent blue eyes, softly curling blonde hair, skin which appeared too delicate to be touched, and a waist that gave the impression she was about to break in half. A faint smile spread on his lips as he thought, "must be the rose where only thorns are plentiful".

'The hotel is at the back,' she pointed towards a heap of sand and rock obstructing the road on that side. 'But you can't go through there. Go down the block and turn left, then by the big tree, turn left again.'

'Thank you.' He said and wondered about the *big tree*. Everywhere he looked, there were giant baobabs, the trees that always looked as if they were plucked out of the earth; and then thrown back upside down.

After filling the tank, he rode down the dirt road flanked by a few houses, until he came to the most amazing thing he'd ever seen. A tree so huge, that someone had turned its trunk into a pub. It was definitely worth one or two rolls of film.

There were six rooms at the small hotel, and all empty. Taking one, he quickly got around to asking for a job.

'What can you do, son?' An old farmer asked as he sat at a table in front of the general store.

'Just about everything, vineyards, wheat farms, and sugar-cane fields, I've worked them all. I can also repair anything with an engine.'

'Good, start in the garage tomorrow.'

Rolling out from under a tractor, Robert found himself looking up a pair of female legs. He had seen her regularly after their first meeting, but never spoken to her again, although he noticed that she often watched him with undisguised curiosity. He was neither interested nor planning to stay so he ignored her inquisitiveness, but lately, he'd been wondering about photographing her. Apologising profusely as the men at the tables made jokes both rude and funny, he wiped his hands the best he could and introduced himself.

'Elizabeth.'

'Don't mind them,' he waved the cloth in their general direction. 'They need distraction.'

'I know,' Elizabeth gave him a peculiar smile. 'People like to talk about you.'

'Only bad things I'm sure.'

'Actually,' her voice dropped to a conspiratorial tone. 'They discuss the fancy equipment you keep in your room. What is it?'

He roared with laughter. 'For being a curious bunch I'm surprised they haven't yet called in an expert. It's mostly cameras, tripods, and lenses.'

'You're a photographer?' Excitement spread on her face. 'The beautiful sets and models; I love fashion magazines but my uncle doesn't let me get too many.'

'Sorry to disappoint, but I'm not that kind of photographer. I like the natural.' He pointed to a cactus a few feet away, and thought that he might as well plunge in. 'I've been wondering. Would you be interested in posing for me?' Perhaps if he put her under a laden marula tree with a giant fan blowing her hair, or dress her in grass and leaves, or smear her with mud and let it dry on her skin.

Their travels through the bush became daily occurrences, everyone riveted as they went about shooting their pictures with a seriousness no one understood.

'I know you have a mother, where is she?' Robert asked one afternoon as he mounted the camera.

The Ndebele costume rustled as Elizabeth climbed up the waterwheel. 'She's sick and my uncle is embarrassed to parade her in public.'

'What's wrong with her?' He queried as he started clicking.

'Do you really want to know or is this merely polite conversation?' She tugged at the blanket about her.

'I want to know.'

'She has mental problems and for want of knowing what else to do, my uncle lets her drown her sorrows.' Sitting down on the platform, she pulled a flask from her bag and offered it to him.

'And it seems so do you.' Waving the flask away, he concentrated on the shot.

'Spare me the sermon, Robert. Besides, unlike my mother, I'm no drunk. But it's always easy to talk if you don't live with it. Rich people are all alike, always looking down your noses at the parasites.' She pulled at the apron and beads around her neck.

'That's not fair. And who said I'm rich?'

'Everything about you, no one could have all that equipment without money.' She pointed. 'Your bike, your boots, your clothes, they are all expensive, unless you stole them. But it's unlikely because I know who you are. I may live in the backwaters but I have heard and read about Powells and all the wonderful buildings they erect. So, what is it you're doing here? Ran away because daddy wouldn't give you enough millions, or is this your way to drown your sorrows?'

They said out of the mouths of babes! 'Does it occur to people that not every rich kid likes to depend on his family's money or name? Furthermore, my father and I have nothing in common. But I think I've had enough.' Snapping the camera off the tripod, he began tidying things up.

She came down the ladder, ran to him, and put a hand on his arm. 'I'm sorry, for saying things I shouldn't and didn't mean. It's just that I know you're here by choice and I have none to leave. How I wish we'd ride into the sunset together.' Her eyes filled with tears.

Reaching out, he hugged her. 'You see how I live; it's no life for a woman. Isn't there something you like to do?'

Sniffing, she wiped her face. 'I could sit and sew a fine seam, bake for the school cake sale, or I can always marry a farmer.' She giggled. 'Which of the above would you choose?'

'Tough choice, but if you married the farmer you could do all three. Life is good here; no one rushes about like they do in the city.'

'If it impresses you that much why don't you stay?'

'Because I can't.' His hand brushed against her face.

Closing her eyes, she put her arms round his neck and kissed him. 'I wish you would.'

'Elizabeth,' he murmured against her mouth. 'We mustn't.'

'I can already see in your eyes that you'll soon be gone.'

Benjamin had counted on Robert running out of money and then crawling home. To his chagrin, nothing was going as he imagined and as weeks became months, he became both hopeful and desperate. Once, the thought crossed his mind that he might have made a mistake concerning Sofia, then immediately dismissed the idea. No woman had that kind of power over any man. As he pondered over his firstborn's whereabouts, he forgot that he had another two sons, who needed him desperately.

Charles had become a thorn in his side, forever involving himself in scrapes with the oddest characters. William had never been an extrovert but now he was becoming a recluse.

Arranging the small packets neatly on the desk, Charles picked one and studied it closely. Opening it, he dipped a finger and rubbed the white powder on his teeth. A friend had said that it was very good, apparently the latest rage in America. 'Hell!' Grabbing a discarded shirt, he tried to stop the nosebleed, a sudden dizziness making him sway against the bedside table. Putting a hand out to steady himself, he knocked the lamp over, breaking it.

Hearing the noise, William walked next door, looked into his brother's room, and saw the broken bits on the floor. 'Must you always do things to upset father?'

Charles waved him away and hiding the bloodstained shirt, told him. 'And since when do I care? I'm going to take a nap, scram.'

That evening at dinner, Benjamin stared at Charles' empty chair. 'Is this to be common practice?'

'He was sleeping this afternoon.' William informed him.

'That's all he does anyway, merely on a road to nowhere. Go call him.' Benjamin was tired of sending servants after Charles and then seeing them walk out the door because of the obnoxious behaviour.

Glancing at his watch, Benjamin knew that ten minutes had passed; yet, there was no Charles and no William. 'What the hell is the matter with those boys?' He asked Munro furiously, pushed the chair back, and stormed out of the dining room. He stopped as he saw William sitting on the top step of the stairway. 'Didn't I tell you to get your brother?'

William looked down, his face expressionless and drained of colour. Then getting to his feet, he started down the stairs slowly.

'Where is he?' Benjamin asked impatiently.

'Dead.'

Benjamin ran to his son's bedroom, nothing preparing him for what he found.

The ambulance and the authorities arrived but there was nothing to do; Charles had been dead since four o'clock that afternoon.

William descended into an endless melancholy, knowing that he was partially responsible for his brother's death, detesting looking in the mirror to see the face of his accuser. The agony of thinking that he could have prevented the tragedy soon drove him into further isolation and the drinks' cabinet. 'Father,' he asked one evening. 'Do you think Robert knows about Charles?'

'If he does, he's not being a good brother, and if he doesn't… Don't you have homework?' Lately, Benjamin always became irritated when anyone mentioned Robert.

William began spending a lot of time locked in rooms, loathing it when anyone intruded. One afternoon, he found himself in his father's study. Sitting behind the desk, he stared at nothing for close to twenty minutes, then as he glanced over the desktop, he saw it; the small key carelessly left in an ashtray. He knew it well; Benjamin carried it in his inside breast pocket. He had always wondered what they kept in the safe hidden behind the panelling of the bookshelf wall.

Removing a few books, he pressed the button in the corner, waited for the panel to slide open, inserted the key, and stared into the darkness. Reaching in, he pulled out all the contents. There were papers, money, some jewellery, and a few large envelopes.

Systematically, he began an investigation of each pile of papers, read the will, flipped through some blueprints and deeds of sale, counted the money, and put it aside. His fingers ran over his mother's jewellery and he recalled how lovely she had always looked. Gently, he returned them to their velvet boxes and pouches.

He opened one of the envelopes. 'What the…' looking closer, he realised he knew the couple in the picture, a very compromising one. Both were in highly successful careers and married, just not to each other. 'Blackmail!' It could not be coincidental that the man happened to be one of Benjamin's most disliked competitors. Going through two other envelopes, he saw the same procedure had followed. No longer interested in the last unfortunate victim, he packed the envelopes and was about to throw them into the safe when one fell and spilled its contents.

Bending to gather the pictures, he stopped, his breath catching in shock. 'Robert!' He paged through the pile feverishly, each picture telling an ominous tale, then grabbing the file, he read it from cover to cover.

Surprisingly, things made sense, yet nothing did. 'He wouldn't!' His hand shook as he held a picture of a heavily pregnant Sofia.

Keeping a neat pile of photographs and a copy of the report, he returned the rest into the envelope and back into the safe. Arranging all contents in their original positions, he locked it again and dropped the key where he'd found it.

Running upstairs, he sat at his desk. Pictures spread everywhere, he stared at them. Tears filling his eyes, he understood what this meant. Benjamin would never allow him to lead a normal life. If he could interfere in his favourite son's life so callously, what would he do to William's now that he was home alone. Charles had often complained at their father's unfairness, knowing that everything Benjamin did was for Robert's benefit, as if they didn't exist or matter. However, Charles wasn't here to see the cruelty and mercenary precision. This wasn't love; it was control; one that brought nothing but destruction.

Closing his eyes tiredly, William wondered if things would have been different had their mother lived, probably not because nothing and no one could stand in Benjamin's way.

Pulling some paper from the drawer, he wrote for a few minutes, then throwing everything into an envelope, he hastened downstairs, ran a few errands, and then went to sit in his father's prized Rolls Royce. The servants who cleaned out the cars found his body next day. And Benjamin buried another son.

CHAPTER FOUR

'I'm a widow,' Sofia whispered as she travelled on the train to Cape Town. After years of companionship, Christopher's life was snatched away by a car crash. One that wouldn't have happened if he'd listened when she protested before he went off to repair a piano during that formidable thunderstorm. She had stared at him at the hospital and thought that they had made a mistake. There was not a wound on him save a hairline graze on the side of his temple.

Everything here was painful, how could she move forward if she didn't let go, especially now that Sister Margareta had also passed away?

She sold the house and furniture, resigned from her teacher's post, and packing most of her clothes and some personal belongings into a few suitcases, left.

Arriving in the Mother City, she spent the best part of a week confined to a hotel balcony. Then, she took long walks along the beach and spent hours at the water's edge.

Last year, she and Christopher had spent their Christmas holiday in Port Alfred. He'd been her companion, her friend, her security, and she would forever treasure the tranquillity he had brought her life. What was she supposed to do with herself this year?

In her suite, she closed the door and stood there a second. Where exactly was she going? Crossing the room, she opened a drawer, took out a photo album, flicked through the pages, and stopped where three mischievous faces looked back at her. 'Hello boys, I'm your Aunt Sofia.'

Entering Lourenco Marques, Robert drove straight to the newspaper's offices. He had spent years criss-crossing Southern Africa as a freelance photographer but lately, he felt the need for direction. Marriage had been ruled out, and he found himself relatively content with memories, even if most times those brought more sorrow than pleasure.

After leaving the Northern Transvaal, he had gone over into Mozambique. Stumbling onto a guerrilla camp, he had almost been executed as a spy had he not been able to convince the local leader that he was a photojournalist; whose very work could highlight their plight. The man nodded approval and let Robert shoot a few rolls of film in and around the village and then set him free.

Months later, he conceived the idea of changing his name, or at least adapting it into something more anonymous. He in no way wanted his father to interfere or become embarrassed by so mundane an activity, of which Benjamin had complained enough. Robert still recalled what Benjamin said every time he saw him clicking the camera that turned out to be his mother's last gift to him. 'It's common, not worthy of a Powell.'

Thomas Robertson, it was close enough but also adequately different for no one to associate it with Benjamin's heir.

'Welcome, senhor Robertson.' The editor greeted cheerfully. 'What have you brought me this time?'

'Hello Pedro, something a little different.' Robert answered in Portuguese and opening a folder let photographs fall over the desk.

'Very good, but your work always is.' Pedro picked one. 'I see what you mean. But if there weren't two sides there wouldn't be a war, and this is what it's about.' He said as he watched the young boy's face on paper. 'I don't know how you get this feeling, it touches the heart. If you were American, you'd have won a Pulitzer a long time ago.'

'You flatter me. Want them?'

'Of course. How much?'

'The usual.'

'When will I see you again?'

'Not sure. Oh, I wanted to show you these as well.' Pulling an envelope from his leather jacket, Robert gave it to Pedro. 'What do you think?'

Silently, Pedro looked through the pack of photographs. 'Now I know why your work is excellent. You're not a photographer but an artist. How long did you wait for this shot?' He studied the picture with the lioness, its cub, and an old experienced crocodile waiting patiently.

'Wars aren't always action, there's a lot of waiting involved. In fact, I'm tired of landmines, mangled bodies, and carnage.'

'You know,' Pedro searched for something on his desk and pulled a magazine from under a pile. 'Perhaps this is what you're looking for. The quality of your work matches any page in here.' He held it up.

Robert studied the cover. 'National Geographic,'

'Keep it. These people are always looking for talent.'

Driving through long streets, Robert noticed that Johannesburg had changed somewhat. Unlike many cities in the world, trees populated it, and he had always been partial to its natural character. He noticed two Powell creations at different levels of completion. Benjamin had to be doing extremely well.

Driving the Land Rover up the hill, he smiled. Only the garden had grown, the house still looked the same. Stopping in front of the palm his mother had planted, he let his fingers run over it.

'May I help you, sir?' A strange servant answered the door.

'I'm Robert and I'm here to see my family.'

'Right this way, sir.' Giving Robert a queer look, the man led him to the study, motioned for him to take a seat, walked out onto the patio through sliding glass doors, and bending over an obese man, imparted his message.

Robert stared in amazement. Something resembling a party was in progress, the pool liberally sprinkled with noisy men and women, but no sign of either of his brothers. Recognition froze him. Benjamin got up with difficulty and advanced to the study as topless women popped in and out of the water.

'Robert!' Benjamin greeted loudly as he chewed on a cigar. 'It's good to see you, my boy.'

'Hello father,' Robert embraced him. 'Baby-sitting for Charles, or is it William?'

'Neither, it's my party. Let's sit.' He pointed to the chesterfield.

'Your party?' Robert looked outside to make sure he wasn't hallucinating, everyone outside was at least ten years younger than Benjamin. 'Then what do Charles and William bring home?' He asked bemused.

'Nothing, they are both gone.'

'And I'll bet you picked their schools. So, where are they, England?'

'No, they're both dead.'

'Seriously father,'

'I am serious.'

A sudden light-headedness hit Robert. 'When?'

Benjamin studied his son with interest. At last, Robert looked like a man. Those rugged looks would drive women crazy and automatically demand respect from fellow men. If only he could keep him here. 'A couple of years ago, we're the last Powells.'

'But... how, what happened?'

'Charles was the first to go, overdosed on some damn drug. Heroin or cocaine, I don't recall. William was weak and couldn't handle the aftermath. He committed suicide.' Throwing the cigar into the ashtray, Benjamin lifted his hands helplessly. 'It's been a long recovery. This is the first time I agreed to let my friends throw me a party.'

'Young women and junkies?' Robert watched a man smoking pot.

'You weren't here, they were. Think it was easy on my own?'

'Sorry father.' Robert passed a hand over his pale face and rose to his feet, took a few steps, sat again. 'It's all such a shock. But why would William-'

'Blamed himself for Charles' death. He'd been in the room minutes before that fatal dose. The servants found him in the Rolls.'

'This is incredible, a nightmare. But tell me.'

Benjamin imparted what he wanted and held back what he felt was unnecessary. '...then I took to food to keep me company.' He touched his mid-rift and laughed.

The sound jarred in Robert's brain. 'Who could guess that so much would change?'

'Yes.' Benjamin agreed. 'Staying?'

'I don't know, but I have to make some decisions. I just wasn't expecting this.' He made a helpless gesture.

'Still designing?' Benjamin queried hopefully.

'Only with my camera.'

'That's not a career, son.'

'It pays the rent.'

'But you could be making a fortune at Powells.'

A disdainful look appeared on Robert's face. 'I see you're still putting monetary value on everything.'

This could be tougher than Benjamin imagined.

Robert frowned as loud shrieks reached them. 'Perhaps I should book into a hotel-'

'No, I'll send them away; it will be as quiet as a convent.' Benjamin knew at once that he'd made a grave mistake. Laughing dismissively, he lit another cigar.

Robert's mood had also changed, going into the sad place he still fought against every day. 'I have to go out, but I'll see you later.'

'Master Robert,' someone called as he reached the Land Rover.

'Munro!' Robert greeted with genuine pleasure. 'After what I heard in there, I wasn't expecting to see you.'

'A lot has changed. And I'm deeply sorry about the young masters.' Munro studied Robert. 'Will you be staying, sir?'

'I had a half-formulated plan but now, I have no idea what to do.' A female scream travelled over the property. 'Is he dating them as well?'

Munro shrugged. 'Where are you staying, sir?'

'Well, here.' Robert extended a hand. 'I'll see you later.'

He was surprised to see the ancient tree, devoid of branches now but still standing. Across the street, the convent looked irreparably neglected but recognisable. Walking over the grass where they had sat so many times, he could almost see her running towards him, long dark hair, beautiful brown eyes, and a smile that always touched his heart. It still hurt and he knew that it always would. Why had she walked out of his life, without explanations, reasons, or excuses? He drove past the house and the store, both looked the same, but neither was. Instead, they hid secrets that he couldn't fathom.

Returning to the house, Robert felt grief. He knew time brought changes, but he hadn't expected this many or this drastic, a deep sadness filling him at not having been home for his brothers. He had loved them dearly and had often felt reprehensible at having left them to face Benjamin on their own. All Charles ever wanted was for someone to pay attention and William, all he needed was kindness. Removing his jacket, he threw it on the bed angrily. Someone knocked.

'Munro.' Robert noticed the other man's nervousness. 'Is something wrong?'

'Yes sir, terribly wrong, and today, I too am leaving. I merely stayed these years to fulfil my promise to Master William. Only, I had no idea that he was going to kill himself, because he was so calm.' Munro pulled an envelope from his briefcase. 'Master William gave it to me the day before he died, making me promise with all that I held dear that no matter what happened I would never let Mr Powell know it was in my possession.

'Since you left, things changed. Your father was impatient and unreasonable with the boys and neither could please him. As you saw earlier, most of the servants resigned and I often contemplated it. Then Master Charles died - heroin they said - and Master William became a shell, blaming himself mercilessly. Hardly a few months had passed and he too was dead. His death was a mystery but most, including Mr Powell, believed it was guilt.

'Many times, I believed the answer lay here.' He shook the envelope. 'But I couldn't bring myself to betray his trust, even in death. Instead, I hid it to await your return as he begged of me. Last month, when I was straightening the cupboards in my room, this thing fell all over the floor.' He placed it in Robert's hand. 'How I regretted not opening it immediately after Master William's tragic passing, because if I had, I might have been able to do something. I must leave now; you'll want to be alone.' Quickly, Munro left the room.

Robert stared at the envelope before tearing it open. Emptying it on the bed, photographs fell everywhere. He picked a few… 'Sofia!' Becoming feverish, he looked through them all. Still not understanding, he opened the file. It was there that he found his brother's letter; pinned to another photograph that tore at his very soul. 'Lord, no!' Feeling ill, he half sank against the bed and onto the floor, and with shaking hands read,

"Dear Robert,

Do not mourn me too much because I have finally accepted that I was never meant to be. For me, life has been a burden, and I cannot wait to be rid of it! Sometimes, I fancied that perhaps I was switched at birth for I often feel that I don't fit in this family. I'm far too weak, to fight, to speak up, to be a Powell…

I have always been good with words but right now they fail me miserably to express the anger, frustration, and hopelessness I feel. And I used to think that you were his

favourite! Imagine what might be in store for me, perhaps a Gulag!

I am sorry for the pain I will cause because now I know how much you truly loved each other! He destroyed not only both your lives, but also your son's in ways I'll never grasp, yet, I know why he did it. He imagines himself our god, to do with our lives as he pleases.

I hate him so violently that I cannot bring myself to wake another morning in his house. No wonder Charles subconsciously chose death, he too craved escape.

Forgive me if you had preferred not knowing, but I found it impossible to ignore.

Your loving brother,

William."

After sending the guests away, Benjamin sat in his chair and puffed on a cigar contentedly, watching the slow whorls rise lazily. Robert was back and if he played his cards right, he might just manage to get him to stay for good. However, as in the past, he could see that no amount of coercion worked. He had to go about this with the utmost care. Unexpectedly, Robert stood in the middle of the study again.

'All I want to know is why.' The blue eyes that could crinkle with amusement were strangely brilliant.

'Why what?'

'Did you honestly believe that I'd never find out? How about this? And this?' Photographs fell on the desk. 'But this has to be the absolute best.' Sofia's clearly visible pregnancy was like a scalpel to his heart. 'And don't you dare deny it.' Robert's voice didn't rise, making it all the more ominous.

Benjamin's face changed with disbelief. 'Where did you get this?'

'William.'

'He's dead.'

'How very convenient for you.' Robert made a helpless gesture. 'Why did you do this to me, Sofia, my child?'

Why pretend? The last he'd heard she had married. 'She wasn't suitable.'

'Because she was Greek or because her father only owned a grocery store?' He stabbed a finger at a photograph and threw an obituary onto the desk. 'But you certainly made sure he got the hotel he wanted. The damn thing probably killed him. She was suitable for me, all I wanted.'

'Think all people are good? I know otherwise. These people are after one thing, moving up in the world as fast as they can. I couldn't stand by and let them do it at our expense.'

'This was about money and how much you think I care for it? There's a pile at some bank and I don't give an iota what anyone does with it. As for my child,' Robert took a breath that came from his very soul. 'What do you suppose my son wanted?'

'We both know he was a mistake and what guarantee is there he's yours? What if in twenty years, when you were married, with your own family, an upstanding member of society, she appeared out of nowhere and put the screws on?'

Robert took a step closer. 'It wouldn't have happened because I'd have been married to her. She was the best thing that ever happened to me and I'd have done anything for her, including working for you, or were you under the impression that I enjoyed your proximity? Who gave you the right to ruin all our lives? Well father, how does it feel to be alone, to know that you destroyed your entire family?'

Benjamin got to his feet. 'Everything I did was for love.'

Robert made an incongruous sound. 'The closest you've ever come to the experience is with money. Well, have it all, I don't want one single cent!'

'But it's yours.'

'Which I refuse to touch!' Gathering everything on the desk, Robert threw it back into the envelope. 'Now I have only one question. Where are they?'

'I don't know, and once all adoption papers are signed that's the end.'

Robert felt weak. 'You never asked us what we wanted. Charles simply wanted love. And William was just a little boy, who wasn't allowed to grow up. I'm tired father, tired of everything about you and I haven't been home twenty-four hours. I'm going, going where no one has ever heard of you or your money, where it just doesn't count! And about Powells,' he waved a hand disdainfully. 'Keep it, sell it, give it away, or burn it down. I certainly don't give a damn!' Walking out, Robert banged the door shut.

How could one individual cause such devastation? That was Robert's uppermost thought as he entered Grahamstown. The other was how Sofia must have suffered imagining that he had abandoned her. Hadn't he thought likewise?

Startled, he looked at the convent he recognised from one of the photographs. Feelings of satisfaction and immense sadness filled him. He rang the bell and almost immediately, a nun appeared at the gate. Quickly, he stated the purpose of his visit.

Without a word, she opened the gate, let him in, and took him to Mother Superior's office.

'Welcome, Mr,' Mother Superior offered her hand.

He kissed it respectfully. 'Powell.'

'And what can we do for you, Mr Powell?'

'I'm trying to trace a young lady by the name of Sofia Andriotti.' He showed her a photograph. 'I realise that many girls come through here but Sofia was different, special, and I'm sure she would have made an impression.'

'May I enquire why you are looking for her?'

He passed a hand over his hair. 'I can barely explain this shambles,' but somehow, he managed. 'We were lied to, tricked! I thought she did this to me, she must have seen it vice versa.'

'Years have passed and some things are best left unsaid.' She raised her eyes from the photographs to his face.

'So said my father, but I'm unconvinced. Some mysteries deserve explanations and none more than this one. It might be impossible to change the circumstances either of us has created but at least, like me, she'll know the truth. Look, I'm not here to condemn her decisions. It may seem as if she chose to give our son away but I know with certainty that my father connived to make it impossible for her to make any other choice.'

Mother Superior glanced at another photograph. 'That is our Sofia. But she's no longer here, moved away last month.' She motioned him to wait for her to finish. 'She needed closure on the past and perhaps she finally managed. The only person who would have known about Sofia's plans was Sister Margareta, but she passed away last year. Your son,' she gave him a faint smile. 'I learnt from the lawyer that he was a most welcome gift to a wonderful couple. Now Mr Powell, you must stop thinking that you'll be able to find him for all information is kept under strict confidential laws.'

A thought crossed Robert's mind. 'Did Sofia become a nun?'

'No, she was a teacher and counsellor, and she married Christopher. As it happens, he's the reason for her move; he died in a vehicle accident.'

'She had a brother in England, do you know his address?'

Mother Superior shook her head. 'I'm sorry.'

'Did Christopher take good care of her?'

'He loved her.'

Angrily, he grabbed his things, climbed into the Land Rover, and drove to Cape Town.

What had he expected? Benjamin made certain they never stood a chance.

Enraged, he paced the hotel room, then, sat paging through the magazine Pedro had given him. Smashing his fist on the table, he dropped it carelessly. It fell open on a page and he stared at it. Getting to his feet, he went down to the docks.

'We're so glad you finally came.' Sarah watched Sofia unpack. 'Since your father's death, Andrea says that you purposely avoid us, or maybe it's England. Isn't that crazy?'

'Crazy,' Sofia agreed.

'Your mother would be so pleased if you stayed; especially now that Christopher is gone. Why didn't you let us know before the funeral? We would have gone.' Sarah studied her young sister-in-law. She was a beautiful woman, with an inherent sadness that made people want to protect her. Yet, she was strong and determined. 'How have you coped?'

'It's an adjustment, but I manage.'

'Apparently, exceptionally well. I've always said that you're superwoman.' Sarah smiled warmly. 'Pity you arrived while Andrea and the boys are away. He's been so busy with the new hotel and they love every opportunity to visit my parents out there on the moors.'

Sofia watched Sarah's struggle for breath and the raised stomach. Who would have believed it? After years of resigned disappointment, three boys had been born in quick succession; and now, here she was pregnant again; probably all the fertility drugs. 'What do you think you'll have this time?'

'After Daniel we're hoping for a girl, but if it is a boy, we'll call him Christopher.'

'Thank you.' Sofia said, highly touched.

The hurly-burly of children's laughter filled the house like a hurricane three days later.

'Boys, boys.' Andrea called above their din. 'I believe there's a surprise for you.'

'What is it?' One asked eagerly.

'Not what, who.' He told them as they stormed up the stairs.

'Thea Sofia.' Three voices shouted and she found herself engulfed in half a dozen small arms.

'They know you well, mama made sure of that.' Andrea announced as he hugged her. 'Almost every day photographs are studied. But it's good to see you.' He pushed her a little away. 'And why didn't you let us know about Christopher? Did you think I'd be too busy?'

'Everything happened so quickly.'

Spending time with her family, although heart wrenching, turned out to be the best antidote for having lost Christopher. The boys were crazy about her and she found herself discovering more of England than anticipated as she often took them out. It was also a chance for Sarah to get her much needed rest before having the new baby and for Andrea not to feel guilty about travelling and leaving her home alone with mama.

Then, without warning, mama took ill.

With delight, little Stephanie was welcomed into the family, but four weeks later, mama became worse. Then within another three, she died. It was then that Sofia was thankful she had come. She would have never been able to say goodbye to her mother otherwise.

Of all destinations, why Johannesburg? Madness had brought her there, because why else would anyone choose a place where heartache was around so many corners?

Taking a suite at a hotel, she wondered what it was she wanted to do, as teaching felt unappetising. During the day, she went out, walked up and down streets, seeing what people did, sold, made, and hoped inspiration would strike.

Crossing a street one morning, she saw a girl sitting on the sidewalk, crying in a most pitiful way. Not only her kind heart but also her years of dealing with people's emotions would let her ignore another's distress.

Leaning over, Sofia asked. 'Are you all right?'

The face that looked up at her was one of pure misery.

Tentatively, Sofia put a hand out to the brown hair. The girl threw her arms around her and sobbed for close to five minutes, or so Sofia thought as she noticed passers-by staring as if they were both mad. 'Let's go somewhere.' Taking the girl by the hand, they walked into a nearby eatery.

"She can't be older than sixteen," Sofia thought, then asked. 'What's your name?'

'Trudy,' the girl sniffed wretchedly.

'Dry your face, Trudy. Then drink your chocolate and I'll take you home.'

Trudy shook her head as tears gathered again. 'I can't go.'

'Why not?'

'My father said never. And my... boyfriend...' more tears fell as Trudy dropped her head on the table. 'I'm pregnant. He just opened the car door and pushed me out.'

Sofia regarded the girl before her. No matter how civilised the world ostensibly became, the more injustices it committed against its innocents. This child, for she was no more than that, had already been used and abused. Not only by strangers but also by the very family who had promised their love and devotion to her. How sad the world was, how hopeless, if it chose to trample on the defenceless.

Trudy was the first and soon there were others, but always more than Sofia liked or could help. Knowing she couldn't possibly carry on with her activities from a hotel - where people were beginning to frown - she bought two adjoining properties and applied to the Town Council to start a Home.

The struggle threatened to go on endlessly and sometimes she felt as if she were learning a new language with the heaps of documents she gathered on her desk. With the backing of a few organisations and religious orders - visionary enough to know that she was rendering the community a service - she earned the respect of some important people. And along the way, she found good people willing to volunteer their time and expertise.

Then, one of the churches came knocking, they did not approve. And didn't Sofia realise that the knowledge of such a place would only encourage young people to disregard morality?

'We should get legal advice.' Belinda, one of the social workers, suggested.

'Did you ever understand a word lawyers say?' Sofia was exasperated. 'We're taking these girls off the streets, off their humiliated parents' hands, and they have the gall to ask what kind of establishment we're running, as if it were a brothel!'

'Don't tell me, tell the judge.'

'Maybe,' Sofia looked thoughtful. 'I'm just so busy, would you mind very much?'

Later in the week, Belinda was in Sofia's office. 'He's here.'

Sofia looked up. 'Who's here?'

'The lawyer. Actually, there are three of them, father and two sons, but only one is here today. Please see him.'

'Okay. What's his name?'

Belinda's giggle somehow resembled a cat's purr. 'Mr Robert Thomas.'

Sofia's head shot up so fast that she gave herself whiplash. But she needn't have bothered; he wasn't whom she imagined.

Rob was a hard but fair fighter, and ever so charming. He saw things through human eyes and when he spoke, it was to touch a chord of sensitivity and understanding. By the time he was through, not only did he have everyone eating out of the palm of his hand but also a firm friendship was established with Sofia.

His brother Peter, Sofia didn't like as much. He had a sneaky side, with a knack for springing surprises on the unsuspecting, often confronting the opposition with unnecessary force, something she found disturbing. She wished she could divorce herself from him.

Zachary Thomas liked to take a backseat, trusted his sons implicitly, and hardly broke his head over the decisions they made.

Then Peter met Patricia, a beautiful redhead from Cape Town. Peter couldn't help but fall in love with the daughter of a man he idolised. Germaine Hillman, undoubtedly the best attorney in Cape Town, had also been one of Peter's professors and the connection between the two young people was instantaneous.

Never could Sofia say that Patricia didn't try, but her family ties were too strong, and with the birth of their first child, those ties intensified. So Peter sold his share of the family business to Rob and went to join his father-in-law at Hillman & Associates in Cape Town.

'Well,' Rob said in Sofia's office after they returned from court after a minor incident concerning one of the girls. 'That problem is solved, how about a celebration dinner?'

Sofia watched him attentively. He was young, handsome, charming, and obviously on the way up. He was also blond, blue-eyed, and his name was Robert Thomas. Every time she heard it, her mind went into a period of her life she preferred forgotten. She could see where he planned to lead the relationship; she had no wish to go there.

'I'm flattered, but no.' She smiled sweetly. 'I intend to keep you as our legal advisor and I won't damage a working relationship with personal conflict. I'd rather have you as a friend.' Her hand went out to his.

'Friends.' Shaking it a little reluctantly, he felt disappointment.

Which was short-lived when a certain Miss Jane Donne arrived in their midst. Jane had recently become an orphan but was too old for foster care. For lack of knowing what to do with her as she had no other family, the welfare services had taken her to Sofia, who took an instant liking to the quiet young woman.

'How did you know?' Rob asked one afternoon as they sorted files.

Confused, Sofia stared at the cabinet.

'That we weren't meant for each other.' His clever blue eyes regarded her warmly.

She smiled. 'I knew Jane was coming. Now, I demand payment, and the first child will do just fine.'

Rob and Jane refurbished the Thomas house, somehow got Zachary to agree to subdivide the property, and built a second house. Before Sofia knew how they had managed it, she had bought the property and was living next door.

Sofia wondered if it was wise, then realised Jane needed a mother as much as she needed a friend, and that Rob knew it too. He had known exactly how to trap her.

Christine Alexandra Thomas was born in March, and for Sofia, it was love at first sight. As Christie grew, Sofia became aware of an extraordinary intelligence and never letting a chance go to waste, she taught the little girl Greek.

'She loves you more than she does me.' Jane complained one day.

'Nonsense,' Sofia laughed, but realised the child wasn't helping by calling her mama.

'Christie, I'm not mama. I'm Sofia.' She certainly didn't want to hurt Jane.

'Fia,' Christie repeated.

'Yes, call me Thea. It means aunt in Greek anyway.'

Things became easier once Christie entered her life, but then, when she was four years old, they got confirmation on what Jane had suspected for while. She would never have more children.

'Is that what the doctor told you?' Sofia sat beside her.

'It's not fair.' The sobs Jane had been trying to control came pouring out.

'I'm so sorry. What does Rob say?'

'He says he doesn't care, but sometimes I think I see disappointment.'

'Don't do that Jane; you'll make yourself miserable if you try to guess what others think. Believe him and love each other regardless.'

'Oh, we do.' Jane wiped her eyes.

'What does your father-in-law say?'

'Oh,' Jane made a gesture with her hands. 'He's the kindest, most understanding man I know.'

Sofia nodded. Yes, Zachary was that. 'And remember, doctors aren't always right. It was the same with Sarah. That's another bit of news, she's expecting again. It's like a Christmas tradition and they've asked me over.'

'Then it's just as well, because I was coming to tell you that we are going to Cape Town. I need a break from all these doctors' tests and awful medication.'

'Yes, change of scenery, air, and routine, will do you good.' Sofia squeezed her hand. 'How is little Gloria?'

'She's terribly thin and with that flaming hair she doesn't look very attractive. What am I saying? She's only two years older than Christie and children go through stages. Actually, we suspect Peter wants to entice Rob down, but he'll never agree. He believes his father deserves more from him.'

The maid disappeared down the hall mumbling something Sofia didn't understand. Turning, she inspected a collection of crystal animals on a glass shelf. Suddenly, she was aware of a pair of eyes peeping from behind a wall. 'Hello Michael,' she greeted.

'Hello.' Slowly, all of him appeared. 'How did you know it was me?'

He was tall, his brown hair neatly parted, intelligent brown eyes regarding her closely, standing just so. She smiled; her father had done that.

She always enjoyed Christmas around her brother's table, as both he and Sarah loved the children in a way she wished the rest of the world could witness. After Sarah's parents left and the exhausted children were taken to bed, the three adults sat enjoying the fire.

Sofia turned to Andrea. 'Michael does this thing when he stands, just like dad.'

Andrea and Sarah looked at each other. She raised her brows and he shrugged.

'Okay you two, what is it?'

'So you've noticed it too.' It was a statement.

Sofia could feel something wasn't right, but she didn't know what was wrong either.

'It's odd because Michael is adopted.' Sarah announced.

How did one react to a shocking announcement like that?

'Actually,' Sarah continued. 'There's something I need to ask. Having worked in this field, you've undoubtedly developed certain senses.' She searched for words. 'At first we debated if we should tell him, but he's too bright, so he would have figured it out himself. For a couple of weeks he asked questions, then, he stopped and I think he changed a little.

'Andrea says I'm imagining things.' Her hand made a fist against her chest. 'It's as if he craves love, not that he's particularly demonstrative. He doesn't hug and kiss like Andrew, Daniel, or Stephanie, we're the ones he expects from, always that little extra, as if he needs reassurances that we love and accept him. We do, madly, he's our first. Did we make a mistake telling him? It can't be easy for a child to accept that his mother gave him away. That the one person he's supposed to trust implicitly just up and disappeared.'

Sofia couldn't answer, feeling as if Sarah's fist had gone down her throat and punched her heart. 'Yes, reassure him.' She croaked eventually. 'But... how is it possible? Neither of you ever said...'

'Because we agreed to stay mum for ten years.' Andrea told her.

'Why?'

'You know how it is, girl messes with boy from the wrong side of tracks, involving two different cultures. All the family wanted was speed and silence.' Sarah informed her.

'What different cultures?'

'Michael is also half-Greek and half-English, which is why it made sense for him to come to us.' Andrea announced.

Sofia stared, unable to find her voice.

'Well, you know we believed we'd never have children, so we registered for adoption.' Sarah carried on. 'Then one day, the man from the agency told us about Michael privately; how the family didn't want him going through orphanages, homes, and the system. They had to hire a fulltime nurse to care for him because the girl refused to see him. Can you believe that?

'But apparently, some of these girls eventually have break-downs, conscience run-ins, guilt trips, and go chasing after the babies, causing torment to all involved, especially the children, so secrecy is of the utmost importance. The law isn't clear on who has what rights so it's best to be cautious.'

Yes, this was the most practised procedure regarding adoptions, especially those that weren't perfectly legal. The memories came rushing back. It felt like yesterday, and hurt like that too.

'So we flew to Johannesburg, met the lawyer, signed the papers, and the nurse brought us the baby.'

A strange presentiment told Sofia to stop asking questions, but she couldn't leave it there now. 'Michael is South African? What do you know about his parents?'

'Nothing, except that they were from Grahamstown.'

Sofia felt as if the floor had opened beneath her feet.

'And that we discovered when we saw his birth certificate. It was a peculiar coincidence, because you were there at the time and we couldn't tell you anything.'

Sofia felt unwell, close to either throwing up or passing out, and she was certain she couldn't move. Her head filled with buzzing, she couldn't think, and something was happening to her heart. She wanted to cry, but there were no tears.

'Are you okay?' Andrea asked.

Sofia shook her head. 'It... the pudding...'

Andrea rose to his feet and pulled her up. 'Go take something and go to bed. You look terrible.'

How could she sleep? She sat by the window, trying to figure out what they'd told her, but nothing made sense. Suddenly, there was a terrible taste in her mouth. As she wiped it, she realised she was bleeding. She'd clamped her teeth so tight that she eventually bit the inside of her cheek. So she started crying, and didn't stop until the sun rose again.

Watching the boys after breakfast, Sofia wondered. "Can it be?" A shiver ran up her spine, her mouth felt dry and her heart pounded. She had to know!

The children started making a racket and Sarah reprimanded them, then turning to her, she teased. 'Which one do you want?'

Sofia gazed at little Stephanie, Daniel, Andrew, and finally at Michael. 'I already have one.'

Everyone stared at her.

'Christie,' she said coming out of that weird place she found herself in. 'I have photographs upstairs.'

Michael was instantly beside her.

'He loves pictures.' Sarah explained. 'There's this one particular photographer he really likes. What's his name, honey?'

'Thomas Robertson.'

She needed to say something because her mind was obsessed with secret places. 'What does he shoot?'

'Mostly, wildlife. He's English but he lives in Brazil. Would you like to see what I have after you show me your photographs?'

They went upstairs together and she gave him the Kodak envelope. While he flicked through them, she studied him. He looked like Andrew and Daniel. Was that because they were cousins? An odd ringing started somewhere. Yes, in her ears.

'She's very cute.' Michael smiled and handed the envelope back.

She followed him to his bedroom, seeing the colourful posters on the walls. 'Are all these Mr Robertson's? They are very beautiful.'

He nodded and made a gesture. 'It always makes me think of my name. Did you know that my second name is Robert?'

Sofia shook her head. She couldn't breathe.

'Mum and dad told me my grandfather asked the lawyer to tell them to give it to me.'

Biting her lip, she tried to stop her furious heart. 'Why?'

'I think it was my father's name. My mother also asked, but she wanted Michael.' He gave her a gorgeous smile. 'It was lucky because it was what dad wanted to call me anyway.' He opened a drawer, pulled out a box, and held something in his hand. 'Isn't it pretty? I guess the R stands for Robert, and the S could be his surname or my mother's initial.'

'Oh lord!' She blurted out and grabbed the back of the chair. The last time she'd seen it was when she'd given it to him as a day-old infant. Why, oh why hadn't she been wiser and known that Benjamin wouldn't stop at merely separating them? That his depth of evil was more than her innocence could grasp. Right now, there was no one she hated more. 'Michael, when's your birthday?' She managed with difficulty.

'The twenty-second of November. Thea, are you all right?' He looked worried as he noticed the laboured breathing.

'I'm not… feeling well.' Wildly, she reached for him, just touching his forehead and the side of his face. 'I need… to…' She struggled for composure. Running to her room, she locked the door and fell on her knees at the foot of the bed. 'Huh…' but she couldn't say or think as the tears started their downward descent. Grabbing a discarded top, she stuffed it into her mouth, so they wouldn't hear her gut-wrenching screams.

She didn't have to pretend that she was ill because something terrible happened to her and she felt as if she were in fact dying. Her heart ached, her head pounded, her mouth was raw and bleeding, and she couldn't eat. Both Andrea and Sarah tried to see her but she couldn't, she simply kept the bedroom door locked and crouched in the corner.

Next morning, finding a little strength, she got up and went downstairs. No, she couldn't be here any longer. It was an effort keeping the tears from falling. 'I need to go home.'

A concerned furrow appeared on Sarah face. 'Is it wise? You look unwell.'

'Yes, I don't feel well. I need to go to sort out all these things.'

'We have good doctors-'

'No, my mind is made up.'

Michael went to stand before her. 'Thea, may I visit you in South Africa? I know I was born there, so I'd like to go. But I wish you wouldn't go.'

Sofia put a tentative hand to his beautiful brown hair and pulled him into her arms. She took a painful breath. How she wished she could tell him that they were knitted together, but as Sister Margareta had said, and Sarah mentioned, she would cause untold harm. 'I'm sorry.'

Sarah watched the scene with undisguised curiosity. Why was it those two gravitated towards each other? A surge of jealousy filled her. He might be adopted but he was hers and she wanted no one coming between them, not even her husband's sister, however wonderful she was. A little coldness entered her voice as she said. 'I think it's none of our business to interfere in Thea Sofia's plans, Michael.'

She went once more to England and once to Athens, where Andrea finally built his grand masterpiece, then she vowed to never again. She couldn't cope with the emotions that ruled her life for months on end afterwards and subsequently, she wondered if she should be thankful or sorry that Michael had never spent time in the land of his birth.

The front-door bell rang. 'It's open,' she invited without looking up. 'Jane, why are you-'

'Do you tell everyone to simply walk in?'

Jumping in fright, a hand flew to her chest. 'Michael! W-where did you come from?'

'The airport, Thea.' He gave her a somewhat impersonal kiss.

'What are you doing here?' There was pure consternation on her face. 'Your father mentioned something about your studies, travelling and hotels, but I never imagined you'd come here. What's the connection?'

'None, I'm here on other matters.' He looked around, as if considering what he should say. 'I'm settling in Lindos.'

She recalled the beautiful whitewashed village, how happy she and Robert had been. 'Why there?'

'I'd like to develop the family land.'

She regarded him. Now that he had reached adulthood, he resembled Robert. How could she forget? 'Andrea mentioned something. So you want to be on your own.'

'I want to see if I have what it takes.'

'I'm sure you do, Andrea is very impressed with your ideas. How long will you be here?'

'Depends,'

'And I can't believe you're standing here.' Gazing lovingly at him, she wished she could hug and kiss him. 'Where's your luggage?'

'At the Grace.' Seeing she was about to protest, he added. 'My business takes me around at all hours, I don't want to impose.'

'What nonsense-'

His hand went up. 'Thank you Thea, but I'm very comfortable. This also gives me a chance to see South African service and hospitality in action.'

Jane appeared minutes later and fell under the charming young man's spell.

Sofia had just called the Home to tell them that she might be late when he arrived the following day. 'Morning Michael, how was your meeting yesterday?'

'Postponed,'

'What are you really doing here?'

'It's a long story.' Dismissing it, he sat down. 'Thea, are you happy working in that Home of yours?'

'Firstly, it's not mine, and secondly, it can run perfectly well without me. Why do you ask?'

'It seems strange that you were a teacher but haven't taught in years. Doesn't it depress you to work there?'

'Every day, and then I see the good we do, how many lives we've helped save.'

'I've often wondered, which is worst, to lose the child or the man?'

The things she could say on the subject, the emotions she would go through if she did, so she chose to say nothing and change the conversation. 'Why are we talking about this? You should be out there, having fun, exploring your country.' He was young, filled with hope, what did he know of broken hearts, dreams, and promises? 'Let me take you out.'

Sofia wondered if he didn't know how to have fun. He was awkward in her presence and sometimes when she gazed at him, she could swear he was paying no attention to a word she said.

It was now the third day he hadn't come around and she wondered if she'd said something to offend him and he'd left without saying goodbye. She tried to imagine what their life would have been like had she made different decisions. Would Benjamin have let her? He had manipulated her life to his heart's content until achieving what he sought and there was no doubt that had she not signed those papers voluntarily, he'd have found another way. Often, she had thought of confronting him, of telling him that he had failed miserably in stripping away her love for this son she adored. But she'd rather go through the rest of her life without seeing Benjamin again.

'Michael?' She was surprised.

'How about a day of fun, my treat.' He gave her a boyish grin that could melt the most implacable female heart, whatever her age.

'Are you okay, honey? I'm not saying you were a stick-in-the-mud, but you look very cheerful. Did this meeting have something to do with a woman?'

'Yes. Now stop being suspicious and let's go.'

'Have you been drinking?'

'Why would I do that in the morning? I'm yours for a day.' He repeated that hypnotising smile and opened his arms.

"Oh lord, don't let him look at me like that because I don't want to let go." 'This must be some woman.'

'Sometimes one thinks, imagines, and guesses. The truth is often staggering.' He announced cryptically.

Shrugging, she let him drag her around; unable to explain why she thought he was behaving differently. After a while, his good spirits infected her and throwing all cares to the wind, she laughed and enjoyed every moment.

'I had a great time, Thea,' he said as they sipped coffee in her living room that evening. 'When my hotel is finished, will you go see it?'

'I don't have much time.'

'And that's an excuse I don't accept. As you said, the Home will not collapse without you. So if you don't go of your own accord, I'll have to figure out a way to get you there.' Getting to his feet, he went to look at the photographs on the mantelpiece and picked one. 'Christie?'

'Sixteen. Isn't she gorgeous?' Sofia smiled fondly
He nodded. 'Where is she?'

'Visiting family in Cape Town.'

Then, he left. She had no idea why he'd come or what he'd done, but something had certainly changed. As always, sadness and heartache filled her, until Christie returned from her holiday.

'How was it?' Sofia queried.

'Okay.' Christie drummed her fingers on the counter. 'Gloria was always falling about, she's a little clumsy. Uncle Peter thought he was being funny and asked if she needed crutches. Then she told everyone that one day she's going to be beautiful, which I believe. Aunty Pat looked at her as if she were a little mouse and said, "I hope so." Did you know they're sending her to a finishing school in Switzerland and then to the Sorbonne in Paris? She doesn't minds the university, but the finishing school... but when we were alone, we had fun. Oh, I bought paints.'

'That's nice, how's little Richard?'

Christie recalled her twelve-year-old cousin. 'Ricky is beautiful. Which is why they've become obsessed with beauty. So, what did you do while I was away?'

Christie was back! What would she do without her? Sighing, Sofia listened for hours. But why couldn't the child talk like this to her parents, especially her mother? Lately, Sofia noticed that Christie had begun preferring her own company. Then again, Jane hadn't paid much attention to Christie's budding artistic abilities.

However, as time progressed, Sofia realised with disappointment that Christie was in fact considering following in her father's footsteps. Especially as Zachary was the biggest supporter of the idea. Christie might not realise it, but this was a disaster in the making.

PART TWO

CHAPTER FIVE

2002

'Boa tarde.' The deep voice greeted in Portuguese.

The woman looked up disinterestedly from behind the desk, then, excitement pouring out of her, she jumped to her feet. 'Thomas Robertson! Where the hell have you been for two whole years?' Her arms flew around his neck as she kissed his cheek.

'Hi Celeste,' after returning the embrace, he looked her up and down. 'Gee, but you look good.'

Her dark eyes danced, a hand throwing her long black hair away from the attractive tanned face. 'So do you. Come tell me what you've been up to.' Pulling him along, she took him to the leather sofa in the corner. 'Do you know how much I hated receiving those thin envelopes? But first, how did you find me?'

'I went to the paper and they told me. Wow, your own gallery.'

'Quite a change from journalism, heh?'

'And it seems you're doing exceptionally well.' He looked at the walls appreciatively.

'My love for beautiful things finally paid off. Besides, you know I'd been doing the art scene at the paper for years so it was a natural evolution.'

'And who can forget that trip we took up Rio Negro in Eighty-five. I worried constantly that the industrialists would kill us for spying on their clandestine activities, and all you cared about were the ruins at Neblina.' He laughed with remembrance.

Aeons ago, she had been the first person he met when he walked into the newspaper offices in Sao Paulo, Brazil. With his pictures and her words, they had been a formidable team, laying bare many a twisted scheme.

Then, as always, things changed. He had known that she was in love with him. Hoping things worked out differently, he tried, but as her willingness for a serious liaison grew, his diminished.

Arriving at her apartment one day, she told him bluntly. 'It's not working out.'

'What?' He had no idea what she meant.

'This thing you call a relationship.' Her hand waved strangely. 'Because, you're never going to let go. I've tried,' the dark eyes drowned in giant pools. 'I've tried to make you forget, but I'm not succeeding.' She drew in breath. 'I know it's a woman, and she's inside you, like a disease one catches in the jungle and cannot get rid of. I will not live waiting for the scraps.'

He wiped the tears tenderly. 'And you shouldn't.'

'That's what makes it so painful, you trying so hard. And to see you all the time just kills me.'

It was then that he moved to the jungle and worked as he'd done in Mozambique, merely coming to the city to sell his pictures. For a year, he stayed away, giving her time to recover. When finally returning to the paper, he saw that although the light of hope still shone in her, she had somehow come to terms with reality. They would be friends and nothing more.

Now as he looked at her, he was glad they had managed to stay in contact most of the time. As she had pointed out, they hadn't seen each other in two years but he had written. 'I moved again, to Xingu.'

'The river?'

'It's close to a village so I actually have an address where you can contact me.'

'Not being able to answer your letters is one of the most frustrating things I've ever endured. I wanted to tell you about all the changes, the gallery. And for goodness sake, why can't you have a mobile phone like all normal people?'

He laughed. 'Imagine that, a mobile phone in the jungle.' Taking a pad from his pocket, he scribbled something. 'Now you have nothing to complain about.'

She folded the paper and placed it in her drawer. 'But you didn't just come to give me an address, you could have written.' She said with realisation.

He smiled. 'I'm here on business. RiverRax, an American magazine, wants to sign me up.'

'That's wonderful. How did they find you?'

'When they weren't looking. One of their people got lost in the jungle and stumbled into a hamlet, where the chief knows me, so he brought the man to my front door. Then, I spent four days trying to reunite him with his group, who incidentally, thought he was dead. Anyway, he's some big shot, who saw my work and liked it, even tried to sign me up right there. I said I would think about it and let him know. I did, and here I am. Now, enough talk, I'm taking you out tonight.'

Like an uninvited guest and with equally unwelcome regularity, the storm broke over Johannesburg, and in seconds, everyone who had been caught unawares was drenched.

'Damn!' Edward exclaimed, dashed across the street to a coffee shop, and immediately made his way to the men's room. Emerging a few minutes later looking somewhat more dignified, he heard someone call.

'Edward!'

'Amanda,' his gaze swept over her with recognition. Quite a smart young woman, she'd achieved fourth place in a class full of geniuses the year they graduated from Pretoria University. 'How are you?'

'Good.' She watched the face, where drops of rain still clung to his eyebrows. The light hair was wet but combed down, and that sardonic blue gaze that she remembered well, was still telling everyone that he was so much smarter than everyone else was. 'I heard about the offer from Baker & Associates, congratulations.'

'It's where I was headed but with this deluge appearing out of nowhere, I'm barely decent to see the tea lady. May I buy you coffee?'

'Thank you but I already have some,' she pointed to a table. 'Join me, I still have fifteen minutes. So, will you commute from Pretoria or become a Johannesburger?'

'Already found an apartment,' Edward pointed to her bulging briefcase. 'Important case?'

'I'm assisting in a child custody battle. But where have you been?'

'I went home to sort out my stepfather's estate and sell the farm, and then stuck around for a while.'

They reminisced about their student days. Laughing as they recalled Professor Steyn, who had a knack for picking up discarded bubblegum with his left shoe.

Amanda glanced at her watch. 'I have to skedaddle or the boss will fry me.'

'Who is the boss?'

'Mr Rob Thomas.' She pointed to a building across the street. 'Whereas you enjoy criminal law, he does family law, excellent mind.'

Edward studied Zachary Towers intently, a perfect example of thirties architecture. 'Do you suppose he'd be interested in me?'

She choked on her coffee. 'Edward, one is not number one for nothing. You get to pick.'

'Precisely.'

Rubbing his head in frustration, Edward wondered why Mr Thomas had taken this case. Evidence was damning enough and pleading temporary insanity due to LSD was hardly going to impress a judge like the Honourable Mr Justice Malan, whose son had been stabbed by a drug addict.

Going into the records room, he searched for a few volumes, placed them on top of each other, and turned… books and files flew and fell in all directions as he crashed into someone who had suddenly come around the aisle. Recovering, he looked into the most beautiful blue eyes he'd ever seen on a girl. Both going down on their knees, they gathered the papers that lay strewn everywhere. 'New here?' He queried.

A smile appeared on her lips. 'I'm Christie.'

'Ah, Miss Thomas,' although she was a little overweight, she also had a pretty smile, long blonde hair, and those amazing eyes. He glanced at her mode of attire. Jeans, running shoes, T-shirt, and a chequered shirt, a girl without self-importance whatsoever. 'Following in your father's footsteps?'

'And not really succeeding. You are?'

'I apologise,' he shook her hand. 'Edward Davis.'

She gave him an admiring look. 'Daddy sings you praises daily.'

'Thank you.'

She glanced at the heavy volumes they had gathered on the floor. 'I could have killed you.'

'They were weighing me down and I needed rest.'

She returned the grin and placed a few files on the table nearby. 'Nice meeting you, but I must dash.'

Pulling another volume from a shelf, his gaze followed her out the door.

During the holidays, she was a type of girl Friday, doing odd jobs for any number of people and he discovered that he derived great pleasure from watching her go about her duties, because more often than not, she blundered somewhere.

'Christie,' Rob emerged from his office. 'Where are those papers? I need them.'

'Yes daddy,' she became flustered in a frantic search.

Opening the top of the copier, Edward suppressed a laugh. Dropping the papers on her desk, he whispered, 'in the copier.'

She disappeared towards her father's office.

Shaking his head, Edward returned to the copier.

Not five minutes later, she was standing in his office. 'Thanks, but I must really stop misplacing things.'

'Sorry if I offend you, but are you always this forgetful?' He asked curiously.

She dropped her eyes. 'It's my love for colours.'

'I don't follow.'

'I was reading the manual. Did you know that it makes six million combinations?' Seeing his look of incomprehension, she elaborated. 'I paint and mix colours so it sounded fascinating.'

Rising, he closed the door. 'Are you dating anyone?'

'No, why?' she asked in confusion.

'Because I would like to take you out.'

'Why?'

'I'm a man, you're a girl, it's done every day.' He smiled.

Of all Christie's acquaintances, none was more pleased than her father was with the budding relationship. Edward was smart, presentable, and unquestionably had a success star that shone above him with brilliant intensity. No doubt, he had an outstanding future ahead of him, and although having an arrogant self-assurance, Rob saw the blatant will to succeed as a healthy sign. Given a few months, Edward would run things blindfolded, while Christie…

Rob was beginning to have serious doubts over her career choice, but that she tried there was no question. It was only fair he let her finish the year and see the results. But if they were anything like the previous, something had to change. There had to be something she liked, she couldn't just be daydreaming every time she became confused.

Edward surmised the situation much the same way; Christie was wasting time at law school. The problem wasn't her intelligence, she had enough of that, but somehow she soon forgot everything he'd spent hours explaining simply because she wasn't interested. But ask about colours! Frustration filled him when she listed exactly how many shades of brown were visible on the bark of a tree, precisely what hue the sky was on any given day.

Weeks turned to months and Edward became part of the family, the Thomas family, because Sofia had taken one look at him and for reasons neither verbalised, neither liked the other. She tried to be polite, to see the charm others perceived and she missed, trying to find the goodness every person is supposed to possess, but in her eyes, he had none. At times, when she caught him staring blankly, she could swear he was doing cold-blooded calculations, not having love thoughts towards Christie. She had spent too long close to raw human emotions not to see that something was amiss.

Edward couldn't explain it either. Her cognitive gaze wasn't enough to scare him off but he wondered why a woman who merely lived for charity could cause him discomfort. Still, that was no impediment in his way, and his way was Christie. Admittedly, she wasn't the beauty he'd envisaged marrying one day, but she was kind, and there were those eyes he could stare at without knowing why he needed to.

Christie also sensed that things were changing, but when contemplating it truthfully, she knew it was pure evasion. This secret desire to escape the hell of law school without having to explain was weakness in the extreme but she just couldn't bring herself to break her father's heart.

'I'm in love.' She announced one evening and sat on Sofia's lounge floor.

Sofia glanced at her. It didn't quite look like it. Christie was a romantic; she loved flowers and puppies, all things soft and cuddly. Christie was in love with romance and love, not Edward, but he was the only one around, so how did she explain it to her?

'You've never said so openly but I know you don't like Edward. Why, Thea?'

Sofia looked up from her book. She couldn't explain the sense of doom she felt when she saw him near Christie. 'Forgive me, I'm probably seeing things where I shouldn't.'

A few days into October, Patricia called Jane. Gloria was back from France and utterly bored, could she come to Johannesburg? Christie agreed immediately and then regretted it. How was she to entertain when exams loomed? If only she could throw all those books away.

Hot days and drenched nights followed each other, bringing relief to cool heads and hot tempers. That year, things felt oddly familiar and intuition told Sofia that all their lives were about to be changed irrevocably.

Gloria arrived dressed in blue silk. To Christie it was as if she had met a cool sea breeze head on. This was no clumsy teenager in need of cheering up; this was a vision of perfection, an instant beacon of attraction for all male eyes.

Self-consciousness filled Christie, her standard attire not exactly the right foil for Gloria's natural titian beauty. 'You look great, Gloria.'

Clear emerald eyes did a quick survey of the other girl.

Christie frowned, Gloria was gloating. People said that if one prayed and repeated it long enough it would eventually happen. By the outwardly transformation,

Gloria must have spent a good deal of time on her knees in supplication.

'Tell me about Edward.' Gloria encouraged. 'I hear he's quite a catch.'

Christie grabbed the matched Louis Vuitton luggage, threw it onto the trolley, pushed it to the car, and unceremoniously dumped it in the boot. Then climbing behind the wheel, barely gave Gloria time to get in before she sped away.

Glancing around the beautiful lounge, Gloria found herself under considerable scrutiny.

'Edward!' Christie became aware of him. 'Why are you here?'

'Sofia requested some files, and then had me carting a desk to her room.'

Christie stared at the glass in his hand. Once, she had eventually asked why he didn't touch alcohol and been told that unfortunately he hadn't given liquor the respect it deserved and that he'd been a full-blown alcoholic at the age of nineteen.

'Water,' he said as he noticed her gaze and then showed her a book. 'Your mom said I could get it from your room. She's next door, should I get her?' He offered, unable to take his eyes off Gloria.

'We're having lunch at Thea's, will you stay?'

'I'm supposed to return.' He sounded unsure.

'Oh, this is Gloria. Acquaint yourselves.' Christie left in search of the servants, feeling a little wounded. No matter how hard she tried, Sofia and Edward would never know each other the way she wanted them to. Why? Sofia was the kindest person she knew, having immense patience and a heart that could endure almost anything. Edward was... she almost giggled; her rescuing knight.

Life changed fast, and not for the better. Suddenly, Christie didn't like innuendoes, as none were directed at her, and this was especially true when all three were together, making her feel like a flat spare wheel. Aware of the intense concentration needed for exams, she tried to push the matter from her mind, failing miserably, feeling as if a vortex threatened to engulf her.

Edward had made a decision concerning Christie, but never imagined Gloria. He had seen the occasional snapshot, but she had been a teenager and although sharing a resemblance with Christie, was hardly worth a second glance. Now, her ravishing beauty quickly became a festering wound of lust.

He vaguely recollected envisaging marriage just weeks previously, but when he compared the two! It was like comparing a swan to a farm duck. "What the hell", he thought and threw all caution to the wind, deciding to follow the hunger that couldn't be satisfied with mere handholding and light kisses; all Christie had condescended upon him. As she prepared for the onslaught of exams, he formulated his attack.

With amused smugness, he realised that he wouldn't have to work particularly hard. Like most women, Gloria was interested, but unlike everyone else, though she teased and tantalised, she obviously remembered that he dated her cousin.

Gloria impressed easily with an inherent knowledge of things Christie wasn't even aware of. She discussed history, literature and art with anyone, and with as much ease as she did the season's fashion; receiving well-deserved compliments. How exciting could life be, spent with a woman whose only interests seemed to be canvas, colour, paper, and paint?

Entering the modern apartment block where everything looked new and clean, Gloria walked down the passage of the second floor and pressed the bell. Edward was sick with the flu and she'd gone to do some of his shopping.

'A speedy shopper, impressive,' he said as he opened the door.

Stepping inside, she nodded towards the walls. 'It's very nice.'

'Growing up on a farm how could I not like green? Though, I don't understand how I don't hate it.' Taking the bags from her, they went into the kitchen. 'Since you're here, care to share lunch? No cordon bleu, but I can do a few decent things.'

She peered into a bowl. Seeing him hover over the counter, she shooed him to the corner. 'Stop breathing on everything.'

'Did I mention that you're looking lovely?'

'Thank you.'

They chatted casually about cooking, difficult dishes, and laughed about hideous flops.

Then as she slid from the stool to take her plate away, he was beside her, pulling her against his chest. His mouth found hers, a fierce probing taking him into ecstasy as his hands reached everywhere, tugging at her dress, trying to get beneath the fabric that rose sensually against her legs. 'I want you so much.' He caressed the fragile neck, his mouth tasting an intoxicating sweetness.

'Ed-ward,' Gloria could barely breathe, aware that she was melting in his hands.

Slipping the bodice off, he stared at the pink lace covering her perfect skin. Bending his head, he dropped kisses all the way up her neck and then returned to her mouth, awakening the fire within. With purposeful movements, he steered her to the bedroom, pushed her against the wall, and continued the kiss that was sending them both over the edge.

Gloria opened her eyes for a second but it was all it took for her to see Christie's face on the dresser. She pushed him away immediately. 'I can't, it's not right.'

'Gloria,' he reached for her.

She stopped him. 'What about Christie?'

'It was never my intention to get involved in the perpetual triangle. Although,' he gave her a lopsided smile. 'I've heard there's something to threesomes.'

Pulling the bodice back into place, she accused. 'This, was merely a trick to get me here, right?'

Seeing her ferocious eyes, he told her. 'It was not intended as a one night-stand, a fling, or whatever you're imagining.'

'I can't believe you!'

'Sorry, but I didn't know how to show you how I feel.'

'That's not the point; you're still dating my cousin. I'm not having very good thoughts towards you right now, so I'd like to hear how you mend this.'

'Marry me.'

Her mouth opened in shock. 'And Christie?'

'We've been dating and I thought it might lead there, but we're just not right. Now that I've met you- Look, I was planning to break up, and I promise I'll do it today, as I can't conceive spending another hour in her presence.'

'Are you serious?'

Smiling, he nodded.

'But... we don't know each other.'

'We can start now.' His arms reached for her.

She stopped him. 'Not like this.'

'What?' He asked perplexed.

She tidied herself. 'I don't know what this is, a game, a dare? Well, if you truly want me, you are going to do everything right. One, get rid of all farcical attachments. Two, you will ask me out properly because as I said, we know next to nothing about each other. Three, you will propose with a ring, and ask my parents' permission. And in case you haven't realised, I won't live in Johannesburg, so there's a choice to be made, and not by me.' She was out the door.

Edward scratched his head. Had Christie been the one dodging sexual advances he would have understood. She was uninitiated in any form of pleasure and he often felt exasperated at her indifference. But Gloria... oh yes, those lips and green eyes suggested plenty and promised even more!

Gloria didn't go home; instead, she went to her uncle's office. Cautiously, she began an interrogation and after hearing what she'd obviously been seeking, departed.

Guilt gnawing, she found Christie in the kitchen; 'Christie, I have to-'

The phone rang and Christie grabbed it. 'Edward. What? Okay.' One brow went up as she put the phone down. 'He's coming over, apparently has something important to discuss.'

'I'm going home.' Gloria grabbed her handbag and pointed to the ceiling. 'I must pack.'

'Why? What were you saying? Are you okay?'

'Yes, and I'm very sorry. But I need to go.'

Sitting on a bench, Christie was still thinking about Gloria's sudden departure, instinctively knowing she was hiding something. Looking up, she smiled as Edward stopped in front of her.

Why was it that sometimes, when he looked at her- 'Christie,' digging his hands into the pockets, he let his thumbs stick out at the sides.

Christie watched the gesture. She had seen it twice before and he had been extremely nervous, just after he had received mysterious phone calls. Calls he'd never told her about. 'What's the matter?'

He cleared his throat. 'You see, it's like this. Look, I never meant for it to happen this way, to hurt you, but I had no idea.' He rambled. 'It's true I considered marriage a while back, but Gloria... I want to marry her. I've already spoken to your father, who isn't impressed and I suppose I understand. I'm moving to Cape Town as soon as I can.'

Blood and anger rushed within her in equal measures, quickly followed by immense shame and humiliation. Why had she pretended she hadn't seen?

'Look, we are sorry. But face it, there's no spark between us and I want,' he searched for words, 'fireworks.'

'Please leave, and never speak to me again.'

'What are you going to do? We'll be family and we can still be friends.'

She rose slowly. 'You break my heart and I reward you with friendship? I don't think so. Goodbye, Edward.'

As dusk fell, Sofia found her sitting in a corner of her garden.

'Go ahead, Thea, say I told you so.' Giant tears rolled down the pale face.

Christie couldn't care less who thought she was being melodramatic. She hurt deeply, wallowed in self-pity, and wanted to cry for as long as it took to make it all disappear. Couldn't they see her life crumbling into insignificance and she unable to do anything about it? Everyone was watching her, knowing she didn't measure up. If nothing else, she knew one thing, she couldn't go through another abysmal year because she knew she was failing the current one. Burying herself in her room, she ate to distraction, soon forgetting everything, including her beloved watercolours. At night when she couldn't sleep, she ate again, watched old movies and cried some more.

A letter arrived from Gloria. Christie took one look at the disgusting thing, tore it up, threw it in the bin, and quickly disappeared out the door.

'Where have you been?' Jane asked impatiently when she returned. 'We were worried sick.'

'I feel sick.'

'Have you eaten?'

'Three burgers, two pizzas, four milkshakes, and I think one hotdog.'

'Good heavens! You're going to ruin your health.' Jane told her in shock.

But Christie was no longer listening. Running upstairs to her bathroom, she threw up. She hadn't felt better while eating, but now she wanted to die.

It was then Sofia decided intervention was necessary. 'I don't blame her for overreacting. He was mean, selfish, and an absolute beast. In a few months, it will all be in the past, the thing is; what do we do until then?'

'You don't suppose she'd do something crazy?' Jane was concerned.

'She's an emotional child but she would never seriously hurt herself. Perhaps if she went away,' a gasp escaped Sofia. 'I have an idea but I'll tell you when Rob gets home.'

Christie stumbled into the kitchen feeling ghastly. What a night that had been, she hated food. Peering through her unkempt hair, she saw Sofia and her mother staring. 'Didn't I leave you here last night?'

'Sit down while I make you tea and Sofia tells you about her proposition.'

'I'm not going!' Was her response, and in rage, she called her father, just to hear that he was in complete agreement.

For weeks afterwards, Christie was dragged around Rosebank from shop to shop. Photos were taken, a passport acquired, a travel agency visited, and clothes accumulated. She should have known better than to half-agree to this crazy idea, but regrettably, even her father had consented to the set-up.

When Sofia announced that Michael had a vacancy at his hotel and offered it to Christie, she knew he had done no such thing. Sofia had asked, or more likely, begged.

She had been adamant that she wouldn't leave, but after Jane went on about terrible marks, failing, eating, depression and her father gave her a lecture over the phone and yet another when he got home, she thought it was worth going to the ends of the earth just to get away from all the nagging. Absence was also the best excuse to avoid making an appearance at a wedding she absolutely refused to attend. Although Edward and Gloria's behaviour had stung Jane, with Patricia's phone call, something had obviously been discussed and she knew that Jane would never spurn the invitation. Christie felt betrayed, expecting her mother to support her more.

Her world was collapsing and she powerless to stop the demolition. Oh but she hated, and silently prayed that she would forget him quickly and forever, never wanting to see the hypocrite's face again! As for Gloria, she hadn't even apologised! She probably had in the letter she'd sent, but Christie had hurt too deeply to read it.

She watched disinterestedly as people got to their feet and moved towards the glass doors. Tiredly, she joined the queue; this was going to be a long trip, and she had with no wish to make it. Perhaps if she crept back into the house, they wouldn't realise she was there until next month. But then, all the sermonising would start again.

Leaning her almost feverish forehead against the cool glass, she closed her eyes, then straightening herself, strapped the seatbelt on, and felt the aircraft move down the runway. Slowly, Johannesburg became small and then disappeared from sight. Everything she knew was in that dark mass.

Tears filled her eyes and angrily, she wiped them away. If only she could fall asleep and wake up with the wound gone. Edward didn't deserve one scrap of emotion, but right now, she couldn't help herself.

She was angry! Angry that he'd lied to her, angry that she'd believed him, angry with Gloria for changing his affections. Then again, it was possible he had never possessed any towards her and choosing Gloria hadn't been difficult at all. The whole thing was degrading. Sofia was right; burying oneself in work would help forget. Sofia should know; she did it herself every day.

Christie wondered about Michael. She had heard enough of him throughout the years, and seen photographs, but she had never been particularly curious, or Sofia overly eager to part information. Which was odd, as Christie knew that Sofia loved him beyond reason. "Funny," she thought. "I never saw pictures of Edward, or his family." The only one she possessed, a mate to the one he had, was stuck in her bottom drawer at home, impulsively taken as they walked past a street photographer. She should have burnt it!

Landing in Athens after nine, Christie realised she had no idea what Michael might look like now. Why hadn't she paid attention when Sofia spoke during the last few weeks?

'Anything to declare?' The customs official asked.

'I don't know.' It was true. She had no idea what the two insane women back home had packed into the cases.

The man looked at her as if she were a moron and told her to open them. There were books, paints, brushes, camera, film, an easel—which she wondered how they had squeezed it in—and objects whose purpose she still had to ascertain. Then she cursed the cases as she struggled to get them closed again.

A man approached her. 'Miss Thomas?'

'Yes.' She watched the middle-aged man. 'Mr-'

'Nicodimus,' he bowed lightly. 'Mr Andriotti's chauffeur. I apologise for not getting here before customs, there was an accident outside the airport causing utter chaos. I suspect you would like to freshen up.'

She raised her brows at his English accent. 'Thank you.'

Giving her a polite nod, he appropriated himself of her cases. 'This way,'

"I need a bath," she thought as she brushed her hair and studied her face; it was bloated. Ramming sunglasses down her nose hard, she stepped out the door and walked straight into a man. 'Clumsy oaf.' Glancing at the handsome face for a mere second, she continued towards Nicodemus.

'Miss Thomas, you didn't see Mr Andriotti?' Nicodimus asked surprised.

'I'm not sure what he looks like. How did you know who I was?'

'Mr Andriotti gave me a detailed description.'

'Really, and how–'

'No matter,' Nicodimus smiled at someone who had obviously stopped behind her.

Turning, she stared at the man she had crashed into minutes ago.

'My apologies for bumping into you so rudely, I didn't recognise you with the glasses.'

Bright pink ran across her face. What a way to meet one's boss. 'Sorry,' her hand pointed somewhere and then she offered it to him. 'How do you do, Mr Andriotti.'

He looked indecisive, as if shaking hands hadn't occurred to him. Then he took hers lightly. 'Miss Thomas. How was your trip?' He asked and then answered himself. 'Like all trips, exhausting. Then you might be pleased by the turn of events. There's two days of business appointments I have to get through, so you'll have to stay with me until the day after tomorrow.' Turning, he started walking away.

She caught up with him; Nicodimus close on their heels. Had he just said "stay with me?" She didn't know how he had been brought up but she couldn't stay with a strange man, in a strange land. Wasn't this how terrible things happened to naïve young women? The nerve of the man, assuming anything was fine

Stopping abruptly, he regarded her. 'I apologise, I forgot to enquire about your plans.'

He was mocking her, knowing perfectly well that she had none. 'There's- nothing.'

'Good.' He continued his walk out of the building.

That was all she needed, a conceited Apollo. He might feel comfortable with his itinerary but this had never been discussed. 'Mr Andriotti,' she walked faster to keep up.

He came to a halt. 'I know I'm supposed to be your employer, but we're also somehow almost related therefore I suggest you drop this formal approach. Michael will do. And if it won't offend you, I'll call you Christie.'

'Huh, that's fine. But,' she shifted her feet. 'I thought we were going straight to Rhodes.'

His hand went up. 'If it makes you feel better, the Athenian is my father's so that makes it home. I have a large enough suite to find it suitable and proper to share with a young woman without intruding on her privacy. There are dozens of people around, choose one and appoint her your chaperone. If I still offend you, I'll move to another floor.'

She gasped and turned scarlet. 'Mr Andriotti, I didn't mean... I don't know what I meant or what I'm saying.' She put her hands to the burning face.

He smiled. 'Actually, I regret my parents and sisters decided to prolong their stay in London. It was my brother Daniel's engagement party last week and apparently, they haven't yet seen the need to stop celebrating. You could have stayed at the house and Stephanie and Jaqueline would have seen to your amusement.'

She noticed Nicodemus seemed to be enjoying himself. "I'm such a conservative fool, better say no more." She thought. 'Thank you.'

Driving away, he sat back in the seat and gazed out the window. Without turning to her, his hand pointed to the buildings lining the streets. 'Thea said something about you favouring old buildings. A budding archaeologist?'

'They're my inspiration. I paint. Well, sort of.'

'Then Lindos will be a great surprise.'

Feeling embarrassed that she didn't know more about the island of Rhodes; she fell back in the seat and gazed out the window half-attentively. Sofia had said enough about it, but as usual, her mind had been elsewhere.

As Nicodimus drove up to a magnificent edifice, she sat up with interest. Marble Corinthian columns with perfectly sculpted volutes went up fifteen metres, a liberal sprinkling of statues of mythological characters adorning an enormous entrance, and an endless black marble floor decking the portico; exactly what she imagined a Greek hotel to look like.

They rode the lift in silence but her eyes darted from colour to texture and back again. Pleasure filled her as they entered the suite. The walls were in camel-coloured damask, sumptuous brocade swags falling in heavy folds on the richly woven carpet, the sofas in floral silks of green, gold, and mustard. A profusion of equally coloured fresh roses adorned a bombe commode.

Michael motioned for her cases to be taken down the passage. 'I have to get back to work so you'll have to spend most of the time on your own. But should you wish to go somewhere, ask for Nicodimus.'

'I do speak Greek so I shouldn't get too lost. So a taxi-'

'No taxis.'

'But the tourists-'

'You are not a tourist, Christie.'

Her name sounded different when he said it. He was taller than most Greek men, his hair an unusual brown, with a wisp that fell across his forehead. A pair of brown eyes examined everything with absolute concentration, the smile, she'd call it hypnotising. The perfect nose, definitely not Greek.

'Conclusion?' He queried.

'About what?'

'You're looking at me as if I were a lab experiment gone wrong.'

She blushed. 'I was thinking that you don't look Greek.'

'That's because I'm half-English. Surely, you know that. But where's the arrogant, bully, presumptuous bit? You acquired that look when I said no taxis.'

'Yes,' her gaze never wavered. 'Why not, I don't need a chauffeur.'

'Maybe, but it's your first time here and I have no wish to be dragged from my business to send out a search party.'

That certainly was plain enough. 'Then it's better I stay.'

'Don't be silly, this is your opportunity to explore.' He put a key in her hand. 'Just don't stay out too late. Do you have drachmas?'

'No.'

'Never pay for anything with foreign money. Here,' he handed her a few notes.

Her eyes opened wide. 'I can't take this!'

'But you are fussy. Spend whatever you want and keep the rest; I'll subtract it from your salary. Now I really have to go, enjoy your day.'

'Thank you, Mr- Michael.' She corrected herself and watched him walk out. "Odd"

An elaborately pleated canopy-bed in dusty pink, grey carpet, and almost mauve walls greeted her as she opened the door. She touched the rich silk of the bedspread. It reminded her of a comforter she'd helped Edward buy once. Tears gathered immediately. No longer interested in her surroundings, she walked into the adjacent bathroom.

Emerging three hours later after a calming bath and relaxing nap, she quickly made her way downstairs.

As if out of a magician's smoke, Nicodimus appeared beside her. 'Miss Thomas,'

'I told Mr Andriotti that you didn't have to.'

'And he said *no taxis*.' He imitated.

She laughed. 'That's very good. But why doesn't he like them?'

'I think it has to do with a character who once tried some moves on Miss Stephanie, his sister.' Nicodimus enlightened her. 'So, where to Miss Thomas?'

'The obvious is the Acropolis and although I do want to see it it's so cliché.' She watched as people walked in and out. 'I'm looking for the real Greece, the places tourists couldn't be bothered with.'

'Then it will be my pleasure to show you.' Nicodimus smiled and led her to the car.

That evening, as she stepped into the foyer, she saw Michael come towards her accompanied by an amazing dark-haired beauty. He stopped. 'Good evening, Christie. Allow me to introduce a very good friend, Evy. Have you dined?' He hardly let them exchange the usual pleasantries. 'Would you care to join us?'

She glanced at his evening clothes, then at Evy's exquisite maroon velvet and lastly at her own jeans. 'Thank you, but room-service is quite adequate. I'm also tired.'

'I'll see you in the morning then.' With a charming smile, both he and Evy walked into the cold night.

Sitting on the bed's edge, she looked at the watch on her arm. Taking it off, she turned it over and read the inscription. "Christie-love-Edward." 'Ha!' Clasping it tightly in her hand, she cried herself to sleep.

Leaning back in the plane, she felt wonderfully drowsy, and closing her eyes, nodded off. Jerking her head up, she stared blankly at the seat ahead of her.

'It seems Nicodimus still knows how to give a young woman a good time. I warn you though, he's married.' Michael said without looking up from the papers in front of him.

'I know, he took me home for lunch this afternoon.'

He stopped scribbling and studied her. 'That's quite a compliment.'

'I thought so too.' Glancing at his briefcase, she noticed a book. 'May I borrow that?'

He followed her gaze, seeing the purple cover where god Helios' marble head was depicted and RHODOS in light green letters printed beneath. 'You don't know much about Rhodes or Lindos, do you?'

'No,' she admitted. Back home, this hadn't been on her to do list.

'No preconceived ideas, you'll enjoy it all the more. I'll give it to you tomorrow.'

She nodded and glanced out the window, seeing nothing except the bright blue sea far below them.

'Clear skies for your arrival.' He remarked as they stepped onto the tarmac and both looked up at the cloudless sky. 'Although, you must remember to wear a hat in summer, the heat is devastating on fair skins.'

Perhaps he wasn't as bad as she imagined. In fact, he'd been nothing but courteous since they met, except for not letting her use taxis. Grudgingly, she also admitted that she'd enjoyed her excursion with Nicodimus.

The drive to Lindos was long and dreary and she couldn't quite keep her eyes focused. Not that there was much to see, everything was dry and bare and after rushing about Athens and surrounding areas for two days even her head was sending out alarm signals. Sinking into the corner of the black sports car, she tried to keep her eyes on the darting olive trees.

'Christie, Lindos.'

Dazed, she stared at the strange surroundings, then seeing him, sat up embarrassed. 'Sorry.'

To their left, at the bottom of a slanting hill a calm sea stretched endlessly. Straight ahead, rising on the slopes of another hill was the pristine village, the beach forming an arc at the bottom of the incline, small craft bobbing gently on the water's mirror surface.

The hill is the rock of Lindos, which dominates the area halfway down the east coast of the island and protrudes out to a height of about a hundred metres, forming two ports, one to the right, which Christie was looking at and another to the left. From this distance, she couldn't tell what inhabited the top, perhaps a castle or a temple. Whatever it was, she was going to love exploring it.

Christie half expected to never wake again. Surprisingly, at seven in the morning, hearing the buzz of activity outside, she jumped out of bed with an exhilaration she hadn't felt in ages.

Stepping onto the balcony, she held her breath. Sapphire-blue waters merged in the distance with the dazzling sky, boats nodding happily on the shimmering surface. How much better everything would look in summer!

'Good morning. Christie, right?' A young woman asked in English as both emerged from adjacent rooms.

'Yes.'

A smile spread on the attractive face as she offered a hand. 'Mary. May I propose the grand tour?'

After walking up and down, left and right of halls, rooms and passages, they found themselves on the terrace for breakfast. Pleasure filled Christie as she saw the old walls towering high on the hill. She had known the view would be spectacular and she absolutely had to put it down on paper. 'It's exquisite. Didn't the locals mind the hotel site?' She questioned as they sat down.

'The land has been in Michael's family for decades so there wasn't much they could do. But he never intended to obstruct or destroy.'

'Do you know what I'll be doing?'

'You're replacing his secretary's assistant. She's getting married and moving away.'

Christie liked Mary instantly, whom she guessed to be around twenty-three. She was what one called cute, smiled readily, had an inherent kindness, and was genuinely helpful. 'I think Thea mentioned you before.'

'Probably; my sister Georgia is married to Andrew, Michael's brother. Let me walk you to the office.'

Stepping into the lounge, images of Namaqualand in bloom hit Christie. There were blossoms everywhere; on sofas, drapes, and even a giant bowl on the coffee table was filled with fresh flowers. There was green, a few hues of yellow, apricot, and lilac in every corner. Michael appeared in the doorway.

'Good morning.' He held the door ajar as she stepped into his office. 'Before we start, may I call you Christie? I do want to encourage the feeling that you are not an employee. People automatically treat you with more respect, as they do Mary.'

'Thank you.' She glanced around the room. Wood-panels, leather chairs, a maroon carpet, and dozens of books. Yet, there was nothing old-fashioned about it.

He paged through a diary. 'I have to return to Athens, so I won't plunge you into anything until Monday. Give you a bit of time to settle in and explore. Are you familiar with office work?'

She'd been right, Thea had begged. 'I used to help my father.' And once, she had filled in for Edward's secretary. They had been close then. She could almost feel the tears.

He noticed the bright eyes. 'That's it for now, Monday, at nine. And here's that book.'

'Christie,' Mary beckoned from the elevator. 'Michael told me he's on his way out again. I have a few errands to run in the village, so I thought you should come.'

They had walked fifty metres down the driveway when Mary stopped, turned around, and pointed. 'What do you think?'

'Beautiful.' Christie studied the three-floor building where warm lights glowed in almost every window, giving it a cosy and inviting atmosphere. Tall palms lined the driveway as if attempting to hug it, the morning sun tentatively endeavouring to shine on the polished brass letters. 'Hotel Helios - hotel sun - I like it.' She pointed to a double-storey house to the left of the edifice. 'What's that?'

'Michael's house.' Mary watched the sad face. 'I realise we don't know each other, but it might do you wonders to talk to someone who's unbiased. And I promise no psyche-analysing.'

'Psychology Major?'

Mary nodded. 'It's my on-off love. Off right now. I'll continue again eventually.' Linking her arm through Christie's, she announced brightly. 'Actually, I can't wait for summer already. We have parties, go sailing, dancing, visit friends, it's just a blast. Not that we can't do some of that now, but summer makes it different.'

Before the morning was over, Christie had blurted out the sad business at Yanni's Taverna. She had never had too many acquaintances and a best friend was non-existent. As she watched Mary across the table, she knew that she had missed out. Reluctantly, she also admitted that there was no one to blame but herself. She simply hadn't shown much interest in anything else but art. Her parents had seen her attempts but rarely commented, except for questioning her inability to complete them. Sofia was often encouraging, sometimes even mentioning art school. Now, she was sorry she hadn't followed that advice.

As the weekend unfolded, Christie realised how much fun could be had if one knew how to, and it seemed she had found a master in Mary. Perhaps if she'd had a fuller life she wouldn't have felt such abandonment.

Mary liked this sometimes-timid girl with the periwinkle eyes. She had loved being included in her sister's escapades and missed the silly things girls do; like midnight feasts, shopping for unsuitable clothes, and hair-dos. For some reason, she hadn't formed that kind of connection with anyone since arriving on the island, although, she had an endless list of friends.

Sunday evening, Christie felt literally numb. There had been a party, where they had danced until their feet and backs ached. She recalled meeting Evy again, along with her brother Paul this time. Both as good to look at as they were fun to be with, and like Michael and Mary, had also grown up in England. Grandchildren of Darius Vissi, a man known for his vision, hard work, and constant good business sense, they too were quickly making a name for themselves in the family giant, Vissi Clothing. Paul with his original flair for design and Evy in advertising. However, her talent didn't stop there, often sending her to the front of the camera where she exploited her extraordinary looks. Who better but the founder's granddaughter to advertise the family wares? It certainly came as no surprise when Mary announced that Michael had just hired her for an advertising campaign in Europe.

CHAPTER SIX

Quiet contemplation was as good a way to end a chapter and begin another. This was Christie's view as she assessed her recent distraught past and faced a more promising future. Then, as always, her thoughts turned to Edward. Had he moved to Cape Town? Would he spend Christmas with Gloria? Had he proposed? Was he remorseful? Fury filled her.

Uncertain about the wisdom thereof, she eventually gave in to Mary's nagging and accompanied her to England for Christmas and New Year. When they returned, she knew that a type of soul healing had taken place, that the bond of friendship was firmly established, and that a different kind of peace had descended.

'I go.' Mrs Kondis appeared with a few files. 'You no mind work late?' She queried in her heavily accented English.

Christie smiled. How could she? February had arrived with bliss. Everything ran smoothly, especially in her little office with the breathtaking view. 'I'm fine, Mrs Kondis. You go have a wonderful evening.'

'Thank you. Goodbye.'

Christie stared at the computer screen. 'What's this?' She pressed random keys, nothing. She tried everything she could think of for close to ten minutes then grabbed the manual and read a chapter on trouble-shooting; still nothing. Irritated, she kicked the waste-paper basket, sending it across the floor. Immediately she went down to pick the mess.

'What happened?' Michael asked as he walked in.

'A mishap.' Returning the basket to the corner, she sat in front of the machine and pressed another key. 'Please tell me what's happening.'

Leaning over her shoulder, he looked at the screen, pressed escape, and getting no response, reset the computer. 'Do you save often?'

She nodded. 'I just thought- Agh, whatever.'

He hovered there, inhaling her scent; there was something hypnotic about it. Involuntarily, he leaned closer.

She had been in close proximity to men before; her father, the reverend, many of her classmates at university, Edward and lately Paul, but never had she felt this. It was as if someone had lit a bonfire and she was quickly burning from her feet upwards. Staring at the screen, she tried to pay attention, but as his body brushed against hers, her mind found the simple task of thinking an ordeal.

Trying to put some distance between them, she realised that she'd be sitting on the floor if she moved another inch. It was impossible to think or remember if your mind wasn't there in the first place. Tomorrow, she would ask again, and make sure she was at least two metres away when she did.

March made its appearance and so did her birthday. By now, nothing Mary did surprised her, so when the chef appeared with a blazing cake at breakfast, Christie merely blushed and wished she could disappear under the table as everyone in the establishment sang a somewhat groggy happy birthday.

'Cake for breakfast?'

'So we can have the whole day to work it off.'
Christie laughed.

The calls from home came late afternoon. 'Where were you?' Jane asked curiously, Sofia saying something in the background. 'We called this morning but you had already left.'

'Mary and I had the day off so we went to Rhodes.' Five minutes later, she was admiring their diplomacy, neither mentioning Edward nor Gloria. She already knew that he'd been living in Cape Town since December and the wedding was to be in May. Realising the subject no longer bothered her, she was grateful Sofia had suggested sending her away. Strange, why didn't it bother her, hadn't she shed enough tears to prove how much she cared? Pushing the thought aside, she wondered where Michael was.

Days later, he stood in her office. 'Where is Mrs Kondis?'

'She left early. Her son arrived from somewhere and sense and order went out the window.' Christie gestured and smiled.

Returning the smile, he pulled a chair and sat a short distance from her. 'I know you celebrated your birthday and unfortunately, I wasn't here. But I didn't forget and bought you this.' He handed her a wrapped box.

'Why, Michael- You didn't have to.' She was disconcerted.

'It's nothing big, but tell me if they're any good.'

'Thank you.' Tearing the paper, she opened the box and lifted the lid. Pleasure spread on her face. Holding the paintbrushes in her closed hand, she put the bristles to her cheek. 'Wow, the very best.'

He laughed. 'One would swear I just gave you jewels.'

'Oh no, these are much better.' Rising to her feet, she offered him a hand. 'Thank you.'

Shaking it lightly, he also rose and fixed his gaze on her. "Beautiful eyes, gorgeous lips…" A hand rose to touch her face, then changed direction and went to his hair.

The office became hot and cramping and she didn't know where to look.

Moving away from her, he took a file. 'I'm glad you like it here and I can honestly say that I've never seen Mrs Kondis this happy.'

'Of course you didn't see her this afternoon, totally mindless.' A laugh escaped her.

'Laughing too. Such a downcast little soul when you arrived. And we must talk again.'

Christie knew that he was more at ease in her presence than she was in his. Because every time he walked into the office or came within metres of her, she reacted in the oddest fashion, with her mind usually being the first to depart.

Lately, she found herself studying him, speculating about his private life, as he was secretive, bordering on the mysterious. There was no denying it; he fascinated her.

Sitting in bed reading, she glanced at the watch on her wrist. As so many times before, she inspected the inscription. Once, the mere sight of those three words - Christie-love-Edward - made the tears flow, now… Shrugging, she climbed out of bed, flushed the object away and knowing she couldn't possibly sleep, grabbed her swimming things.

On she swam as crazy notions rushed through her mind. Okay, good, she was over that mess, but those other ideas... Almost hearing muscles screaming for mercy, she stopped, stood in the darkest part of the solar-heated pool, and glanced over the small garden; glad Michael had made certain hotel guests couldn't come this way. Unexpectedly, she saw him about to dive in, straight at her. 'Michael!'

Startled, he found her in the shadows. 'What on earth are doing at this ungodly hour?' Diving in, he came up within a metre of her. 'So?' He watched as she moved to the light; covered in winter clothes, he hadn't noticed that she'd lost weight. Right now, the wet look was fantastic on her.

'I couldn't sleep.' She started moving towards the steps.

He followed. 'Please stay.'

'I've done enough.' She also preferred to be dressed when having a conversation.

'What's wrong?' His hand went to her wrist. 'Please don't be shy.'

That was all she could be when he was this close. She felt the drop of water gather at the tip of her nose but before she could wipe it, he did, causing goose bumps all over her body. She averted her gaze.

'Are you homesick? It's quite natural.'

She wished he would disappear.

'Why can't you look at me today?' He studied her a second. 'Did you find a boyfriend? Who is it, Paul?' His grip tightened as he felt a jealous rush.

'No,' she told him in confusion.

'Not a very good liar.'

The impertinence! 'May I have my arm back?'

'Then if it's not Paul, I suggest you disclose his identity so I may know what his intentions are.'

'And I think you're overstepping your authority.' Turning to go, she found her wrist in a vice.

Christie,'

His tone triggered something that was wild and primitive, calling to the very essence of her. Turning, she saw the very thing mirrored in his eyes.

Merely giving a tug, he pulled her to him and wrapped both their arms around her back, letting his body touch the length of hers. He was bare-chested and she, not exactly dressed in the wet costume. The contact was electrifying and his body reacted accordingly. His mouth opened over hers, and his tongue set out on a slow exploration of a wonderland that was cold and sweet, the combination utterly enticing.

She'd been kissed before, just never like this. Edward's kisses had been... absolutely nothing, and his presence had been the promise of escape from all she detested. This was something else altogether, a flame that seared her from the inside out, demanding she surrender, and it begged for her very soul. Thereafter... where would she be; his heart, his bed, or the same place Edward had left her? No, this would be worse, so much worse, and a complication she had neither bargained for nor wanted. Pushing him away, she ran to her room.

Walking into her office later, she saw the white rose on her desk. Turning, she saw him. Heavens but she was upset.

'Christie,' he seemed tongue-tied. 'There's no excuse for what I did. Forgive me?'

She wondered how anyone refused him anything, especially women. The thought made her furious and she knew he could see it in her eyes.

'Look, I don't go around doing things like this.' He didn't know how to label her reaction. Didn't she like it? Or- was she frightened because no one had ever kissed her that way? He could tell she didn't know much about kissing.

"Then why did you?" She wanted to scream.

From that moment, he went out of his way to be polite, but for some idiotic reason, also decided that they should dine together every Thursday, saying something about getting to know each other better, family time, friendship, and whatever nonsense she couldn't recall. She hated it. She didn't know what to do, where to look, or what to say. He on the other hand, seemed to have no problem whatsoever. Thankfully, Mary was always there to alleviate very uncomfortable situations.

Her sixth sense also told her that the truce was temporary, that there was an underlying current lurking beneath the façade, and that one day it would explode. She found it disturbing and hoped that she wouldn't be the one on whom he intended his target practice.

Christie tugged at her sweater in disgust. 'I need new clothes; everything has been ruined in that laundry.'

Mary laughed merrily and rose to her feet. 'It's April, have you actually looked in the mirror since December? See you at two then, we'll go shopping.'

Driving to Rhodes, Christie watched the sea avidly, wanting to remember the exact hues. Until now, she had been highly disappointed that she couldn't go out because of the rains. Michael had declared the ruins out of bounds as it was slippery and dangerous and as he so high-handedly pointed out, there was no hospital in Lindos should someone fall and break a leg, or injure himself worse. Since no one went up there, no one cared, but she did. Now, hints of sultriness, warming breezes, changing currents, and the days of spring were more than a promise.

Wandering through the medieval castle in Rhodes later, Christie felt captivated by its antiquity.

Mary's only remark was; 'it's old, big deal.'

Christie studied the thick walls, the dry moat, the Arsenal Square, and the seahorse fountain. Walking up the Street of the Knights - a long, straight and narrow cobbled street, lined with sombre facades of the Inns of the Tongues and various nationalities belonging to the order of the Knights Hospitalers of St John - it brought images only she could see. She touched the walls and studded doors with caressing gestures.

They stopped to talk to a group of street artists, Christie quickly becoming engrossed in a discussion of colour blending with a young man named Nichola. Every minute or so, Mary pointed to her watch. Reluctantly, Christie eventually moved away.

'I don't know what you see in this stuff.' Mary commented. She was happier eating some sweet cake with a ton of nuts and a gallon of syrup.

'I've seen this one, now I want to see the others.'

'What others?' Mary asked worried.

'Ruins. There's Ialyssos, Kamiros, Kalithea, Monolithos,'

'Today?'

'Over the weekends, the weather is really good now.'

'Can't you ask Michael or Paul? Or how about that Nichola we just met?' Ruins were definitely not her forte and she knew better ways to spend an afternoon than listening to debates in praise of antiquities she regarded little better than rubble.

'Nichola may be nice but is also a complete stranger, Paul I don't want to encourage, and Michael is never around. Besides, he's my boss, so it's hardly appropriate.'

'Do you two get along?'

'What kind of a question is that? He tells me what to do, and I do it.'

'Yes. Let's go have lunch, walking aimlessly makes me hungry.'

Sitting beneath brightly coloured umbrellas, they enjoyed their *souvlakia* and the view at the Mandraki *plaka*.

'I love it here.' Christie gazed at the moored yachts a distance away.

'And it loves you right back. How are you doing where Edward is concerned?'

'Haven't thought about him since- don't know and no longer care. I should've known better, but didn't, so I guess I did learn something. Sadly, I expect he'll eventually fall flat on his face and I pity Gloria, because she's the one who will be there.'

Christie stared at the reflection in the mirror. Did that face belong to her? Passing a brush over the hair one last time, she hurried down to work. As usual, Michael was nowhere to be seen; making her wonder if he worked as hard as Mary affirmed. Through Mrs Kondis, she heard he had finally agreed that the ruins were safe to visit, so she already knew where she was spending part of her weekend.

Armed with easel, bag, and straw hat, she headed for the inviting structure. 'My castle,' she announced gazing at the thick black walls framed against the cerulean sky.

The ascent was steep as it wound on the side of the hill and she stopped often, taking the opportunity to survey the silvery sea below. Arriving at the stairway leading into the beckoning darkness, she tried to count the stairs as she ran up, giving up at forty. A gate or door no longer existed at the inner entrance, and she stepped into the tranquil dusk.

She followed the patches of sunlight until she reached the ancient propylaeum, rows of decrepit columns standing guard. 'No wonder ancient Greeks were good athletes,' she mumbled as she stared at the stoa and grand stairway. She'd been reading about the island and all its treasures and had discovered that this was the Lindian Athene.

Reaching the ruins' edge, she peered over the sheer drop to the rocks below, seeing a small lagoon with a white structure to the right of its shore, the port of St Paul. She set up the easel and pulled her drawing pad from the bag.

Much later, she glanced towards the sun, trying to guess the time, maybe near six. Sitting on the wall, she packed the things away, her fingers running over the brushes Michael had given her.

That day, she had thought it peculiar; until she discovered he often bought personal gifts for his staff. Disappointment filled her; the gesture no longer as special as it had first implied. Pulling the manual she referred to often, she perused a chapter. A shadow fell across the pages. Her heartbeat accelerated as she lifted her eyes. 'What brings you up here?'

'I thought you might be with Mary, but she made a face and pointed towards the heavens.' He grinned. 'I wasn't sure what she meant until she said, what's dark, broken down and really old? Here,' he offered her an ice cream cone.

'Thank you, but I was about to go down.' Taking the cone in one hand, she removed the hat with the other.

His eyes followed the movement, seeing the new haircut. 'Your hair looks- nice.' There were better adjectives, really good ones he'd like to whisper in her ear but knowing her, she'd be offended. She was becoming extremely good to look at, so good, his body was developing a mind of its own whenever she was around him. Her arms were strong and toned and although still white, he knew that summer would turn them golden brown. His gaze dropped to her exquisite ankles and well-defined calves. He looked up again. She was beautiful, and there was the hot coal that sat in the pit of his stomach.

'Thank you.' She knew there were a million topics to discuss, even the weather being an option, but that self-consciousness she always felt in his presence reared its head.

'Called home lately?' He sat down.

'Everyone is fine.'

'And you?' This impersonal area she liked to stick to was annoying.

'It's peaceful here, I like it.'

'Is peace what you're looking for?' He considered his next words. 'I know you and Mary get along, but aren't you bored? Don't you want to mix with people your age, go clubbing, dancing,' hopefully she didn't, because he'd been noticing how just about everything that was male ogled her. It made him fume. 'Mary says Paul and Evy often call with invitations, but you turn most down. Why, or am I being dim and your interest lies elsewhere? I recall questioning you before, but to this day I have yet to have my curiosity satisfied.'

She recalled that day too and the memory of that kiss made her feel shy and annoyed. How was she to tell him that Paul didn't interest her and Evy- those beautiful dark looks were enough to turn any man's head? Why shouldn't he behave like the rest? And it was common knowledge they saw each other regularly. He called it business but she wasn't so sure. "I'm jealous," she realised, so her next words ground out crossly. 'I don't care about clubs or dancing and I do spend time with people my age, most of them anyway. As for my private life,' she felt a rush of blood to her head. 'It's exactly that.'

'Temper temper.' A grin spread on his face.

'I do have one, but you're yet to meet it.'

'Really, hold still.' Grabbing the serviette, he was about to dab the corner of her mouth, when the gesture assumed sensual proportions. 'Chocolate,' he whispered, thinking he'd rather lick it off. Dropping a hand against the soft curve of her neck, he pulled gently and let the tip of his tongue touch the corner of her mouth, pleasure filling him as she shivered at the contact.

It was a feather-light touch but her heart rate rose alarmingly. Why hadn't Edward stirred her this way? Hadn't she loved him? She already knew that. What she didn't know was this. Was it lust or love? Was she falling in love with a man whose very smile could bring a tornado to a standstill, whose presence triggered hidden hungers, who was the very epitome of manhood? Placing her hands on his chest, she felt his heartbeat beneath her palm. For a crazy moment, she grabbed the shirt, pulled him closer, and opened her mouth.

Taking her face in both hands, he felt his heart leap; she was giving him permission. He entered her mouth gently, letting his tongue just touch the tip of hers.

Something ran from her head to the very centre of her being and opening her eyes, she looked straight into his. Then jumping to her feet, she raced all the way down the stairs.

In her room, she tore her clothes off and climbed under the shower, trying to rid herself of his touch and smell, trying to forget how he made her feel. This feeling that told her to let go, as much as it told her to hang on.

Someone knocked. Throwing her bathrobe on, she went to open it. Physical pain lodged in her innards as she saw him.

'You might want these back.' He handed her the easel, bag, and hat.

'Thank you.' She dropped her gaze to her bare feet and refused to look up again.

He banged a hand on the door, startling her. 'Who's this man who has such a hold on you that I revolt you? Don't worry; I won't touch you again.'

Did he just speak a foreign language? And the rest of the day was absolute torture.

As a child, Gloria had not been the epitome of beauty, Christie was. Wherever they went, people stared, at Christie for her appealing blonde looks and at Gloria because she was gangly. Perpetually clumsy and accident-prone, Gloria knew nothing would ever change, secretly resenting her cousin for being almost perfect; just as her brother Ricky was. Christie was excellent at just about everything, knew Greek, and had a talent not many noticed but Gloria knew was becoming as important as breathing.

It had become tradition that Christie spent every second Christmas holiday in Cape Town, and peculiarly, those were the worst times Gloria endured, yet, they were also the best times she remembered.

One morning, they stopped to watch a pavement painting competition. A man walked up to them and asked. 'Trying out?'

Gloria laughed. 'I can only draw stick-people.'

He turned to Christie. 'It's for a good cause. All proceeds go to street children.'

Going down on her knees, Christie drew and coloured.

'It's good, even if rough.' The man commented later. 'Should consider lessons,'

Gloria saw it as a novel way to pass time, then realised this was Christie's true passion, and that she was seriously considering art school. Feeling pangs of envy, she snorted. 'And who will take over from your father and granddad?'

'Are you going to study law?'

'I don't have to, Ricky will.'

'Granddad thinks I should be a liberated woman-'

'Yes, that's how it works in families such as ours. They're expecting you to take over, just as daddy expects Ricky to, and me to go to Europe.' The eighteen-year-old Gloria announced assuredly. 'We can't choose, it's been decided. Paint all you like, but it's only a hobby.'

Soon after, Gloria left for Madame Vidal's finishing school. There, she found it extremely boring to sit through hours of political science, art appreciation, flower arranging, menu planning, and luncheon organisation, not to mention French diction and how to set a table. She could have learnt half of that from the servants at home.

But through her resentment one ambition kept her going, driving her to achieve excellence at everything she had first disliked, to be better than Christie. It wasn't that she hated Christie, she never had; she merely wanted to be good at something too. After a year, she left for the Sorbonne. There, she discovered that not unlike Christie, she too was talented. However, unlike Christie, her talent was not a hands-on type of art. Her genius was in assimilating knowledge at record speed.

She learnt about galleries, palaces, museum, and all that was worth knowing about the art world, and in the process acquired wit and a delightful way of speaking. However, that hadn't been her only triumph, something that impressed more than the knowledge that was now such an integral part of her had also taken place during those four years. Her body filled out in all the right places, her face changed, and her hair no longer caused people to gape. Now they did that in admiration.

Returning from Paris, Gloria was happy to attend parties for a while, then realised that she no longer had much in common with most of the girls she had shared school.

'I'm bored.' She complained. 'I think I'll ask Christie to come visit.'

'There's a boyfriend so I don't know if she'll want to leave him.' Patricia announced.

'Let's ask him along then.' Gloria looked at the calendar. 'No, Christie is still busy with classes. I have a better idea, if aunt Jane doesn't mind, I'll go to Johannesburg. And then they can come back with me for Christmas.'

Knowing her beauty was now comparable to Christie's, Gloria arrived with a little rivalry in her ego. Instead, there was no competition whatsoever, disappointment making her feel like a deflated balloon. Was this what she'd been jealous of, or was it possible that she had twisted the past? However, that jolt was incomparable to the one when meeting Edward. Now here were two satellites moving in opposite directions around two different planets.

That she was immediately attracted to him was undeniable but she hadn't expected him to reciprocate so unashamedly, literally forgetting about Christie.

The predicament became unbearable and she doubted Edward's intentions, often speculating whom of the two he was about to crush. Then, he set her up and proposed! Wondering about his earnestness, she set down a few conditions, then went home, both because she felt deceitful and because she needed a response that appeased her guilt. For all she knew, he was playing them both for fools.

'Gloria,' Patricia rose from the sofa in surprise.

'Oh mom,' everything came tumbling out hurriedly. '…I couldn't stay and look at Christie. I feel awful.'

'Do you love him?' Patricia didn't know what else to say.

'I don't know. I like him, I'm attracted to him. It's all up to him now.'

'Go upstairs and get ready for dinner. I have to call Jane.'

Pat began by apologising profusely, wanting to hear how Gloria's *faux pas* influenced family relations.

'It's not your fault,' Jane conceded. 'And it's possible it's not Gloria's either. Dating and proposing are two different things. Perhaps we read more into the relationship than we should have. And many times I wondered why he bothered at all.'

'How is she?' Patricia commiserated.

'Bad enough. Honestly, I'm not surprised by the turn of events. She ignored him most of the time, leaving Gloria to look after his amusement. What did she expect to happen between two attractive people?'

When Gloria opened the front door one early December morning and Edward stood there, it completely bowled her over. Having a man who went to such lengths was heady. Then sense settled in. How could she be so callous and hurt Christie this deeply?

Both Rob and Peter regarded Edward wearily, as each was concerned with his own daughter's well-being, and neither liked what he had done to the other.

Rob felt foolish because he'd thought so highly of Edward, even having contemplated the possibility of one day letting him take over. So much for that now.

Peter wasn't certain how to view the young man who was about to become his son-in-law. That he had looks and ambition was certain, but what else was going on in that smart head of his?

Edward spent two minutes worrying about straying from his carefully laid plan, then, he shut the door on the past. Spending the five months prior to the wedding demonstrating how much he loved Gloria, he eventually assuaged Peter's misgivings. He found his own place and job, making it abundantly clear that he expected nothing. Besides, he did have the nest egg from the sale of the farm and apartment, so it wasn't as if he came across as needy.

The church service and reception for a hundred guests was like something out of a fairytale. There were silvers and crystals, bows and flowers, everything so perfect Edward knew that it could never be improved upon. He savoured every morsel and enjoyed more than every drop that was set before him, wanting to remember everything.

Twenty minutes from the cottage Patricia had procured for their overnight stay before flying to Mauritius, rain crashed down in waves. Swearing through his teeth, Edward cut through the shroud of water, finally arriving at their destination in complete darkness. Parking the car, he quickly jumped out, and ran into the cottage.

To Gloria's surprise, he didn't come out with an umbrella; instead, he stood on the doorstep, gesticulated furiously. Drenched to the bone, she stepped into the welcome warmth of a log fire and laughed. 'Talk about unorthodox.'

Kicking the door shut, he gazed at her oddly, and passed her a towel. 'Do you need anything from the car?' He went to the drinks cabinet and grabbing one of the bottles, took a large swig.

'Of all the days Edward,' she dried her face. 'You fall off the wagon on your wedding day?'

'I'm celebrating,' he tilted the bottle again. 'This day deserves something special.'

'And I need dry clothes.'

'Wait,' he drank the bottle down to half.

She stared, unable to think why he'd do this after being sober for so long. 'Edward, please stop.'

He finished the bottle, sat it down on a table, and then pulled her into his arms, initiating a kiss that was both wild and violent, hands feverishly tearing at everything that was cloth.

Taken aback by his single-minded objective, she tried to push him away.

With one tug, he tore the silk blouse open.

'Ed-ward,' she gasped.

'Sshh.' Dragging her roughly along, he pushed her onto the carpet, immediately following her there.

Dread filled her and suddenly, being out in the raging storm was more appealing. 'Edward, not like this, and you're drunk.'

He didn't listen, becoming merciless in his assault, pulling and ripping at her clothes. She tried to fight him off, to push him away, but he was too strong, keeping her pinned to the floor, never showing compassion or saying the words she anticipated. She screamed; fear and pain spreading on her face at the punishment he dealt not only her body but also her senses.

All colour drained from her face, she turned onto her side with difficulty, then, got onto all fours, and stayed there until finding the strength to rise. Clutching the shredded remains of the silk blouse to her chest with one hand, she covered her mouth with the other, endeavouring to arrest the uncontrollable sobs. Unsuccessful, she disappeared into the bathroom. Trying to combat the giddiness, she leaned over the toilet bowl, threw up, and sank onto the floor.

Her eyes struggled open. "What a dreadful nightmare". Turning slowly, she saw Edward lying contentedly on the other pillow.

'The princess awakens.' He announced in excellent spirits and pulled her naked body beneath the covers towards his.

Warm rays crawled across her face as she awoke gradually, her body feeling as if it had been spun at high speed in a cramped washing machine. Revulsion filled her as satisfied snoring floated in the air.

Careful not to disturb him, she got out of bed and went into the bathroom. Submerging herself in hot water, she pulled her knees up, dropped her head, and vented the horror of the previous night.

How could this be happening? Hadn't he said he loved her? Where was that man who had made love to her in her room back home as her parents laughed downstairs, where were those hands that had caressed her that morning when he found her down by the beach, and the arms that had held her tenderly as they lay spent in his bed? She didn't know this man, she didn't like this feeling, and she didn't understand this game.

Was this how every bride felt? What did she do now? Walk out or demand an explanation? If she did the former, where did she go? Her parents weren't even home. They were in Barbados by now, enjoying a well-deserved break.

Did she turn to one of the servants for help or one of those people who had attended the wedding? She hardly knew most of them, even the young women who had been there were closer to strangers than friends. Did she call aunt Jane or uncle Rob? What about Thea? She'd probably tell her she had everything she deserved for breaking her cousin's heart.

She had to go out there, face him, and see where this was leading. Eyes drowning, she got out of the tepid water and threw a robe on. Opening the door, she took cautious steps.

'Feeling better?'

Colour disappearing from an already ashen face, she closed her eyes; then turned to see the sardonic smile on his lips. She wiped her eyes with the back of a hand. 'Huh… breakfast.'

'I'm not hungry.' Moving to the middle of the bed, he threw the covers over and patted the place he had vacated. 'Playing hard to get again?

Staring at her bare feet, she then raised her pain-filled eyes. 'How could you?'

'I had too much to drink and my plan didn't exactly transpire as I imagined. And I was teasing you, giving you a bit of fantasy.'

A shiver ran through her. 'You thought I wanted that? It was...' how could she even put it into words? It was the most humiliating experience she had ever endured; something she had never expected from a man, much less a husband.

'I wasn't thinking, now, come here.' But she didn't move and he noticed her head go up a little tartly. She was making a decision and he was not going to like it. 'No, wait.' He jumped out of bed, went to get a glass of water, grabbed a bottle of pills, took three out, and put them in her hand. 'Drink those, you'll feel better in a couple of minutes.'

Looking at the handsome face, she wondered if she hadn't imagined the horror, or at least part, but the pain she felt was real. Her eyes filled with tears; maybe he was sorry. Taking the pills, she swallowed them down.

Edward was upset. Gloria lived up to none of her promises and he felt taken in! Previously, she'd been like fire but now that passionate semblance belied a coldness only found in the deepest Siberian gorges.

After five days in Mauritius, he was bored with life, marriage, but mostly, Gloria, and his thoughts started straying to Christie. Why? She had never inspired much.

But the more he brushed it aside, the more her blue eyes danced in his head. Then, Gloria made a mistake; she suggested they cut the honeymoon short and go home.

He was considering the same, as he couldn't imagine three months - the time she had asked her father to give them to travel, ostensibly to get to know each other better - of nothing but looking at her. What he did know was that she wanted to escape.

'Bored already?' A cynical grin appeared on his face.

Looking towards the secluded beach, she saw the sparkling water embracing the white sand, the sky a glittering blue, the two palms leaning a little carelessly to the right. It should be exciting; instead, it was torture.

'I'm surprised,' he mocked. 'Willing to let all those people know you didn't enjoy yourself, the ones who looked at me as if I were the dirty rag? Want to prove them right?'

Turning quietly, she went to stand behind the sliding door. What did he know, lately, she just didn't feel well.

Approaching, he put a hand to her hair. Shrinking away, a look of pure dislike crossed her face. Fury filled him and closing his fingers in the silky strands, he gave a hard tug. 'Come on Gloria, let's make love.'

She took a step away. 'You no longer know what it is.'

'Neither do you, Miss frigid.' Grabbing her wrist, he pulled her close to his body. And there it was again, he wanted the blue eyes. 'Even in all her inexperience, Christie had more soul.' If he couldn't have fun any other way, then he'd make her squirm.

'Leave me alone.' She tried to pull herself loose.

Grabbing both hands, he forced them behind her back and pushing her against the wall, kissed her. Sometimes, when he closed his eyes, he could imagine Christie.

Releasing her, he announced. 'If I wanted Christie back, she'd be only too obliging.'

Gloria snorted. 'Yeah right, and if you think she's waiting for you at home, think again.' Turning, she went into the bathroom.

He knocked. 'What do you mean?'

She opened the door. 'Oh yes, you don't know. She's been in Greece since November. Rhodes is a beautiful island; blue skies, fantastic beaches, exciting clubs, interesting men- especially now that the weather is warming up.'

'Why would she go there?'

'Michael gave her a job.'

'Who the hell is Michael, and what kind of job is this?'

'Thea's nephew, he owns a hotel in Lindos.'

His eyes narrowed, not liking the sound of this. 'How much will you bet that I can have Christie again? She's in love with me, which is more than I can say for you; you just hated the fact that she had something you didn't.'

'Is that right, and what kind of sick bet is that? I know Christie, you don't. No matter what story you tell, she will never take you back.'

'You're right; we've been on this damn island too long.' A thought crossed his mind. 'Is Sofia's nephew married?'

'No he's not.' Her lips curled as she enjoyed the potential outcome.

Sofia had never liked him, never wanted him near Christie, now he knew why. She'd been looking for this opportunity, and he'd given it to her on a platter! Glaring at Gloria, he saw the mocking smirk. Grabbing her, he struck her twice with the back of his hand.

Tears filled her eyes as her cheeks burnt and hurt, and trying to take a step away from him, she fell to the floor, where she crouched. She heard his footsteps receding, and then coming towards her again. "Lord," she begged. "Please don't let him hit me again."

Dragging her up, he had pills and water in his hands again.

She shook her head. She didn't like how she felt when she drank those things. But he dropped them into the glass, where they dissolved, and then he put the glass to her lips, and forced her to swallow the contents.

Perhaps hours, days, or weeks passed, she wasn't certain, because her mind had become a separate entity.

After getting the information he wanted from front desk, Edward placed a call.

'Michael Andriotti.' The well-timbered English voice answered.

'Well, how did I get the big guy? I was looking for my girl.'

'Excuse me?'

'Christie. On second thought, let's keep it between ourselves. She and I were, are... fill in blank. I've heard you have a grand place out there so I'm coming to check it out.'

'Who are you?'

'Edward Davis. I just thought it fair to give Christie the heads-up that I'll be arriving with the wife, since she went there because of me.' He rambled on for a few minutes. 'What women do for love; anyway, tell her that we're on our way.' He disconnected then grabbed the phone again. 'Yes, check the schedule. We need to get to Athens within the week.'

'How was the-' Mary stopped. Maybe it was too soon to ask.

Christie knew instantly what she meant. No, it didn't bother her. 'The wedding was a great success, Gloria was stunning, everything perfect, the usual.'

'How does it make you feel?'

'Sorry for Gloria; otherwise not worth another thought.'

'Then what troubles you?' Mary noticed the pinched look. 'Why don't you go out with Paul? He's eager.'

'I'm not ready for involvements.' Christie waded out of the pool and wrapped a sarong about her waist. The way things were going she wondered if she would ever be.

'And Christie,' Mary called after her. 'Don't forget dinner at Michael's.'

Friday morning, Mary noticed Christie talking to a young Swede. "Strange," she thought. Christie was charming and unaffected; in fact, the most approachable person she knew, and most people sensed it too, yet that wasn't what she'd seen at Michael's house last night. When they were within metres of each other, it was as if... 'Oh hell,' Mary swore with realisation.

Concern filled her as she saw the bigger picture. Christie was sweet and on the rebound, and he- being utterly selfish if he took advantage. Then again, he had no idea of Edward's existence, because Christie had obviously decided that tormenting him was a good way to go, and hence, his confusion at her resistance, and he'd been particularly recalcitrant last night, as if he were raging mad.

Paging through a report, Christie felt tired, not physically, but emotionally and mentally. What was that mess last night? He was upset about something again and she with no idea what she might have done. This attraction was a huge inconvenience because she'd prefer to loathe him. If only there was a switch, she could snap off at will!

As if brought by telepathy, he entered the office, and as usual, she knew that he was in a murderous mood.

'Where's Mrs Kondis?'

Glancing at the clock, she wondered why he bothered to ask. 'I'd say home. Anything I can do?'

He pushed the door shut. 'Apparently, you've already done plenty.'

She already didn't like his tone. 'Can you actually specify?'

'I knew there was a man, why not just admit it?'

What was this man business? 'Who are you talking about now?'

'Edward.'

Of all the stupid things he said, that was definitely not the expected one. 'Edward! How—'

'I found out? Lover boy called for bookings. And guess what?' Sarcasm laced every word. 'His wife is also coming along. What the hell Christie, a married man? Is this why Thea sent you out of the country?'

Why were they coming here, who had suggested it, and what had Edward said? 'I think it's none of your business.'

'You bet it is. You may not like it or agree with it but that's just the way it is. Damn it, Christie!' He put a hand to his forehead. Heavens, but he was upset, and confused. He could have sworn she was inexperienced. 'I will not tolerate improper behaviour by anyone in my employ, is that understood?'

How dare he? He didn't know the first thing about her! Something she had never known exploded as she got to her feet. 'Hypocrite! You do whatever you wish and I must conform to your double standards? I propose you set an example first.' It was true, what were those two kisses about, fun? And now he was issuing orders? 'I think I'm quite capable to look after my own affairs. You don't like it, fire me, or should I simply resign?'

But that little speech only provoked him, the word affairs not sitting well with him at all. 'You didn't understand me. You are not going anywhere but abide by my rules. You will not leave Lindos for any reason whatsoever because I absolutely forbid it that you conduct an adulterous rendezvous with your lover and then have the village discussing it as if it were a cheap soap opera.' Without another word, he left the office.

Sitting down wearily, her hands flew to her face. "How can I despise and desire the same man this intensely?" She knew how and she had only herself to blame for being ensnared by good looks, eyes that were constantly alert, and a sharp tongue that often lashed out in sarcasm.

'For all the steps mankind has taken forward, men sure have taken few where relationships are concerned.' Mary said as she walked in ten minutes later. 'But obviously, you're not doing much where this one is concerned.'

'Meaning?'

'Michael. Men are such frauds. It's okay for them, to have as many flings as they wish, but when they hear about the one guy in a woman's past-'

Christie made a wild gesture. 'He discussed this with you?'

'Discussed? No. He just told me adorable Edward is on his way, so he's fuming silently, which should bring him to boiling point by the time Eddy arrives. I hope he's not going to embarrass you, himself, and the entire staff when Edward gets here by punching him, instead of shaking his creepy little hand and pretending to be having a whale of a time. Then again, perhaps it will do him good to suffer a bit as he's used to getting his way.' Mary studied her friend for a second. 'It's obvious there are feelings involved here.'

'Yes, of intense mutual dislike.'

Christie felt claustrophobic. Edward and Gloria would be here in a few hours! How would she survive, especially with Michael watching her like a hawk? What reason could they possibly have to come here? Had the world run out of places for newlyweds to visit? Had they imagined that she hadn't hurt? Who had suggested it? Then they had better get here soon because she was going out of her mind.

Covering the computer with its dust cover, she turned to switch the light off. 'Edward!'

'Christie?' He soaked the indescribable picture before him and gave her a bear hug. 'I leave you for a few months and this happens.'

"And I thought I was in love with this fool." 'Gloria?' She managed.

'She's very tired. Will you join me for dinner?'

"Is he for real?" She glanced at Michael and seeing a phoney smile, turned back to Edward. 'I'm busy. How long will you be staying?'

'Well, we have three months, so we're citizens of the world.' He laughed.

It grated her nerves. "I'll bet this was his idea." She tried to sound casual as she looked meaningfully at Michael. 'Edward likes interesting buildings, I'm sure he'd enjoy a tour. In the meantime, I'd like to go say hello to my cousin.'

'Cousins?' The threatening eruption was hard to miss.

Seeing Gloria was like meeting a stranger. Her eyes fired up one moment then dropped in total mortification the next, no longer as sure of herself as she'd been months previously. This was the old Gloria, the meek child who cried when people made her unhappy. Automatically, Christie reached for a hand; to become immediately aware of an abnormal trembling. And she knew; she knew something bizarre was unfolding before her very eyes! Leaving minutes later, she felt the need for quiet reflection, away from this person Edward called Gloria but she didn't recognise.

Gloria thought she was supposed to do something, but kept forgetting. They had flown here and she imagined that she was supposed to know where here was. She felt unwell, shakings and headaches attacking her constantly, making her feel as if she could no longer formulate thoughts. Her mind rode a never-ceasing Ferris-wheel and she had no clue how to stop it. Edward had become kindness personified, looking after her with immense patience, even getting her medication that obliterated every body and mental pain, but it felt so strange.

'Edward,' she ventured as soon as they were in their suite. 'I think I'm allergic to the pills.'

'You will do what I bloody tell you.' He announced savagely.

Walking to the village, Christie wandered through a few narrow alleys and then left at the other end, just where the small forest began; the one everybody called the park. Sitting on a rock, she watched the calm sea below, the twinkling lights along the shore, hearing people laughing and singing. Why was it that things looked different from a distance? Everyone seemed happy but she knew it was a mirage. Not everyone was, she wasn't, neither was Gloria. She wished they had never come here because now she was going to worry constantly.

The situation must look baffling to Michael but she absolutely refused to explain his erroneous conclusions. His arrogance was contemptible; he had no right to sit in judgement of anyone, least of all her. He was taking his role of protector far too seriously and she absolutely detested his unfairness. As if the thought conjured him up, she saw him approaching from the path, the last house casting strange shadows over him.

'What was so important that you had to follow me here?' She queried.

'Before I start, how long have those two been married?'

She shrugged. 'A couple of weeks,'

He looked as if he were about to explode. 'In all my years I have never met a woman with less kindness or compassion, not to mention being utterly selfish and destructive. That you are considering carrying on whatever you had with that man, is detestable. He's a pompous fool and she- she's as fragile as a sheet of glass and I cannot believe what you're envisaging.'

'Look at me,' she got off the rock. 'This is me not caring what you think.' In some cultures that was probably a death sentence for a woman, but she doubted he'd hurt her even if he was hopping mad. Turning her back on him, she returned to the hotel, locking herself in her room. If either he or Edward knocked on her door, she would break their jaw.

Days later, Mary wondered how Christie endured this melodrama Edward had so viciously set up, then realised that her friend was stronger than many people believed.

She couldn't wait to see how she'd put Edward in his place.

'You know,' she commented casually. 'From what you said, I expected a tart, but Gloria is not like that at all, just very quiet. But Edward… now there's a mystery. Like a sly fox he is. I don't trust him, and neither should you.'

'I don't. And I never met that weird human being in my life. I don't know what he's done to her but he sure has done something.'

CHAPTER SEVEN

Seeing Edward approach the pool, Christie was immediately on her guard. It was as if a shroud had lifted from her eyes. She didn't like anything she saw, especially as she considered the possibility that he might be hurting Gloria. Why oh why had Michael given him permission to use this pool?

'Hello,' he greeted cheerfully. 'Heard you're an early riser.'

'What do you want?'

Wading in, he stopped beside her. 'Why didn't I really see you before?'

'Because neither I nor my feelings mattered.'

He made a face. '*Touché*, but now it doesn't have to be that way anymore.'

'And how is it supposed to be? Oh yes, friends. No.'

'What if friendship is the furthest thing from my mind?' He gave her a glance, as if it was self-explanatory.

'Then I'd say I just got lost in this conversation.'

'I'm talking about us.'

'That's just it Edward, there's no us.'

'There could be.'

'What exactly are you implying?'

'I know you're sceptical, but I didn't know I cared. How could I guess that you had crept into my heart while I was thinking of other things? I need you.'

Incredulity appeared on her face. 'And where exactly do I fit in, your bed? You're out of your mind to even imagine that I'd consider it.' She started walking away from him.

He grabbed her arm. 'We'll go home and-'

'I'm not listening to this drivel.' The sorry thing was that he seemed to mean it.

A smirk appeared on his face as he pointed towards Michael's house. 'What, you think Mr Big Shot will marry you? Not now that he believes you're my mistress. You have so much to learn about men.'

Yanking her arm free, she went towards the stairs, then turning, she told him. 'I may be naïve but there is nothing I want to learn from you. And who gave you the right to insinuate lies about our past?'

Without warning, he pulled her into his arms and kissed her.

She froze, standing like a rock, immovable and unfeeling.

'Acting the miss iceberg, are we?' He let her go.

Her hand flew up, striking him across the left cheek. 'Don't ever touch me.'

He grinned. 'You want me as much as I want you. Well, you're a woman scorned so you're entitled to your little tirade. But,' he gave her an odd look. 'There is a time limit.'

It was a strenuous situation. Christie tried to avoid Edward like the plague, and Michael as much as was humanely possible. Mary watched bewildered and thought the predicament felt like a time bomb on a short fuse. Christie couldn't sit still for longer than a few minutes, spending endless hours hiding in the local ruins, as if she were on a permanent high, and Mary fully expected her to have a nervous breakdown within days.

That was exactly the point, most people couldn't think of walking up those endless stairs every day and she figured Edward would behave likewise. Dragging the easel around was cumbersome, but for peace of mind, she'd walk up there every hour.

Suddenly, strong arms grabbed her from behind. Startled, Christie spun around, a paintbrush in her hand. 'I'm busy.'

'There was a time when you wanted me to hold you. True, on the incompetent side, but a brave attempt nonetheless.'

It was as if he merely opened his mouth to bait her. Best ignore him.

'It should have been you I tricked to my apartment. And I'll bet anything it would have been most enjoyable making love to you.'

She coloured at his expression. 'You'll never know, will you?'

'Given my proposal some thought?'

She felt like laughing. 'Are you serious?'

'Absolutely.' His eyes ran over her indolently then stopped on her mouth. 'I used to hate your mindless chatter. Now, I'd endure anything to be with you.'

She took a deep breath and a step back. 'I don't know how to put this any plainer. Stop this, it makes me extremely uncomfortable.'

'Sorry I care.' He said theatrically.

Christie's sapphire eyes flashed furiously as she packed her bag. Then she pointed angrily. 'You want to be here, it's none of my business, but don't interfere in mine. And if you're under the misconception that I'm allowing you to terrorise me then you're sadly mistaken. Tread softly because it doesn't take much to make a phone call.'

His eyes narrowed, she was bold. 'To whom?'

'Uncle Peter. Think I wouldn't dare? Try me.'

'My, finally full of fire. And wow, counterattack, I'm impressed. Truthfully, I prefer you this way.' He reached for her face.

Seeing the gesture, she swung the bag as if to strike him. Then grabbing the easel, she rushed down the great stairway, his laugh jarring loudly in her ears.

Reaching the lobby, she ran into Gloria. 'Great.' She did a half-turn, intent on avoiding her, then changed her mind and walked back.

'Painting again?'

Christie wondered why she persistently got the feeling that Gloria never knew what to say around her, or if she did, she couldn't find the right words to express it. 'Yes.' She watched her cousin with interest. 'I'm on my way to the village, want to come along?'

'Lovely place.' Gloria agreed as they reached the trees.

'I feel as if I've always lived here. The people are wonderful, especially Mrs Kondis, who's always asking me to lunch or dinner.' Yes, if it weren't for the kind woman, she would have already lost her head and pushed Edward over one of the cliffs.

'You didn't ask me here for the view.'

Christie gazed quizzically at her. She actually looked coherent. 'No. I feel it's time we settled some things.'

Gloria looked down at the beach. 'Do you love him, or want him back? Because if you do-'

'No to both questions, in fact, I don't even like him. Know what he was? A convenient way out. Look, you did hurt me, but now it all feels far removed and silly, as if it happened to someone else.' She propped up the easel and pointed. 'What do you think?'

Gloria looked at the canvas. 'Such a pity you never pursued art.'

A smile appeared on Christie's face. 'According to you, this was a hobby. Law was expected of me.'

'When did I say that?'

'Before you left for Switzerland.'

'And you listened?' Gloria's eyes glistened unhappily.

'Ah, there you are.' Edward interrupted. 'So, what were you discussing?'

'My artistic ability or lack thereof.' Christie told him coldly. And why was it she got the distinct impression that he didn't want Gloria to be alone with her?

He perused at the work. 'What do you know, you're actually improving.'

Christie forced herself to calm down. She was still annoyed over the episode earlier and simply hated being in his presence. 'I should get back.'

'Yes.' Edward waited for her to pack everything.

She was furious at the dismissal and looked at Gloria. The little spirit she had seen but a few moments ago had already been extinguished.

Thursday evening, Christie hoped a twenty-four-hour virus got hold of her. Since Edward and Gloria had arrived, Michael had included them at the dinners and she hated all those awkward moments and conversations. Then she noticed with disappointment and distaste that Edward had become reacquainted with alcohol, and she witnessed a quickly disappearing faculty as he clung to his drink.

How did she discover if Edward was hurting Gloria, when Gloria wasn't willing to impart information? On three occasions Christie had watched him do battle in court, he'd used allusion quite successfully and she wouldn't put it past him doing so now, especially as he sought to coerce her into submission. The nasty thing was that his intimations were often based on truth. Going down to the bus-tours kiosk, she bought a ticket to Kamiros, hoping the ruins' solitude was inspirational.

In ancient time, Kamiros was the second largest town, situated on the north-western shore of Rhodes. The hill, where the acropolis is, is u-shaped and in the centre, there is a gentle sloping valley. Public and religious buildings are perched on the higher part of the slope while residential habitations spread down the hill. Columns and outside walls are no taller than five or six feet, and mostly everything else is flat or just a couple of feet tall. Now, it's mostly bare through either erosion or tourists' spades, but it still brings them in hordes.

Returning home, Christie couldn't say she was closer to enlightenment, just half-numb.

However, days later, she knew Kamiros had nothing to do with the way she felt. Dropping her head on the desk, she wished she could ignore the agonising pain. Rising slowly, she told Mrs Kondis that she needed to be somewhere.

An hour later, she stared at the doctor. 'Can't I take something?'

The elderly man shook his head and reached for the phone. 'I'll call Dr Dionidis at the hospital and make the arrangements. All you need to do is get there.'

'I never did hear of an appendix that just went away'

'Who shall I call or would you prefer the ambulance?'

'That's very kind but someone might actually need it. Let me go tell the boss.' Getting to her feet, she cried out in pain.

'Sit down Miss Thomas; you are in no state to walk anywhere again.'

Minutes later, Michael stood in the consulting room. 'Why didn't you tell me you were sick?'

And why did he irritate her the moment he appeared?

Reaching for her arm, he pulled her up, making her wince. 'I'm sorry,' all of a sudden his voice became soft, as if he were truly concerned, making her cry. 'But when Christie, when are you going to learn to talk to me?' And gently, he lifted her into his arms and took her to the car.

She stayed in hospital six days and in that time, she saw everyone except Edward. Not that she wanted to see him, but she wondered what could possibly occupy his time, as Mary told her that none of them had seen him for days. And on the flipside of that, she was glad Michael and Mary drove Gloria in to visit her. It was gradual, but she was seeing a change, as if Gloria was going through a detoxifying process.

One morning, she tried particularly hard to guess, question, and snoop, but Gloria was not ready to share. Impatience and annoyance; that was all she felt around Gloria and Edward.

After returning to Lindos, she made it a point to spend most of her free time with Gloria, who, looked almost happy if quiet and Christie put it down to Edward's absence. She wished she knew what he did. But it was almost certainly something seedy because this was not the same man she had met.

Crossing the lawn, she saw Gloria sitting under a palm tree. Right, this insane situation needed a resolution and probably a revolution too.

'Gloria,' she began. 'Does Edward love you?'

The beautiful emerald eyes looked startled. 'What makes you ask such a question?'

'My concern for you. Edward doesn't act like a newlywed and you don't seem to be enjoying this absurdity either. What are you doing in Rhodes when there's Corfu, Crete, or Kos? It doesn't make sense.'

'Edward is in charge of our travelling arrangements.'

'And finding his pockets lined with your father's money, does wonders for his ego. Does he hurt you? Please let me help, or do you think that I'd gloat? I'd never do that.'

'No marriage is perfect and the sooner you learn that, the better. It's hard trying to build a life when two people are as different as we are. Forget the bed of roses.'

'And I'll bet yours is particularly thorny. Now look me in the eye and tell me without crying that you're ecstatically happy. You can't. So when you return home, how will you hide from your parents?'

'Drop it.'

'Please don't be fooled into thinking that your problems will miraculously vanish.'

'I have to try make things work.'

'How in heaven's name do you make something horrible work? If it's like this now what will it be like next year? And what if there are children?'

Gloria rose from the chair. 'Stop interfering.'

'Why can't you see that he's making both our lives hell?'

'I'm warning you, Christie, stay out of my life.' Gloria said shakily.

'No, you get out of his. And since you refuse to fix this, then I will.' Christie told her equally upset, as she too jumped to her feet then looking up in frustration, she saw Mary and Michael.

Gloria opened her mouth, but nothing came. Tears welling in her eyes, she ran away, with Mary on her heels.

'I'd like to see you in my office.' Michael said and turned his back on her.

She raised a hand to knock but as if sensing that she was there, he opened the door, and almost dragged her inside, unceremoniously pushing her into a chair.

'What is it with you? Didn't I warn you to stay away from that man? I should have you locked up because you are certifiable. All I see is this monopolising beast devouring everything in its path.'

He raised a hand and for a second she imagined that he might strike her. Instead of showing fear, she rose to her feet, within inches of him. 'Are you quite finished? And what is it you're trying to prove, that you're better, why, because you're a man? I will have you know; I'm sick and tired of your judgemental attitude. You're my boss, not my guardian, even less my father, whom I still listen to although I'm no longer obliged to. You say different words but your method is the same. Bullying someone weaker than you is easy, isn't it, which is what both of you do to me, continually. And, don't you touch me disrespectfully again because I am not a silly female desperate for kisses from the boss. Count me out of your club. As for Gloria, I better than anyone here know what's best for her.'

'That man is trouble and all you'll get from him is a broken heart.'

'You should know, you use the same tactics.'

He was not following her reasoning at all. 'Christie, believe me when I say that I care about your welfare. You never said why you came here; now, it's all I see. And I simply hate watching him stringing you along.'

Was that what he believed? With Edward opening his mouth, who knew what had come out. 'Why can't you ever be civil to me?'

'Point taken and I apologise.' What else could he say to an infatuated woman? 'But how wise is a liaison with that egotistical nut? Married men make continuous promises, which they never keep, and they rarely leave their wives for their mistresses. Can't you see? Edward will only cause you grief.' Heavens, but this mess made him angry.

'Can I ask you a question?'

'Of course,'

'How daft do you think I am that you swallow such hogwash? And why is it easy for you to believe him, but not me?' She left his office.

She stormed into the elevator crossly. Why did people find nonsense easier to believe than the truth? A few people came in and she continued the ride, when everyone got off at the next floor, she realised Edward was beside her. She glanced at him disinterestedly.

'Fortunately, Gloria is not inclined to leave me.'

'You listen to me, I will not be intimidated.'

'Or what, you call Uncle Peter? If I see him, how shall I put it? Michael might just have an unfortunate accident.'

She froze. 'Leave Michael out of your warped games, he has nothing to do with this.'

'It depends on you, doesn't it? You see dear Christie, I can have Gloria and you and get rid of Mr Annoyance along the way too, which will give me as much, if not more pleasure. He's a huge irritation and I can't wait for an excuse to dispense with him. I suggest you keep your mouth shut.' His eyes bore into hers. 'And Gloria is no longer your concern.'

'Blackmail is a criminal offence.' Her heart pounded.

'And you're hardly an expert on the law.' Waving cheerily, he walked out of the elevator.

CHAPTER EIGHT

Hearing the door open, Gloria pretended she was asleep. This was hell but she couldn't see a way out. Edward climbed into bed and she smelled ouzo. Best stay away. Moving closer to the edge, she suddenly found him right behind her.

'Christie,' he slurred, yet his voice was soft and caressing. 'I love you so much.'

'Edward,' she began, but never finished. Tomorrow was soon enough.

Suddenly a light went on, followed by excessive swearing. Opening her eyes, Gloria saw him standing in the middle of the room, his hands on his head.

'You tricked me.' Pointing accusingly, he advanced towards the bed.

'I tried to tell you-'

'There's your punishment for hoodwinking me. I should have stayed in the plan, but I didn't know that I needed her so much. You realise I'll never love you.' He glared at her.

Her eyes filled with tears, and slipping out of bed, she threw the gown on. This was no time to feel vulnerable. 'I want an annulment.' She declared.

Surprise showed in his eyes. 'How are you getting this done? Do you know what you have to prove to get that right?'

'I'm sure I'll find something.'

He became mocking. 'You're suddenly very brave. What happened, skipped a few pills?'

'Blackmail me all you wish but I refuse to drink that poison again. And I won't live waiting for what will never be.' She wiped her wet cheeks.

'Maybe you're right; Christie might need to see some sort of commitment.'

'Forget it, she doesn't want you, she wants Michael.' She was in an impossible situation but she knew what love and desire looked like.

He struck her with the back of his hand.

She stumbled, fell, and hit her jaw on the bedside table. A shaking hand went to her mouth, wiping the blood. 'Hit me all you like but you can't change facts.'

Grabbing her by one arm, he pulled her up, his fingers digging into the soft flesh. 'Cold passionless female, never underestimate me. I wanted you, got you, and what a mistake that turned out to be. Now, I want Christie, and her I shall have, and I want her more than anything I've ever desired.'

She tightened the belt about her waist. 'I failed her once, not again. Therefore, I've changed my mind. There's no annulment, no separation, and no divorce. I'm keeping you away from her.'

For the second time that night, he struck her. 'I'll never love you, only Christie.'

'You're not in love, Edward. You're obsessed.'

'As cheerful as a town hit by a cyclone.' Christie stared at the sunglasses and silk scarf. Then without warning, she pulled the scarf aside, gasping as she saw the ugly bruise. 'He hit you!' She felt sick. Squeezing Gloria's trembling hand, her own eyes filled with tears. 'Oh please, please don't let him do this.'

She was so enraged that she had to leave. If he could do this to Gloria, what else was he capable of? A fear she had never known filled her, something that wasn't visible but felt in the depths of her soul.

She had barely reached the grand stairway when she saw him. Blood boiling, she strode purposely towards him, her indignation obvious.

He leaned nonchalantly against a column.

'It's absolutely criminal.' His indifference exasperated her. 'Touch her again and I will have you removed from this island by whatever means.'

Moving swiftly, he grabbed her face and pushed her against the column, his thumb digging into her neck, making breathing difficult. 'Do not cross me.'

'Or you hurt Gloria again? Do and a Greek jail will become home sweet home.'

He gazed at her, so beautiful; the deep blue eyes full of unshed tears, the sensual mouth. Tightening his grip, he thrust her further against the column. 'I've been reduced to my knees, and suddenly, I find it repulsive to crawl and beg. Now, I'll tell you something I expect you to take as law, do as I say or else. Think Gloria has it bad? Wait until I deal with Michael, for there's no chance in hell that he'll possess you before me.' Leaning forward, he kissed her roughly then he let her go.

Running, she bumped into a stranger at the bottom of the great stairway; his long black hair giving him the look of a cutthroat.

What exactly did she or Gloria know about Edward? Nothing, except that he already had a drinking problem since his teens. He had barely mentioned the past, or volunteered meagre scraps of information, suddenly making it all very mysterious. Was it possible there was something to hide?

After Mrs Kondis left that afternoon, Christie paced the office. What was she supposed to do?

'Christie,' Michael said from the doorway. 'There's something I'd like to ask.'

She wanted to think about Edward, to know what was going on. 'Can it wait?' She drummed a hand on the desk.

'Then come see me before you leave.'

She grabbed the phone, dialled quickly and waited a few seconds. 'Mr Peter Thomas, please.'

'Who may I say is calling?' The secretary asked.

'Christie, his niece. I need to speak to him urgently. It's about his daughter.'

'Please hold.' There was a short silence and then a quick connection.

'Christie, what's this about?'

'Where do I begin? Gloria's life has become one hell after another and I have no idea what to do. Did you know that they're here? Edward's sick idea. Yesterday, he hit her. Since they've arrived, he hasn't stopped being an absolute beast to her and pesters me constantly with the most indecent proposals.'

'If this is true, why hasn't Gloria called?'

'Because either pride, blackmail, or whatever that shaking is-' that was something she was still unable to comprehend. Gloria's body was somehow out of control, although she seemed to be improving. 'I know she's a grown woman, but right now, she's one without power because he has taken it from her. How do I stop him? Now, he says he wants me back. I told him not to bother me but it's like talking to a snake. Uncle Peter, please believe me when I tell you that your son-in-law is dangerous.' Her voice wavered. 'Please do something, because if you don't, you'll get her back in a body bag.'

Michael looked up from his PC as he realised she was leaning against the wall. She was unhappy, that much was clear and he couldn't explain what it was that he felt because she made him crazy. Surges of love, lust, and desire culminated in stages, intensities, and at different tempos; turning him into something even he had trouble recognising, and he found the phenomenon both exhilarating and depressing, as he couldn't resolve the situation. He'd given it a fair attempt at starting a relationship, but she had soon dampened progress with her erratic behaviour. One thing he knew, he wanted her as he'd never wanted another woman.

A smile appeared on her face; one that told him someone brought love thoughts to mind. Jealousy rushed through him. He wanted to be that someone, the only one she would think about like that. 'What's going on?' He asked.

'Uncle Peter will be here soon.' She announced tiredly. She was sick of this, and she wasn't going to tell him funny stories anymore, because he was probably the only one who could actually help her. 'You have no idea the pandemonium Edward has created. He hit Gloria!'

'When?'

'Yesterday, and then ordered me not to tell. That if I did he'd-'

'That he'd what?' He prompted.

If Edward hurt Michael... It was as if a dagger lodged itself in her heart. She gazed at him. Heavens, she loved him. She made a helpless gesture. 'I've probably aggravated the situation. And to extract revenge, he'll just hurt her more.'

'He's not going near her again.'

'And how do you propose to do that?'

'By having her moved to the house and him deported.'

An odd sound escaped her. 'Under what law? Besides, it happens almost every day in the village and the police are still to do something about it.'

'Yes, nothing is as perfect as it seems.'

'Mrs Kondis is trying so hard to set up a safe-house and to have the layabouts arrested. But if they are, how will the women survive? They have no education, no means,' she did a half-turn. 'But sure enough, they have children.'

'I'll speak to Dimitri and see what can be done. Now, to warn Gloria.' He reached for the phone.

She waved a hand. 'I'll go tell her. What did you want to discuss?'

He smiled, rose to his feet, and went to stand before her. 'I was going to ask you out on a date.' Seeing confusion on her face, his smile widened. 'I have been known to act like a gentleman.'

Her heart was about to come to a standstill. 'You and me?'

'Why are you so surprised?'

'The last time I did this was with Edward, I don't want to go there. Then there's this rule about the employees- You are not very democratic.'

'I may have been harsh in that respect and I still have reservations. However, as I also said, you are not exactly an employee. So?' He regarded her intently.

'It's so out of the blue and with all of this happening-'

'Yes, skip dinner. You and Mary must also move.' Seeing the face of protest, he added quickly. 'Until Gloria's father gets here, you stay together, away from that crackpot. Christie, do you possess an evening gown? I've been invited to a grand opening on Saturday.'

'I still don't understand why you're asking me. Is Evy busy?' Did he have to be this close?

'I don't know because I didn't ask. Is this a problem? Would you rather not go out with me at all?' He straightened her collar and then tucked a stray lock of hair behind an ear.

Was this what he did to women, use this bizarre power that turned her into a fool? The power that was so intense, she thought she would die if he didn't touch her. She leaned her face into his hand.

This was promising. A thumb rubbed gently against her chin, then he pulled her against his body and his lips brushed across hers. She didn't resist, but he knew something wasn't right yet. 'Are you afraid of me?'

No, but she was afraid of something else. Unable to stop it, a tear slid down the side of her face, and she dropped her gaze. 'But like Edward, you are going to mess me up and break my heart.'

Suddenly, he understood all the crazy behaviour. He lifted her chin, so she could see what burned in his heart. 'No, Christie, this is where I want to be.' Wrapping his arms around her, he kissed her slowly, tasting her gently, igniting her, getting a response that made them both feel physically weak. Reluctantly, he tore himself away. 'Don't worry; I'll still prove I'm not like Edward. You're right, my behaviour was reprehensible, and I'm sorry. Okay, you go see Gloria and I'll find Mary. Then, we'll deal with Edward. And afterwards,' he gave her an intriguing smile. 'We'll surprise each other.'

Christie glanced around the Hermes suite, extremely attractive in beiges and salmons, the beautiful travertine marble giving it an opulent luxury, exactly the surroundings Edward thrived in; except, he was never here.

'Any particular reason for today's visit?' Gloria queried.

'Yes.' Christie stared at the bruise, feeling rage again. 'Do you know where Edward goes all the time?'

'He tells me nothing, and honestly, I no longer care.' Gloria poured herself a Perrier from the bar. 'In fact, I have some news that might please you. I asked Edward for an annulment, and then it was a divorce. That's how I got this.' She touched her face.

'No one should be glad over a broken marriage, but this one! I fear for your life.'

'It's possible I should be celebrating but all I feel is degradation. How did I get myself into this, you,' Gloria's eyes filled with tears. 'But we didn't know. Please Christie, please promise that you'll never be tempted to reconcile with him.'

'I'd rather eat glass.'

Gloria knew she meant it. 'Why are you here?'

Hearing the key in the lock, they stared at each other. Instead of waiting for him and taking her leave, Christie ran to the adjoining bathroom and hid behind the door, where she could see into the suite.

'If it isn't my lovely wife.' Edward bowed theatrically.

Gloria put the glass down. 'Where have you been?'

Taking quick steps, he towered above her. 'Making lots of money, and all on my own. But I'm sick and tired of this inquisition.' Grabbing her arm, he twisted it until she cried out. 'And didn't I warn you to shut your mouth? Now, Christie is defiant, which, as it happens, is quite the thrill.'

'Please let me go home.'

'Home,' he asked as if not comprehending the concept. 'Ah, away from me.' Reaching in his pocket, he pulled out a leather wallet. Taking out her passport and airline ticket, he dropped them in the ashtray and deliberately set them alight.

Christie put a hand to her mouth to cover the gasp.

'You may go anywhere you wish.' Grabbing Gloria's discarded drink; he poured its contents over the small fire. Then turning around, he left again.

As if in a trance, Christie came into the room and put her arms around her cousin. 'Oh, Gloria, who is that man?'

'Miss Thomas,' the barman greeted. 'What will it be?'

Christie felt as if she was high. 'Whiskey, and make it a double.'

His brows shot up. Everyone knew she was no drinker. 'Something wrong?'

'To say I'm rattled is an understatement. This day has been unpredictable, unnerving, frightening even.' Now, she hoped Michael succeeded in getting rid of Edward, fast. 'Have you seen Mr Davis?'

'About fifteen minutes ago. Was on his way to the Harbour Master. Business, he said.'

Her interest was pricked. Earlier, Edward had mentioned money. 'What kind?'

'No idea. That strange character who hangs around him doesn't look like the hard-working type.' Realising she didn't know whom he meant, he elaborated. 'Tall, dark, and not handsome. They're constantly scheming in corners.'

'Oh, it must be the man I bumped into the other day.'

'Please be careful, Miss Thomas. He does not look friendly.'

'I know what you mean.' She swallowed the drink in one gulp, tears springing to her eyes. Then, with a wave, she left.

'Miss Thomas,' the desk clerk smiled as she stopped beside him. 'Going for one of your famous walks?'

She returned the smile with a faint version of her own, her mind squarely on Edward. Perhaps she should follow him. 'A short one.'

'Enjoy it.'

She smiled, feeling shy, exhilarated, thrilled, and everything else as she recalled Michael's behaviour earlier. Excitement filled her, now this felt like an adventure.

Strolling briskly, she watched the houses with interest, here and there seeing modern structures rising above the traditional dwellings. Stopping, she turned and looked at the hotel. She couldn't think of another place as perfect as this. Yet, right here, an awful tragedy unfolded. Quickening her step, she hoped she got to Manoli, the Harbour Master, in time to discover what it was they were concocting.

Her mind turned to Gloria. But perhaps she shouldn't think or she might need more than a double whiskey to come to grips with what she had heard. Yet, in an extraordinarily frightening way, it all made sense. Gloria became upset when Christie announced that her father was on his way. True, Christie taking charge implied Gloria was incapable. However, wasn't temporary embarrassment better than constant humiliation?

Approaching the house noiselessly, she wondered if Edward had come here or gone to the office, where Manoli spent most of his time. Two cats stretched and groomed themselves with intense concentration, completely unaware that she had entered their yard. Seeing the flower-box on the windowsill, she bent to smell the yellow blooms. As she did, a noise came from within, as if something had been bumped and broken. Noticing the open door, she knocked lightly and took a step inside. The man wasn't a recommendation to the human race but if he had fallen, or hurt himself, she should assist him.

A sort of dining-cum-sitting room lead towards the centre of the house and she knew the noise had come from there. A deep male voice reached her, one that didn't belong to Manoli, but neither was it Edward's. Then Manoli answered, behind the closed door, disagreeing over something she couldn't understand.

Turning towards the entrance, her steps were arrested by a sound she had never heard before, a sound that made the hairs on her body stand on end, a sound she could never forget because it was followed by the most horrible noise she had ever heard another living creature make. Two more blows followed. Utterly horrified, she found herself paralysed against the wall, just where the curtain started. The doorknob turned and she prayed that if she stopped breathing, whoever was about to walk through that door wouldn't see her.

It was as if the man had used a paintbrush and liberally splattered red paint all over his clothes. Her eyes became rooted to his blood-soaked hands. Grabbing the curtain, she pressed it into her mouth and bit hard, so she wouldn't scream and give herself away. Looking behind him, a wave of nausea ran through her as she saw Manoli contorted on the floor, deep gashes to his chest and head, a lake of blood reaching the door.

Flinging the object into the room, the man grabbed what looked like a club from a hook on the wall. Christie shuffled her feet together and closed her eyes with fear.

'So, it's over.' An English voice said.

Turning her head, she saw Edward. Both men became aware of her presence simultaneously. As something heavy fell against her head, pain shot through every part of her body. Everything became blurred, then dark, and the floor rushed up to meet her.

'Have you seen Miss Thomas?' Michael asked as he stopped at front desk.

'She went down to the village.'

Michael took an envelope from his pocket. 'Will you see the police captain gets this as soon as possible? I couldn't reach him on the phone as he's out somewhere.'

Now what she was up to was anyone's guess because her antics forever surprised him. One moment there was that fiery temper that unsettled him and the next she was so sweet that all he wanted to do was sit somewhere watching rain, drinking hot chocolate, and making love to her. He recalled the kiss earlier and groaned. No, using the same tactics as that crackpot Edward was hardly the way to win her over. Romance, that's what Christie needed, and from tonight, he'd change all her preconceived ideas. Christie wasn't any woman; she was the one he wanted.

He had barely removed his jacket as he entered the house, when he saw his butler. 'Milo, are the ladies settled in?'

'Quite comfortably. The police captain is also here to see you, sir.'

'Excellent,' Michael passed a hand over his hair. 'Good evening, Dimitri. Glad you reacted to my message so speedily.'

'What is it you want to see me about?'

'Where does the law stand in connection with domestic violence?'

'Tough area. Men refuse to recognise women as equals so the courts follow this mentality and dislike being bothered. In fact, everyone pretends it doesn't exist. Why do you ask?'

'Can we use it to deport someone?'

'Who?' Dimitri asked curiously.

'Edward Davis.'

'The wife should make a formal complaint. But before we continue, the Harbour Master was killed.'

'Good heavens, how-' Michael said in shock.

'And unfortunately, he's not the only one who got into trouble today. The doctor is doing everything possible and the ambulance is already on its way.' To verify his words they heard the siren in the distance. 'Michael, do you have any idea why Christie should be at Manoli's house?'

'What?' All colour drained from Michael's face.

There was police and neighbours everywhere. Then the questions began, why, what, when. Who knew? He sure didn't. 'Enough,' Michael announced angrily. 'I don't know why she's here. What I do know is that it's impossible for her to do what you're suggesting and then knock herself unconscious. So when someone figures this out, I'll be at the hospital.'

The nightmare unfolded. Hospital personnel rushed back and forth, X-rays were taken, and he was left in the dark.

Christie's brain was swollen and contused from the impact, and the pressure had to be relieved. Dr Dionidis had contacted a neurosurgeon, who was flying in from the mainland.

Then Dimitri appeared and brought perplexing news. There was a stranger involved in this chaos but he'd never seen him. His name was Costa - a criminal - whose poster was plastered on the police station's wall. Then it became worse. Edward was somehow embroiled in the bedlam as well.

Michael seethed. Not only at Edward, but also at himself for not having realised sooner that Christie was in more trouble than he'd imagined. So the triangle was; Edward, Costa, and Manoli. Why?

'Edward is bad news and I don't put anything past him. Have you questioned him?' Michael queried tiredly.

Yet another mystery, no one had seen him since that afternoon. Some people swearing they'd seen him board Manoli's boat with Costa. The boat was missing, so Dimitri assumed it was true.

Costa was apparently a delightful character. He'd been on the run for two years, with quite a list of accomplishments: armed robbery, manslaughter, and the reason why he'd jumped bail; art fraud involving millions worth of German art. Nothing made sense so Dimitri had gone to question Gloria.

'What did she tell you?'

'Edward is unstable.'

'That much I know.'

'I mean he has serious mental problems.' Putting a hand in his pocket, Dimitri pulled out an empty pill bottle. 'Imagine this. You have a condition but instead of taking medication, you feed it to your wife. What do you expect to happen? That's how he got her to come to Rhodes, drugs and blackmail.

'Those first pills made a sane person feel as if she walked on air. She wanted to stop taking them but Edward always managed to slip them into her food or drink. Then a while back, he became involved with something - their get-rich-quick scheme obviously - and started forgetting. Feeling lucid, she called her doctor back home and queried the medication's side effects.

'So while he intoxicated his wife, his own mind went downhill. If it weren't that he had become otherwise preoccupied, she could have been irreversibly harmed. Thankfully, she disposed of the medication because she couldn't chance him feeding it to her again; but he continued blackmailing her, threatening to harm her teenage brother. Christie was made aware of this, minutes before she walked down to the village, and she may have confronted him.'

When Dr Dionidis told him that the neurosurgeon had arrived and Christie was in theatre, Michael took a deep breath.

'Mr Andriotti, you have to go home.'

'But Christie-'

'Young man, there's nothing you can do here. That surgery is going to be hours. There's plenty time for you to rest and return. She is serious but not dying. Trust me; we're taking good care of her.'

And so he'd gone home and called her parents.

Sitting yet again at the hospital, Michael recalled Peter Thomas' swift arrival and departure. A decisive man who was discerning and able, he took quick yet gentle control over his emotionally wounded daughter. Had Gloria been in familiar surroundings, the ordeal would have been hard enough but in an alien environment, it had become beyond endurance and they watched helplessly as she slowly disappeared before their eyes in the space of hours. If it weren't for Mary's constant supervision, Michael suspected that she might have lost her mind, as Edward clearly intended.

Then Dimitri called. The coast guard had found Manoli's boat, near Turkey. Costa was in custody, but there was no sign of Edward. The police had also discovered what business they'd been involved in; Icons. They'd stolen Icons and Religious artefacts, which explained the partnership with Manoli. There was quite a haul but no longer everything; a lot had already disappeared into the black market, and it would be near impossible to recover. They simply walked into homes and churches and helped themselves. Dimitri had alerted ports and airports, so if Edward was on Greek soil and tried to leave, they would know.

Disconnecting, Michael went to stare out the window. The night air was clear and crisp but he didn't notice. Someone played *bouzouki* in the distance, a slow mournful tune but he didn't hear, his mind in the land of memories. None of this was her fault, it was his. Had he paid attention, he would have seen that she needed his help. He sighed deeply, aware that he had no idea how to handle the feelings of guilt and inadequacy.

Then thankfully, Jane arrived.

Apart from sitting at Christie's bedside, she questioned Michael and Mary continuously. Patricia had called and informed her of Christie's conversation with Peter. How was it possible, none of them had imagined any of this, she asked, how had they been so wrong? How had he hidden it so well? It was all very alarming and perplexing.

Now, every day, they watched doctors perform something called a PERL test - Pupils Equal and Reactive to Light - and stimuli tests, which involved electrical shocks, pinches, and pinpricks; but as always, Christie remained unresponsive.

The doctors hoped, they prayed, everyone waited, and nothing changed; but they refused to accept what the neurosurgeon said, that Christie might stay like this a week, a month, or a year.

CHAPTER NINE

'As I told you on the phone, she's doing well, physically.' Dr Dionidis told Jane and Michael from behind his desk. 'We ran some tests and the neurosurgeon does not suspect brain damage. Unfortunately, she sustained both direct and indirect head trauma, so there is a concern. At first, we considered hydrocephalus - that's an increase in the volume of cerebrospinal fluid in the brain - but thankfully that's not the case.' He paused. 'Sadly, there is always the possibility that a condition may become permanent. However, both the neurosurgeon and Dr Papacostas, the psychologist, are hopeful that-'

'What condition?' Michael interrupted.

'Retrograde amnesia, or in layman's terms, selective amnesia.' Dr Dionidis saw their dismayed expressions. 'Which means, not everything is gone. Thankfully, I already knew Christie so I assisted Dr Papacostas in creating her profile. Chunks of her past are gone but she still reads, writes, and speaks English and Greek. Although she is physically well, we insist she stay here until she develops a sense of security. She recalls Lindos, even if a little jumbled, so that will be our next step in creating a safe environment for her.

'The largest gap seems to be from April to present, and as for her life in South Africa, there are some problems too. Remember,' he looked at Michael. 'You filled me in how the incident happened; she has no recollection of it. Edward is a total blank. She does not recall ever meeting this man. Dr Papacostas seems positive about a complete recovery, but there are confusing and conflicting emotions, and as this starts running its course, there will undoubtedly also be bouts of depression to deal with.'

Michael left the office feeling cheated. So angered was he at that moment that he knew he would have snapped Edward's mean neck had he been around.

She had precipitated this wave of information when she demanded that everyone tell her the truth, but as she recalled little, Christie seesawed between depression and yearning to make all the pieces fit. Then she agreed that trying was better than burying herself under self-pity. Although by no means easy to accept that a piece of her life had disappeared, perhaps it would also be exciting to rediscover what had been.

She liked this part of the hospital's gardens. There was an uninterrupted view of the azure waters blending into the frothy horizon and she felt she could see forever. Forever was a long time, why did she expect everything to change today? She put a hand to her strangely cropped hair with a silent hope. That her memories might return as her hair grew into its former glory.

'May I?'

Seeing the end of a crutch, she looked up. 'Hello John.' She shuffled left as he sat on the right side of the bench. 'How's the leg?'

'Much better, thanks. I just feel like an idiot.'

She recalled his story two days previously. He'd been standing on the deck of his boat – which he rented to tourists – when a sudden gust of wind had swung the mast around and he, trying to avoid being knocked over, ducked, misstepped, and twisted his ankle rather awkwardly.

'I hear you're leaving tomorrow. How do you feel about it?' He asked.

'Mixed feelings. The doctors have done all they can, so now it's all here.' She pointed to her temple.

'Lindos will definitely become more cheerful with you back. I told you I also stay out that way, so would you think it presumptuous of me if I called sometimes?'

She watched the tanned face, the friendly brown eyes, light brown hair gently blowing around one ear, and the short beard. For a second, he reminded her of someone. Someone she seemed to like. A gentle smile appeared on her lips. 'You're the first friend I've made since the accident; I'd like you to.'

'Then count on it. We'll have lunch, picnics, and do fun things-'

Both turned their heads as they heard a woman's voice.

'Doesn't she ever stop?' John moaned and got to his feet with some difficulty. 'I have never seen a physiotherapist who takes her job as seriously as that one. I'd like to stay but she'll see me and drag me to the torture chamber. Sorry, I must dash.' Slowly, he limped away.

During the drive home, Christie kept to that eerie silence both Mary and Jane dreaded and both felt as if she disappeared into another world, one where neither could reach her. Christie glanced in their direction, sensing the invisible yet very much felt barrier erected between them.

Until today, she had been sheltered and cocooned; now, she had to go face a frightening world. Dr Papacostas kept telling her that trying was a better way to battle obstacles, that good or bad, she should endeavour to recover every memory. Perhaps, but when feelings of helplessness hit her, tears and the sanctuary of a dark room seemed the only solace.

Realising the threat of becoming a burden, Christie wondered what she was equipped for. She recalled the two years of law, pathetic. Painting… For some reason, something had happened in her brain. When Mary brought two canvases to hospital because she didn't believe that she painted, she felt grief-stricken because she couldn't recall having produced them.

'Where are we?' Christie asked as she opened her eyes, hating the grogginess her medication brought.

'Lindos,' Mary announced as she navigated the hill.

Christie sat up and stared at the hotel and then the house. 'It's beautiful.'

'Isn't it?' Mary brought the car to a standstill.

Michael opened the door. He wanted to hug her but had no idea how much she recalled. And then he saw it. It was minuscule, but the step backwards was there nonetheless. So he offered his hand instead. 'Welcome home, Christie.'

'Michael-'

He turned to Jane. 'I'm going away for a few days so everything is at your disposal. Dimitri is aware of it.'

As hours became days and then weeks, things began to change. Dreams, images, and names would suddenly fill Christie's head and she queried their significance. Perhaps Dr Papacostas hadn't said all those things merely to placate her after all.

'Christie.' Michael called as he saw her sitting in the garden.

'Hello,' she shaded her eyes to look up at him.

'Would you like to go for a drive?' He asked eagerly.

'And work?'

'There's nothing pressing.' He offered his hand and waited. He'd noticed her reaction around men. She didn't seem aware of it, but he was. However, today, something was different. She gave her hand and let him tuck her arm through his. 'Please inform Mrs Thomas that we're going out for the day.' He told one of the servants and turned back to her. 'Everyone deserves a break and you've been cooped up too long. You need a new routine and I'll see about walks around the village, just not alone.' With Edward still missing, he hardly wanted to imagine her walking into him. Costa had sworn enough times that the knock to her head had been accidental but as they now knew Edward to have some mental challenges, that put a very different perspective on things.

Watching part of the road they took every Tuesday and Friday when going to her therapy was hardly interesting, but today she enjoyed the sun's rays as they played on the water's surface. Gazing at Michael, she asked. 'What do you think of my painting?'

He was tempted to flatter her but seeing the keen expression decided against it. 'Promising, and the only way you'll know is by trying.'

'Sometimes I'm so frightened. I look at those pictures and think I'm intruding in someone else's life. It's as if I expect another Christie to come knocking, someone who's going to tell me to get out because I'm usurping her place.'

Bringing the car to a halt, he turned to her. 'I know we can barely imagine what it feels like, but this is you. Dr Papacostas says you need time and patience, then, we must all have it.'

She followed him to Mario's Taverna, a little place almost completely hidden by a vine that had to be at least fifty years old. But once they sat down at the table, she had an uninterrupted view of a shore kissed by whispery white waves. 'Was I ever here?'

'Possibly, but not with me. Apart from driving you to Lindos once and to the hospital another, this is the first time I've ever taken you out.' He might as well continue. 'Christie, what do you remember of our friendship?' What else could he call it?

'Not much.' She dropped her gaze.

He did his best to hide the dismay he felt.

'But,' she said brightly. 'I do know that you are kind, very considerate, and smart. I'd say we can get along fine.' Her eyes became intensely blue. 'Did we get along before?'

For once in his life, he was speechless. He made the so-so gesture.

'Then I'll say this. If you'll give me a second chance, I'll give you one too.'

'Done.' Reaching across the table, he pressed her fingers tentatively.

She returned the gesture, liking the feeling of safety she felt in his presence, but then she took her hand away. 'Life is too short to stay mad at anyone, even if I can't remember the reason.'

Would she understand if he explained? One day, he'd probably have to, but that wasn't today. 'You wouldn't want the gentleman to be embarrassed into admitting all his faults.'

She smiled. 'Is that an apology?'

He nodded.

'One of these days, I will know why you're apologising. And it might be sooner than you think.' A gorgeous smile appeared on her face and leaning across the table, she whispered, as if telling him a secret. 'Crazy dreams, disorganised ideas, and jumbled memories; it's quite a mess, but my life is slowly returning. That's why I ask so many questions. I have to know where it all fits. Dr Papacostas is very positive.'

'Let's go for a walk.' He removed his shoes and pointed to hers. 'It's easier to negotiate sand.'

With the tide coming in, they walked up and down the beach, sat on an outcrop, and chatted for hours. Then they searched for shells and watched the occasional gull plummeting into the blue abyss for a snack.

Michael announced. 'I'm famished.'

'Me too.' She laughed as she realised the gulls had inspired the idea.

They left after an enjoyable meal, then drove to another beach, and walked around a piece of land Michael had recently acquired. When late afternoon found them travelling back home, she couldn't help but doze off in the comfort of the leather seat.

He gazed at her adoringly, knowing this was what he'd tried to achieve but failed miserably due to his nasty jealousy. Both had constantly misinterpreted what the other said; would they do it again? This time he opted for straight talk, as soon as she was ready to hear it. 'We're home.'

'Thank you for today.'

'We'll do it again.' He fought the urge to touch her, to kiss her.

That evening, as she prepared for bed, her mind drifted to the day's events, speculating about their previous relationship, instinctively reading something he wasn't telling. Could it be they'd been more than friends? But had they been that at all?

She woke with a start, hearing the rain pelt the house. Somewhere, a shutter banged and if she didn't close it, it would probably wake everybody else.

After closing the kitchen window, she poured a glass of milk and took a step back. 'Aahh…' She cried in fright and dropping the glass, smashed it on the floor.

'Why are you in the dark?' Michael switched a light on, and exclaimed in pain.

'What?' She asked alarmed and took a step towards him.

'Stand still Christie, there's glass everywhere.'

'Sorry, but you snuck up on me.'

'Which brings me to my original question, what are you doing?'

'I came to close the shutter.' She pointed.

'Same here.' Reaching her, he lifted her onto the kitchen counter. 'Don't move.' Opening a cupboard, he took out a bucket, then going down on his haunches, began throwing pieces of glass into it.

'It's not every day one sees a man cleaning a kitchen floor.' She grinned at his bare back.

'I must find a plaster.' He looked at the floor where he was leaving a trail of blood.

'Sorry about that.'

'I'll survive.' Rummaging in a drawer, he opened a box, wiped the wound, and covered it. Pulling hands-full of paper towels, he began mopping up the blood and milk.

'Where did I like to go for my walks?'

He looked up at her. 'Don't get any ideas. You are not to go anywhere alone.'

'You think Edward still wants to hurt me?' She put a hand to her neck. 'I was just in the wrong place.'

'So Costa said, but I'm taking no risks.'

'You?' She snorted. 'May I get down from here?'

He glanced at her bare feet. 'Wait there.' Taking a broom from a corner, he swept most of the tiny pieces of glass into a spade, then, he stood in front of her. 'I'll take you to the passage, in case I missed something.'

'I'm perfectly fit-'

He picked her into his arms. She stiffened and he tightened his hold, pulling her closer, so she'd rest her face against his bare chest. Her body relaxed. Hell, why did he do that? Now he wanted to keep on walking to his bedroom. Instead, he dropped her onto her feet in the passage. 'Goodnight.' He told her and slid his hands down her arms.

She merely stared. Then as soon as he turned his back, she put her hands to the fire in her face.

Christie liked Martha, the young woman Michael hired to look after her needs. She was very attentive, obedient, and always appeared within seconds when called. She was in fact more of a companion than a servant; as she was a smart girl who loved reading, laughing a lot, and just having a good time.

'Martha,' Christie descended from the windowsill where she'd been sitting and went into her room.

'Miss Thomas,'

'I'm going down to Yanni's Café.'

'Should I come with you?'

Christie regarded her. 'Not today. But, will you look after my mother? She doesn't look very happy lately. Ask her if she wants something and see if you can give it to her.'

'Yes Miss Thomas. And please be careful and don't go to lonely places.' The last thing she needed was to lose her job, or worse, unleash the boss's wrath.

Christie had been sitting quietly for about ten minutes listening to a heated debate on hooks and gill nets when she became aware of someone beside her. She looked up, 'John!' She shook his hand lightly and pointed for him to join her. 'How's the leg?'

'Good.' Pulling a chair, he ordered coffee. 'How's life treating you?'

'Well, and everyone is so kind.'

'It's always easy with a pretty girl. I believe I never saw anyone as beautiful.' Seeing her head drop shyly, he reached for her hand.

She pulled hers away immediately. 'So, how's the boat rental business?'

'Swedes,' he smiled. 'This is their year. Have you ever been sailing?'

Was he about to invite her? The thought unnerved her. 'I don't think so.'

'Don't worry,' he said as if aware of her reluctance. 'I won't ask until we know each other better and you tell me you'd like to go.'

'Thank you.' She relaxed. 'I wanted to ask so many questions, but that woman,' she giggled as she saw John's face. 'I'm surprised she didn't get herself married to you.'

'There's a scary thought, since I'm already married.'

'Oh, I wasn't aware.' She searched for a gold band that was non-existent.

'Separated. Don't be sorry, it was a mistake. One should be discerning where a life partner is concerned but I jumped right in. Who knows, I might still get lucky and find someone like you.' Registering her discomfort, he began discussing the merits of preserving some archaeological sites. Then he glanced at his watch. 'I apologise, but I have to go. May I still call you?'

'Of course,'

Michael noticed that Jane was finding her stay akin to lugging a millstone around. He understood that she missed Rob, their home, all the activities she was accustomed to and obviously loved. As the weather turned cooler, she was becoming gloomier, and realising that she might have to spend Christmas in Greece, she was feeling trapped.

Before she became utterly despondent and thought of dragging Christie back home, he checked with Dr Papacostas and told Christie to return to work. Besides, Jane's depression was hardly conducive to Christie's recovery. She needed to be busy, not sitting at home wasting time waiting for doctors' appointments.

Days later, he suggested Jane return home. Christie was doing well and she no longer needed constant supervision, and there was Mary and Martha. He could also deal fine with her lapses of memory, and it was no train-smash if she messed up occasionally.

With Jane gone, he wanted to treat Christie. What he wanted to do was date her. No, it was more than that but he wasn't sure she was ready, or if it was a good idea right now. There were still too many missing pieces, and he didn't want to confuse her.

Mary also needed a break. She too did more than was required. All anybody had been doing was follow doctors' orders. So he sent them to his parents in Athens for a week He imagined both could do with some shopping, and just plain lazing about.

Christie realised instantly why Michael loved his sisters so much, they were gorgeous, and full of fun. When the three; Mary, Stephanie, and Jaqueline got together, it was like meeting a carousel. They were unstoppable as they just did things. And refreshingly, they were also the most accepting girls she had ever met, neither having a nasty intention in their characters.

They ran into Evy on the second day, and she came around every day after that. Then Saturday morning, Christie witnessed something she had never seen before. The five caused pandemonium when they went downtown. Christie had never seen traffic brought to a standstill; she did that day. In fact, being part of the cause. Someone recognised Evy as Greece's top model, Stephanie and Jaqueline as the young socialites they were, and she and Mary although not known, people figured they had to be somebody important if they were together.

Christie found it both fascinating and infuriating that people tripped over themselves to serve them. She had never seen anything like it and she imagined this was what it felt like to be a celebrity. It was flattering, yet she hated it.

When they returned to Rhodes Sunday evening, Evy decided to follow them to Lindos. Christie noticed that she didn't like it when Evy mentioned Michael. Then she realised that she was jealous! And while away, she'd had fun, but she'd missed him terribly. So much in fact, that she hadn't been able to eat properly.

When she saw him in the lounge, as if he'd been waiting for them impatiently, her heart leapt.

He greeted all three, making sure Christie was last. He hadn't been able to get her out of his head, night and day. Heavens, he'd missed her. 'Okay, now that everyone is here, who's hungry?'

'What's dinner?' Evy asked curiously.

Mary intercepted. She'd noticed the look on his face, and she guessed that he'd appreciate being alone with Christie. 'We had quite enough at your parents' lunch today, thank you. Therefore, we will go take nice showers and then join the dancing room where the gorgeous Sampaio Moreira is strutting his stuff. But you should eat Christie; you hardly touched food while away.'

'You must have visited every shop.' Michael stared at the small hill Milo was gathering in the middle of the room.

'Almost,' Mary searched for a bag. 'Now, you have to excuse us, we are going to co-ordinate our evening.'

Evy had no choice but to follow her.

'How you two bought all that must be some kind of record.' Leading her to the kitchen, he busied himself around the stove and counters. 'May I serve?'

'Please do, it smells really good. What's this?'

He pointed with a spoon and named the dishes.

She savoured a mouthful. 'Excellent.'

'Some wine?'

She had to take pills in the morning, but that was over twelve hours away. 'Just a little,'

Pouring a glass, he put it in her hand, his fingers covering hers briefly. Seeing her clutch the glass and swallow the contents at one go, he refilled it. 'Like it?'

'Very nice.' His proximity filled her with confusion. She gulped half the second glass to calm her nerves.

'What's this about you not eating?'

'I wasn't hungry.' She dismissed and emptied her glass.

'Must get more of this.' He grinned looking at the bottle.

'Yes. No. I mean, I shouldn't have anymore.' Nevertheless, she did.

Rising to his feet for some reason, he brushed against her. 'Finish your dinner.'

'I'll try.' She felt breathless.

'There's still dessert.'

They continued for a few minutes in silence. Then everything became strange, as if she didn't know where she was, his voice echoing in her head. 'Michael,'

Leaning over, he looked into the beautiful blue eyes and pressed his lips against hers

She responded, opening her mouth invitingly. Taking advantage, he tasted her deeply. Then stopped, she was barely breathing. 'Christie,' he called, holding her face between his hands.

'I need to…' she said faintly and half-fell off the stool.

Steadying her, he wondered why her body felt limp. Picking her up into his arms, he took her to the bedroom and dropped her gently onto the bed. Sitting on the edge, he removed her shoes and opened the buttons on her cardigan. She moaned. His eyes fell on an old medication box. 'Oh crap!' Grabbing the phone, he dialled. 'Good evening, Dr Papacostas, Michael Andriotti. Sorry to disturb you at home but I may have done something,' and he explained Christie's symptoms.

'It's a chemical imbalance. Let her rest and drink lots of water, skip the dosage tomorrow and then start again. Make sure she can breathe at all times and she'll be fine.'

'Thank you, doctor. And while I'm on the line, may I come see you next week?'

'Sure.'

Looking around for her nightclothes, he found the cute pink pyjamas on the chair. 'Sorry sweetheart, but this is not how I pictured taking your clothes off for the first time.' So there he sat on the bed, glad that she was back, carefully undressing, putting her pyjamas on, grinning as she mumbled and spoke absolute nonsense in her intoxicated state, and loving every second of it.

CHAPTER TEN

Evy was throwing a goodbye party. She was on her way to Australia on a modelling contract and naturally, she had invited them. She had also invited Michael, but for some reason, he'd chosen not to attend.

'Why did I agree to this?' Christie asked as they stopped outside the sprawling white villa on the hill.

'Because Dr Papacostas encouraged you to be adventurous. Stop fretting, and remember,' Mary winked. 'Evy's uncanny instinct for lame ducks, she'll try to fix you again.'

'I've noticed.' That was Evy all right. Always trying to fix things, people included. And she'd done that in Athens. Mary was the student but Evy was the practicing shrink.

'Go mingle.' Evy told Mary brightly. 'This is our chance to get to know each other better.'

Mary looked at the two and wondered if she hadn't made a mistake. In Athens, Evy hadn't been able to get too close because Michael's sisters had been around but now they were alone. Amongst their circle, Evy's interest in Michael was well documented; Michael's in Christie was as well known as the whereabouts of Pandora's Box.

'I'll be fine.' Christie said as she noticed her friend's apprehension.

She was being silly, Christie was not helpless, so she made a beeline for Paul.

Appropriating herself of Christie's arm, Evy led her across the room. 'Pity you never took an interest in my brother. Though, I'd say he's not particularly broken-hearted.'

Christie saw Paul in an involved discussion with two pretty girls, and automatically making a spot available for Mary to sit beside him. She'd always noticed that between those two. They were so close, they couldn't even see it.

'Rather like Michael and me; we are over even before we began. Being a little older, he always looked so sophisticated, somehow reminiscent of a Greek god; and that's exactly where he stayed; out of reach! He's great to look at, is an exceptional conversationalist, and ever so smart.' A sigh escaped her. 'Do you know that he doesn't have to say a word to tell you that you're wasting your time? Which is why he chose not to be here. Work...' She made a dismissive sound. 'Therefore, I've finally decided to concentrate on my career, which he tolerates and makes use of, but doesn't even pretend to like. There has to be a semblance of self-respect because a girl shouldn't keep making a fool of herself. So what is it I do next? I accept work Down Under in the hope that he'd ask me to stay. Know what he did say? Good luck.' She snorted. 'I know I'm a fool, silly, even childish,'

What was she supposed to do with the revelation? But okay, now she knew he wasn't interested here.

'Christie,' Paul greeted.

She was thankful for the interruption. 'Hello.'

'Paul, be a darling and see to Christie's entertainment while I chat to someone.'

'My pleasure,' he turned to her. 'As always, you look lovely, but I'd love to dress you.'

'Excuse me?' Christie frowned.

'Oh no, I'm sorry,' Paul said embarrassed. 'I mean my designs.'

She sighed relieved. 'Maybe I should come around.'

'Please do, I have the most gorgeous fabrics I'd love to see you in.' After twenty minutes into a conversation on Vissi Clothing, he excused himself to return to the two girls.

Christie took a few turns through throngs of people and realised she wasn't in the same part of the house anymore. She opened a door, it was a bathroom. About to walk away, someone pushed her in. Startled, she swivelled around. She knew Anthony from passing and knew that he was somehow related to Evy, and, that he was never alone; his cousin Alex followed him like a shadow.

'*Tikanis, agapimo*. Darling,' Anthony mocked. 'The boyfriend left you alone?' Kicking the door shut, he thrust her against the wall.

She wriggled fiercely, trying to get her arms in front of her chest. 'You've had your fun, now let me go.'

The door-handle turned and Alex walked in.

How was she to fight two monsters? 'Anthony, Alex, we can discuss this.'

'Why?' Anthony pressed his body against hers, his face inches away.

Her heart pumped wildly, the breathing raised a notch, her voice stuck in her throat, and she went blank. "What do I do?" Bringing her arms up with a strength she wasn't aware of possessing, she pushed and shoved him with both fists. Surprise and pain forced him to let go, but as he did, his right fist flew out and struck her around the left eye. Bolting for the door, she hoped Alex was as easy to overcome. All he did was stretch a foot.

Tripping, she went sprawling across the floor. As she struggled to keep her balance, she saw the two idiots running out of the room.

'Oww,' she complained as she put a hand to her head.

'Christie?' Paul entered the bathroom and helped her to her feet. 'What happened?'

'Huh, Anthony and Alex came in and sort of attacked me.'

'Aren't you supposed to be at a party?' Michael was visibly surprised.

'I drove the girls home as there was some trouble.' Paul announced apologetically as he dropped Mary's car keys on the table. 'The doctor says she's fine.'

'What, who?'

'Christie-' Paul never finished the sentence.

Michael was instantly beside her. 'What happened?'

Considering the possibility that she might have been in actual danger, she started shaking; probably delayed shock. Without thinking, she threw her arms around his neck.

His arms tightened about her, his mouth brushing her forehead. 'Will someone please explain?'

'Anthony and Alex Soros forced themselves on her, as a joke, and scared her witless.'

'What kind of reprobates do you allow into your house?' Michael was livid.

Paul was equally cross. 'The house was full of people, how could I guess that they had their eyes on her? They simply picked whom they imagined the easiest prey. Besides, it was my sister's party, I did not invite them.'

'Please don't be mad at him, it's not his fault.' Christie intervened. 'Now I just want to go lie down and forget the sick episode.'

'What did the doctor say?'

Christie touched her tender eye. 'I'll just have a bruise.'

'Did you fall?'

'Anthony punched me when I fought back.'

He was more than livid; he was dangerous. He had done many things that he wasn't proud of and said others that had inevitably hurt someone, perhaps even more than he realised, but never had he raised a hand to another man, even less a woman. A love he'd never known filled his heart. This was more than physical; it was something that began in the depths of his very being. 'I could murder right now.' He ground out.

'They said it was a joke.'

'One I find repugnant.'

'Morning,' Christie greeted wanly as she entered the dining room, a horrible reddish bruise around one eye. 'Evy! When did you get here?'

'An hour ago.' She stared at Christie's face. 'I'm very sorry about that, and I think you should put some ice on it.'

'Yes, I'll get something.'

'Well,' Paul rose and helped his sister. 'We need to go, as you still have packing to do. Once again Christie, I apologise.'

'Thank you, but it wasn't your fault. And I regret having contributed to ruining your party.'

'I definitely need to revise my list of friends. But it will have to wait until I return from Australia.' Evy glanced at Michael. Whatever reaction she'd expected, was non-existent. Instead, he had acquired a grim expression as he watched Christie. In that look were all the explanations Evy had never received and those she had, which hadn't made sense. She recalled all her efforts, the useless attempts, the wasted calls. He had made up his mind a long time ago!

Mary, who had also been paying attention, announced quickly in what she imagined was a perfect Australian accent. 'That's great mate, and be sure to bring us a koala.'

Everyone laughed.

'Philistines,' Mary pretended offence, glad she'd successfully diverted Evy's thoughts, even if temporarily. How Evy had never suspected which way the wind blew was still a matter of astonishment because it was all she'd been able to see for months. Then again, both Michael and Christie were adept at hiding things. She guessed Evy needed to vent a little at the realisation that she'd been wasting her time for ages, so she left with the brother and sister.

When alone, Michael turned to Christie. 'How about a great surprise?'

'What kind?' She queried curiously.

'The kind that you have to wait for. I'll see you in an hour.'

She was paging through the painting manual on her bed when the phone rang. 'Hello.'

'Morning Christie, how are you?'

'John! I have a headache.' She touched her face carefully. 'What are you doing today?'

'I'm taking some people over to Faraklos. So, what's this I hear about last night?'

She sat up startled. 'Are people talking?'

'What do you think?'

Hearing a knock, she told Martha to enter. 'Sorry John, did you say something?'

'You forget everyone pays particular attention to influentials, especially Darius' grandkids. I heard someone had the audacity to hit you. Who's this worm?'

She told him quickly. Then her heart turned peculiarly as she recalled Michael's concern. Wondering what Martha wanted, she looked up. 'Michael! John, I have to go.'

'Can we go out sometime next week?'

'Call me.' She returned the phone to the bedside table.

'And where do you know this John guy from?' Michael pointed vaguely.

'Hospital.'

'What's his surname? I might know him.'

'I never asked.'

'Does he live in Lindos?'

'He said he stays out this way.' Jumping off the bed, she grabbed a jersey. 'Let's go.'

'In a minute. First, I want to know.'

'Know what Michael?'

'Why haven't you mentioned this John guy before?'

'Because I understand his wish for privacy. What's with the interrogation?'

'Christie, we know nothing about this man. Have you been out with him?'

'You are paranoid. I do have some idea on how to look after myself.'

'Yes, but this is Greece and men still have odd notions concerning women.'

'Including you?'

'I'm not archaic. So, what do you know about this John guy?'

'I don't know much about "this John guy", except that he's nice. What's wrong with that?'

'I don't know this man from a bar of soap and he might try taking advantage of you.'

'Two already did.' Christie touched her face.

'See what I mean? Is it wrong I'm concerned?'

'No, just don't freak out all the time. Can we please go now?'

It was a silent drive, each busy with his own thoughts, Michael feeling as if he'd been kicked in the ribs. Now who the hell was John and why hadn't she mentioned him before? As far as he knew, she had never been in danger, or had she? "What am I doing?" Last time, jealous rage had made a mighty mess of things, was he about to repeat the blunder? But when he thought of her with another man, it drove him insane.

'Do I hear the sea?' Christie asked when he stopped.

'Yes. Xristo,' Michael called in Greek.

A deeply tanned man appeared. 'Right on time, boss.'

'Will you have someone take my car home?'

'No problem.'

'Do you like sailing?' Michael asked as they started down the path.

'I have no idea but it sounds wonderful. Do you have a boat?'

'Two weeks old and now we're sailing it back to Lindos.'

'This is that piece of land you bought.' She recognised, and then turned her head at sounds in the distance. 'Are you building something?'

'Yes. But that's a surprise for another day.' Seeing excitement spread on her face, he pulled her into an embrace as they stepped onto the jetty. 'Before you drown yourself.'

A thousand butterflies lived in her stomach and every now and then, all flew in single file towards her throat. She stared at the beautiful yacht bobbing gently on the sapphire surface. 'Does it have a name?'

'It will.' He helped her on deck.

They spent pleasant hours drifting slowly along, again talking about things she couldn't discuss with anyone else. It was peculiar, she loved Mary dearly, yet it was Michael, who truly was her confidant. People said that men and women couldn't be friends for long without sex interfering, and although she was beginning to feel its pressure, she knew that this friendship was equally precious to him.

She studied him. Yes, she could see interest because sometimes, he took deep breaths, and there was that dead-give-away he wasn't even aware of; he bit his bottom lip as he stared at her mouth. Yet, he never dared go over that imaginary line.

She knew she liked him best of all the men she knew, she felt safe around him, and she was possessive. She didn't want anyone to look at him, to touch him, to... It wasn't like, it was more than that. 'I have such a headache.' She complained.

'I'm not surprised.' He watched the deep red bruise, feeling angry again. 'Regrettably, I have nothing on board but water and fruit.'

Standing up, she glanced over the side. 'I feel dizzy.'

'Then sit down. You might be seasick, or concussed. Would you prefer to lie down?'

'Maybe,' she said weakly.

He helped her downstairs to the stateroom. 'You look pale.'

Before she could lie down, she swayed as if she were about to faint, leaned against his shoulder, and closed her eyes. 'Thea knew! She just knew he was no good. Mom, shame, and daddy must have thought he was the answer to his prayers because I was hopeless.' She opened her eyes and looked straight at him. 'No wonder you apologised in advance, you did like to tighten the bolts.'

'What's happening Christie?'

'Can't you hear what I'm saying? Without warning, I have just about everything in my head!' She burst into tears on his shoulder.

For a moment, he didn't know what to do. Then wrapping his arms around her, he too closed his eyes. Thankfulness filled him, perhaps now things could get back to normal.

A tearful Mary greeted them at the door, and neither could understand why she was crying. When she calmed down, she eventually told them that Andrew, Michael's brother had called. Her father had had a stroke, her sister was pregnant and suffered from high blood pressure, and that she needed to pack.

'Yes, go. I'll call Andrew.' Michael said and disappeared into the study.

'Many stroke victims recover completely, he probably will too.' Christie consoled and put an arm around her friend's shoulders.

'I wish you'd come with me. If there's a person who inspires survival, it's you. How do you manage without going crazy?'

'I have wonderfully caring friends.'

Next day, Christie felt as if she had surfaced from a whirlwind. Rushed trips were always exhausting, especially if involving medical emergencies and tears and Mary had shed her fair share, not only for her father but also for her sister and her still unborn child.

Everything became quiet, and both she and Michael realised that they were alone in the house. This was a village, on an island, in Greece, where conventions were still adhered, so before a smidgen of gossip could lift off, Michael requested Martha sleep in the house. Chaperone she wasn't but at least it looked better to the people down in the village.

Christie had barely dressed when the phone rang. It was John. He wanted to know if she was working. If not, would it be possible for her to join him for a picnic at the park? Why everyone called it that, she didn't know. But it did have some magnificent views. She didn't feel like joining him anywhere but she had the day off and what else should she do until going to Dr Papacostas?

'What time should I expect you?'

'There's a bit of a problem. I'm still down at the harbour and I have to get back straight after ten. If I walk up there we're cutting it short. Would you mind very much meeting me at Yanni's? And I apologise that I have to leave you there again. Is that too ungentle manly?'

That suited her better. 'I enjoy walking.'

He smiled broadly when he saw her sitting at *their* table. 'I'm glad you could come. How are you?'

'Lonely, Mary went home.' They began walking down the cobbled street.

'This is why I called.' He regarded her for a moment. 'You're basically alone in the house.'

She saw where his mind had gone and didn't like it. What was this obsession about how things looked? And why did she get the feeling he was jealous? Goodness, no!

He seemed to follow her train of thought because he changed the conversation by asking if she liked a particular Greek dish. After discussing food for a few minutes, he queried. 'How's your memory?'

'Improving.'

'Do you recall the accident now?'

She nodded. 'I do, but I can't visualise Edward. I know what he looks like, but I have no recollection of meeting him or speaking to him. Isn't that strange?'

'Perhaps you're not as ready as you think you are. But today, let's not talk about any of that and just have a good time.' He plucked a flower and handed it to her. 'What's being done about the creeps?'

'I don't understand their behaviour but I refuse to enrage myself further by having a slandering match in court, therefore, I'm dropping it.' She twirled the flower in her fingers. 'Do you ever hear from your wife?'

'When she wants something.'

The more he spoke about life, the more she thought that he was a man with deep hurts. Perhaps it was in the way he became furious within seconds, or the way his voice changed when something displeased him.

Taking a few bites of what he offered, she found herself comparing everything he did to Michael's ways, the contrast striking her as unusual. It was like comparing a bland grape juice to the best wine, the one far outweighing the other's insipid qualities.

'Does Michael mind when you go out?' He asked as they ended their meal.

'He isn't crazy about me walking about alone but he realises I'm entitled to my friends so he has calmed down.'

'I'm glad you think of me as a friend.' He moved closer.

The action didn't please her and getting up quickly, she bumped into a rock.

Steadying her, he left his hand on her arm. 'Why are you always running away from me?'

Trying not to show how much his action bothered her, she pulled her arm away. 'Please, John, this is not what I'm looking for. May we go back now?'

He was disappointed, but she couldn't encourage him into something that was going nowhere. As she watched him throwing things into the basket and folding the blanket with sharp movements, she knew that it was much more than disappointment.

Michael told her in a matter-of-fact voice that he was going to meet someone in Athens, that he'd be staying over for two days, and that she should enjoy herself while alone. Gazing at him, she saw a smugness she didn't like. That meeting had nothing to do with business and she wanted to know who it was. Was it a woman? The idea drove her crazy. But she daren't ask.

Jealousy coursed through her for two days and she hardly slept. She recalled why she'd been afraid of a relationship before, but then, she hadn't known some things. Now, she knew those and a few others. Edward wasn't around to fill his head with rubbish, he wasn't interested in Evy, and he wanted her. Why didn't he pursue intimacy, when she knew he burnt with desire? He'd been to see Dr Papacostas a few times. Could they have discussed something she wasn't aware of, and if so, what?

She sat in quiet contemplation during breakfast, missing him, and hating being alone. She knew he had entered the room before she heard him. Her hands trembled and grabbing the coffee cup, she gulped.

'Good morning Christie,' he greeted in an odiously good mood.

'I need to-' she started to rise. 'Thea! What on earth are you doing here?'

'Michael called a few weeks ago and began a dreadful begging pilgrimage,' Sofia laughed and embraced Christie. 'How I've missed you.'

'But… I never thought you'd leave.' Christie was dumbfounded.

Sitting down, Sofia poured herself a cup of coffee. 'And your parents are arriving next week. Or haven't you realised that Christmas is in ten days?'

Christie wondered why he'd done that. But when she saw that expression on his face - the one that reminded her of a child looking for a well done - there was no place else she'd rather be. 'I don't know what to say, except, thank you.'

He watched her with undisguised interest, noticing how the blue scarf accentuated the colour of her eyes. Gazing at her mouth avidly, he imagined what it would be like to make love to her, to have her respond, as he knew she could. The images accelerated his pulse. He pushed the thought out of his mind and announced. 'The weather bureau says Saturday will be a perfect day, so I'm treating the two of you, plus a few friends to a day of sailing.'

'That brings back memories.' Sofia recalled Robert; he'd rowed them up and down the coast one holiday. She glanced at her son. What a pity he'd never known his father.

'Are you awake?' Michael asked outside her bedroom door Saturday morning. 'There's a call for you.' A pregnant pause followed. 'John is not getting through. It's the phone in the hall.'

'Okay.' Jumping out of bed, she threw her gown on, ran out the door, past him, down the passage, and picked the receiver. 'John.'

'Morning. Did Michael wake you?'

'No. How are you?' Sometimes, he was just irritating.

'Fine. Would you like to go out today? The weather is absolutely perfect.'

'We're going sailing.' Her eyes lit up. 'Why don't you join us?'

'Firstly, I don't think Michael likes me, and secondly,' his voice dropped. 'I received divorce papers.'

'I'm sorry.' She commiserated.

'I thought that I'd feel nothing but I'm quite depressed.'

She made up her mind instantly. 'Is ten o'clock okay?'

'Does that mean you'll come?' He was elated. 'I rented a car so I'll come pick you up.'

'That's nice. I'll tell them not to wait for me. Where are we going?'

'A drive to Plimiri, some lunch along the way and then back home. Is that respectable enough?'

'Yes, thank you. I'll see you at ten.'

Going to breakfast, disappointment filled her, but her kind heart wouldn't let her leave a suffering soul lonely on a day like this. She would never be able to enjoy herself. Sitting at the table, she wondered if she should mention it between bites of toast or leave it for the coffee. Michael would blow a gasket because he didn't like "this John guy". She fancied telling them that she had caught a twenty-four hour virus. She hadn't had one of those in ages. 'I apologise, but I can't go.'

They looked at her in surprise.

Michael's suspicion was evident. 'Why not?'
'I changed my mind.'
'Does this have to do with John's call?'
'Maybe.'
'I thought you said you'd like to learn to sail.'
'Still do, just not today. This is more important.'
'Well, then that is that. Thea, when you're ready.'

She had expected his interference but not his disregard, and it hurt that he seemed to be sweeping it away so casually. Biting her lip, she bade them goodbye, somehow expecting him to deliver a final word, even if one that upset. Instead, he didn't give her a backward glance.

The outing began slowly. John drove up a mountain where they had brunch at Genadi, in what he said was the prettiest place but she couldn't quite see the beauty amidst so much dryness and rocks. During the meal, one thing disturbed her, his hand kept straying to hers, squeezing it repeatedly. The first few times, she thought this was merely his way, but as the morning progressed, she started imagining blatant sexual advances. Whenever encountering men - perhaps unfairly - she always compared them to Michael and as all left her indifferent, John rattled her. She brought up the divorce three times, in the hope that he forgot her hand, but three times, he changed the subject. After a while, she wondered if there were any papers or even if a wife existed.

Then it was on to Plimiri, and she actually enjoyed walking up and down its short and narrow roads, visiting the tiny shops sandwiched between tavernas, ceramic shops, and frilly tablecloths.

After coming down the mountain, he stopped alongside a tiny bay and invited her for a stroll along the deserted beach. The idea made her nervous but she decided to ride it out. Then he held her hand, presumably imagining that she would trip. She'd rather he let it go. Looking up and down the beach, she saw not a soul. 'It's late.'

Pulling her down with him, she fell against his chest. 'John,'

'You are the most desirable woman I know,' he whispered and kissed her, his hands moving down her back, pressing her against him.

She didn't find the contact exceptionally pleasant and disentangled herself. 'Please take me home.'

'It's Michael, isn't it?'

'Will you take me home or should I flag someone down? I told you I can only be your friend, why must you spoil it?' Turning, she started walking towards the car.

He came alongside her. 'Why couldn't it have been me?'

All of a sudden, she felt pity. 'I'm sorry, John, but there are things we can't control.'

'Yes,' he agreed.

For a moment, she imagined that he was about to protest more, to put his case forward, and make her see his point of view, and not necessarily by reason. A cold shiver ran down her spine. He might have noticed, or not been aware of it at all.

The drive home was quick and quiet, Christie sitting on the edge of the seat as close to the door as possible, her hand tucked into the handle. Before he got out of the car, she was standing outside the front door, a sigh of relief escaping her. 'Goodbye, John.'

Finding the house deserted, she went straight to her room, took a shower, and lay on the bed mulling over the day's events. John was strange, his rocketing moods leaving her bewildered. Why did she attract unbalanced men? Was it her fault, theirs, or was the world filled with odd characters? But he was right about one thing, she didn't want anyone but Michael to touch her.

The moment they sat down to dinner, she knew Michael wasn't in the best of moods. Thinking it best to avoid him for at least a day, she went to the veranda afterwards.

'Did you have a good time?'

'Okay.' She speculated at his reaction if she told him that she had loathed it.

'Ask John around, I'd like to meet him.'

'He's very busy.' And after today, she didn't want to.

'Not for you.'

'He likes me, what's wrong with that?'

'Nothing, but we still don't have much information. Do you at least know his surname?'

'No.'

'Christie, do you know in what danger you could be placing yourself?'

Getting to her feet, she told him tiredly. 'I don't particularly want to discuss John. Goodnight, Michael.'

That night, the wind blew almost gale force, the rain pelted the house mercilessly, and the tree outside her window groaned. Hugging the bedcovers, she tried to sleep, but an inexplicable noise continually disturbed her slumber. She wondered if Rhodes had snakes. But it wasn't a hiss she imagined hearing, more like a whooshing sound. For all she knew there was a burst pipe in the air-conditioner.

Michael felt sneaky about it, but what recourse was there? Christie wasn't forthcoming and he worried, and not simply because he was jealous. He was in love with her, there was no denying that, but the anxiety he felt every time she walked out the house was something he couldn't describe. So he'd asked Dimitri to look into John's little secret world. Because what else was it? He didn't know who this guy was and he knew everybody.

'So?' Michael urged.

Dimitri glanced at a paper in his hand. 'Nothing unusual. His name is John Kanakis. Cypriot, but can't string two decent Greek words together. Has been around a couple of months, married-'

'Excuse me?' "What is it with her and married men?" He thought annoyed.

Dimitri repeated himself. 'Yes, married, but apparently divorcing. Rents a house down Pefki way and owns a boat, which he hires to tourists or takes them out himself. Comes in every morning, or stays over. That's about it. Want me to dig further? My colleague in Pefki says this is a quiet man, who doesn't like trouble, but that's no reason to assume anything.'

'I wish he would come to the house. I tried to speak to him twice but he was out both times. I left invitations to come see me, but he never showed.' Michael looked thoughtful. 'If you got hold of his wife, I'd like to know why they split.'

'I'll put someone on it right away.'

Under Dr Papacostas' careful direction, Christie had salvaged her former life, except for Edward. She knew the course of events that had brought her here, even recalled conversations they'd had, verbatim, but no matter how hard she tried, even under hypnosis, she couldn't recollect physical contact with him whatsoever. It was as if her brain saw him as a mistake to be obliterated.

After Christmas and her parents' departure, Christie thought that sleep had left right along with them. Something in her room startled her awake most nights.

The technician came, fiddled with pipes and wires in the air-conditioner and declared it faultless. She smiled satisfaction for three days and then knew the man was paid for naught.

On her way to the office, she walked past the newspaper stand in the lobby. The headline caught her eye. Turning pale, her hand flew to her mouth and she rushed to Michael's office.

'Michael,' she pointed to the newspaper in his hands. 'You have seen it.' The headline announced that Anthony and Alex Soros had died in the Rhodes marina.

He nodded. 'I see it has affected you.'

'It's terrible. Do the police have any idea how it happened?'

'I called Dimitri and he told me they're classifying it murder, but he didn't disclose details.' Michael told her.

She turned paler. 'But… who would do such a thing?'

'They were trouble-makers, and nasty, so they riled someone up. Are you going to be all right about this?'

She shrugged. 'I suppose.'

'I see you've started painting again. How is that going?'

'I often think that I'll never know as much as I did before, which wasn't much by anyone's standards. I'm reading a lot but can't say I always understand the information.'

Glancing at a document, Michael heard the complaining tree outside Christie's bedroom. He wondered if it would survive the night. A repetitive slamming began nearby.

Going to the window, he turned the lever on the wall. Suddenly, the sky became blindingly white, a bolt hit the tree and instantly, flames poured from its centre. A thick branch tore off and he watched in astonishment as it was propelled into the air. Seeing its trajectory, he knew exactly where it would land. He ran.

The shutters flung open. Peering outside, Christie realised they would be ripped off their hinges if she didn't close them. Thunder and lightning tore through the night as she reached for the handle, the sound of smashing glass filling the room. Rain, wind, and something of great strength rushed in, making her jump in disbelief. Turning to run, it caught her, smacking her shoulder, pushing her forward. Losing balance, her hands flew out to stop the fall but succeeded only in pulling the small table along.

Michael stared. The branch lay in the middle of the bedroom as if carelessly tossed there, water wetting and wind blowing everything about. 'Christie!' He called above the noise. Clambering over the obstruction, he saw her pinned down. Fear filled him as he lifted the weight off her and his hands ran along her body, searching for broken bones. 'Christie, please answer me.'

She looked at him. 'Michael,'

'Thank God!' He hugged her.

She turned her head to look at the mess all around them. 'What happened?'

'What on earth were you doing?' He shouted just as the noise subsided.

'I was trying to close the shutters. How was I to know a tree would come flying in?'

'I'm just so thankful you're all right. Let's get out here and call the doctor.' He pulled her to her feet.

'I'm fine, except for the ugly bruise I'm going to have here.' She rubbed her shoulder.

'Don't ever scare me like that again.' He kissed her.

It began tenderly, making her dissolve, making her head spin in a most alarming way. 'Michael,'

'You're all I think about, what would I do if something happened to you?'

The tree must have hit her harder than first anticipated.

'Don't look at me like that. I love you, please say something.' He urged.

Her eyes filled with tears.

'Christie?' Had he just made the mistake he dreaded? He had purposely not pressed intimacy so she would find herself and know her mind. Now in a moment of panic, had he destroyed everything?

'How, huh,' she hiccupped. 'What are you saying?'

'That I'm in love with you. I didn't mean to frighten you but the idea of losing you... I'm rushing you. Or is it John?'

She shook her head. 'No. I love you.'

Sighing, he tightened his hold, his face close to hers. 'Then will you marry me?'

She broke into sobs.

He wiped the tears. 'Marry me and I promise that we'll be very happy.'

'I'm sorry; I didn't expect you to be so prepared.'

'You want to see prepared.' Grinning, he led her to his room, opened a drawer, searched for a few seconds, and grabbed a box. 'I love you so much that I picked it out months ago. I'd sit staring at it, wondering when was the perfect moment.' Snapping the lid open, he took out the ring and slipped it onto her finger. 'I'm done waiting, let's be married as soon as possible. Say, a week?'

She laughed through the tears. 'You're crazy, my parents just went back.'

'Michael, Christie,' Sofia came down the passage.

'In here.' Michael called.

Sofia stopped as she saw them in each other's arms. 'Why is it people wait until disaster strikes to say what they should have said before?' She picked Christie's hand where the diamond heart glistened blindingly. 'About time. And am I to presume this isn't to be a long engagement?' She didn't wait for a reply. 'Honestly Michael, you had to make it difficult and wait until Jane was gone. Who's going to help me now? But first,' she pulled Christie to her side. 'Michael, I would appreciate it if you moved up to the hotel. We can't have the village going mad.'

CHAPTER ELEVEN

Christie stared at the heaps of samples and listened passively at the limitless information the wedding-planner imparted non-stop. She was trying to be sensible, but he kept making suggestions that diverged from everything she had ever imagined. At least, one thing was going as she wished, Paul was designing her wedding gown and she was enthralled at his clever ideas. Then thankfully, Mary returned and with her, came Stephanie and Jaqueline. In their company, Christie found it easier to sit through endless hours of consultations as all had very distinct opinions, which were rather *avant guard* and quite funny.

'I thought I saw you coming this way.' Mary sat on the garden bench. 'There are people everywhere and I don't know what they're doing. If I were you, I'd elope.'

'Don't give me any ideas. All I wanted was a calm wedding, but it seems I started a state fair.' Christie picked one of Mary's hands. 'You've lost weight.'

'It was the stress of seeing both my father and sister ill. But he's recovering well and Georgia's medication is working so that's all that matters.' Mary shifted on the seat. 'I've got some news. I've been offered a scholarship in the US, which I cannot refuse. So, it's psyche on again.' She smiled. 'Imagine, me living in New York for a year.'

'I think Michael has some friends there. Or at least close by.'

'He does, I met them last year. They have the cutest kids. Speaking of which, will you two be starting a family right away?'

Christie flushed pink. It was a valid topic but she felt extremely self-conscious. 'I don't think we should.'

'Then if you need help choosing something, I'll take you to see Dr Dionidis.'

'Thank you, that's sweet of you.'

'I thought you might need a guiding hand because I suppose you've ever needed anything?'

Christie shook her head.

'Good for you.' Mary patted her hand. 'And I'll tell you something, not to scare you but because I think you should be prepared. Andriottis love intensely and that means physically too. Once they've made up their minds; that's it. With them, it's a case of life or death. You'll see what I mean when Andrew and Georgia, and Daniel and Cathy get here. I find it frightening because when I look at them, I understand what dying of a broken heart means. But you have nothing to worry about, you love like that too.' Hearing a footfall in the distance, she looked up. 'There comes Thea, let me go ask if she needs help, because every time Jaqueline helps something goes wrong.'

'Christie,' Stephanie called. 'Phone,'

'Hello.'

'Missed me?'

Why did the mere sound of his voice make her feel disheartened? 'John, how are you?'

'Good. I was away so I thought I'd better call to apologise for my horrid behaviour last time.'

This constant fixing was a definite problem. Mistakes happened and one had to move past them. With John, it was perplexing. 'Actually, I have news of my own-'

'Then come tell me at Yanni's. I haven't unpacked, but bags can wait.'

He must really have been away if he hadn't yet complained about the engagement. Taking a parka from the hall closet, she slipped it on, left the house, and hurried down the well-worn path. She sat down and ordered coffee.

'Hello.'

Turning quickly, she saw John appraising her. 'Hello.'

'Is there something different about you?' He asked as he sat opposite her.

'Not that I'm aware of. How was your trip?'

'Excellent. I needed rest and asked for a good hiding place. They sent me to Halki.' He laughed. 'There's no electricity out there. Well, there is in the village, if you can call it that, but not where I stayed. It was total peace, nothing but nature and me.' He studied her. 'Every time I see you, you're more beautiful.'

'John,' she tucked a few strands of hair behind an ear.

'You said you had news-' as if propelled by a spring, he jumped to his feet, grabbed her hand and stared in disbelief. 'What-?'

She smiled. 'Michael.'

'I know who gave it to you.' He sunk back into the chair as if a heavy load had just fallen on his head, his face drained of colour. 'The sacrifices I've made.'

All at once, she was frightened. Coffee untouched, she rose from the chair and walked away.

He was soon beside her.

'If you have nothing decent to say then don't bother. It's true I liked you, but if you misinterpreted, I apologise because I never meant to lead you on, or to give the impression that we might have been more.' She faced him squarely. 'I don't know what sacrifices you're referring to but whatever it is, it was of your own initiative, and I think it unjust that you try making me feel guilty. Believe it or not, I m sorry we part under these circumstances because we could have been friends.'

Gazing at the dress spread out on the bed, Christie knew she had never seen another as beautiful. Although it resembled her original design, it was as different as any bride's gown she had ever seen. Paul was a genius.

Jane walked into the room. 'You're not even dressed!'

'Nerves,' Mary announced. 'I'm going to make tea.'

'Good idea. In the meantime, Stephanie and I will help you.'

'I have a knot right here.' Christie complained with a hand against her stomach. 'All I want to do is throw up.' Then without warning, she ran to the bathroom and did just that.

Glancing at the dress, Jane turned to Stephanie. 'Honey, please go tell Mary to bring dry toast as well.'

Christie appeared in the doorway looking ghostly white. 'Did you feel like this on your wedding day?'

'Nervous yes, not nauseous. Do you suppose that you could be pregnant?'

'Way off track, mom.' Christie attempted a smile. Since this morning, she'd been having some strange ideas. Edward had told Gloria that he loved her; Michael told her that he loved her. "Stop scaring yourself," she thought. "You can't believe that he'd hurt you like that." She needed to speak with Dr Papacostas. 'Mom, may I have five minutes alone?'

"Autumn leaves," Michael thought as he watched her approach, and hoped that this day would soon end because he hadn't been able to eat since the previous evening. But when she finally said, 'I do' a little unsteadily and he placed the gold band on her finger, that strange knot diminished somewhat.

Christie wasn't certain what she did afterwards and in what order, but she vaguely remembered eating, being toasted, dancing, and a lot of hugging and kissing. One thing she recalled vividly, the way Michael looked at her. She didn't think that his eyes had been anywhere else since she had come down those stairs.

'The bride's bouquet,' Sarah Andriotti announced and taking Christie's hand, took her up a few steps. 'Go on, honey. But please do your best to avoid my daughters.'

Turning her back on the assembled women, Christie threw the flowers high into the air, landing them neatly in the eighteen-year-old Jaqueline's hands.

'Gross,' she exclaimed and stuffed the bouquet in her sister's hands.

'No way.' Stephanie said and throwing it over hit Sofia as she walked by.

'You have got to be kidding.' Sofia quickly disposed of it by planting it in Evy's hand, who, reacted as if it were toxic and quickly passed it on to Mary.

'Well,' Christie smiled as everyone burst into giggles. 'It seems everyone in this room will soon be wed.'

'Come along, darling, or you'll be late.' Jane announced as she hugged her.

Emerging from the bedroom, one of the hotel staff approached them. 'This came for you, Miss Thomas,' he smiled apologetically. 'Mrs Andriotti. A boy from the village delivered it.'

'Thank you.' Glancing at the envelope, she saw no name or address. Then as everyone seemed to be in a hurry to be rid of her, she dropped it into her handbag.

The drive wasn't long but it was dreary. Michael had been particularly secretive over their honeymoon plans and she wondered where he was about to take her. It was something she couldn't explain to anyone. She loved him madly, yet when she thought and imagined what Edward had done…

She knew she should say something but it was a while since she had imbibed alcohol and mere days since stopping taking medication; all that champagne had gone to her head and made her drowsy.

'Mrs Andriotti, we're here.'

Snapping her eyes open, she looked at him and then at the rings on her finger. 'I didn't dream it.'

'No, we are married.'

She stared at the wonderful wooden creation before them, it somehow pointed to American origins.

He glanced up at the sky. 'Do you know where you are now?'

She nodded and wondered if they would also go sailing.

'May I carry the bride over the threshold?' And without waiting for a reply, he swept her up into his arms and walked to the front door. 'Weather permitting, I'll show you around tomorrow, there's a storm brewing.'

No place could be more inviting. In a fireplace, acting as partition between living and dining room, roared a huge happy fire.

'You may unpack.' Michael told her as he walked towards a door, then stopped, turned, and smiled. 'While you were in dreamland, I brought the bags in.'

Xristo had left them a light meal on the table near the fireplace, but neither had much of an appetite.

Michael poured two glasses of champagne and handed her one. 'We've already had far too much and everyone made all the frivolous and clichéd toasts we could hope to hear.' Giving her a smile, he became serious again. 'May we love and understand each other always, and when we fight, and I have no doubt that we will, may we have the patience to listen to the other's point of view. And afterwards, may we be courageous enough to ask for forgiveness even when we're not wrong. But above all, may we never say goodbye.'

She smiled, nodded, and tried to hide a yawn.

Taking her glass, he encouraged. 'Go get ready for bed. I'm going outside to check things, I want to make sure Xristo left enough wood.'

He'd been right to warn her because he made a racket knocking and pushing things about. After a shower, she put the silk nightdress and gown on, went to the kitchen, and then just walked through the place, for no other reason than to calm her apprehension. When he eventually came in, he was dripping wet. It had started raining.

Thoughts of Gloria rushed into her head, the horror images making her skin crawl. No, she couldn't believe Michael was anything like Edward.

Coming from the bathroom, he watched her. She was adjusting the nightdress straps nervously. Bracing himself, he walked over and fell on his knees before the armchair. 'Christie,'

The vision of him wearing only a towel made her melt somewhere inside, which was followed by that inexplicable uneasiness.

'Sweetheart, are you afraid?'

She dropped her gaze and made an incongruous gesture. 'I don't know. Edward raped Gloria on their wedding day.'

'Dear lord! When did she tell you this?'

So she told him about that terrible day, about what she'd learnt about Edward and that somehow, he'd dragged her mind and emotions into a panic pit. 'When I imagined him perpetrating unspeakable horrors, it filled me with dread. And that's what he counted on, on Gloria being helpless and me hysterical.'

'I feel so stupid.' Cupping her face, he wiped the tears.

'It's just- I've never been with anyone.'

'Sweetheart, I know this.' He took her hands and kissed the fingertips. 'And that's why I didn't press for intimacy. We'll have an adventure, at your pace, without rushing. Do you know why I visited Dr Papacostas? Because I could feel something wasn't right and I'm serious that I never want to frighten or hurt you. You're not aware of it but I always noticed your hesitation. So if tonight is not the night, it's not. We're going to be married forever, there's time for everything.'

Even when he acted crazy and out of character, she knew a secret beauty existed in him, and here it was, laid at her feet. 'I'm nervous, not petrified.'

'Then will you trust me?'

'Yes.' She whispered, knowing that she always had. 'Just love me.'

'I do, body, and soul.' Pulling her up, he slipped his hands under the silk on her shoulders, letting the nightdress and gown sink into a shimmering pond around her feet. His eyes roamed over her almost naked body, drinking her in, becoming intoxicated. Letting his fingers glide down the column of her neck and then the line of her shoulders, he felt the strength beneath the velvety skin. Gazing into her eyes, he told her in a low voice. 'You bewitch me.'

His mouth was gentle, waiting for her want to unfurl. It was maddening, he wanted wild, passionate, but he couldn't frighten her. Hands running up her back, he brought her closer, making her body melt into his, so his fire would ignite her. His body telling hers that this was the only thing it could think about now.

Picking her up into his arms, he covered her face with kisses as he carried her across the room. Dropping her onto her feet, he took a faltering breath; how he wanted her.

Guiding her to the bed, he told her. 'Look at me, Edward is not here to frighten you. Touch me, and you'll keep it here,' he touched her temple. 'And feel and taste my love, to safeguard it in your heart.' He let the finger run down the side of her face.

She closed her eyes and parted her lips; when his mouth covered hers again, she felt her body burst with need. Reaching out, she finally let go of Edward's spectre and became lost in Michael's wondrous touch. 'Show me.' She asked breathlessly.

His eyes shone with delight, and he did, not merely the physical love, but the one that came from the depths of their souls for each other, making them both cry.

She awoke slowly, with Michael draped over her. He'd kept his promise, being as gentle as he could have been and she felt wonderful. Moving a little, his skin made hers tingle. She wanted more.

He'd been awake when she began to stir and finding the fire of unquenched desire almost impossible to bear, he discovered the simple act of breathing a laborious effort.

He wanted to run his hands over her body, to explore all the secret places, to kiss her mouth… But he didn't move, letting her experience the safety of his embrace.

'Michael,' she called softly.

He put the light on, propped himself up, and looked at her. 'Yes, my love.'

She lifted a hand to his face and he swallowed hard. It was true; she had the power. 'Make love to me.'

It rained for three days and they enjoyed every minute. There were picnics in front of the fireplace, some hours of reading at the bay window and small marathons watching the torrent from under a blanket, but mostly, they satiated their growing craving for one another.

'You named her after me!' Pleasure poured out as she read the bright blue name on the yacht's side. 'I love you.'

'Good.' He kissed her with gusto, patted her behind, and helped her up. 'Come on, there's work to be done.'

'Where are we going?'

'Around the islands. The sea is rough so I don't want to become too adventurous. Sure you wouldn't have preferred Paris, Bali, or some other exotic location?'

'No, you chose exactly right.'

'We'll do the exotic bit next year.' He became serious. 'Actually, Dr Papacostas suggested I didn't take you far away, in case your subconscious fears about Edward materialised. The last thing I wanted to do was frighten you as he did.' His voice dropped to a whisper. 'Yet I did with my unfounded jealousy.'

Resting her face against his chest, she sighed. 'I was afraid of him but never of you, just thought you very weird; one minute, politeness personified and the next, that fury! I was thoroughly confused trying to guess why you kissed me, or why you would be interested. Okay, perhaps as an enticing pastime, Edward suggested as much.'

'And we know what a smart jerk he is.'

Drifting along with no timetable to keep, they spent their days making discoveries about each other and the places they visited; walking up and down cobbled streets, seeing every ruin, and sometimes spending the night in a tiny room in some small hotel tucked away on the side of a hill.

As the CHRISTINE glided slowly into the Rhodes marina, Christie watched Michael. How was it possible that one man could be exceptional in so many areas? With him, there were no two-ways or in-betweens; it was all the way or nothing. She'd been like that once, but then... Edward became the escape from everything she loathed; Michael presented a highway to everything she loved.

With interest, she watched the panoramic array of kaleidoscopic craft. This, a mere handful compared to what the marina would take during the hot months. Thrilling, exciting, adventurous she thought of them, and the people who owned them. Next summer, they would join this wondrous world of fantastic discovery, and then she would take her easel and paints. For days now, she had been getting the strangest cravings for the feel of brushes in her hand and the smell of paint in her nostrils.

'Christie, do you need anything?' Michael asked as he secured the ropes.

'Such as?' "Hope I'm doing these sails right."

'I made a list of supplies we need. It's on the table.'

Perhaps she should get more conditioner; her hair was starting to feel harsh from so much salty air. Going quickly inside, she picked up the note and perused over Michael's neat English handwriting. Unable to find the pen, she went into the stateroom. Rummaging in the dressing table, she noticed a discarded envelope in the bottom drawer. 'I forgot about this.' Inspecting both sides, she couldn't see name or address. Returning to the galley, she took a knife, slit one end open, and poured its contents onto the table. There was a note and two Polaroids taped together. Her brows lifted curiously. Only one way to find out;

"Christie,
Would Michael do this for you? I think not.
Edward."

Reaching for the Polaroids, she separated them and stared uncomprehendingly, then, blood drained from her face. Dropping the pictures as if they burnt holes in her hands, she turned quickly, bumped into the cupboard, and knocked two pans down.

Michael was appreciating Christie's sail work when he heard a strange thump and things falling about. Racing down the stairs, he found her crouching on the floor, holding her head tightly to her knees. 'What's wrong, sweetheart?'

Giving him the most pitiful look he had ever seen, she threw her arms around him and burst into tears. 'He's never going to stop.' She sobbed and pointed. 'I'm frightened, Michael, afraid for you.'

Grabbing the discarded pictures, he glanced at them and then jumped to his feet as recognition filtered into his brain. 'Where did you get these?'

She passed him the note.

His eyes ran over the words quickly, and then he stared at the pictures again. 'We have to call the police.'

Nodding, she wiped her eyes. 'He'll never stop tormenting us. And now, he's become homicidal.'

Sitting opposite them, the Inspector scribbled in his book. 'Mrs Andriotti, where did you say you got these photographs?' He stared at them in the plastic bag, his glasses balancing precariously on the tip of his nose.

'On our wedding day, just before we left. I simply forgot about the envelope.'

He watched the face before him. Over the months, he'd seen it many times in the papers and down at the police station, and every time it seemed, in connection with some calamity. There was the Harbour Master's death, millions of drachmas worth of stolen Icons and artefacts - apparently Davis' idea of a get-rich-quick scheme - and now the Soros' murders. He wondered why someone as beautiful as she could inspire such chaos. Pushing the glasses up with the pen, he then pointed it at the photographs. 'One thing intrigues me. Were they chosen at random or is there a message only you understand?'

'My wife didn't know them but I'm sure you've heard of their antics.'

'Yes, they were most disagreeable and in permanent trouble. Nevertheless, this is a murder investigation. The culprit must be found.'

Michael recounted the incident after which he had felt an ire that was hard to describe.

The Inspector listened in silent immobility, his eyes fixed on Christie's face. No picture had done her justice, not even the ones he'd seen of their wedding weeks previously. He was beginning to understand what drove that foreigner Davis to such madness, as it was imminently clear that her husband too was besotted. He glanced at Michael, who sat holding her hand, perused the statement, looked up at them again, and announced. 'Then you too had a motive.'

'If you think I killed them and then played this sick prank on my wife, you're crazier than Edward. All I did was punch Anthony.'

'What, when?' Christie asked in shock.

'Not the day they died, the day of the party. Paul and I went to see them. Anthony insinuated, insulted, and then hit Paul; I had to defend him. We should have pressed charges, because then, they would have been behind bars and not dead.' Michael motioned towards the pictures.

'Where were you the day of the murder, Mr Andriotti?'

'Probably at work, ask my secretary.'

'But you can't possibly think...' Christie couldn't finish.

'It could be a clever ploy.'

Michael banged both fists on the table. 'I didn't touch the little creeps again although I was sorely tempted. Check the fingerprints on that note and pictures, your answer is there.'

The Inspector rose. 'We will, but so are yours. Are you planning to go somewhere?'

'We were about to start back home but I'll sit idly by until you are satisfied I had nothing to do with that.'

'Thank you and I assure you that I'll delay you no further than is absolutely necessary. Good day, ma'am.' He put a hand to his temple. 'By the way; who is this Paul you mentioned?'

'Now look here, Inspector-'

'Mr Andriotti, I need to verify your story.' Opening the book again, the Inspector pulled a pen from his pocket. 'Surname and address, please.'

Michael told him. 'Yes Inspector, now do you think that I killed one and he the other?'

'Every avenue must be pursued. I'll see you again.'

They watched the Inspector walk down the gangway in silence.

'I'm scared, Michael.'

'Don't be, he's only doing his job. But if they had done it right and found Edward, this wouldn't be happening. The question is, how much damage will he wreck before being caught. I just can't believe that he's been around as late as-' realising how frightened she was he stopped. 'It was stupid to mention Paul.'

'Edward's message is not implication. It's a warning that he still wants to hurt you.' Giant tears rolled down her face.

He put his arms around her. 'Please don't cry.'

Christie was in the galley when the Inspector returned two days later. She desperately wanted to know the news but her knees felt weak. Pacing nervously for a few minutes, she then bolted up the stairs.

'Mrs Andriotti,' the Inspector greeted cheerily. 'I was telling your husband that he was right in guessing that Mr Davis' fingerprints were on everything. Nevertheless, this is a serious crime and these things must be done. The handwriting also matched the samples Captain Dimitri sent from Lindos. I hope you will accept my sincerest apologies. And now you may continue your journey.' He bowed towards her.

Michael placed his hands on her shoulders. 'Christie, if he meant me real harm why would he do this first? He meant to scare you, and obviously succeeded. Now put this out of your mind and let us lead a normal life. The police have begun a search all over again and he knows it. He's a saboteur, who simply drops his bomb and runs, he'd never put himself at risk. And do you know why he got rid of them so easily? Because they were drunken fools. Like most criminals, Edward is also a coward, picking on the weak and defenceless, I'm neither.'

Then he began a discussion on late Gothic architecture, so she understood that he was not afraid. After a few minutes, she did respond, eventually taking part in the conversation animatedly as they started walking along Mandraki.

'Don't you just hate it when they build a glass tower right next to one of those?' He pointed in the direction of the high castle walls rising above the fir trees. 'But I doubt excessive modernisation would be welcomed by anyone, especially the tourists. Mentioning tourists, have you ever seen our artists at work? We have a few around, even this time of year.'

She grinned. 'I know them better than you do. Whenever we came to see Dr Papacostas, Mary and I always wandered around.'

'Then there's nothing I can show you today.'

'On the contrary, I'm never bored around ruins or paint.' She looked around. 'We should have gone through the Gate of the Harbour; they tend to be more around there. But after being cramped so long on a boat-'

He came to a sudden halt. 'Don't you like being cramped with me?'

'I love being cramped with you.'

He pulled her close and kissed her.

They came upon the group rather suddenly. 'Hello,' she greeted.

'Christie,' almost all said in unison and then the marriage congratulations and jokes started.

She smiled at their friendliness and camaraderie. 'Let me present my husband, Michael.'

'We wish you much happiness.'

'Thank you very much. Where's Nichola?' Christie queried.

One young man pointed behind her. 'He gets the drinks.'

Turning, Christie smiled broadly. 'Hi Nichola, how have you been?'

'Good.' Putting a bag down on the ground, he shook her hand. 'Sorry I did not come to the wedding, but I was visiting my family in Thessalonika and did not see the card until I come back three days ago.'

'I thought that might have happened, therefore, I'm not upset. Go ahead, I don't want to disturb.'

'So,' Michael whispered in her ear. 'Which one do you like?' He pointed to the displayed works against the wall.

'Actually,' Christie went to stand behind Nichola. 'I want to paint like him.'

Michael eyed the work critically and nodded. 'This is definitely the most impressive watercolours I've seen in a while.'

Turning his head, Nichola smiled, then, flicking through his folder, he asked. 'What do you think?'

'Nichola, it's me!'

Michael touched it gently. 'Beautiful! Not only because it's of my wife; but also because it's excellent work. Is it for sale?'

Nichola shrugged. 'I cannot afford to be sentimental. But perhaps it is a wedding gift-'

'That's very kind, but I'd rather buy this one today. You can make us another.' Michael had seen how vigorously Christie shook her head when Nichola mentioned giving it away. If clothes were an indication to prosperity then Nichola needed money fast. Taking a chequebook out, he scribbled quickly, tore out the page, and put it in Nichola's hand.

'I cannot accept this!'

'Why not? I could go buy a masterpiece which would cost the earth but wouldn't please me as much.' Michael paged through the folder. 'It just occurred to me, I've been looking for original work for the hotel. Interested in the commission?'

Nichola's eyes seemed to pop out of his head. 'I don't know what to say.' He looked down at the cheque. 'I still think it's too much.'

'Nonsense, you are talented and should be making a living now, not some auction house after your death.'

'Sorry,' Nichola offered a hand. 'I'm staring and completely forget my manners. Thank you, not only for the money but also for the commission.'

'Just give us some time to settle down.' Michael wrote on a card. 'But on that date, I expect to see you in Lindos.'

Homeward bound, Christie was excited about the future. Not only was she going to share it with Michael but also with Nichola. He was brilliant and she dearly wished to paint as well as he did, because now was the time to start seriously. Watching the sinking sun as it hid behind grey clouds, she wanted to record the exact hue of purple the rays sent across the gleaming water.

Arriving home, they found it deserted, the servants informing them that Sofia had gone to stay with Andrea and Sarah for a while and would afterwards return to South Africa. Michael reacted quickly. Getting on the phone, he almost ordered Sofia to go nowhere, and then to return to Rhodes. Christie and Sofia laughed at his obstinacy, neither comprehending it.

'Oh, there's one more surprise,' he told Christie after dinner. 'And you'll love this one.' Covering her eyes with one hand, he guided her through the house. 'What do you think?'

Her eyes opened and so did her mouth in delight, her hands flying up in astonished pleasure. Throwing her arms around him for a second, she immediately let go again. 'It's perfect!' Turning in a complete circle, she stared at what used to be the veranda, now turned into a studio. Completely enthralled, she peered out of windows, gazed at the skylight, and hugged him again. 'I love you.'

He tucked the blonde hair behind her ears. 'We'll invite Nichola to work from here.'

'Do you know how much I can learn just by watching him? And I'd be delighted if he agreed to give me lessons. There are things I don't understand and I desperately need someone with an art education to teach me.' She went on excitedly.

'I know. So you see, my invitation had a dual purpose.'

'Thank you.' She told him as her eyes danced happily.

The following Monday, Dimitri was in Michael's office. 'The judge has finally set the trial date. He's met with Dr Papacostas and he's satisfied Christie is competent and able to be a good witness.' He glanced at a file. 'About John; do you still want to know?'

'Was there anything unusual?'

'All normal stuff.' Dimitri threw a photo onto the desk.

Michael stared at the strange face curiously. 'I don't know what I expected. Did you ever speak to his wife?'

'My Pefki colleague did, on the phone. She told him that they had simply drifted apart. In fact, she hasn't seen him in a year.'

'It just makes me feel better knowing that Christie was never in any real danger.'

CHAPTER TWELVE

Sitting with a book in Christie's studio, Sofia looked up from the page, studied the young face in front of the easel, and thought that Christie could never look more beautiful than she did now. Christie had always been that, but being neck-deep in unhappiness, she'd neglected herself, just as she did her studies. When she thought that this loving girl could have married that fruitcake Edward, she got the willies.

Now seeing the two people she loved most together, was more than she deserved.

'Stop dreaming Thea, come have a look,' Christie called.

'Sorry, darling.' Rising, Sofia went to stand in front of the easel. 'This is what you've been doing?'

'Like it?'

Sofia watched herself on canvas. 'It's nice. But don't I look… er, sad?'

'Not exactly, it's more wistful, perhaps even yearning.'

'You see that?'

'Not always. Sometimes, it's as if you're waiting for something, or someone.' Christie rubbed her hands on a cloth. 'I need to find my Gum Arabic.'

'While you analyse me, I'll go see what's for dinner.'

'Where could it be?' Christie mumbled as she hunted in the newly redone bedroom. Looking towards the bed, she realised that workers had been everywhere and someone might have kicked it under there.

Going down on her knees, she threw the bedcovers up and crawled under the bed, spreading her hands across the carpet. Finding nothing, she turned on her back and let her hands touch the wood above her. 'Wonder where he found this.' The four-poster being of somewhat antiquated origin had a flat wooden frame where the mattress lay. Trying to guess its age, she let her hands run all the way up to the headboard. She stopped; her fingers had found something thin and pliable. She followed it all the way to the leg and there discovered some type of container. She gave it a tug, it came off easily.

Quickly wriggling herself out from under the bed, she stood up and stared at the strange objects in her hands.

It was somehow reminiscent of the small cartridges used for making soda drinks, a small black box on top, with a red button on the side, and that thin pliable tube dangling like a snake. Walking down the passage, she asked. 'Martha, have you seen a bottle of binding material, it's called Gum Arabic.'

'Yes ma'am, it's in the hall closet in a green box, should I get it for you?'

'Thank you and take it to the studio.' She walked into the lounge and asked. 'Michael, what's this?'

'Have no idea, where did you get it?'

'Under my old bed. I was searching for Gum Arabic and found this instead.'

Within minutes, Michael had the servants look at the device but no one knew what it was, where it had come from, or who had put it there. Finally, Martha ventured, 'Sir, do you suppose that it could be a bomb?'

'Christie, put the thing down and don't touch it again. I'll ask Dimitri to come take it away.'

Dimitri entered the room accompanied by another police officer. 'Good evening, Michael, Christie, Mrs Watson. Your call sounded urgent, anything the matter?'

'Any idea what that is?' Michael pointed to the Parsons table.

Dimitri gave the object an interested appraisal. 'Looks like a gas bottle, even if small. I'll have the lab look at it.' He pressed the red button with a pen and a whooshing sound filled the room, followed by a thin spray from the tube, a peculiar pleasant odour reaching him. 'Chloroform,' he announced, and quickly took a step back.

'That's it! That's the sound that kept me awake!' Christie announced with realisation, all colour draining from her face. She turned to Michael. 'I didn't imagine it, there was something in that room.'

'We'll have it dusted for prints and tests done to the contents.' Dimitri told them as he placed the bottle in a plastic bag, bade them goodnight and left.

The answer came five days later.

Glancing at a report in his hands, Dimitri watched the anxious faces before him. 'As I told you before, the substance in the bottle was chloroform, or trichloromethane as the lab called it; either used to induce unconsciousness, or the opposite effect. Doctors use it to put patients to sleep before surgery. The box on top was a remote control to release the substance. As you noticed before, the smell is pleasant and in the quantity released, was almost impossible to detect.

'Still, the lab technicians say that it is a most dangerous thing to do and believe that over-dosage was a strong likelihood with the crude instrumentation used, and that serious harm was intended. It can cause serious respiratory, cardiac, and liver problems. Sadly, again, Edward's prints are everywhere. I just can't imagine when and how he got into the house, unless he hired someone.' He looked at Christie. 'He's determined when it comes to you but the inconsistency of his methods is something we cannot fathom. He killed two men who attacked you, yet he jeopardised your life. How do we find someone like that?'

Christie stared out the window. 'What I don't understand is why it never happened when I was awake, which is why I couldn't trace it. So how did he know when I was asleep, was he spying on me?' An involuntary shiver ran down her spine.

'Perhaps we should have the place searched.' Dimitri suggested.

'Tear the house apart if need be, I'm not having anyone live in fear of a maniac. Isn't there something you can do to find out if he's still around?'

'Believe me Michael; I want him locked up as much as anyone. But as you see, apart from the fact that he's insane, he's also resourceful and likes to play dangerous games, especially with your wife. And for your sakes I hope he's no longer in the country.'

Three police officers arrived in plain clothes from the mainland. They spent the day going from room to room. When they emerged late afternoon, they had a bag full of listening devices and a camera. And all had been found in Christie's old bedroom.

Christie refused to let Edward terrorise her with his invisible tentacles but as the trial loomed, she dreaded the disorder it would bring and the ugly memories that were to resurface. With Michael's support, she knew she could survive more than she had expected, but increasingly, she wished she could just let go and take no part in the inevitable invasion of privacy.

Apart from that dark cloud, life was the rollercoaster that was living with Michael. He was smart, hilarious, unpredictable, and totally in love with her. And that very fact; filled her with a bizarre fear. One that told her that all this was too good, that it couldn't last, that someone would stop it. She felt like Cinderella; just before the clock struck twelve, and then everything she was becoming accustomed to would disappear. However, unlike in fairytales, here, prince charming might find that getting rid of the ogres was tougher. Because she had no doubt that Edward was not yet done with them.

What she wouldn't give to paint like Nichola, he always made it look so easy. But now, finally, only a week remained before his arrival in Lindos. She should pack everything away, because her lack of technical expertise was giving her headaches, and then they would start from scratch.

Sitting on one of the high stools in the kitchen, she watched the cook as he went about checking cupboards and the refrigerator, writing endless lists as if they were starving. Didn't the man rest? She smiled as he mumbled in his native tongue, something in a Slavic dialect.

'Goodness, Milo,' she said as he entered the kitchen carrying a small but heavy crate. 'What have you got there?'

'I don't know madam, it's addressed to you. It arrived at the hotel and the porter sent for me.'

Surprised, she got off the stool and waited for him to put the thing down, pry the top open, and pull masses of shredded paper out. 'I hope it's not one of those empty box jokes. Ah, there's something, another box.'

'Let me take it out for you, madam, it's rather heavy.' Milo pulled out the second box and placed it on the counter.

'Here's a card.' Opening the envelope, a smile appeared on her face. 'It's a late wedding gift. I wonder from whom,' she flicked the card open. 'Oh! Thanks Milo.'

'Should I take it out?'

'Go ahead.'

Something wrapped in bubble-plastic appeared on the counter, and pulling the tape off, Milo revealed a magnificent bust. This was no ordinary piece of rock carved in some dingy workshop for tourist consumption; this was the genuine article, and she was certain it was at least a few hundred years old.

'Very nice.' Cook noted.

Milo also nodded approval.

'Yes. Thank you, Milo. Just leave it there until I find a place for it.'

The phone rang and Milo answered it. 'Andriotti residence.' He listened a few seconds. 'I'll be right over.' He returned the receiver to its place. 'Madam, there seems to be some confusion regarding parcels at the post office.'

'Yes of course, go sort it out.' Walking away with the card, she read it again.

"Dear Christie,

Let me begin by offering my sincerest apologies for my abominable behaviour last time we saw each other. When in your company, I usually make a fool of myself and on this occasion, I find it inexcusable because rightly, you owe me no explanations whatsoever.

It would therefore make me eternally happy if you accepted this gift as a token of my friendship and good wishes.

I'm leaving Rhodes. If you could find it in your heart to spare me an hour, I would apologise in person, for you deserve better than a few lines on a note. It would also contribute greatly towards clearing this guilty conscience. I'll wait at Yanni's on the... at four o'clock.

Your humble friend,

John"

'That's today.' She felt flattered by the gesture. After all, as he admitted, he had behaved badly, and it was only proper she thank him personally for such an exquisite gift. Grabbing her coat and scarf, she ran out of the house.

Pleasure filled her as she glanced at the bright blue sky. Finally, the days were getting warmer again. Was it only sixteen months since she had arrived? It felt as if an eternity of experiences had taken place. She was married to a most exciting man, whom she had fallen in love with twice - she smiled at the idea - and a long road of discovery lay before them. She breathed in deeply, as if to take in physically the happiness she felt.

Making her way down one of the narrow streets, she studied the brightly coloured shutters. Just like eyes. Some closed in laziness, others half-open, and the rest wide-awake. Standing still a moment, she took another deep breath. How she loved being here. Then she ran down the street, reaching Yanni's at ten past four, fearful that he might have already left.

Unexpectedly, he was before her. 'Hi, Christie. It's always such a pleasure to see you. Please, let me start by apologising for my nasty character.' He smiled.

'Hello, John, thank you and I accept your apology.'

'How is married life treating you? Don't answer, extremely well.' He winked.

This was a definite improvement on the last John. 'I'm glad you approve.'

'Of marriage, always have. Although mine was an ugly disaster, I still believe the right woman will come along. Would you like to go for a walk?' He saw flickering doubt. 'A short one, I have to finish packing if I don't want to miss my plane.'

Falling into step beside him, she queried. 'Where are you going?'

'Home, I've had enough of foreign places to last me a lifetime. To be blunt; I hate it here.'

'What a shame. I like it so much that it never occurred to me that someone else might find it unpleasant. What's Cyprus like?'

'Okay. This is my place, at least for another hour. May I offer you some refreshment?'

She looked around nervously.

'With my record, I don't blame you. Quick tempers are so unbecoming.' Opening the door, he walked in. 'Leave it open, the taxi will be here shortly.'

Since when was paranoia normal? She stood in the entrance uncertainly. 'What time is your flight?'

He pointed to a chair and glanced at his watch. 'I have to be on board in two hours so I may have to race all the way up and down the mountain.' He laughed. 'At least I'll get some thrills on my last day.'

'Thank you so much for the beautiful gift you sent us. But somehow, it feels wrong to accept.'

'Why?' Pulling a case from the top of the cupboard, he dropped it on the bed.

Her gaze travelled around the room, it was bare.

'You're wondering how I can afford such a fine piece. Ever heard that looks can be deceiving? Don't let my meagre belongings fool you.'

'I apologise. But where did you make such a find?' She stared as he began transferring clothes from the drawers to the suitcase on the bed. Odd, it was as if she was having a *déjà vu* moment. 'Have you always been in the tourist business?'

He disappeared into the bathroom then reappeared with a shirt in his hands, dropped it on the bed and leaning against the door, pushed it shut so he could get something in a box. 'People will suffer almost anything to achieve a goal.'

'Of course; and you were working through your separation.' She commiserated. 'Sorry it didn't work out.'

Walking next door again, he turned on a tap.

She stared at a monitor on the corner table, an uneasy suspicion beginning to fill her.

His muffled voice reached her. 'I hear your memory is completely restored. Do you recall how we met?'

'At the hospital.'

'So very unromantic, don't you think? But I meant back home.'

As he re-entered the room, she jumped from the chair with fright, turned pale, and suddenly found it difficult to breathe. He no longer had a beard, his hair was blond, his eyes blue. 'Ed-ward! It... it's impossible. You're...' Her hand flew to her chest, trying to stop her racing heart

'As you can see, I've had ample time to mingle and blend in. I've even been home, via Cyprus, and my handsome face plastered on the airport walls. How's that for idiocy?'

"I'm going to faint," she leaned against the wall, her gaze falling on the monitor. That's how he'd known what she was doing, saying… Why hadn't she recognised him, his mannerisms, his voice…? Why hadn't the police known? She reached for the door; locked! 'I want to-'

'I know you believe I always want to hurt you. That's not my intention today.'

Her voice rose. 'I want to go home.'

'And into Michael's loving arms. But when you hear what I know you'll never go there again.'

She covered her ears. 'Open this door.'

'You can't imagine what peculiar behaviour is going on. Did you know that you're part of a most intriguing cover-up?'

She swivelled around. 'What do you want? You always want something!'

He pulled two papers from his pocket and waved one. 'Michael's birth registration. Now why do you suppose Sofia had it? Because she's his biological mother.' He saw her mouth open in shock. 'Don't believe me?' He waved the other. 'Here's his original birth certificate to prove it. Fascinating, isn't it? However, that, is nothing compared to who his father is. Know what's really sad? Even Michael is oblivious to Sofia's deceit. And worse, according to the law, you cannot be legally married. Why you ask? Because he's your half-brother. Imagine Christie, you travel half across the world to meet and marry your father's bastard son.'

Something had hit her, only she wasn't sure where it had struck because her whole body was numb. 'N-no… You're lying!'

'Am I? But don't take my word for it, ask Sofia. Didn't you wonder why she wanted to send you here? All these years she's been grooming you for him. Now, who's mad?'

'No!' She struggled with the door handle. 'No! Let me out!'

'Right here,' he pointed. 'Mother, Sofia Andriotti. Father, Robert Thomas. It's yours.' He stuffed the papers into her hand and turned the key.

Bolting out the door as if chased by the devil himself, she was almost knocked down by a taxi. She ran through the winding streets, knowing nothing she had heard was true. She stopped abruptly, stared at the crumpled paper, and felt the tears of fear run down her face. 'Robert Thomas,' she repeated to herself.

It was an official paper, the well-known purple stamp from the Department of Internal Affairs glaring back at her. Everything swam in front of her. Leaning her head against the hot wall, she held onto it with both hands.

Breathlessly, she burst into the study from the garden.

'Where have you been?' Sofia looked up with a smile, which died instantaneously. 'Christie?'

With a streaked face, Christie shoved the paper into Sofia's hand. 'Is it true?'

'What's wrong, sweetheart?'

'Look at it! Is it true?'

Straightening the paper, Sofia could never have guessed or expected this moment. 'Dear lord!' She exclaimed, and against her own wishes swayed, her trembling hand going out for support. 'Where did you get this?' Her voice was barely above a whisper.

'Is it true?' Christie demanded, but the reaction she had just witnessed was conviction enough.

Sofia nodded, her eyes filling with tears. 'Christie-'

'How could you do this to me?'

'Does it really matter after all these years? It was better this way-'

'For whom?' Christie screamed near hysteria. 'I trusted you...' impassioned hands grabbed at her chest. 'Where's your heart, Thea? How could you?' With a flick of the wrist, she snapped the paper out of Sofia's hand and walked out of the study. 'How could you let me marry my own brother?'

Sofia reacted in shock. 'Christie!'

Rushing down the passage, Christie sobbed, 'how could you? How could you?'

Sofia became highly agitated. 'Heavens, where did she hear such lies? Christie, let me explain-'

'Sorry, not today.' A voice said behind her.

Turning quickly, Sofia's hand flew to her mouth. 'Edward! How, what, I mean-'

'How I found out? I may be going insane but I'm no idiot. Thought you were rid of me, no, I'm rid of you.' Lifting his arm, he struck her with the marble obelisk he'd just picked up from the desk.

Locking the study door and dropping the key into his pocket, Edward walked down the passage. If he had timed this right, only cook was around. Going into Christie's old room, he looked for his gadgets. The place was clean. He had wondered why transmission had suddenly ceased but he thought it was the tree's fault. It no longer mattered. Letting himself out the window, he stopped at the next one. Peering inside, he saw her, filling cases, tears streaming down her face. He clenched his teeth. 'I will have you.' Then, he sauntered towards the taxi.

Walking into the house, Michael thought it strangely quiet. 'Good evening,' he greeted cook. 'Where are the ladies?'

'I don't know, sir. But I could swear I heard them shouting at each other earlier.'

Michael frowned. 'Are you sure?'

'That's the problem, sir, I'm not. I walked to the study but it's locked so I must have imagined it.' He pointed to the bust on the counter. 'Mrs Andriotti received that this afternoon. Then she went out and I didn't see her again.'

Michael appraised the bust. 'Very nice. Do you know who sent it?'

'There was a card but Mrs Andriotti took it.'

Seeing the studio in darkness, Michael went into their bedroom, took a shower, and wondered why the bed and floor leading to the dressing room was strewn with clothes. As he towelled his hair dry, he saw the envelope on the desk. Picking it up, he opened it and glanced over the short note. It was Christie's handwriting but it looked different, as if she had been unable to hold her hand steady, as if the paper had been out in the rain.

"My dearest love,

We promised that we would never say goodbye, but like most promises, we have to break it. I'm sorry for leaving without explanations but I cannot face you and repeat this horrible thing...

I beg you, don't try to find me because we can never be together again, and that, is the biggest heartache! My fear that this wondrous heaven could not last has happened; yet, I have no regrets and much to be thankful for.

All my love, always,
Christie"

He stared at the paper as if it were on fire. 'Okay, the joke is over and you have scared the living daylights out of me. Christie?' He called as he quickly slipped into his shirt and pants.

Two hours later, he thought, "I'm in hell." All he'd been able to establish after kicking the study door open and finding Sofia in a pool of blood was that Edward had been in the house, almost having smashed her head in, sending her into emergency surgery and Christie to places unknown.

As hours passed and Dimitri and his men got to work, they finally ascertained that Christie had taken a taxi to the airport, but never got on a plane, another taxi driver swearing that he'd taken her to the harbour. He had thought it unusual but in the state she'd been in, he doubted she was aware of what she was doing.

Those had been the most miserable two days of her life, but Christie knew that no matter what discomforts she endured from now on, it could never compare to the black hole she had just encountered.

It hadn't been difficult to get a passage on the ship and for that, she was thankful. Offering wads of money, they would have taken her all the way to China, but all she had wanted to know was their destination.

'Egypt.' One of the men on deck told her.

'May I see your captain?'

He turned out to be a kindly middle-aged man who somehow understood that she was in a crisis. Checking her passport, he nodded. 'There's plenty room,' and refused to take more than was necessary.

The voyage wasn't pleasant; she developed seasickness from the moment the anchor was hoisted, relegating her into an almost continuous stay in bed.

On arrival in Egypt, the captain called a taxi and had her driven to one of the lesser-known hotels as she requested, shaking his head with immense pity. How could such a lovely girl be suffering so much?

The first thing she did after being shown to her room was have a shower and then collapse on the bed, thinking that exhaustion would drive her into a dreamless stupor. Instead, she lay for hours staring at the ceiling, tears running down her face.

Eventually falling into a fitful sleep, she later cursed the morning light for waking her and with it bringing reality. 'I have to think,' but that soon brought back the tears. How could this be happening? Where should she go? What would she do?

After dressing and going down to breakfast, she went out to the market nearby. Another time the dazzling colours and textures, the smells and variety of goods on display, would have enthralled her, but today, she was lost to the world, living inside herself.

Returning to the hotel, she lay on the bed staring at the ceiling once more. Turning on her side, she reached for the handbag and pulled out the crumpled paper. How could Sofia have done this to both her and Michael? And what about her father... he couldn't possibly know. She sobbed for a long time afterwards, holding the paper in a fist. Then she reached for the phone.

It was a warm autumn day when she arrived in Johannesburg but it could have been the coldest because she didn't notice. Glancing around, it felt as if she had been gone for an eternity. She had left the country with a bruised ego and now returned with a life in tatters. Tears sprang to her eyes, which she quickly hid behind dark glasses; then hailing a taxi, she gave the address to the driver.

'Christie,' Jane greeted without surprise. 'Everyone is frantic, especially Michael.'

'Where's daddy?'

'He was here but then had to go to the office, he's very concerned. Were you aware that Edward almost killed Sofia? She's still unconscious in intensive care. The criminal almost bashed her head in.'

Christie bit her lip. 'I need a bath and rest. I haven't done much of that in days.'

'Aren't you at least going to call Michael? He's terribly worried.'

'This is why I had the taxi driver call first and ask if he was here. I wouldn't have come in otherwise.' She turned from Jane's prying eyes. 'May I borrow some money?'

'How much do you need?'

Christie named a sum.

'All that, what for?'

'Huh, there's travelling, rent, all the necessities.'

'What about your husband?'

Christie's eyes drowned in giant pools. 'We can no longer be.'

'I don't understand anything. Michael says you didn't fight, that he hasn't slept since you left. Calls every hour or so to hear if-' Jane realised her mistake.

Christie struggled to get the words out. 'Can you lend me the money or should I sell these?' She gazed at the rings and watch, her fingers going to the earrings Michael had given her for her birthday. 'They should be worth something, and I have Thea's pearls-'

'No! You can't!' Jane said in shock. 'I'll write you a cheque. Cash it whenever you wish but please don't do anything you'll regret.'

'Regrets,' Christie's voice was mournful. 'I have none. Can you write it now?'

'If it makes you feel better.' Opening a drawer, Jane took out the small book, wrote quickly and tearing out the page placed it in her daughter's hand. 'You know you can't believe anything Edward says.'

'Please, mom, I'm very tired and have no wish to discuss this with anyone, ever.'

'You should, or it will tear you apart.'

Lying on the familiar bed, Christie stared at the bedside lamp as if answers were forthcoming. Would this pain ever subside? 'Oh Michael.' Burying her face in the pillow, she sobbed until she drifted into a weary slumber.

Jane took her a dinner tray and announced that Rob would like to see her. 'What happened, did Edward frighten you again?'

But no one could make her repeat this horrible secret. Climbing back into bed, she requested they leave her alone, refusing her father entrance when he knocked, knowing that she would feel worse if she saw him.

Sleep was impossible and getting out of bed quietly, she walked down the passage, then, stopped as she heard Jane's voice.

'And how am I supposed to keep her in the house until you get here? No, she refuses to talk. All she wants is money, lots of it. She threatened to sell the jewellery if I didn't help. I wrote a cheque.'

Returning to her room, she dressed, closed the bags again, and lovingly removed the engagement ring, earrings, and the watch. Along with the pearls that had belonged to Sofia, she dropped everything in the bedside-table drawer. After making sure the house was enveloped in sleep, she took the cases downstairs, made a quick call from the kitchen phone, and walked outside into the darkness.

Jane cried when she entered the room in the morning, realising instantly that her daughter was no longer home. Sitting on the bed, she took the small note and read;

"Mom,

I apologise for leaving without saying goodbye but I cannot run the risk of Michael finding me. The temptation to return would be too great, and that is something I can never do.

I want everyone to know, but especially Michael and Captain Dimitri, that Edward and John are the same person.

The jewellery is in the drawer; keep it as payment for the money you gave me. Thank you. I beg your forgiveness if I've hurt you.

Your loving daughter

Christie"

Jane stared at the pieces in her hand; the watch alone was worth what she had written.

'Give them to Michael,' Rob said when he appeared on their doorstep hours later.

'What?'

'These.' Jane dropped them into his hand. 'She's no longer here. Oh, and this, I think you should contact the Greek police immediately.'

Michael perused over the note. 'But... this is ludicrous!' He denied vehemently. 'Dimitri investigated John, he's from Cyprus, and I saw a picture!'

Rob and Jane shrugged their shoulders.

Michael called Dimitri and told him.

'Are you sure?'

'How do I know? Christie isn't here to confirm or deny anything.'

'If true, this explains how he got so close without detection. But why would the wife lie? I'll look into it.'

Christie was inside the bank as soon as it opened its doors and fortunately, the manager still remembered her. Afterwards, she went into a travel agency, asked a few questions, and took a pile of pamphlets and travel guides. Walking down the street in Rosebank, she suddenly changed direction and went into a gallery she hadn't visited in years.

Walking in, she took a left turn and stopped to gaze at a painting she had known most of her life.

A man approached her. 'Emmett, know his work?'

'I met him briefly at one of his exhibitions years ago, but I've just returned from overseas so I'm not up to date.'

'Then let me have the pleasure of showing you around. Are you an artist, an art lover, or a student?'

CHAPTER THIRTEEN

Regrettably, Sofia alone was privy to Christie's possible whereabouts, but she was dead to the world and Michael knew that every passing minute was in Edward's favour. Thankfully, Sarah arrived from Athens so when Jane called, he rushed.

If possible, he felt worse when Jane gave him Christie's note. Fruitless days followed, he felt helpless, and unable to solve anything, he returned home.

He had always been exacting, but also fair and open-minded. Now, he was hard to please and plainly refused contradiction. He was heartbroken, everyone knew it, but he wouldn't admit it so although all felt sorry for him, no one dared mention Christie's name.

Reporters arrived with the commencement of the trial, knocking on every door in the hope that each would be the one with the exclusive. Hotel and village closed ranks and refused to discuss Christie with outsiders, sending the frustrated writers into wild leaps of speculation as to what exactly had taken place; her picture spread over most front pages.

Then, Sarah called from the hospital. Sofia was awake, but instead of providing answers, all she did was weep.

Now, sitting at Sofia's bedside, he waited for the explanation that would solve this shambles.

'Mi-chael,' she said groggily as tears welled in her eyes. 'I'm sorry I couldn't stop her.'

'What happened, Thea?'

How could she guess that the secrets she had guarded for so long would be used with such devastating effect? How had Edward discovered it, but worst of all, how did she explain? Once or twice she had imagined what it would be like if Christie married Michael but never had she set out to influence either in that direction.

Then along came Edward. That she disapproved of him had nothing to do with Michael. The man was something she could neither tolerate nor understand and she could not comprehend what loveable Christie saw in him or why he was interested when it was obvious he wasn't even close to being in love. He had looks and brains but no heart, the morals of a starved wild beast, and it was impossible for her to imagine Christie spending the rest of her life happily married to him.

'Thea,' Michael called again. 'I need to know.'

They might have given her sedatives but those could never prevent her from thinking, remembering. Now, how did she give plausible explanations without digging up deeds she had prayed stayed buried forever?

Wiping her eyes with the back of her hand, she realised how astute Edward was. He knew she was pressed between two impossible places; and whichever she chose, Michael would feel the brunt of it, tasting the pain that had obviously been intended by whatever course she followed.

Why, she didn't know, but this had been Edward's aim, to harm Michael at all costs, to ransack his emotions, to strip him bare, and destroy him. Edward being in possession of such knowledge would not rest until he wrecked the desired vengeance for perceived wrongs. Worse still, she knew this was not the full extent of his viciousness.

'Why did she run, Thea?'

'Edward is evil and filled with hate, has utter contempt for the right thing to do, no scruples whatsoever, greed that can fill a vault, and complete disregard for human life. I know that I shouldn't judge, but I can't help it because this shouldn't be happening.' How many times had she wondered what would happen if she told? Everyone's life would change; how much hurt!

'Don't you see, Christie is my world and I can't function without her?' Rising, he went to stare out the window. 'I have to know.'

'And you have no idea what you're asking.'

'Damn it, Thea!' He snapped angrily. 'I'll deal with it.' Eyes filling with tears, he sank back on the chair, took her hand in his, and dropped his head on the bed like a small boy. 'If you love me, and I know you do, help me.'

'Oh darling,' her hand was gentle on his. 'You should have seen her face when she came home. The poor baby was horrified and I didn't make it any easier. She misinterpreted, thinking Edward was right. If I'd stayed calm and explained the error right away- but confusion was his ally that day.' She had made a mistake all those years ago, in her ignorance letting Benjamin beat her. Now, what difference did it make if she alienated her entire family? 'If it weren't a matter of urgency that she leave after he tore out her heart, I'd be dead and then what would you know?

'I have no idea how he discovered it but he was always quick at grasping situations so the merest trace of suspicion must have sent him digging. But naked truth never satisfied him; he always embellishes. I saw him do it in court, it's quite frightening.' She gazed at him for an instant. 'He discovered your biological parents' identities and I can see how his mind went into overdrive trying to use the knowledge to its best nasty advantage. As usual, he wasn't satisfied with facts, because that birth certificate was horribly twisted.

'When Christie heard what he said, she went crazy, and so would you. Running home, she shoved the hideous thing in my hand and demanded to know if it was true. I looked at it and thought… I don't know what but she saw my reaction. Shock is not the word to describe it, which was his intention, and in the state I was in, I said yes. Only after she blurted out the most ridiculous outrage did I realise what that document implied. I couldn't believe my ears, but she was no longer listening. I called out to her, trying to rectify the mistake, but he stopped me.'

'Okay, I follow the part of a forgery. So the next question is; what did he change?'

'I just wanted your happiness.' She looked away. 'And I think you had it, which is why he couldn't stand it.'

'Thea, what did he change?'

She sighed tiredly. 'Your father's surname was conveniently absent. But to add insult to injury, he decided that adding her father's identity number would be the final touch.'

'Delete Powell, leaving Robert Thomas.' Michael said as one solving a riddle. 'He added her father's ID number,' he took a moment to process the extent of the information. 'She thinks we're related?'

How did he know? She had never told, or had she when he'd found her near death on the study floor? Had Edward? Her head spun and filled with strange buzzing. 'I… I don't understand.'

'I apologise, Thea,' he put a hand to her forehead. 'It was never my intention to give you such a jolt.'

'But… how?'

'Remember when I went to South Africa? That's when the trail I'd been following ended. No one hid the fact that I was adopted, so my parents had to be someone. One day, before I left home, I decided to cut through the heaps of magazines I'd accumulated, so paging through one, I saw a face that could have easily been mine. His name was Robert Thomas Powell, and that he happened to be South African was somehow coincidental. There was a woman with him in the picture, the writer Janet Scott. I'd read about her in the gossip columns so I thought, "any beginning is as good as another." Not altogether certain, I made an appointment to see her. I had barely entered her hall when she announced;

"After all these years, yet another Powell enters my life. I suppose you're her son?"

'That was already a clue in the right direction, because she also saw the likeness.'

"Whose son?" 'I asked.'

"Sofia's, of course. He just couldn't forget or let go. Then again, I did trap him into that hell of a marriage. Kids do crazy things and I did my fair share."

'I didn't immediately think of you because Sofia is a fairly common name, even in England.'

"So, what is it I can do for you, Mr-?"

"Andriotti."

'She laughed.' *"Heavens, did I hate that name. Everywhere I looked, he had scribbled Sofia Andriotti, especially after we were married, to drive me nuts no doubt. And there was an insignia he drew on just about everything. An entwined R and S…"*

'I must have looked ill because it was then she realised that I didn't know. Concerned, she invited me in and we spent the afternoon unravelling secrets, paging through photo albums, and it was there that I met Benjamin's underhandedness. Regrettably for you, as soon as he discovered the relationship, he started plotting with Janet. Yet, somewhere, you also made a decision. It was that that made me angriest!

'But I couldn't understand the twist. Why was I with my uncle? I was seething, resentful. I went from one emotion to the next and back again, trying to come to grips with the way I felt, towards you, my father, everyone. But above all, I felt betrayed.' He looked tired. 'In a roundabout way I asked mum and dad about my adoption. The bit they knew wasn't helpful because they never met Benjamin.

'So I flew to South Africa to meet my grandfather. Unfortunately, I'd asked Mrs Scott to inform him that I was on my way. Now there's the strangest person I have ever had the misfortune to meet. Even went as far as having me checked out before agreeing to see me.' He smiled ruefully. 'Imagined I wanted a chunk of Powells. But in the meantime, I was looking for a confrontation with you, meaning to tear your heart out, just as mine had been, knowing you hadn't wanted me.'

'Oh Michael, I can't even begin to explain...'

'Unbelievable as it may sound, Benjamin exonerated you. Never have I met a more mixed-up character. First, he wonders what I want and then tells me a story that made my blood curdle with its cruelty.'

'How I regretted what I did. Having nightmares for years, praying constantly that you were safe, loved.'

'You didn't know where I was?' He asked surprised.

She shook her head. 'I had no clue until you were ten, the same year you found out. It was such a shock. Sarah told me you were adopted, you told me about your name, and showed me the ring. How I hated Benjamin, even more than before.'

'You were eighteen, easy to manipulate, and Benjamin was a grand master. Then, he lost his family and became a lonely old man. I suppose I believed him when he said he was glad to share the burden of guilt. He also gave me the letters you had written to Robert and a file that made my stomach turn. And when he told me how Robert learnt of my existence… Discovering that although scared, you wanted me, that both of you loved me, was salve to my hurt.'

He spoke for a long time afterwards, telling her about things she had never known or understood, Benjamin's depth of wickedness hitting her full force, sometimes making her cry and at others, bringing bittersweet memories. And discovering that Robert had searched for her relentlessly broke her heart all over again. Why hadn't she believed him more?

'Know another crazy thing he did? After establishing that I wanted nothing but information, he asked if I'd consider moving to Johannesburg. First, he tries to protect Powells and then, as much as offers it to me. I was almost tempted, but of course my decision would have had more to do with a pair of blue eyes.' A smile crossed his lips. 'But I had no wish to be near a man who had done such damage to his own family.'

'Do you still hate me very much?'

'I did while a raging outcast, one burning desire keeping me going; to know who I was, countless nights spent trying to figure out where I came from, where I fit in, why I was given away. When I discovered that both you and my father would have never given me up willingly, I could no more. I merely felt hollow for I could do nothing about mending what had been so viciously torn. And then I was glad mum and dad got me.'

Explaining the tale to the family took more than anticipated.

Sarah broke down and accused Sofia of blatantly planning it. 'I knew you were up to something years ago.' She pointed. 'How could you know, keep quiet all these years, and then just spring it on us? You're not taking him away from me.'

'Mum, please.' Embracing Sarah reassuringly, Michael let her cry against his shoulder. 'Thea isn't trying to do anything but help me. If this happened when I was a boy, it might have caused problems, but I'm a grown man and I've known for years. When did I behave differently? You can't lose me whatever I discover; I'm your son for life.'

'How is it possible?' Andrea asked dumbfounded.

'Dad, for goodness sake,' Stephanie said looking at the sombre face. 'We knew someone was his birth mother, so what if it's Thea? Please stop believing she's not human. And be thankful, because before today, he had no blood ties. Now, he's actual family.' She glanced at her sister.

'Exactly,' Jaqueline joined in. 'He's still our brother and your son. Now, grow up all of you.'

'How odd that they should share the same name,' Jane said after hearing the story. 'No wonder my poor child shed blood tears when she heard such horrible lies. I agree with Michael, we are going to need more than what he and Rob are discussing. Posters and pictures in newspapers will only work locally, what about the thousands of towns she could be in?'

The cottage didn't have much in the way of furniture but it was adequate for what needs she had, as those weren't many. Taking the paintings and sketches out of the folder, Christie spread them throughout the room to give it a sense of home, but as she gazed at them, she couldn't control the tears and so packed them away again. Now she wished she had brought her paints and easel, for they might help pass the eternal sleepless nights. But all she had thought about that awful day was to run, almost wishing she were back in a coma so she couldn't think, remember, or feel!

Curiously, the small community wondered what had brought this beautiful creature their way, or the reason for her solitude, but perhaps someone was to join her later.

Shyly at first, Christie answered the waves from her nearest neighbour, a woman of about thirty, who seemed to enjoy entertaining every Sunday.

When Christie had gone into the Rosebank gallery, she hadn't been thinking of where to go or what to do, but the knowledgeable assistant had mentioned something that intrigued her.

'Are you perchance one of those people who always sell themselves short?' He asked curiously.

'I'm not sure what you mean.'

'There are those who are good, know it and have swollen heads, and there are those who are good but have no idea that they are. Into which category do you fit?'

'Into the "I have a lot to learn before I produce work like this".'

'But today it's exceedingly easy to learn whatever one wishes, there are courses and workshops. Johannesburg alone has about a dozen different events every weekend for any number of artistic avenues, why not enrol? I can put you in touch with the right group. Alternatively, if you are more adventurous, you can join an artist's community. There are hundreds throughout the country, gaining popularity very fast. I have some literature around.' Going to a desk, he opened the drawer, and searched through heaps of papers. 'Nowadays, everyone has to advertise and this is the artist's way. Not everyone succeeds professionally, so many have turned to teaching. There's detailed information on what each community offers and produces.' He pointed to a pamphlet.

'Thank you.' She glanced at the masterpiece in the distance.

A knock at the door brought her back to the present and she glanced quickly at the mirror. Every time she saw that short dark hair, that feeling of strangeness filled her. This had been a last minute idea as she realised that Michael would probably send her picture to every imaginable medium.

A woman's head appeared above the half-door. 'Hello, I live over the hill that way.'

'Hi. I hope you don't mind that I walk all over your property.'

A charming smile appeared on the pretty face, the shoulder-length black hair flicking from left to right, the deep blue eyes crinkling at the corners. 'If I minded I'd have erected walls. You're welcome to go anywhere you wish.' Opening the latch, she entered and her gaze swept around the room, noticing its barrenness. 'Actually, the real reason why I'm here, the gang is curious and would like to meet you. Okay, maybe not all of them, but I am, more because you rented long-term. You are obviously not on holiday so that makes you a resident. Every Sunday, we get together for lunch at my house. It's just a group of friends; mostly painters, sculptors, writers,' her eyes fell on the folder. 'If that's what I think it is, you'll fit right in. I'm Sandra, what's your name?'

Her life had changed, she wasn't going to change who she was. 'Christie.'

'Am I being nosy if I ask why such a beautiful woman is in Harristown alone?'

'Huh, well, you see...'

Sandra put her hand up as if to stop traffic. 'Let me guess, there's a man in this story.' Seeing Christie's eyes glisten, she reached for one hand. 'I apologise. May I make us a cup of tea? I brought you some of my blends.'

'Thank you.' Christie stared out the door. 'Have you lived here long?'

'Six years, and wouldn't trade it for anything on this earth.' Sandra busied herself around the small stove. 'I came to visit a friend after a disastrous love affair with a married man and only wished to die,' she grinned as she filled a kettle. 'Then I met Donald, my husband, and have been laughing ever since. We are not what one would call a growing community but there are a few bachelors around. Would you like to date sometime?' Sandra caught sight of the wedding band. 'Maybe not. Anyway, if you change your mind let me know, we can always import one from somewhere.' She was struck by the immense sadness on Christie's face. 'Come over on Sunday, everyone talks about their work. Something to take your mind off things, even if only for a short while.'

'You're very kind and I'll think about it.'

Daytime wasn't too bad as she occupied herself with various activities. She watched the roosting cormorants, crabs in the small rock pools along the beach and there were the endless walks she took across the dunes, but the nights were filled with heartache, pain, and unquenched longing. She never knew one could cry so much and eat so little.

Sunday arrived to find her lonelier than ever. If only she had a radio. She also needed supplies that the little shop down the main street lacked. Dressing slowly, she felt ghastly.

'I'm glad you're here.' Sandra smiled when she appeared on the kitchen doorstep.

'I didn't come for-'

'Please stay.'

'Thank you.' Christie entered the kitchen. 'Do you know where I can get paints?'

'You might have to go into Bellasdorp as our little shop isn't big enough to accommodate everyone's whims.'

Christie nodded. 'What kind of public transport is available?'

'None, you stand in front of the Post Office at seven in the morning and someone will give you a lift. We have a guest today.' Sandra announced as a tall man entered the kitchen. 'Donald, I told you about Christie.'

He shook her hand with a sure grip. 'Hello, Christie. I hear you paint, what medium?'

'Watercolours.' She liked this man instantly. He had a way of looking straight at people, as if his gaze was assurance enough that he cared.

He grinned. 'Can't imagine what Jeffrey will say about that.' Then grabbing two trays, he was out the door again.

'Who's Jeffrey?' Christie asked curiously.

'A friend who doesn't believe that watercolours is a proper medium.'

'Then he and I will have nothing to discuss.'

'Don't you believe it.'

Without warning, the house filled with people, coming and going in every direction as they carried plates, dishes, and bowls. Christie wondered how many more were still to arrive when a small boy stormed in.

'Mommy, look what I found.' Putting his hand up, he showed Sandra a beautiful brown shell.

'That's lovely. Brian, say hello to Christie, she's the lady from the cottage.'

'We walked there. Uncle Jeffrey says it's desso… desso-something.'

'I think he means desolate.'

'Mommy, I'm hungry.'

'We're eating soon.' Sandra dropped a kiss on his head.

Christie felt like an intruder. As if reading her mind, Sandra reached for her hand and together they walked outside.

'Everyone,' Sandra called. 'This is Christie, introduce, and acquaint yourselves.'

There were a dozen or so hellos and Christie was glad no one made a fuss over her. She couldn't handle questions right now.

Lunch was a disorganised ritual; no one sat in the same place for longer than seven minutes. It was during one of these exchanges that a darkly tanned man sat beside her.

'What do you do, Christie?' He asked.

'I'd like to start painting again.' Glancing up, she saw Emmett. He looked older than she recalled, his face reminding her of wrinkled leather, the lines crossing his skin in interesting patterns. Ever since she started painting, she had tried to emulate his style, even if not using oils.

This man could have been famous, yet he preferred to live far from crazy city life. Years ago, he'd been the toast of London, but it hadn't changed him. Instead, he'd come to live in Harristown, permanent population, three thousand, endearing himself to his compatriots, who revered his work and respected his privacy.

He returned the gaze with a smile and stared down at his plate. 'Ah.' Surveying the face intently, he then studied her hands. 'Did anyone ever tell you that you'll look magnificent on canvas?'

'I agree.' A man she hadn't noticed said across the table.

Looking at him, Christie recalled Nichola's portrait, the one over the mantelpiece at home. She told them flatly. 'I'm no Mona Lisa.'

'Definitely, you're beautiful.'

Sandra studied Christie. She looked young and vulnerable, an almost physical anguish emanating from those expressive eyes. 'Stop embarrassing the girl, Jeffrey.'

'Where's the girl?' He said while appraising Christie.

Christie pretended to be interested in the salad. Then turning to smile at the ageing woman beside her, she asked. 'Brenda? Am I being inquisitive if I ask what you're working on?' Noticing undeniable interest in Jeffrey's gaze, she shut him out. She was beginning to think the place deserved merit and did not want to leave because of yet another man.

Opening her eyes, Christie stared at the clock on the small table, six forty-five! She would never make it to the post office in fifteen minutes. Might as well go tomorrow. Resigning herself to another empty day, she was startled to hear a car engine outside. She scrambled to get dressed.

'Christie, are you in?'

'Morning Sandra, I'm hopelessly late. I was exhausted, something I never experienced in Greece.'

Sandra's brows lifted with interest but before she could delve further, Christie sat down and dropped her head between her hands.

'Appetite or no appetite I'd better eat something.' Christie said faintly.

'You're as white as a sheet,' Sandra put a hand to Christie's forehead. 'No fever. Besides, you look cold not hot. I'll make you some breakfast.' She rummaged in the cupboard, found the bread and taking two slices popped them into the toaster. 'Do you sleep?'

'Not particularly well.'

'You're probably rundown, short of vitamins, and good food. Were you ever this thin?'

Christie shook her head. 'I just can't to do anything about it.'

Removing the toast, Sandra put the kettle on. 'You're lucky you came now because we've just had the electricity put in. Most people don't mind but others complained so much that we thought it a good idea to upgrade a little.'

'This is your place?'

Sandra nodded. 'We're actually considering selling it. We have the house and as you see, it's large enough for all our needs.'

'Is that tea ready? I'm so empty I could faint.'

'Here we go,' Sandra placed a mug before her.

On their way to Bellasdorp, they chatted about this and that but Sandra couldn't help noticing Christie's determination to avoid personal questions. This was no ordinary woman; she was intelligent and charming, having a deep kindness she showed everyone, but above all she was a mystery and Sandra loved those. 'You mentioned Greece, did you stay long?' She began tentatively.

'Long enough.' Turning to the window, Christie wished memories could be switched off.

'Do you speak the language? Oohh, your husband is Greek.' Sandra said with realisation. 'Won't say another word.'

Bellasdorp wasn't much larger than Harristown but it seemed to meet most needs of the ten thousand people in the area adequately. There were the usual amenities: clothing stores, one or two supermarkets, garages, three schools, a few churches, one hotel and a hospital, and she particularly liked the way it was sandwiched between a few rolling hills and a slow river. But best of all, it was more than a thousand kilometres away and one of those places where people didn't pay particular attention to what Johannesburgers did. That suited Christie perfectly.

Sandra pointed to an art shop in a strategic corner. 'Go see if you find everything you need while I run some errands, and there's a coffee shop. Give me three hours.'

Christie finished quickly and then walked down the street. Seeing doctors' consulting rooms, she peered inside.

"Why does one feel so vulnerable lying on an examination bed?" She thought. The middle-aged man smiled kindly but it didn't help much. Then he asked a few questions, disappeared, and a nurse appeared.

'Why do you need so much blood?' Christie asked as she watched the vial fill up.

'You may be anaemic, diabetic, or simply rundown; the doctor always makes certain.' The nurse told her before leaving the room.

'Which is it?' She asked twenty minutes later when the doctor returned.

'I have a rule; always do the simplest test first. If it's not that one, then send the blood away. So here's the verdict, you are definitely stressed. However, if you follow a good diet, take adequate exercise, and rest, you should be in splendid shape at the end.'

'What end?' Fear filled her.

'Your baby's birth.'

She knew she was falling but she neither could nor wanted to stop. Fortunately, he caught her before everything turned black.

When she came to, she wished she had stayed in that oblivion. This was too horrible to contemplate. Why? Why was she the one on who birth control failed? She wanted to cry, she wanted to scream, she was speechless. All she could feel was her heart's rhythm in her ears.

Driving home, Sandra knew Christie was deeply troubled, something tearing her apart. 'Here we are,' she said, bringing the 4x4 to a standstill in front of the cottage and helped carry the few parcels.

'Thank you for taking me today.'

She sat at the table, staring at the shopping bags. Holding the pill bottles, she studied them. 'Oh Michael, what have we done?' Dropping her head, she let the wave of sobs take over her body, until she knew she could cry no more.

Her mind took her down many paths that night; to places she had never been, neither considered, nor imagined an option, especially as she speculated about the doctor's reaction if she requested a termination. To go to some back street, she would probably end up dead, not that the notion didn't sound almost pleasant. And even if able to prove incest, she doubted any court would be in a rush to grant her an abortion.

Getting out of bed before morning, she opened the top half of the door and watched darkness slowly turn into light.

Walking over a few patches of wild-grass, sand, and rocks, she went towards the shore. She liked it here as not too many people came this way, and found a spot where she could sit on a boulder and work. Carefully balancing the easel on the sand, she put a blank paper up. Perhaps she should draw something first. Opening the new box of paints, her eyes fell on the brushes, nothing compared to the ones Michael had given her. "It's always going to hurt." The image of Michael brought love-filled memories and she wished he were here to hold her, to tell her that everything would be all right, that they would survive. A slow tear trickled down her face. If only Edward had left them alone. He had been mean and cruel. But Sofia, how could she have done this?

Angrily, she drew a question mark. How much did her father know, what was Jane aware of, had Andrea and Sarah known? No one but Sofia knew. So if she had taken such pains to conceal it, how had Edward unearthed such information? Questions without answers; that was all she had.

'Hello.' Jeffrey greeted as he peered from behind the easel.

'Hi,' she stared at the paper, then pulled it off and made a ball of it.

'So, what's on your mind?' Sitting on a nearby rock, he picked a handful of sand.

She glanced at him disinterestedly. 'You may have heard of privacy.'

'Sure. The question is, is it always good for one's well-being?'

'You may have a point there. What brings you this way?'

'I was up at Sandra's and she said you looked depressed yesterday. Actually, she said she couldn't explain what you looked like. We don't know each other well but I figured a little company might do you good.'

'We don't know each other at all. But thank you for your kindness.'

'I'm here for purely selfish reasons. I just had to see you.' He grinned boyishly.

Gazing at him, she was aware how handsome he was, especially when he smiled. He was taller than Michael and quite muscular, which seemed unusual for an artist. When he moved, strength rippled beneath the shirt. His golden hair reached the shoulders and he waved it out of his hazel-brown eyes almost constantly. His face was covered with something between stubble and a beard, a shade darker than his hair, rather giving him a feline appearance. As she ended her scrutiny, she asked. 'Really, why?'

'I couldn't get you out of my head.'

A knowing smile appeared on her lips. 'You do this to every new woman in town, right?'

'Think what you like, but it's true.'

'I believe you. The thing is, Mr-'

'Ferris, but call me Jeffrey.'

'I'm married.' She waved her left hand.

Rising from the rock, he held her fingertips. 'You have beautiful hands. In fact, the whole of you is beautiful.' His eyes travelled to her chest and then her mouth.

Colouring at the blatant sexual observation, she pulled her hand away and told him pointedly. 'I think it's time I started work.'

'Any completed work around?'

'No.'

'Then this is my excuse to go up to the cottage. Of course, I won't come to look only at pictures. Am I embarrassing you?'

'I think you'll eventually embarrass yourself.'

'You're a mystery to me.'

'Ah, so that's what you can't resist.' She dropped the pencil, aware that no work would be accomplished while he was around.

'One minute you blush at something I say and the next you look me straight in the eye and tell me you're not interested.'

'Sorry if I disappoint you.'

'On the contrary, you're a challenge. I don't think I've had one of those.'

'Poor Jeffrey.' She said with a straight face and then burst into laughter, the sound breaking over the noise of the waves. Realising it was the first time in weeks; she thought she ought to enjoy it more. 'What?'

'It's like the tinkling of bluebells in a summer field and now that I've heard it, I cannot live without hearing it again.' He grabbed his chest as if he were dying of cardiac arrest.

'You're incorrigible.'

He stayed a few minutes longer, then, jogged down the beach again.

Picking a brush from the box, she felt its bristles. A shadow fell across her. Looking up, she saw Emmett.

'You'd think I'd be able to see everyone coming and going up this beach.'

'Did I startle you? I saw you from my boat.'

'You're most welcome, but I think I should go.'

Helping fold the easel, he tucked it under his arm. 'Do you eat fish? I caught some.'

'If you stay, I'll make it for lunch.'

Reaching the cottage, she dropped her things on the table and pointed for him to sit down. Taking two fish from the bag he had left in the sink, she started cleaning them. Running to the bathroom, she threw up whatever she had in her stomach, reappearing minutes later with an ashen face.

'Mmm,' rising from the chair, Emmett offered it to her. 'I'll do the fish. Isn't there something you can take?'

'I do, it's just some smells,'

'I suppose you suffer most in the mornings?' A smile appeared on his weather-beaten face as he searched for a frying pan. 'How I know? You don't look the squeamish sort to me.'

'Please don't tell them, I just found out myself.'

'So, your husband doesn't know.' Seeing her eyes fill with tears, he remarked without malice. 'And you don't seem particularly thrilled about it either.' Throwing the fish into a bowl of flour, he gave it a few turns.

'I'm not feeling sorry for me, just for an innocent who doesn't stand a chance.'

'Life's a funny thing so don't you go giving up on it yet. There's always a surprise around the corner.'

'I'll say. Do you believe in miracles?'

'I'm not religious but I do believe in the miracles of nature and life.' He placed the cooked fish in front of her. 'Smells different doesn't it?'

After the meal, Christie made him coffee and then quickly cleared the table. 'Please stay.'

'Mmm,' watching her at the sink, he asked. 'May I see some of your work?'

She dropped the folder on the table. 'Be honest and tell me if I should stop now.'

He paged through it in silence. Afterwards he glanced at her. 'No, you're definitely gifted. Why aren't they completed?'

'I know something's wrong, but unable to fix it, I rather start a new one.'

'Did you ever take classes?'

She shook her head. 'I began on my own.'

'It shows. You're having problems with perspective and technique.'

He pointed to Sofia's portrait, the one she should have burnt!

'Had you chosen oils you wouldn't be having as much difficulty. Why did you choose watercolours?'

'I like the way the pictures glow, they always look so fresh.'

'That they do; now you have to learn the right techniques. You're trying to do here what we do with oils. It's impossible to achieve the same results with watercolours.' He glanced through the folder again. 'You have all the inspiration here, now fix them.'

'Will you teach me?'

He gazed at her through the chinks of his lids. 'I suppose I could try.'

Emmett was a demanding although kind teacher when she did make the inevitable mistake, and in the beginning, she made more than were welcome, merely compounding the fact that she lacked greatly.

To her surprise, he didn't let her paint immediately. 'Draw,' he told her. 'Draw everything you see, but remember perspective and balance.' And he gave her a book that he'd obviously made good use of decades previously.

Weeks later, he invited her to go see his work, so she could study practical application of knowledge. Sometimes, she stayed to work on the assignments he gave her and knew that if she learnt half of what he knew, she would be great indeed. She also found that this commuting between their two dwellings occupied a great deal of time and discovered that she was less inclined to linger on all the things that hurt so much.

It was he too who took her to the next doctor's appointment and she was quick to realise that giant feelings of paternal proportions were developing; as if she were the daughter he'd never bothered to have but now was grateful for. Her heart warmed and she found that being around him was also an excellent obstacle in Jeffrey's obstinately determined tracks.

As she became part of the intimate group, she knew that the odd dish and salad bowl was hardly an expression of the gratitude she felt towards Sandra, who was kind and comforting even when not aware of it. Then the idea struck her. Every Friday afternoon she would take Brian and have him stay with her until Sunday morning, when they returned for lunch, so giving Sandra precious personal time.

She enjoyed the little boy's company and apart from keeping her busy, he was an insight into what awaited her, and like Emmett, yet another barricade in Jeffrey's way. The man was infatuated and although she kept building walls she didn't see his interest dwindling. Alternatively, perhaps she was going about it all wrong; his interest might be increasing because she put herself out of reach.

Reaching the house one Sunday, Brian ran into the kitchen and greeted. *'Kalimera, tikanete?'*

Everyone stared.

'Good morning; how is everybody?' Christie translated.

'Poli kala, esi?' Brian answered himself.

'Well thanks, and you?' Picking a bunch of grapes from the table, Christie put one in her mouth and lifted herself onto the kitchen counter.

'You're teaching him Greek?' Sandra realised.

Brian, enjoying being the centre of attention, repeated a few more sentences.

Jeffrey turned to Christie with interest. 'Who taught you, a Greek boyfriend?'

'Don't pry, Jeffrey.' Sandra warned.

'My aunt.' Recalling Sofia, tears hadn't sprung. Christie felt all the better for it.

Entering the kitchen and seeing her on the counter, Emmett immediately held out his arms.

'Oh Emmett,' she kissed his cheek. 'I'm not sick.'

The gesture seemed odd to Sandra, who could have sworn there was nothing intimate between them, but to Jeffrey, it was an expression of familiarity.

'I have an announcement to make.' Christie took a second. 'I'm pregnant.'

Jeffrey stared.

Sandra wasn't certain what to think, was it Emmett's? 'How far are you?'

'Four months.'

Sandra breathed a sigh of relief.

'Emmett, Jeffrey,' Donald entered the kitchen. 'Care to give me a hand?'

When they were alone, Sandra queried. 'You'll be contacting your husband?'

The beautiful face filled with sadness. Lowering her head, she said simply. 'No.'

'You don't think he should know?'

'If this was a regular marriage; it's not.'

Hearing the end-tail of the conversation as he returned for something on the counter, Jeffrey brightened at the words. He knew he was being selfish, as he saw her suffer every time she spoke of that unknown man, but why should he care? The more he knew Christie the more his impulse to protect her grew; something he couldn't explain because he'd never felt it before. She was different, rare, and ever so desirable, though, this pregnancy was something he hadn't counted on. There was nothing like a baby to bring two people who loved each other closer and she loved her husband desperately. He wondered about the man. If he hadn't loved her back, then he was a fool.

'This is a huge burden to carry alone.' Sandra became aware of Jeffrey's extraordinary interest. She had witnessed countless liaisons and together they had often laughed at some odd idiosyncrasies. Christie was different, and for the first time, it affected him.

Lunch didn't centre on mediums and vehicles that Sunday. Everyone more interested in discussing the arrival of the baby, all having opinions, sharing ideas, and giving advice.

'I'll have to carry a book around to write down all these things.' Catching Jeffrey's gaze, Christie knew she had to do something. She liked him but her heart belonged to another. So how did one convince a stubborn blind man that he was about to fall off a precipice?

CHAPTER FOURTEEN

Celeste stared through the net hanging around her hat; a quick after-thought as she got off the plane and realised how many bugs circled one's face in the jungle. Glancing at the man who guided the boat, she then looked at the other two who sat in front and asked in Portuguese. 'When will we be in Xingu?'

'This is Xingu.' One pointed to the river waters.

'I know that,' she snapped in irritation. 'I meant when will we get to Mr Robertson's house?' She was no jungle person. Why was she here?

'We are going upstream, tomorrow.'

'What I wanted to hear.' She smacked a hand against her neck, knowing something had just drawn blood. And night was still ahead.

'Thomas!' She called as she ascended the wooden steps leading from the river to the small hill.

Turning, he stared at her as if she were an apparition. 'Celeste! What the bloody hell are you doing here?' He said in English.

She answered likewise. 'Looking after your business.'

'This must really be important, let's hear it.' He retorted in Portuguese.

'That's it? No hello, how are you, how was your trip, come in the house?'

'Sure. Hello.' He ran down the few steps separating them and embraced her. 'How was your trip?'

'Terrible.' She stared at the wooden house a distance away. 'It looks nicer than I imagined. Still, it's not the city. I'll never understand why you like this.'

'Where do you expect me to shoot jungle life, at the zoo?'

'A panther is a panther.'

He laughed. 'Okay. But why didn't you let me know you were coming? I would have met you down-river. And what if I weren't here?' Linking his arm through hers, he led her to the sprawling veranda. 'So, what kind of business do you have in mind?'

'An English magazine has approached me to do a spread on your work, with an interview and models-'

His hand went up. 'You mean a fashion-shoot?'

'Sort of, but not exactly.'

'You've wasted your time, Celeste.'

'Before you say no, let me explain what they have in mind. And the money-'

'If you think any amount would make a difference, then you don't know me.'

'And have I ever?' A little hurt entered her dark eyes. 'Anyway, I promised SMITTEN that I'd inform you and the rest is up to you. I don't want to be accused of withholding information.'

'You didn't have to travel a thousand miles to tell me this, a letter would have sufficed, or better yet, you could have declined on my behalf.' Going inside, he returned with two bottles. Putting them on the small table, he sat on the opposite chair and studied her. 'You're really interested in this, why?'

'Because your work deserves to be seen by more than the few who buy RiverRax.' She pulled three magazines from her bag and dropped them on the table.

He picked one and flicked through it. 'What is it SMITTEN sells, fashion?' He stopped on a page. 'What can ten pages in a fashion magazine, do for my work that I can't?' Standing up, he stared at the distance where an endless wall of green hid everything from view. 'I don't need this, neither the money, nor the aggravation.'

'But Thomas, the entire issue would be dedicated to your work. And they're willing to pay a small fortune for the privilege.'

'Sorry Celeste, go back to Sao Paulo and tell them that I decline.' He told her seriously. 'So, staying or going?' He pointed to the boat on the river.

She looked at her watch. 'If I leave now, what time will I get to the plane?'

'Definitely quicker than it took to get here. About six O'clock.'

'I'm tired, so I'll stay. Maybe tomorrow I'll understand why you like it here so much. And don't tell me anything else anymore. I'm going to give you a couple of months to think about it. Keep those.' She pointed to the magazines. 'Perhaps they'll remind you that there is another world out there.'

'What do you think?' Christie watched Emmett's face.

'Never knew anyone could learn this fast. And motivation certainly helped.' He smiled. 'You'll probably be able to take part in exhibitions soon.'

'If I enjoy them as much as you and Jeffrey complain, then I don't know what to look forward to.'

'I suppose it depends on who your *agent* is. Newa is unconventional but truly loves art so we find it easy to put up with her screwball ideas, but above all, she's honest.

Years ago, I had some fancy name looking after my affairs and then discovered that I was being robbed blind. There's no way on earth Newa would do that to her artists.'

'Where is she? Brenda and Jeffrey mention her as if she's constantly around but I haven't yet laid eyes on the woman.'

'Consider yourself lucky she's touring Europe because that woman is exhausting. However, your luck is ending. If I recall correctly, she should be making an appearance in the next two weeks.'

'Do you think I have anything half decent to sell her?'

'How many times have I told you to ask? But you're too proud.'

'It's not pride. I need to learn to cope on my own and you have already helped by giving me lessons. I'd like to buy the cottage, there's the doctor, and the baby is coming. I sold three the other day, two to a tourist from Namibia. But he might have sensed desperation. Perhaps if I found a job- But in my condition, who would want to hire me?' She regarded him. 'So, anything?'

Emmett studied the works against the walls then pointed left. 'Try those.'

'I thought you said they weren't good.'

'Never said they weren't good, I merely told you they lacked. I see you've been working on them again. Don't you sleep?' He peered at them critically. 'Most interesting, any gallery would be pleased to have them. But I suggest you see Newa first, she has an uncanny sense for talent, and if she likes them, doors will open.'

Christie studied her work judiciously. She put major effort into everything she did now; painting from the heart, and it showed. Perspective, composition, colours, and combinations were now automatic. She glanced at the study of emotions she had begun. Emmett had sat staring at them in silence and then at her. She pointed to them. 'I thought those.'

'Let people see your progression and start at the beginning, yours are very good now.'

That was the basis of their relationship, trust. He was the father she no longer had. Many times, she had been tempted to write to her mother, Mary, and Evy, especially now that she was the face of an international make-up brand and Christie often saw her in the glossy magazines. But that meant postmarks and she couldn't chance it. This was a new life, new friendships, and these she should encourage. Yet, she dreaded to show her heart, fearful of losing again.

Jeffrey was an amusement, but she made sure to neither do nor say anything to either encourage or hurt, as he often reminded her of a little boy who simply couldn't get his hands on a desired toy. She wondered how much was genuine feeling, and what was mere stubbornness.

One afternoon, he found her sitting on the dunes. Jogging for a few seconds, he fell to his knees. 'Here again,'

'It's beautiful.' She couldn't tell him that she felt close to Michael, that she remembered passionate kisses, and making love to the sound of waves...

He pointed to the setting sun. 'Not just that, it's ravishing, scorching, sensual,'

Exactly, but she had to fill her mind with other things. 'Is there someone looking after your house in Cape Town?'

'Two students. The agreement is; I give them free lodgings and they look after the place. I call a week before returning and that gives them time to dust and fill the fridge.' Lifting himself, he held his hand out to her. 'I'll walk you home.' Pulling her up, he put a hand to her face and dropped a kiss on her lips.

Turning, she walked away.

Catching up, he declared. 'I hate your husband, because he has spoilt you for other men. You never say a word but I see it in your eyes, you're always remembering, comparing, and no one lives up to him.'

'I know you can't understand but I didn't leave because of trouble between us. And although we have love, reality prevents us from being together.' She looked wistfully over the endless sand. 'I would do myself a favour if I fell in love again, but I can't.'

'Every time I look at you, I know where your thoughts are. If you were anyone else, I'd have given up ages ago, but something about you. I like my women, yet, I haven't been able to look at another since you walked into our lives.'

'Please Jeffrey, don't dream about me.'

'That is all I can do. I wish I met you before he did, that I was in your head as he is. I'm jealous! I'm jealous of a man you may never see again and yet you're excruciatingly faithful to. I want that kind of love and devotion.'

'And maybe you'll have it, but not from me.' Her soft hand touched his bearded face. 'Just try be my friend.'

'If another woman said that I'd laugh my head off.'

He hadn't made advances since then and she was thankful, welcoming the peace and tranquillity of not having to fight him off because she did like him. He had a better heart than he gave himself credit, but she could never love him the way he wanted or deserved.

Arriving in Cape Town, Christie noticed with interest that some streets had changed somewhat since her last visit. Beautifully coloured buildings, new shopping centres, and malls had darted up, increasing the cosmopolitan feel of the Mother City.

Sandra peered at some of the buildings. 'Have you ever been here?'

'Years ago.'

'On holiday?'

Christie merely nodded.

Newa was a surprise package. When Emmett, Brenda, and Jeffrey spoke of her, Christie imagined a tough Amazon. Instead, she was tiny, ultra feminine, who talked non-stop, her eyes darting in rapid movements, displaying her spontaneous and intelligent nature. She brightened and filled a room simply by entering it. With masses of blonde hair swishing around her as she moved, Christie knew it would be tricky trying to pinpoint her age; probably somewhere between twenty-five and forty-five.

Her office was an image of her character, covered in bright coloured posters of art exhibitions from around the world. Christie stared at a particular Chinese one.

Newa followed her gaze. 'I need constant reminders of where I've been.' One dainty hand pointed to the walls. 'I absolutely adore them all, although, some were gifts from friends.'

Christie was over the moon with what Newa paid her. Turning to Sandra happily, she told her. 'I can buy the baby some pretty things. Not only that, as a token of appreciation, I'd love to take you out. Anywhere particular you'd like to visit?'

Sandra wanted to decline, but seeing rare enthusiasm, she couldn't bring herself to. 'How about that new place at the Waterfront?'

'It's a date.'

As dinner ended and they got to their feet, Sandra watched Christie's face. 'You need rest. But wait until you get to the eighth month, lying down is the only activity you find interesting.'

Passing through two tables in the full restaurant, Christie had to stop in front of a woman.

'Christie?'

Horror filled her. This was something she had not considered. Grabbing Sandra's arm, Christie almost dragged her out of the establishment. 'Please,' she pleaded. 'Just get in the car and drive.'

'Do you mind telling me what just happened?' Sandra queried as she sped away.

'That was my cousin! What are the odds of something like that happening?'

'More than you realise, we picked one of the trendiest spots in town.'

After wrestling with the face that was just too familiar, Gloria reached for the phone.

'Watson residence,'

'Good evening, Thea. Hope I didn't wake you.'

'Not at all, we always go late to bed. How are you, Gloria?'

'Well, thank you. Any clues?'

'I never realised there were so many unbalanced people in the world. Fortunately, all those calls are picked up by the answering machine on the separate line we had installed. We wouldn't have a life if the house phone rang like that.' Sofia stopped. Perhaps she shouldn't be discussing unhinged human beings with Gloria. Lord knew the child had suffered enough. 'Michael seems positive. I'm just glad his people are reliable, because this could be his ruination.'

'Yes. Is he around?'

'Arrived yesterday, do you need to speak with him?'

'Thea, I think I saw Christie tonight.'

'What, where? Michael,' Sofia called. 'Pick up the extension, Gloria saw Christie.'

'Hi, Gloria. How is she, what did she say?' He asked eagerly.

'Nothing, she pretended ignorance. She cut her hair, changed the colour, so darkness made me a trifle unsure. I tried to follow but lost them in the crowd and barely watched them drive away.'

'She was with someone?' He felt his heart tighten.

'There was a woman with her.'

'How did she look?'

'Different.' She knew what he was thinking. 'Michael, she's hiding, why would she give herself away? But do come down and perhaps we can get some information.'

He flew to Cape Town and paid regular visits to the restaurant. No one remembered much, he felt like smashing tables, and like every other lead, disappointment soon followed. But despite another setback, he was glad to see Gloria smiling again.

After a week, he left for Johannesburg. He had received calls like this before, from strangers, after Christie's picture had appeared in the papers. People had called from all sorts of places swearing that they had seen her in Bloemfontein, Nelspruit, Durban...

Paging through the financial section of the newspaper, Benjamin closed it in boredom and threw it aside. Absent-mindedly, he opened the main section and his eyes fell on the pretty face. 'Greek hotelier still searching for South African-born wife.' His finger ran across the article. 'How the hell did this happen?' He saw a strangely familiar parallel, but this time he knew nothing about it.

His brows lifted. So, Sofia had somehow discovered Michael's whereabouts. Perhaps Michael had told her, after all that was why he'd come to the country years ago.

Michael had impressed him, and unexpectedly, Benjamin had felt the desire to know his grandson better, impulsively offering him a position at Powells. Not that he intended to let Michael run anything, but who knew, though not born into the name, he might be the one who truly deserved it.

For obvious reasons, Michael hadn't been in a forgiving mood, telling him that he neither wanted nor needed one cent from his empire. Many people said those words without meaning them, secretly hoping to gain something from being associated with Benjamin; Michael did, especially when he told Benjamin exactly what he thought about his methods of operation.

In those minutes, it was as if Benjamin were looking at Robert again, reliving the last time he saw him, and the regret he felt was something he could never impart to another human being. Then turning his back on the old man, Michael hadn't contacted him since.

People said time healed; perhaps if he showed the concern he was feeling, Michael might give him another chance. Lifting the phone, he dialled a number and left a message.

Benjamin arrived early at Powells next morning. In fact, he hadn't slept well. This business of the missing girl was affecting him strangely.

Someone knocked.

'Come in,' Benjamin called and shook the young man's hand. 'Pleased to meet you, Mr Hamilton.'

'Same here.' Hamilton watched Benjamin's white hair. 'Actually, I'm here more out of curiosity than anything else, as I know that my father worked for you.'

'Almost thirty years ago.' Benjamin pointed to the chair. 'To get right to the point, there's a job I think only you are qualified for. You're the best private investigator around and I wish to hire you.'

'What does this entail?'

'Finding a young woman. I once asked your father to do something similar, it turned into a tragedy, which now I think only you can mend.' Benjamin saw Hamilton's incomprehension. 'Time makes people see things differently and I intruded in things I should have left alone.' He gave an edited version of his past deeds.

Hamilton was quiet for a while, as if ruminating over the information. 'Who do you want found?'

'My grandson's wife.' Benjamin pointed to the picture. 'But this time, I'm making certain of the facts before I take steps. I'm not making the same mistake twice.'

Hamilton perused the paper. 'As I understand it, she left Greece of her own free will. Perhaps like last time, this is none of your business?'

'See what that's about.' Putting a hand in his pocket, Benjamin pulled out an envelope. 'For travelling expenses, as you might have to start in Greece if this has to make sense. I want to know everything, if they were happy, if he hurt her, if she did him. But no one is to know.'

'Are you sure you have good intentions?'

'Absolutely. I never hid from your father what I wanted, why start now?'

'There are a few court cases at which I have to give evidence, so it might take a couple of weeks. But in the meantime, I'll get my underground sources digging.'

'I hoped you could start sooner, but I'll wait, as I don't want to entrust this to anyone else. Thank you, Hamilton.' Benjamin offered his hand again.

Hamilton shook it quietly. Perhaps it wasn't entirely true that some old dogs couldn't learn new tricks.

Peace about Edward had finally reached Christie. He was mad and no one could change that. He could no more be held responsible for his actions than she could for the typhoons in the Far East. He needed help, fast. She just hoped either he or someone close to him realised the urgency thereof and did something about it.

"Loneliness is an unbearable beast," she thought constantly. The perpetual yearning was growing into monstrous proportions, the worst time being at night when she was alone with her memories, her heart aching in ways she hadn't known possible. Punching the pillow, often violently, she buried her face in it and cried. When the heartache was overwhelming and crying only made things worse, she painted until weariness took over and reached a trance-like state.

Emmett shook his head, too aware of her fatigue, wishing he knew what secrets caused her such pain.

Sandra also worried. The girl was tearing herself apart and there was nothing she could do but watch. She had grown very fond of Christie, thinking of her as a younger sister and hoped Christie would open her heart and share those deep hurts.

Christie looked lost for words. 'Move up to the house? I don't know, Sandra.'

'What's to know? You could go into labour in the middle of the night. We'll fix the yellow room.'

'I like to paint.'

'Because you can't do anything else. You need company, Christie.'

Christie wanted to say no, but she knew it was a wise decision.

The transition was quick, as there was nothing to take but her clothes and painting materials, and after three days, it felt as if she had been there for weeks.

Newa arrived unannounced, as Christie and Emmett sat on the beach. Christie no longer painted there, the easel was too cumbersome to carry, and generally, she felt too hot to sit for long periods under the ever-warming sun. Emmett and Jeffrey offered to fetch and carry but she disliked disrupting their lives as they too had work to finalise.

Christie stared, wondering how she could balance herself on those alarmingly high heels on the sand.

'Emmett, where's the work you promised me months ago?' Newa dove straight in. 'I said I'd come, so here I am. Christie, I came especially for yours. And Emmett, tell Brenda I definitely want to see this stainless steel thing she's working on and is so secretive about. Oh, I have to tell you,' a beautifully manicured hand rested on Christie's arm. 'One man really liked your work and bought three, and promised to be back for more.' They started walking towards the house.

Newa had seen many wonderful, horrible, mediocre, excellent, and just plain bad works, but nothing prepared her for what this young woman had produced, her eyes and mind taking in every colour and brush stroke. But these were not about art; these were about the rawness that runs through every living creature. Christie had woven an extraordinary mixture of human and mythological creature together.

'Imagine what you'll produce at forty.' Newa said. 'Words are useless, these are unreal! And I don't want to sell any; I want everyone to see them first. Emmett has taught you well.'

'And we've barely scratched the surface of what I must learn.'

'What's particularly exciting is that nothing is usual through your eyes. I noticed it in that first lot you brought me. I can go to any number of art schools and buy a thousand landscapes, all beautifully executed, perfect techniques, marvellous compositions, the works, but none will appeal to me the way these do. You speak to the soul, and I see you are brutally honest. That is scary.' Staring at one, Newa shivered.

'Life is far from perfect, I merely mirrored it.'

'Have the others seen them?'

'Only Emmett.'

Newa talked a long time about awakenings and style and Christie wondered how such a tiny person could go on for so long without stopping for breath.

Finally, Newa announced, 'I absolutely love it when I come upon fresh and original ideas.' A curious sound escaped her. 'Every year around November/December, I put on a show for new artists. I was one short and being away didn't give me much time to search the schools. Now, here you are! Interested?' She asked excitedly.

'I've never done anything like that, am totally unprepared, and look at me.'

'It's not a huge event. Every artist gets one section of the gallery and a few people are invited; people who can help your careers along; other artists, CEO's, that sort of thing. It helps with exposure, commissions, just a little promotion.'

'Would I have to be there?'

'It would be great but not essential.'

Brian stopped in the doorway and said something.

Newa made a face. 'What on earth is that gibberish?'

'He paid you a compliment in Greek.'

'And since when does he speak the language?'

'Christie lived in Greece and she told me the stories of the Greek biology.'

'Mythology,' Christie corrected.

'She had a castle.' Brian continued.

'Hardly, it's one of those ancient Greek temples.' Christie dismissed. 'Newa isn't interested.'

'But I am, and it also explains your classical inspiration.'

Newa left that afternoon, after making Christie promise to keep everything under wraps, already trying to formulate the plan that would complement the work.

The truck arrived two days later and the men packed everything in. Brenda's sculpture, Emmett's work, some of Jeffrey's, and Christie's.

Suddenly, she was sorry to part with them, wondering if she wasn't being hasty and rushing into things that should have taken her years to achieve.

'Something wrong?' Emmett queried as he saw the concerned furrow.

'Isn't it too much too soon?'

'Your work speaks for itself, let people see it too.'

She was unconvinced, but she needed money, or she, and soon her child, wouldn't be able to survive on the meagre sales she made to tourists.

The weather brought ever-warmer breezes and Christie was beginning to find most things a strain. She had taken to painting small portraits of Brian, the household pets, the servants, her friends and just about every piece of furniture she laid eyes on, but above all, she was definitely sleeping too much.

Sandra treated her as if she were an Arabian princess because every time she looked up, there she stood with loads of fruits and vegetables. 'We have to save that figure of yours.' She said.

Christie looked in the mirror and both burst out laughing.

'Hello,' Sandra stuck her head into the room just off the patio where Christie had set up her studio. 'There's a man here looking for art.'

'Okay,' Christie grabbed the cloth and wiped her hands.

A tall man in his mid thirties walked in. 'Good afternoon.' He greeted politely.

'Hello, Mr-' Standing up, she shook his hand.

'Call me Ian.' His eyes took everything in quickly. 'Mrs-'

'Andriotti, but you can call me Christie.'

He looked around with an interest she found fascinating, then eventually, chose a work depicting Lindos; the ruins visible in the background. 'I like this, is it a real place?'

'It's real, but as far away as the mountains on the moon.'

'I beg your pardon?'

'Should I wrap it?'

'Thank you.' He gave a cursory glance at others she had against the wall.

In the weeks that followed, she ran into him three more times and couldn't help but wonder why she thought he was strange, why he asked so many questions, and always in such a way that she often answered too truthfully. Shrugging, she hoped he'd be more careful in future when going near large bodies of water. She'd heard that he had capsized a boat and gashed his forehead - for which he received seven stitches - and pulled a muscle in his right leg so badly that he needed physiotherapy.

CHAPTER FIFTEEN

Sitting behind the wide mahogany desk, Benjamin pursed his lips. He had sent Hamilton out ages ago so his story had better be a good one. 'What happened?' He asked as the man limped into his office.

'I had an accident.' Hamilton placed a large flat package against the wall

'Did you find her?'

'Yes.' Quickly, Hamilton related his tale.

'You found her because she bought a house?'

Hamilton smiled. 'Checking official records is one of my specialities and there's good success. People can't change names on important documents and they tend to forget that databases are creeping into everything. I've gathered informers in all provinces and it pays off. She buried herself at the ends of the earth.'

'Is she all right?'

'Perfectly. Oh, congratulations, you are about to become a great-grandfather. Before the accident, I went around to see what went on. At first, I thought I had made a mistake because she doesn't look like the picture in the papers, but whatever the colouring, it's her. I suggest you let your grandson know as soon as possible.'

'I'll do that. What's that?' Benjamin pointed towards the package.

'She's a painter. In fact, Harristown is full of them. I bought it for myself but you may borrow it, in case your grandson needs convincing.' Hamilton tore the paper open. 'This is the backdrop to their place in Greece.'

'You've done a good job, Hamilton. As I knew you would.'

'Better than my father?'

'We did mess things up. Why did she leave Greece?'

'No one talks about her back there, especially if you're foreign. They think you're a reporter and everyone becomes tight-lipped. However, I did hear bits and pieces of a story about an accident, a court case, stolen art, and some guy, who caused hell. No one would give a decent explanation and the papers refused me permission to see back copies. I tried to talk to the police but they seem even more suspicious than the public. I had another file but lost it during the accident, even lost my digital camera. So unfortunately, I have only this and some photographs. ' He threw a thin file onto the desk and pointed to his head. 'I tried to write down as much as I could remember from the previous file.'

'It doesn't really matter now, does it? You found her. Perhaps my grandson will shed light on that. Thank you, Hamilton.'

'It was a true pleasure, Mr Powell.' Hamilton left with a smile on his face.

Benjamin reached for the phone. To his chagrin, he got an answering machine. Half irritated; he left a message.

Newa was legendary for unusual parties and although many didn't appreciate her sense of art or personal style, few dared pass the opportunity as she often made the social columns. Loving themes, she usually had all guests or herself and her *helpers*, dressed in whatever took her fancy. Patting the list now, she wondered if anyone would cancel. Watching the calendar, she grabbed the phone and dialled.

'Hi, Christie, can't you make it?'

'Sorry, I'm too uncomfortable.'

'Why is Jeffrey the only one coming?'

'Emmett says you give tiring parties and it's enough he suffers for his own, Brenda is Brian's baby-sitter, and Sandra and Donald my designated drivers.'

'Emmett exaggerates and the rest are excuses.'

Newa knew she had outdone herself; all she was concerned about now was what people would think. It wasn't really concern, more a dislike for those who could look down their noses when someone came up with an original idea, as if it were wasted. She looked magnificent in the scarlet *himation*, the gold braiding reflecting her hair colour with flashes of light. Readjusting the shoulder strap and the glorious mane, she stepped outside her office. Touching something here, adjusting there, she drifted through the entirely white draped room. Taking one last look, she leaned against a wall.

Jeffrey appeared beside her in blue, frowning heavily. 'Was this really necessary? I feel stupid.'

'You sort of look like a Greek god,'

He pulled at the shoulder strap. 'How the hell would Christie have held one of these up?'

'That's quite a crush you have on her.'

'What is it with women; do you all go to intuition school while men aren't watching?'

'Ah yes, the frustration of being unable to get what you imagine you want. Look, our first guests. You take that side.' Smiling, Newa walked towards a few people. The Stewards, Warrens, and Perlmans came. Peter Beckley arrived with a gorgeous blonde and Joseph Osborne actually brought his wife along.

'Peter, Patricia,' Newa greeted warmly. 'I'm so thrilled you're here.'

'And we're thrilled you didn't ask us to wear those.' Patricia eyed her up and down. 'It suits you though.'

'So, this is your lovely daughter,' Newa watched the young woman curiously. 'Have we met?'

'I don't think so but you might have seen her around. Gloria.'

'Pleased to make your acquaintance,' Newa smiled, not able to stop staring at Gloria as she disappeared among the crowd.

'It's going great, even if I feel like an idiot.' Jeffrey whispered in Newa's ear later.

'Stop complaining. Have you seen Patricia's daughter? She reminds me of someone.'

'Where is she?'

'Can't miss her, has flaming red hair.'

'Redhead, haven't had one of those yet.'

'Oh for goodness sake, Jeffrey! No wonder Christie knows better than to get involved. She'd be yesterday's news if she had ever encouraged you.' Newa told him harshly and then glanced at the clock on the wall. 'We should go through because everyone is desperately impatient.'

Clapping her hands, she stood in front of the columns, the backdrop startling white. There she stood in scarlet, masses of blonde hair cascading down to her waist, the contrast spectacular. 'Ladies and gentlemen, the moment you have been waiting for,' and she made one of her beloved speeches.

Scanning the room with pleasure later, Newa's eyes fell on Gloria. The young woman had what Newa could only describe as the most astonished expression she had ever seen. Patricia had said that she was knowledgeable; it would be interesting to hear her opinion. Walking over, Newa stopped beside her and gazed at the woman's portrait. 'What do you think?'

Gloria didn't turn to look at her. 'Wherever did you get them? This,' she pointed to the one alongside as Jeffrey joined them. 'It didn't look like this when I last saw it but it is the same one.'

'You couldn't have seen them; it's a recent acquisition and all originals.' Newa said.

'I know that, what I don't know is where-' Gloria peered at the signature. 'CAT, that stands for Christine Alexandra Thomas, my cousin. Where is she?'

Newa exchanged a curious glance with Jeffrey. 'I couldn't possibly reveal my artist's whereabouts without permission.'

'Apparently, this is the first time you're being overly secretive. Christie's visible absence tells me she requested it.'

'May we go into my office?' Of all days, this was the worst to cause a scene, and seeing determination in Gloria's countenance, Newa knew the possibility of an exceptionally ugly one had just surfaced.

Jeffrey stared as Gloria smoothed her hair. He had seen Christie do it a thousand times. The oddest feeling filled him. He knew this woman was a stranger, yet, it was as if he already knew her.

'Look,' Gloria said in softer tones. 'I understand you're loyal friends, who think she needs protecting, but her husband needs to know where she is.' Seeing their impassive faces, she knew this was going to take more convincing. 'You don't have to help me, but what do you suppose will happen the minute my parents realises whose work this is?'

Newa sighed. 'I'm returning to the guests, you two sort it out whichever way you want.'

Donald glanced at Christie. 'It's eleven o'clock and you should be in bed.'

'I can't sleep.'

'Regardless, you need rest.' He returned his attention to the papers on the coffee table.

Appearing with three mugs of hot chocolate, Sandra sat beside Christie. 'Don't worry, it will be fine.'

'That's what you think. I'm being greedy, aren't I? It should have taken me so much longer to get here.'

'Are you always this positive?' Sandra noticed the pale face. 'Are you okay?'

Christie shook her head and took a deep breath. 'I'm so stressed about this day that I think I've been in labour for the last two hours.'

Sandra spat chocolate all over the carpet. 'But you're not due until–'

'Tell that to the baby.'

The drive to Bellasdorp wasn't long but today it felt endless to Sandra, who thought her knuckles would be crushed as Christie held onto her hand tightly.

'I'm so tired.' Christie cried hours later.

Sandra wondered if she meant physically or emotionally. 'Then close your eyes and sleep.'

'But I need–'

'Christie, they'll bring him after you've rested.'

'That's right.' A nurse announced firmly.

Unwillingly, Christie closed her eyes. When she opened them again, dawn was breaking, the weak daylight filtering through the soft curtains in the quiet room. She glanced around without much interest. It was small. A wide window on the one wall, a bathroom opposite and Sandra curled in an armchair at the foot of the bed. Sandra had once suggested that Cape Town was perhaps a better choice for the delivery, she had declined, feeling as if that would expose her unnecessarily.

'How do you feel?' Sandra approached her. 'Do you want to know about the exhibition?'

Christie knew something was amiss. 'They hated it.'

'No,' Sandra told her quickly. 'It was a great success.'

'Then what's wrong?'

'Your cousin was there with her parents. Apparently, she cornered Newa and Jeffrey and is on her way down here tomorrow, or rather, this morning.'

Christie turned paper-white, a trembling hand going to her temple. 'I knew I shouldn't have agreed to it. What do I do now?'

'Maybe it's time you stopped running.'

'You don't understand. She'll tell Michael and he- I can't see him, ever. Oh Sandra, what am I going to do?'

'Well, first of all, see your son. I'll go ask the nursery sister to bring him.'

As soon as the cot was wheeled into the room, Christie held out her arms to the small bundle. Putting him on the bed, she unwrapped the cocoon, inspected the little body, and counted his toes and fingers. 'Sandra, how can one tell if a child isn't normal?' She asked as the tears fell.

Sandra looked at her strangely. 'Why would you think your baby isn't normal?'

Christie wiped her eyes. 'Please Sandra,'

'Here's the chart.' Sandra pulled it from the bottom of the cot then looked at Christie with concern. No, this wasn't a question; it was something altogether different. 'I'd better ask the doctor to come explain, because you have a phobia about this child.'

And the doctor did, trying to put her mind at ease. 'I have delivered hundreds of babies and this one in no different.' Smiling, he too wondered why the girl worried so much.

'So,' Sandra asked after the doctor left. 'What are we to call this handsome fellow?'

'Michael Thomas.' Christie's eyes clouded over. 'I'm so unhappy.'

'Tell me something I don't know. Open your heart Christie, because if you don't, you will go mad.'

Stretching his legs on the bed, Michael stared at the ceiling. How he wished none of this was happening, but above all that he had told Christie about his biological parents while he'd had the chance. That would have surely stopped Edward dead in his tracks. But who would have guessed that a scrap of paper could be used with such skill and malicious intent on the one person who was devoid of scheming wickedness?

He glanced at the clock; it was late, or early, depending on how one looked at it, and his thoughts went back to that evening. He was sick of running around in circles so he'd gone to pay the police a visit.

'Try Hillbrow,' one of the men suggested. 'It's a maze and easy for anyone to disappear in. Actually, it seems the scum of the earth decided to hide out there; prostitution, drug-dealing, murder, robbery, to name a few. It's just one of those places.'

'No,' Michael denied heatedly. 'Christie would never go to a place like that.'

'Why did she leave, Mr Andriotti?' The officer watched him with interest. 'We all read the papers, yet no one knows why you're looking or why she left you.'

'She didn't leave me, but it is a personal matter and we're in no rush to have family secrets out on the media's wash-line.'

'Yes,' the man nodded disapprovingly. 'You rich folk like to do everything on the quiet.' It wasn't hard to see that the man before him was well to do. The suit alone was probably worth a months' salary. 'As I see it, you'll have to wait for her to return on her own.'

'You're the police; can't you do better than that?'

'She's over twenty-one, hopefully of sound mind, in a foreign country. Did you tell her she couldn't come home? Was she happy?'

Michael punched the wall. 'Yes she was. We had just got married and I would never prevent her from coming home whenever she wished. I would have brought her myself. Can't you see? We were forcibly separated.'

'The best I can do for you is to send her picture to all police stations. Apart from that, there isn't much else. She has no criminal record, is a grown woman, and free to do as she pleases.'

'That's where you're wrong.' Exasperated that they couldn't do better, he left.

Climbing out of the taxi, he gazed at the buildings, the Hillbrow Tower in the distance. 'What has that maniac done to us,' he muttered. 'And I have no idea how to fix it.'

Walking down the street, four prostitutes soon accosted him, a man sold watches, another, condoms, and a third *great stuff*. Not every street, building, or establishment looked seedy but there was an eerie feeling to walking down some streets alone. Then he saw a woman with a short bob and he ran to her. It was just another business deal. One could easily go mad imagining someone like Christie in a place like this.

'Michael,' Sofia called outside the door.

Snapping his eyes open, he got up. 'Come in.'

'Morning, honey.' She glanced at his clothes. 'Where were you?'

'I went to the police and they suggested I go dig the dirt in Hillbrow. Can you imagine Christie there?' He stopped as he saw her face. 'What?'

'Gloria called again. I waited up but it got so late that I never heard you come in. She knows where Christie is.' She saw a bewildered look appear on his face. 'She went to an exhibition and recognised Christie's work.'

Michael sat on the edge of the bed, as if he couldn't stand, speak, or breathe. 'Is she absolutely certain?'

'There's no doubt. Call her, she'll tell you.'

Reaching for the phone, he stood up and dialled the number. As he waited, he hugged Sofia. 'Oh mom, my prayers have finally been answered.'

She couldn't have stopped the tears had she tried. 'I'll be down, preparing breakfast.'

Minutes later, he entered the kitchen, a wide grin on his face. 'I could run there on an empty stomach.'

She smiled. 'Probably, but I suggest you don't try. Now I recall, a man called yesterday, said it was a matter of the utmost importance.'

'When I get back.'

'Eat your breakfast and I'll call the airline.' She reached for the phone. It rang. 'Good grief. Watson residence,'

'Mrs Watson, I left a message yesterday. Did you deliver it?'

Looking at Michael, she pointed to the receiver. 'Moments ago.'

'Then stop wasting time and give him the damn thing, Sofia.' The voice told her sharply.

'Who is this?' She asked with affront.

'Benjamin Powell. Now let me speak to my grandson.'

She had a mind to put the object down; instead, she handed it to Michael.

'Hello?'

'Michael, be in my office in half an hour. I have important news.'

'Who is this?'

'What's the matter with you Andriottis? It's your grandfather.'

'I thought I told you-'

'That's fine and I don't care, but what about your wife? I have everything, including her street address. And in case you think I'm pulling a fast one I also have photographs.'

Michael was stunned and angry. 'Wasn't once enough for you? Who gave you the right to spy on my wife?'

'If I hadn't taken it upon myself to do so, you'd still know as much as you did last week. Now get down here and come get this pile off my desk.'

'And I made myself perfectly clear that I wished for none of your meddling, ever.' The man was crazy and who knew what he was after? 'And you're a little late, not ten minutes ago I heard of her whereabouts.'

'You have no reason to believe or trust me but I'm serious that you should come here before going in heaven knows what direction. I doubt your informant gave you all the facts.'

'I don't have time for this; I need to get on the first plane-'

'Which doesn't leave until nine, and I've already booked you on it. Now stop wasting time and come see me, I've sent the car.' Benjamin slammed the receiver in Michael's ear.

Michael was furious. 'Charming man, and up to his old tricks again. I can't believe he had the audacity- And what does he mean I don't know everything?' They heard a car horn outside. 'Half an hour, that's all he's getting.'

Walking over the granite floor at Powells, Michael could barely hide his annoyance. How dare he? Looking around disinterestedly, he saw Benjamin waiting for him. For a moment, he imagined the old man meant to embrace him, but only a hand came out in greeting. He shook it half-consciously. Was this how one greeted one's grandfather?

'I would have had this information sooner had the investigator not had an unfortunate accident. He told me an amazing story about Christine.'

'Christie,' Michael corrected him. 'And who gave you the right to intrude in matters that absolutely do not concern you?'

Walking down the passage, Benjamin took him into his office. 'Pretty girl.'

'What about Christie, I don't have all day. But before we go any further, what do you want?'

'Nothing, not even a thank you. Years ago, you, like your father, accused me of destroying this family. As harsh as that statement was for me to accept, I know it's true. Now, I've had a lifetime of regret and although amends can never be made, I can at least attempt to give you your life back.'

'Fair enough. So, where-' Michael stopped, that was a picture of Lindos. He went to it immediately and traced the temple, as if he were trying to find her. 'Where is she?'

'In some place called Harristown.'

'At least Gloria got it right this time.'

Benjamin continued. 'Bought herself a cottage and that's how the investigator tracked her down.' He placed a photograph on the desk.

Michael walked over. 'She lives here?'

'Used to, now she stays with friends.'

'Why would she do that?'

Benjamin studied his grandson's face. 'You don't know, do you?'

'Know what?' Fear gripped him.

'Before I explain, may I ask why she left you?'

'It's a long story and neither of us has all day.'

'There's always time for family. So, just the basics.' Benjamin encouraged.

'She believes we are brother and sister.'

'Good heavens! Are you?'

'No!'

'Then how did she come by the assumption?'

'A mutual friend kindly pointed out that both our fathers are called Robert Thomas.'

Benjamin made a face. 'But you're a Powell.'

'It must have slipped his mind.' Michael added sarcastically.

'So she just up and left?'

'It's more complicated than that.' Michael gazed at the photograph again. 'What is it I don't know?'

'She's expecting.'

'Expecting what?'

'What do you think, an elephant or a rabbit? A baby, you fool.'

Michael's face drained of all colour. 'That's impossible, we'd just been married. Who's the father?'

'Don't go idiot on me. She was already pregnant when she left Greece.'

'Oh lord, and she's been alone all this time! Where are the rest of the pictures?'

'Here,' Benjamin passed him the file.

'Who's this?' Michael asked and then did a double take as recognition filled him.

Benjamin pointed to a close-up. 'Hamilton does not make mistakes.'

Michael's heart twisted oddly as he saw a full-length picture, her hand resting on her raised stomach, a faraway look in her eyes. A knot found its way to his throat as he went through the pile. 'Huh... What... when did you say the plane leaves?'

'Everything is arranged. The driver will take you back home and then to the airport. But I should've anticipated this and kept my plane free.' Benjamin smiled. 'Another surprise I have for you.'

'I appreciate your help but I don't need a plane.'

'Not the plane, but who's in it.'

'Someone I know?' Michael asked disinterestedly.

'It's possible but improbable. As soon as this is resolved, we'll have a family reunion.' Benjamin grinned.

'My father?' Michael looked up keenly

Benjamin shook his head. 'I doubt we'll see him again, your brother.'

Michael furrowed his brows in surprise. 'Why would Andrew or Daniel-'

'None of those, your father's other son. To be given two grandsons after losing my entire family is more than I deserve and I'm beyond gratitude.'

'How is it possible?' Michael asked curiously.

'Robert was always a wanderer, so he met some girl up north.' Benjamin chuckled. 'As if to rub my face in the fact that neither needed my money, nor my name, both succeeded alone. Imagine what you could have accomplished had you been born under my roof. You would have been my future as none of my sons had it, except Robert I suppose. I didn't only break his heart, I wrecked his life.'

Michael glanced at his watch. 'All this is very interesting but I don't have time to be discussing long lost brothers.' He rose to his feet. 'Thank you, grandfather.' Shaking Benjamin's hand, he turned to walk away then stopped. 'Okay, so my curiosity can be satisfied, what's my brother's name?'

'Edward Davis.'

CHAPTER SIXTEEN

Sitting in the plane, Edward shuffled the photographs on his lap, then leaning back in the seat, he closed his eyes and recalled the first time he'd got confirmation that the man he believed to be his father, wasn't.

He had just turned seventeen and finally accepted that his mother, Elizabeth, was different, her mind not altogether clear, often unable to distinguish between reality and fantasy. It was a tragedy because she was both smart and beautiful. Mystifyingly, she mumbled and babbled and Edward was too intelligent to miss the insinuations, and over the years, suspicion that Sebastian Davis wasn't his father mounted.

That summer, a particularly heavy storm descended over the farm, and he and Sebastian ran to the barn to make sure the animals were safe. Returning to the house, they discovered Elizabeth missing. Both became frantic, knowing she would catch pneumonia, as she had no sense to get out of the downpour. Their search began immediately but after three hours and no sign of her, Sebastian called emergency services. Highly agitated, Edward couldn't wait and continued his own search.

Standing in the middle of the yard with no idea of what path to follow, a blinding flash fell towards the east, where the trees were. Running there, he slipped between the barbed wire and recalled frequently hearing her sing *My Favourite Place* when going in this direction. He had tried following her a couple times but he'd soon lose her among the baobabs. If he'd imagined it important, he would have solved the mystery of her disappearances, but he'd never seen it as such; and everyone knew that some of those trees had good hiding places, so she'd probably discovered one. As he went around a tree now, a hand literally appeared from inside and pulled him in. Startled, he stood in the engulfing darkness.

'Robert,' Elizabeth embraced and kissed him.

Shock kept him immobilised for a second. 'Mom,'

'Remember?' Her hands caressed the face she couldn't see.

'Mom, I'm Edward.' Forcefully removing her arms, he asked. 'Who's Robert?'

'Edward,' recognition filtered through. 'I didn't see you come in. Why are you soaked?' She seemed to be searching for something. 'Where's your father? Robert, stop pretending to be Edward. I missed you so much.' She reached for him, pressing her lips to his again.

Edward pushed her away. 'Are you crazy, I'm your son!'

'My mother was crazy; ate poisonous berries, couldn't tell the difference, and died. I know about berries. They're saying I'm crazy too, aren't they? And who knows, perhaps so are you.'

Edward knew fear as he grasped the hidden meaning of the whispers that had followed him throughout the years. Tears pouring down his face, he pulled the shirt off his back and ripping it into strips, gagged her so he didn't have to listen. Then tying her hands, he picked her up into his arms and took her home.

'Why didn't you tell me?' Edward demanded after they were alone again.

'Tell you what?' Sebastian flopped into a chair tiredly. 'That she's ill, that she cannot be cured, that her cognitive senses are gone?'

'I knew that a long time ago. I'm talking about my father.'

'I'm your father.' Sebastian told him sharply.

'Believe whatever you wish but I'm not your son.' Edward shouted above the noise. Then standing stiffly as if uncertain what to do, he disappeared into the raging storm.

Two things happened simultaneously over the following months; first, he became acquainted with alcohol, as he tried to numb his fear of the debilitating disease. Second, he began interrogating Elizabeth, sometimes learning a little, and sometimes nothing at all, as her memory seesawed between reality and that place he was beginning to dread. And he swore, swore that as soon as he left this hellhole, he would confront the man who had left his mother. Every Robert Thomas would be tracked down, investigated, and the right one dealt with, especially now that her mind was slipping quickly.

But life wasn't done dishing out painful blows. Returning from school one afternoon, he discovered that Sebastian had finally succumbed to the nagging tongues and given up, having Elizabeth locked away in an institution in Johannesburg.

Edward was super smart, had excellent reasoning abilities, logic, and debating skills second to none. So on completion of his high school career, Law seemed like the perfect fit. Newly excited about life, he left for Pretoria.

His mind was a wondrous place, capable of the most intricate plans and he began a methodical search for every R Thomas between Pretoria and Johannesburg. It was time-consuming, expensive, few fitted the profile, and who knew? Perhaps the man had moved away, emigrated, or died! He hoped not, for that would deprive him of vengeance. And somewhere in between, he vaguely recalled a holiday when Sebastian died.

Studies over, he was no closer to knowing anything that was worth attention, and exhausted, as he'd given his all to achieve number one, he went home. Strange symptoms emerged and fearing his mother's words prophetic, he was also sensible enough not to ignore the signs and diligently visited a specialist.

Discovering that he too had inherited the crippling disorder was frightening until a programme that promised a degree of success was suggested. Elated, Edward realised that unlike Elizabeth, his future didn't have to be bleak or filled with spells at institutions, as long as he took his medication and followed the therapy guidelines.

Then one evening, when he stepped onto the farmhouse's porch, he knew that he'd already been there too long. Selling everything he owned, he went straight to Johannesburg. When Baker & Associates heard he was looking, they came knocking.

Unexpectedly, Amanda walked into his life and introduced him to a Robert Thomas he had missed. For the simple reason that the man's personal number was unlisted and the small practice registered under Zachary & Sons, Mr Thomas' recently deceased father. At last, he had the perfect candidate! And could it be coincidental that both practiced law?

Growing in confidence and renewed hope, he set forth on a path of achievements, and finally brought himself to start visiting Elizabeth.

Most times, she wasn't certain who he was, but at others, there was an astounding lucidity and it was during one of these that he told her, 'guess what, mom? I'm working for my father.'

'And is your grandfather as fierce as Robert claimed?'

'I don't know, he's dead.'

'Well, it's not as if Benjamin was immortal.'

'Zachary, mom, Zachary.' Edward stressed, wondering what path her mind had taken.

'Who's Zachary? Your grandfather's name is Benjamin Powell.'

He recognised the name; he'd seen it not four blocks from here, an hour ago. There had to be a mistake.

'Imagine, Edward, you, grandson to one of the most powerful men in the country. Sebastian insisted we marry quickly when we discovered I was pregnant but I doubt anyone was fooled, especially as it became common knowledge that he was sterile. I sent him to find Robert but he only saw Benjamin, who had no idea where his son was. Sebastian returned years later but still the same thing. I don't know if Benjamin would've helped or liked to have known you, but Sebastian decided that you were his.'

'So I'm a Powell, not a Thomas?' If true, this was just too incredible.

'Oh, I see what you thought.' She said with realisation. 'No, your father's name is Robert Thomas Powell.'

'That still didn't give him the right to abandon you.'

'Robert? No, he never guessed I'd fall pregnant. I told him I was on the pill, even showed him the box.' Elizabeth giggled. 'They were my mother's. My uncle was old-fashioned but he was not prepared to risk her having more children. Come,' she invited. 'Let me show you.'

'Who's this?' Edward stared at a familiar face.

'Your uncle Charles, see the resemblance? That one,' Elizabeth pointed to another magazine picture. 'William. But it's no use going to look for them, they're both dead.' She took the obituaries. 'I don't have any pictures of

Robert, and he such a talented photographer. Look, I even posed for him.'

What did he do now? Stay with Mr Thomas, court Baker & Associates, or go to Benjamin? He was also dating Christie… He made a face; where was that going? Nowhere! Then not many weeks after, on the very day Gloria entered his life, fate revealed another secret.

He'd gone to Sofia's house to drop some files. As she was thanking him, she asked if he would mind taking a small desk upstairs to her bedroom. He minded but said okay. Irritated, he pushed it roughly against the bedside table and the force knocked her wedding picture over. Picking it up, he studied Christopher and Sofia on their wedding day, thinking it an unorthodox decision for a Greek girl to make back then. Men, yes, he knew many foreigners who had married English or Afrikaans girls, but he hadn't come across many of the opposite.

Returning the frame to its place, he noticed the photograph was skew. Giving it a shake, he realised it wouldn't straighten due to an obstruction at the bottom. Sitting on the bed's edge, he opened it, pulling away a paper that had been stuck to the back. He stared at the birth registration, not really surprised as he considered where Sofia worked. 'Wonder whose secret she's keeping. Name, surname, father's name, and mother's name white-out.' Whistling softly, he rummaged in the medicine cabinet.

'Edward,' Sofia's muffled voice came from down the hall. 'Do you need help?'

'All done.' Folding the paper, he put it in his pocket, returned the photograph to its place and went downstairs.

Sofia stopped at his side. 'Thank you. Sorry for the manual labour when you were only delivering files, which I should have picked up.'

He smiled. 'It's not a problem.'

'I've prepared lunch. As you know, Gloria is arriving today. Care to join us?'

'Thank you but I need to get back.' He didn't but he was too curious about the paper in his pocket, and he would meet Gloria tonight.

'Are you going past next door?'

'Yes ma'am. Should I give Mrs Thomas a message?'

'Lunch is ready, and,' she pointed to a bunch of flowers. 'Will you take those?'

'Sure.' He crossed the two gardens and walked into Jane's kitchen. 'Mrs Watson says lunch is ready, and here are the flowers.'

Jane smiled. 'Thank you, Edward. Staying?'

'No. I lent Christie some books, but there's one I need, may I get it?'

'Help yourself.'

He ran upstairs to Christie's room, opened the cupboard with art materials, and searched for ear buds and a bottle of thinners. Good he actually listened the day she carried on about removing paints and inks. Sitting at her desk, he took the paper out of his pocket and stretched it out. There were four choices, name, surname, father, and mother. Carefully rubbing the white grime away, he saw it had been blackened with marking pen; he continued rolling the ear bud carefully, then held the paper up towards the sun. A broad smile appeared on his face.

Name; Michael. Surname; Andriotti. Father; (completely scratched out). Mother; Sofia Andriotti. Had Sofia and

Christopher lost a child? Had she been unable to deal with the grief? Then why wasn't Christopher's name on the birth register? He studied the paper again. She was eighteen when this child was born. He looked at the official stamp, Grahamstown, 22-11-1970.

Hearing a car drive up, he knew Christie and Gloria had arrived. He grabbed a book, sprinted to the kitchen, poured himself a glass of water, and walked into the lounge seconds before Christie and Gloria did. Svelte was the first word that entered his mind as he saw Gloria. Now that was a woman to pursue.

Edward could hear the animated conversation. He hesitated a moment, then stepped out.

'Edward,' Christie smiled. 'Joining us?'

He looked embarrassed. 'If Mrs Watson will allow me.'

'Of course, didn't I ask you earlier?' Sofia wondered what had changed his mind.

Edward only added monosyllables as the four women discussed Paris, London, and Cape Town. He had to admit, he was always amazed at Sofia's food; she cooked like no one he knew. 'Mrs Watson, you are a fantastic cook, you have a beautiful house, and you are an awesome woman, why didn't you remarry?'

Sofia studied him a few seconds. 'I never considered it again.'

'How old were you when your husband died?'

'Almost twenty-five.'

He shook his head. 'Too young, and when you married?'

'Twenty-one.'

He choked on his food and coughed. This was interesting; the child was out of wedlock. With her husband to be? 'Did you meet your husband at school?'

'No, I was at University when I met him.'

Well, now he knew. 'Did you always live in Johannesburg?'

'No, we were in Grahamstown.'

'I'm serious Mrs Watson, you should have remarried.'

A gentle smile crossed her lips. 'I'm married to the Home now.'

'It's not the same.' Briefly, he flirted with the idea of revelation. But what would that accomplish except stun everyone that she'd had a child?

As he gazed at Gloria across the table, he felt his pulse race. He turned to look at Christie. Except for the blue eyes, it was as good as staring at the salad. No, he was no fool.

Seeing the vision of perfection he never imagined possible, Edward became obsessed with the desire of possessing Christie, wanting to be in control, jealousy and envy consuming him, as he wondered if Michael had succeeded where he'd failed, or rather, not given thorough thought to - her bed.

Within hours of arrival, he felt the silent but mean war. Often, both Michael and Christie were on the verge of shredding each other, but an overwhelming intensity existed between them and he knew exactly where it would lead if he sat idly by. No man would separate her from him, but definitely not this one, whom he disliked intensely. Perhaps it was the Andriotti name that riled him up.

Christie's stubbornness was infuriating and he tried to coerce her into obedience, ultimately resorting to threats. In retrospect, drugs would have effectively wiped out her fighting spirit, just as they had Gloria's. Eventually, he issued his ultimatum, hoping she heeded it. But as Gloria had said, Christie repudiated every advance.

In wild frustration, he began exploring the surrounding areas, and it was during one of those excursions that he encountered Costa. Spending countless hours in each other's company, Costa spoke of his past, and suddenly, Edward knew how to make money, lots of it. Greeks loved Icons and Religious Art; it was everywhere, quite old, and valuable.

Then one Thursday, at one of those stupid dinners, the conversation took a detour into Michael's life.

Mary kept the conversation going as Christie found it difficult to behave near normal when in the presence of both men, as for Gloria, she was simply useless.

'Michael,' Edward said animated as he sipped Greek coffee. 'You have a good thing here; better that some places I know back home. Have you ever been to Africa?'

Michael nodded. 'I was there, just not long, but I'm planning to return.'

Edward looked intrigued. 'Business ventures?'

'Not sure yet.' Intentionally or not Michael's gaze rested on Christie.

'Of course it would intrigue you.' Mary said matter-of-fact. 'As you were born there.'

Edward stared. 'I thought you were English, from the way you speak. Oh, I get it; your parents also lived there.'

'Did they, when?' Christie asked curiously, as she knew they never had.

'Only dad, before he married. My mom only visited.'

Edward looked as if he was having problems adding two plus one.

'Before you injure your brain,' Gloria said tartly. 'Michael is adopted.'

Mary and Christie exchanged a curious glance. What was that about?

'Will you two excuse us?' Mary said quickly as she noticed Edward's glare, and motioned for Christie and Gloria to follow her down the passage.

But the news had obviously been something of a surprise to Edward. 'We actually have something in common; I was also adopted, by my stepfather. Did you ever want to know who your real parents are?'

'No. Besides, I'll always be an Andriotti.'

'Of course.' Edward said. 'Do you even know where you were born?'

'It's some place called Grahamstown.'

A peculiar expression appeared on Edward's face. This was a weird turn of events. And why was that date running in his head? 'So when's your birthday, or did they make one up?'

'No, I'm told the twenty-second of November 1970 is my actual birth date.'

If he weren't sitting down, he would have had to, as Edward thought he would start sweating as he hid the leaping excitement. Again, he wondered what to do with the information, as it was becoming progressively more outrageous. Who knew? Maybe he'd hit the jackpot when he finally figured out who the father was. But hell, was it all confusing as well. Had Sofia just handed him over to her brother?

Christie's presence in Manoli's house was something neither had expected and Costa's quick reaction was one of those things people don't usually foresee. As soon as it happened, he knew… and he feared for her life because he couldn't envision living without her.

Realising the police's determination to get him behind bars, Edward travelled to Turkey and later Cyprus, searching for one of Costa's associates, one with very special abilities. Had Dimitri really expected to succeed when money spoke the language of greed? It was astounding how far a few notes could go, even going as far as buying a new persona - John, and a wife. A woman who had no idea what had happened to her husband and needed money.

Yet again things didn't go as planned. As he grasped at Christie's amnesia as a second chance to gain her trust and later love, she still shrunk away from any man who wasn't Michael.

For lack of knowing what else to do, he broke into Michael's house, placed the chloroform under Christie's bed, and bugged the room. He watched, listened, and learnt what took place in the house, and now and then, he released the chemical. When he heard about the idiots who dared attack her… Had they imagined that they could hurt her and get away with it?

Aware that lack of medication was fuelling instability, he took a break away from the island. When on his return she announced her engagement, his rage grew so thin that he was sorely tempted to teach her a lesson but dreading his growing lack of control, he travelled to Cyprus then back to South Africa. He needed to see his doctor.

After his evaluation, which he didn't like one bit, he sat clueless at home, wondering what his next logical step should be. Then unexpectedly, he chanced upon that interesting folded paper again. Yes, it was time to go digging once more.

Playing the role of adoption lawyer to perfection, he flew to Grahamstown and got his hands on those sealed records. He suspected that more than friendship had existed between Mr Thomas and Sofia and that had been his plan, to unearth that juicy bit. However, would Sofia approve of such a union if that were true?

The saying was; be careful what you wish for, for you just might get it. Oh yes he got it. He'd looked for the truth and here it was in all its glory. Robert Thomas Powell was Michael Andriotti's father. Edward fell into a chair in shock, becoming pale and dizzy; his head spinning in a most alarming way. This was a dreadful nightmare because things like this were not possible. He despised Michael, how could he be his own half-brother? The concept was too horrible to contemplate or accept. In stunned disbelief, he sat staring at the papers. Then, it dawned on him...

After dropping that bombshell, he returned to South Africa, not only to escape detection and arrest, but as he'd told Christie, he was through playing moronic John. It was also imperative he continue his treatment in peace because he would need to be there for her, now that she no longer had a husband.

Seeing his comfort zone disappearing and turning unpleasant, as both Rob and Peter Thomas tried to track him down, he introduced himself to Benjamin.

Realising the old man might not take kinship at face value, Edward came prepared with Elizabeth's photographs, newspaper clippings and letters she had written, never sent but saved, and presented himself as an orphan.

Benjamin was utterly amazed, somehow imagining that Robert had never touched another woman after Sofia.

Nevertheless, he welcomed this unknown grandson eagerly, excitedly telling him that he wasn't alone, that there was another, one Benjamin could only admire from afar. Edward hid his ire and said how marvellous it was to discover that he had a sibling; one he would love to meet!

If Benjamin wanted to atone, he must do it in his own time. Unlike Michael, Edward wanted everything; respectability, power, money, but above all, he desperately wanted the Powell name. Because once he had that, what could anyone do to him?

Benjamin bragged and boasted about Michael, driving Edward to the edge of murder, making it impossible to forget the prejudices life had bestowed on him, so he started plotting again, wondering how he could rid himself of the old man and later his brother. Because if a man could not be found to pay for his own sins, then his son would do just as well. Besides, Michael had not only beaten him in the family stakes by being Robert's first-born and Benjamin's favourite, but he'd also taken the one woman Edward wanted.

Now, how he regretted having lost Christie! But when comparing the cousins all those months ago, any man who'd said that he preferred Christie, would have been called mad. How could he guess that the chubby caterpillar would turn into a beautiful butterfly, or grasp the power she truly possessed over his heart?

What did he do to make her love him again? Destiny had chosen her for him but he blinded, pursued something he imagined better, turning his back on his true love. It was more than he could bear and the fact that he shared blood with her husband was disgusting.

Turbulence brought Edward back to the present with a jolt. Throwing the copies he'd made of Hamilton's report aside, he got up, and went into the cockpit.

After a furious exchange of words the previous night, Gloria fully expected Jeffrey to leave first thing in the morning with only one purpose in mind - to warn Christie. Instead, she managed to extract a promise that he would wait for the decent explanation she owed him as they drove to Harristown. 'Morning,' she greeted tiredly, as she hadn't slept much. 'I appreciate you keeping your word.'

Dressed simply in jeans, shirt and a hooded jersey, she looked younger, definitely not the glamorous woman he'd seen last night, reminding him so much of Christie, that he found it disconcerting.

'Morning. You do realise that Newa called last night.' He held the vehicle's door open.

A concerned expression appeared on her face. 'Do you suppose she'll run?'

'That remains to be seen and I hope I'm not going to regret this. You started on some kind of narration yesterday but I was soon confused and wondered to whom I owed my loyalty. Oddly, something tells me I should listen, whether I like it or not.'

'I was desperate yesterday, today-'

'I'm fond of Christie and if you think I'm dropping you, unannounced, on her doorstep, you're mistaken. So, what shall it be?'

Gloria shifted in the seat, as if trying to control her nerves. 'Few outsiders know what's really going on.'

'Then I'm extremely privileged to be added to the list.' He said as he drove away.

She ignored the sarcasm. 'It started when Christie met Edward, my ex-husband.' Her voice dropped to a whisper. Even after all this time, it still seared her heart.

'Is this a family feud?'

'Just madness.' Gazing out the window, a far-away look crept into her eyes. 'Things could have been different and perhaps the disease wouldn't have manifested. He was considering marrying her when I came along. But you have to understand, he's insane.'

Jeffrey listened in silence as Christie's mystery unfolded. As Gloria spoke, he realised that she too had suffered greatly. Not once did she mention intimate details, but he could imagine what had taken place from the way her voice trembled, her hands twisted and shook, and her eyes filled with tears, which she desperately tried to hide.

'...so when Edward discovered that both uncle Rob and Michael's father coincidentally shared the same name, it was a Godsend to his warped mind. Imagine Christie's panic. She simply disappeared and Michael couldn't get an explanation from Thea until it was too late.'

'All these months, she's been under the impression that she's married to her half-brother?' Jeffrey became agitated. 'I didn't mention, which is why I wanted to be present when you saw her, she's pregnant! Well, no more, I called Brenda this morning. Christie went into labour last night. She's no fool and the implications! And I can barely believe what you've just told me.' He nodded. 'You're right, Edward can't be allowed in the world of the sane. He has to be found, stopped, and locked up.'

CHAPTER SEVENTEEN

Michael sat as if under a spell, wondering how he'd got home and then to the airport, although he vaguely remembered the chauffeur. When Benjamin said, "Edward Davis", he felt as if Powells had literally collapsed around him. Colour leaving his face, he sunk back into the chair as if his legs couldn't support him. 'It can't be.'

'I was just as surprised.'

Michael's mind raced as he realised what Benjamin had been saying. 'Where is he?'

'I don't know; it's the first time he requested permission to use the plane.'

'Who's this Edward, or more importantly, did you tell him about Christie?'

'It was such good news, and you weren't home when I called.' Benjamin accused.

'Can we find out where he's gone? If this is the same Edward… do you know what he's capable of?' Michael saw confusion on Benjamin's face. 'You don't understand, grandfather, Edward is extremely dangerous and there's no telling what he'll do when she refuses to accompany him.' A nervous hand passed over his eyes. 'What does he look like?'

'Here,' Benjamin opened a drawer and took out a photograph.

Michael simply shook his head in disbelief. Why him of all people?

'Is he really dangerous?'

'Not only that but he's also insane. And he's the one who caused this bedlam to start with. You had me investigated; didn't you do the same with him?'

Benjamin shrugged apologetically. 'He had letters, photographs, and clippings. Everything he said made sense, and of course, there's his looks. He's a Nichols, Elaine's side. A most disagreeable development as the boy seems to have quite a head on his shoulders.' Benjamin pointed to the report. 'It's yours.' An odd look crossed his face as he recalled having given him another, years ago. If only he'd done things differently.

A feeling of helplessness swept over Michael. 'Whatever I do, it's already too late.'

Going around the desk, Benjamin put a hand on his grandson's shoulder. 'Get down there and do what you must to save your family.'

Now, as Michael sat staring unseeingly, he knew this was going to be the longest trip he would ever undertake. Because there was no doubt in his mind, that Edward was heading for Harristown.

There was a glimmer of sunlight in the horizon when Edward landed in Cape Town and he was in a bad mood. Running to the car rental counter, he filled the necessary papers in a rush, acquired a map, and without thanks to the pilot, disappeared down the tarmac in the rented vehicle at break-neck speed.

After a dreary drive on the highway and two secondary roads, he turned off a small patch of road, stopped, looked at his watch, and saw that he had been driving for longer than three hours. This could only mean one thing; he was lost. Studying the map, he then drove a few minutes until finding the route-marker. 'How the hell did I get here?' He asked exasperated and banged his fist on the dashboard. 'I hate these insignificant places.' Putting his foot down, he raced in a different direction. To his horror, he got lost again while taking what he imagined was a shortcut across two roads.

Abruptly, he came upon a house half-hidden on a cliff. Climbing out, he knocked. No answer. 'Damn all this sand and rocks.' Getting back into the car, he drove down the gravel path. Seeing an old man on the side of the road, he stopped and asked. 'What's this place called?'

'Ashville.'

'Doesn't anyone live around here?'

'Plenty holiday houses, but the people stay in the cities.'

'Can you tell me how to get to Harristown?'

'Go to the petrol station.' The man pointed straight ahead. 'It's easy from there.'

'Thanks.' After kilometres of more sand and dirt, he arrived at a junction, the antiquated petrol station in one of its corners. Glancing at the fuel gauge, he thought refilling a good idea. 'Is this petrol or diesel?' He asked another old man, as he couldn't tell the difference through the black grime covering the pump.

'Petrol. How much?'

'Full tank.' Taking the map out, Edward wondered where exactly this junction was. 'Do you know how I can get to Harristown?'

'Two ways.' The man gave him a toothless grin. 'One, turn left at the T-junction and go through Bellasdorp, and then you drive on the other side. Two, turn right and go straight to Harristown.'

Edward pulled a paper from his briefcase. Thankfully, he'd had the good sense to copy Hamilton's file and pictures. 'Know this place?'

'Many times I went to Mr Donald's house. You a relative?'

'A friend, so, how do I get there?'

'It's down by the sea. The main road is not straight but you must follow it to the end.'

'Thanks.' Edward placed a few notes in the old man's hand. 'What's your name?'

'Jacobs.'

For once, someone gave proper directions. He detested it when strangers only confused him more. Grinning, he drove twice around the cul-de-sac, then stopping, he walked to the entrance.

'Hello. May I help you?' Brenda asked as she opened the door.

'I'm looking for an old friend, Donald McKewan. But I might have misunderstood directions and got lost.'

'You're quite right, this is Donald's place. Unfortunately, he's not in.'

Disappointment showed on Edward's face. 'What rotten luck, I just drove four hours to pay him a visit.'

'And look as if you could do with some refreshment. Come in.'

Emmett appeared at the door, followed by Brian. 'I thought it might be Jeffrey.'

Edward went down to the little boy. 'You must be Brian.'

'Something cold?' Brenda queried as she motioned to the sofa in the living room.

'I don't want to put you to any trouble. Is Sandra home?' Edward glanced around the room curiously.

'Christie had a baby.' Brian announced loudly.

So, she had the brat! A few more questions and he would know where she was. But how many hospitals could there be in the area? Unless she had bypassed the one in Bellasdorp and gone somewhere else.

Brenda brought him a juice as Emmett watched him with interest and asked a few questions about his friendship with Donald. Edward answered generally, laughed a lot, and lied outrageously.

'So,' Edward asked casually. 'Where is this baby?'

'In Bellasdorp,' Brian piped up quickly.

'I think I should go. I'll call Donald and plan better next time.' He shook Emmett and Brenda's hand. 'Nice meeting you.'

Driving at a speed any traffic officer would consider reckless, Edward arrived in Bellasdorp, stopping only once in front of a house where children played in the yard to ask directions to the hospital.

It was a typical South African hospital; a long, double-storey brown edifice, with most windows open, as it was a warm November day.

Knowing men walked in and out of maternity wards at all times, he strolled down the passage, reading names, peering into rooms. He stared, no matter what colouring, she was always beautiful. Opening the cupboard, he took the suitcase and filled it with her belongings. Then he shook her lightly. 'You've been a busy girl.'

Instant fear showed on her face, instinctively pulling the bed-covers closer around her. 'Ed-ward! Why... how did you find me?'

'Let's go.' He glanced at the drip and pointed. 'How many more do you need?'

She could try delay him until Sandra or a nurse returned, but the gun tucked in his belt certainly put a different perspective on things. 'Only this one.'

'Good. Where's the baby?'

'In the nursery. You can't be suggesting-'

Hearing a commotion at the end of the passage, he opened the door a fraction. 'What the...' He was taken aback to see Gloria. She was with a man; who gesticulated and spoke quickly to Sandra. 'Change of plan.' He grabbed the drip, took her by the arm, marched her down the passage, turned the corner, and away from where the excitement was taking place. They crossed a cemented courtyard that led to the laundry, going towards a fence. Thankfully, the gate was unlocked. He dragged her along a grassy patch and arrived against a tall building. Why was everything difficult?

Peeping around the corner, he saw the main street shops a few metres away. One man was loading shopping bags into the back of a 4x4, then, he returned to the store.

'Come on.' He urged.

'I...' Christie leaned against the wall.

Pulling her, he opened the 4x4's back door. 'Lie low.'

'See you next week, Stephen. And enjoy your stay.' A man's voice said outside.

'Thanks, I will.' Stephen climbed in, put the 4x4 into gear, and drove away.

Edward waited ten minutes then sat up. 'Stephen,'

Startled, Stephen applied brakes and zigzagged to the side of the road. 'Who the hell are you?'

'I'm commandeering this vehicle.' Edward glanced at the shopping bags in the back. 'Where are you headed?'

'Home.'

Edward looked pensive. 'Where?'

'Ashville.'

'Is your family there?'

'I'm alone. What is this about?'

Edward showed him the gun and motioned for Christie to sit up. 'From now on, I'm in charge. If you choose to disregard good advice, I can always put a bullet in your head, is that understood?'

'Perfectly. Where to?'

'Home.'

Christie felt light-headed and wished the house was somewhere nearby because all she wanted to do was pass out. But eventually, Stephen stopped the vehicle. Edward got out before him, opened the driver's door, and without blinking, shot him in the thigh. Whether from shock or physical exhaustion, she slipped from the seat in a dead faint and into Edward's arms.

'Christie,'

'W-what,' she whispered in the coolness of the bedroom. 'What happened?' But seeing Edward's face, she recalled immediately. Sitting up, she felt her head swim, as if she were going to be sick. 'How could you?'

'He'll live. It's insurance against escape attempts.'

'Where is he?'

'Behind the cabinet in the lounge.'

'What?'

'There's a secret room, a sort of pantry, safe, or something.' He explained.

'Is he all right?'

'Can bleed to death for all I care.'

She gasped. 'May I see if he needs assistance?'

'You will do nothing but lie there until later. Enjoy your sleep.' He left the room and closed the door.

Rolling onto her side, she felt the tears seep from the corners of her eyes. This was unlike any physical pain she had ever experienced. It was right in the middle of her heart, a pain that couldn't stop or heal unless he disappeared from her life.

Why had this obsession befallen him? The madness that would destroy them all if someone didn't stop it. Occasionally, he behaved sane, as he was doing towards her now, and she was thankful because she was in no condition for a confrontation, either physical or emotional. The tragedy was that it wouldn't stay like this for long. When that hidden monster made its appearance, there was nothing or no one who could stop it, and unluckily for Stephen, he would probably be the main recipient of it.

Closing her eyes, she hoped that when she opened them again, all this would be a horrible nightmare. That she was back in hospital.

'Dinner is served.' Edward placed a tray on her lap.

'Stephen?'

'He's not exactly hungry. His name is Stephen Lint and is apparently in advertising. I'll give him something later.'

'May I see him?'

'I detest this bad habit of yours; always wanting to help someone. Oh all right,' he agreed as he saw her tearful eyes.

'This man needs urgent medical attention.' Christie announced. 'The bullet is lodged. It will become infected, he'll develop a fever... he could die.'

'What do you want me to do, take the damn thing out? I'm no doctor.'

'We can't let him suffer. And without the bullet he'll feel better.'

'He doesn't need to feel better, he needs to feel dead.'

'It doesn't look too deep. You just need a pair of tweezers…' she gulped.

'Oh, stop those tears. Go back to bed and I'll see what I can do.'

She covered her head with the pillow when she heard Stephen cry out, wondering if Edward was being as careful as he possibly could or if he had changed his mind.

'I didn't kill him, if that's what's worrying you,' he told her as he sat on the bed's edge.

The gesture disturbed her greatly but she made no comment.

He continued. 'Just given birth but still so beautiful, and if I weren't stupid, he would have been mine, we'd be together. What am I saying? We are.'

She was in no mood for chatter so Edward filled the gap by talking non-stop. And so she found out about things she'd been wondering about. How had he found her? How long did he think they could hide like this? Where would they go? He had it all sorted out in his head. 'But now, I want to know how you've been, if you've missed me.' He said finally.

Before today, things had been bearable; there were new friends, work, and soon there would have been her son. Then, as before, he had turned up and made sure it all changed. If she weren't careful, he would sink her into a swamp of despair. Dejectedly, she turned away from him, in no mood to partake in his idiotic conversations.

Stephen developed the expected high fever and Christie feared for his life as Edward mumbled back and forth from the sofa to the kitchen with cold towels in his hands. He'd never had any patience and she imagined this was grating on empty reserves.

'Let me look after him,' she offered.

Hours passed, with them taking turns looking after Stephen on the sofa. During one of her shifts, she tried the kitchen door; locked, no key in sight, she hadn't expected anything less.

Next day, she realised what a mistake it had been to be up so long, but Stephen was better and that was consolation enough for how awful she felt.

Waking from a long sleep, she found Edward sitting on the chair staring at her. Hating it, she realised he would keep doing it until... until what?

'Absolutely the most beautiful thing I've ever seen and I feel like making love.'

She grabbed the covers in fright.

'Do I scare you that much?' He arose, went to sit on the bed, put a hand to her face, and asked softly. 'Just tell me one thing then, did you ever love me?'

They should have had this discussion when they broke up, but he'd been in a rush to be done with her and she'd felt wounded. In a way, she should thank him for not wanting her. What she would have missed if she'd never met Michael. How she loved him. 'I thought I did, I was wrong.'

He watched the blue flames he often saw in his dreams. 'When I think about what I did to us- I had no idea what I had. My salvation is that you have a good heart and will eventually overlook all my misdeeds.'

'How's Stephen?'

'In other words, you no longer care for this discussion. He's much better and sends his appreciation.'

Pandemonium had reigned supreme at the hospital, no one believing that such a thing was possible in Bellasdorp. Doctors, nurses, police everywhere, and still no trace of Christie. Michael thought that perhaps he should be used to it, but wasn't and would never be. He felt tired, exhausted, limp, and a million other things, but above all angry. How could anyone endure the insanity that destroyed everything in its path?

Then, looking up, he saw Gloria standing before him, her eyes filled with tears, and her arms with his son.

Staring at the small sleeping figure, he put a careful hand to the blond head. Was this little person part of him and Christie? The thought did something to his heart. Leaning over, he picked his son, that extraordinary feeling coursing through him; and both gladness and intense fear filled him.

The story was an open secret; everyone in Harristown and Bellasdorp knew it but as if by some unspoken agreement, the locals reacted as those of Lindos, few repeating it to the swarms of reporters, who had suddenly swooped on the small communities. Increasingly, the residents were closing doors on their faces the minute they asked a question pertaining to Christie, many thinking she deserved better treatment than she was getting. She had always been kind, friendly, and shown a good moral upbringing. Here, that was important.

'Should we expect a ransom note?' Captain Rossow, a man of about fifty, asked from behind his desk.

'No, Edward only wants Christie.' Michael announced tiredly.

'There's no proof of kidnapping; just that her room is empty and her things are gone. Except for what you say, and the little your friends know, there are no witnesses to verify this story. The hospital staff saw nothing. Are you certain he took her by force?'

Michael looked dangerous at that moment. Turning, he walked out of the police station, got into the Land Rover Donald had lent him, and drove back to Harristown.

Walking into Sandra's house, he saw Gloria feeding Michael Thomas. Smiling, he passed a hand over his son's head and sat down.

'You look tired, Michael.' Gloria noticed.

'That's just the thing, I can't close my eyes. I feel as if she slips further away every time I do. This isn't Greece, I have no idea who to see, what to do. So far, I haven't been able to protect her at all.'

'Go lie down, even if you can't sleep. Don't worry about Michael Thomas, I'll keep him tonight.'

'Thank you.' Michael walked to Christie's room and lay on the bed. As her scent filled his senses, he fell asleep.

'Mr Andriotti,' Captain Rossow greeted as Michael walked into the police station next morning.

'Any leads?'

Captain Rossow shook his head. 'We have no idea how they got out of town. He arrived in a rented car, left it outside the hospital, and there are no reported stolen vehicles. What direction did they take? Is there an accomplice? This is holiday land so we are checking houses in a sixty-kilometre radius. But they could be anywhere.'

'No,' Michael said with conviction. 'Let me tell you about Edward. He derives great pleasure from rubbing people's faces in his insane genius. He'll disguise himself, walk right past and we have no idea it's him.'

'Still, he can't keep her hidden forever. Everyone knows Mrs Andriotti, which is good because people remember. I know I asked this before and you didn't like it, but are you certain-'

Michael cut him short. 'How many women do you know who would leave their new-born child to go with a maniac, whom she's petrified of.' He put a hand to his temple. 'In Greece, he was living a stone's throw away. You have to think as he does.'

'Perhaps a profiler might give us an insight into his personality.'

'And reveal things you won't believe. His mother is in a mental institution; call her doctor. That is information from my grandfather.'

Contrite that he had been careless where his newest grandson was concerned, Benjamin had called Hamilton and asked him to investigate Edward.

'Then again,' Michael continued. 'Why not try Gloria's in Cape Town? And what about Christie's in Rhodes? See what's going on, everyone seems lose it around him. But if he values his life, he'd better not lay one finger on her.'

'You shouldn't be saying such things in a police station.'

'Then you find him first because if I do and he's harmed her in any way you'll have to lock me up as I'll more than lay my hands on him.' Michael's anger was quickly rising. 'Brother or no brother I want him out of our lives. I want my wife and my life back. I have a son who needs a mother. This is my family, can't you understand?' Storming out of the office, he walked all the way down the street, then realised he'd left the Land Rover parked in front of the police station. Walking back more calmly, a flash burst just ahead of him. He looked up, reporters.

Feeding his son, Michael thought how fortunate Michael Thomas was. He didn't miss Christie, his little heart didn't constrict in pain, and as long as someone fed and put him to sleep, he was satisfied. The longing would come later, as it had done with him. Never could he complain about his adoptive parents, yet he couldn't forget the yearning he'd felt from the moment he'd discovered that someone else had given him life.

When as an adult, filled with anger and rejection he discovered that malicious trickery had separated his family, it had been a bitter pill to swallow. Until Christie's disappearance, he hadn't understood how Robert had felt when he couldn't find Sofia, and later, their child; now that he did, he also knew why Robert had never returned. Now also feeling Sofia's sorrow at being wickedly deceived. What had he known at eighteen? Absolutely nothing!

At least Christie had found good friends. He had worried about where she lived, what she did, whom she saw, and sometimes when he looked at Jeffrey, jealousy twitched, as there was no doubt that deep feelings existed, something that went beyond friendship.

'Sorry to disturb you but your grandfather is here.' Sandra told him.

'It figures, as he's unable to stay out of other people's affairs for longer than a few days,' he said annoyed.

From the moment Benjamin arrived, everyone became edgy. In a few hours, he was issuing orders as if he owned everything for miles around. Then, he raided the police station, and spelt out his expectations.

Captain Rossow stared at Mr Powell, and Hannes, the sergeant, wondered where this would lead. Then, captain Rossow told Mr Powell clearly, what he thought about his methods of operation and never to give an order because it would simply be ignored. Hannes thought Mr Powell would die of affront, and as he was about to answer in anger, Michael looked at him and said *"drop it. This is their job; they don't need your meddling"*, Michael looked angry too. Mr Powell opened his mouth a few times but when looking at Michael; thought better of it and *"dropped it"*.

Michael became increasingly irritated with the old man's attitude. Benjamin went about as if the past was a clear sky, while he saw the storm clouds, and he prayed worse weather wasn't on the horizon for all of them.

It was obvious from the first that Sandra's house, although large, could no longer accommodate anyone else and everyone breathed a sigh of relief when Benjamin took residence at the local, if rather small hotel, and in three days as many employees resigned from their jobs.

'No wonder he split the family.' Jeffrey told Gloria as he watched her rocking Michael Thomas. 'His bombastic ways can drive anyone to suicide.'

'And I'm glad Michael doesn't take any nonsense. Now, I also see where Edward got his strange ways, it's uncanny how alike they are. The only difference being that Edward is insane.'

'Sure he didn't inherit that from him too, Benjamin appears quite mad to me.' She giggled merrily and he knew that Christie had been right. Love and infatuation were different.

Gazing at him, Gloria wondered why life was so complicated. Why couldn't she have met a man like him, when she still trusted in romance and life, when she still believed that anything was worth trying?

'Gloria,' Jeffrey called a second time. 'Michael Thomas is fast asleep. Would you like to put him down and go for a walk?'

They often did and now she realised that he never spoke about himself, that he always led her into conversations where they discussed Edward, as if on purpose. For the first time, she was aware that she spoke of him as if he were a stranger, as if she'd half forgotten what he'd put her through. Suddenly, it felt good.

'Where on earth is your mind today?' Jeffrey queried as he watched the emerald eyes.

'I'm sorry,' getting to her feet; she cuddled Michael Thomas and dropped a gentle kiss on his forehead. 'Give me a few minutes?'

'Take all the time you need, I'm going nowhere.'

Unexpectedly, his words meant more than this moment. She smiled. 'I won't be long.'

Watching her disappear inside the house, Jeffrey knew that he would never be the same again. How could he have imagined himself in love with Christie? But he already knew the answer. She had been the promise of things to come, the window that gave him a glimpse of Gloria, knocking him breathless that his innermost secret desires had a touch of reality. No wonder he had felt overwhelmingly protective towards her, she was almost a carbon copy of Gloria. But now that the original was here, he saw how tender and fragile she was. How did he not damage the delicate soul and reinforce the little strength she had finally found?

'Ready.' She announced at his side.

'Any particular place you'd like to visit today?'

She took a mere second to answer. 'Would I be disturbing you if I asked to see your work?'

'No, it would be an honour.' He had sometimes laughed when people told him what they thought of his work, and at others listened with interest and been truly surprised at the conclusions people drew of his character as interpretations were often completely off the mark. Now, he couldn't wait for her opinion.

There were a few misses but overall she did well as she analysed and studied.

'Newa was right, you are knowledgeable,' he told her as they arrived in his bedroom where only one piece adorned the wall above the bed. 'Tell me about this one.'

'Was this your blue period?'

'A comedian too, what else is a man to ask for?'

She looked at the painting and then at him. 'If you did this, why don't you use the technique anymore? May I?' She pointed to the bed.

'I'll take it down.' Removing his shoes, he quickly jumped on the bed and dropped the painting on it.

She studied the work for a few minutes, then, turned to the frame itself. 'I may be insulting you but I don't think you did it.'

'Why would you say that?'

'First, this technique hasn't been used in the last fifty years, which makes it older than you are. Second, I doubt these blends have been heard of for longer than that. Thirdly, that is not your signature. Fourth, discoloration is about a hundred years old and I'd say so is the frame, and it has never been taken out of here.' She made a face. 'How much off the mark am I?'

He looked seriously at her. 'A few years, it's ninety-five.' Then, his face crinkled into a smile. 'That's brilliant, Gloria. Only Emmett and Christie know I didn't paint it.'

'Then who did, because although it is different, there are also many similarities.'

'A great-great-uncle. He was the only other Ferris who had the bug but it seems no one thought much of his talent, so he committed suicide. When I discovered this as a ten-year-old, it was all I wanted to do. As with him, I struggled for every paintbrush, tube and lesson I eventually got. But unlike him, I managed to pursue my dream and do moderately well.'

She watched him for a quiet moment. 'Why did you test me?'

'It was not a test you needed to pass, it was mere curiosity.' Slowly, he took her hand in his, feeling tremors run through her. 'Don't be afraid of me, I could never hurt you.' Caressing the side of her face, his hand moved beneath the glorious hair. Uncertainty and fear appeared in her eyes and he was overwhelmed with feelings of regret for the pain she had suffered. Dropping his head gradually, he kissed her with a tenderness he hadn't known he possessed, then, letting her go, he whispered. 'When you're ready, I will be waiting.'

'After Edward,'

'I know you're scared but I'm not him, and you mustn't believe anything he ever told you.' He returned the picture to the wall. 'Gloria?' He questioned as she stared out the window. Turning her to face him, he saw the tears.

'I don't want you to want me if all I do is remind you of Christie. I've already been through that once.'

'For a while I wasn't sure but now that you're here I understand. I was searching for you and because you're so alike, I thought she was the one.' He gazed into her eyes. 'Do you know how quickly I'm falling in love with you?' Very gently, he wrapped his arms around her and held her tight against his heart.

Christie dreamt about means of escape as the days passed exceedingly slowly. She had seen in films how prisoners drew lines on walls to keep track of time, now she understood how they felt. True, she had considerable luxury, as Stephen's house was anything but plain or ordinary, but both she and he were prisoners nonetheless.

With interest, she watched the windows. Did they have to be so narrow? It was probably impossible to squeeze through them. But if she managed the feat, where exactly was here? Her body was healing but she'd still never manage great distances on foot. She glanced at the walls. These weren't modern structures, but pointing to an era when security was a necessity against invaders. Suddenly, it was as if she were looking at a miniature fort, now also understanding why the windows were so narrow. They had been built that way to stop bullets, arrows, and anything else an assailant might have in his arsenal. Now she also understood the secret room behind the cabinet with the thick wooden door and the tiny window. It had probably been a jail, a storeroom, or simply a place of safety when attackers had penetrated the outer security. How had Edward discovered it so quickly? But he was naturally suspicious, so he must have looked behind every nook and cranny.

Every day, both morning and afternoon, Edward locked Stephen behind the cabinet, her in the bedroom and went somewhere; she wondered if he took the 4x4. She knew he sometimes left the kitchen door unlocked, but doubted the keys to both garage and vehicle were lying about, and she speculated as to how far she would get. Knowing him, she could just picture him sitting on a rock nearby, waiting out of sight for her to make that fateful mistake. Up to now, he'd been reasonably considerate but if she ventured out the door, there would be no guarantees.

Having Stephen around helped keep Edward out of her hair, as the two often sat in the lounge talking about any number of subjects, especially extreme sports, of which Stephen seemed to be a devout follower. Sometimes, she got the distinct impression that he too was thinking escape, and she became frightened for him. If Edward smelled a rat, there was no telling what he would do. She hoped Stephen used the common sense he seemed to possess and saved himself further serious injury.

Edward chatted as if the two had always been friends and Christie noticed with alarm how every tale he told was far from reality. He began a long saga on Gloria's powers of seduction and she cringed when he left out all the horrible bits he had perpetrated. Often, she felt like correcting him, but knowing that getting involved was asking for trouble, she let it pass and tried to concentrate on one of Stephen's books.

Stephen gasped and she wondered what they were discussing. Paying particular attention, she heard a detailed account of the Soros' murders.

Time dragged on and she was getting more than an insight into the painfully twisted character. Surprisingly, she felt great pity. Sorry for the mind that was being eroded; or perhaps sorry that he had never stood a chance against the curse that swept over his existence.

Jacobs sat in his favourite place - the rocking chair on the small porch - as he watched the evening sun sink lazily. Slowly, a car appeared over the dusty horizon. He smiled with recognition.

'Hello sergeant, many speed fines today?' He said cheerfully as the driver pulled up.

'Hello Jacobs, no, everyone has been driving well.' The sergeant grinned and climbed out of the patrol car. 'Fill her up and pump the tyres.' Leaning carelessly against the door, he queried. 'Have you seen any strangers around lately?'

'People pass through every day.'

'I mean strangers who haven't been in our area before but are staying now.'

'One man, he was here this afternoon.'

'What does he look like?'

'Blond, blue eyes, well-built,' Jacobs made a fist.

'Is he here?' The sergeant spread a few pictures on the bonnet.

Glancing through them, Jacobs pointed. 'This one.'

'You're sure?' The sergeant saw Jacobs nod. 'Anyone else with him?'

'He told me he wanted to buy his wife some clothes, but I never saw her.'

'Do you know where he's staying?'

'He always drives Mr Lint's 4x4 so I asked him why. It's his cousin. Why do you have his picture? Is he a criminal?'

'The police in Harristown and Bellasdorp think so.'

'Harristown,' Jacobs scratched his head with recollection. 'Now I remember, the first time I saw him he was looking for Mr Donald's house.'

'You're absolutely certain it was this man?'

'Yes.'

'Well then, thank you, Jacobs.' Climbing back into the patrol car, the sergeant drove away. Over the horizon, he stopped. This was too good a lead to pass up.

CHAPTER EIGHTEEN

Darkness greeted as Christie opened her eyes. It wasn't easy to have relaxing naps, but apart from worrying constantly, there was nothing else to do when Edward left them locked in the house and went on one of his excursions. She watched the windows wistfully, what a pity Stephen had left those narrow gaps. An eerie darkness enfolded the house tonight. She clicked the bedside lamp, no electricity. Wearily, she got off the bed and went to join the two men in the kitchen.

'Hello,' Stephen greeted from his usual chair, where Edward always tied one hand to the back.

Candles flickered hesitantly, casting dancing shadows on the walls, and she felt a bottomless sadness, recalling one night when she and Michael had filled the yacht with candles. They had laughed, as they considered how they'd be rescued if there was a fire, and then... how they had loved. Feeling Edward's hands on her shoulders, aversion filled her. Biting her bottom lip, she tried to control the nervous heart, and fixed her gaze on Stephen. His face spoke volumes. If he could, he'd grab her and run.

'Hungry?' Edward queried.

'No.' How could she eat when all she wanted to do was puke?

'I have a surprise.' Opening a cupboard, Edward brought out a large bag. 'I realised you didn't possess an extensive wardrobe so I went to town and bought a few things; must try them on as I guessed your size.'

'That's very thoughtful.' She noticed Stephen was miming something. His hand went up as if holding a glass and his finger made half a turn against his temple, Edward was drunk. That sure put a nasty spin on the evening. Stephen had reason to worry but he had no idea what Edward became when inebriated.

If only they'd known earlier how far he was going. But he never told them anything, making certain neither attempted a step out the door even if they could manage to get out of their respective cells. He had created an irrational world, from which no one would escape. A knot lodged itself in her chest and before she could do anything about them, the tears brimmed in her eyes.

'Don't cry; I'll give you whatever you want.' Edward misconstrued her reaction.

Now that was almost a joke. 'I don't feel well.' She returned to the bedroom, where she cried for a long time. How much more of this could she endure?

'I have the bag here.' Edward's voice came through the door.

'I'll get it tomorrow, I'm tired.'

'And I want to see you in one of the dresses tonight.'

She couldn't be bothered about a fashion show right now, but something in his voice told her to comply. Opening the door, she stuck out an arm, where he draped a floral creation over it and put a candle in her hand.

Walking out of the bedroom, she saw the living room dotted with candles. 'Where's Stephen?'

'Where he belongs.' Rising from the sofa, Edward approached her.

'Can't you let him out?' She hated feeling vulnerable.

He stared at her. 'How could I not see that you were merely in disguise?' Both hands came down on her shoulders. 'And don't ask me to let Stephen out again; I'm in no mood to watch him drool all over you.'

She shifted uncomfortably. 'He does no such thing.'

'Then there must be something wrong with him.'

Shrinking from his touch, she tried to sound matter-of-fact. 'May I go?'

Eyes closing to slits, he reached for her hand, seeing her reluctance to produce it. 'When are you going to forget?'

Her gaze dropped to the wedding band on her finger.

'Look at me when I ask you a question.'

Lifting her eyes, she saw something that frightened her, the look that said he meant to hurt her. 'I should go-'

'There's no marriage, why wear it?' Unceremoniously, he pulled her into an embrace.

She tried to push him away. 'You're hurting me.'

'I want you to love me, to desire me the way you do him. I've heard you cry and come to watch you sleep. And knowing that he has made love to you fills me with rage! It's then I could kill you!'

'Don't you see? It's Gloria all over again. And then you'd tire of me too.'

'Never! I despise him, despise you, yet, you're all I think about. How I've hated these months I wasn't able to see you. I knew you'd leave and I tried to follow, but you were quicker than even I expected. Not knowing where you were, or who you saw was hell.' He dropped to his knees. 'My dreams are filled with you. Tell me what I must do to convince you.'

When times like this came what did she say? Did he mean what he asked, or was it a type of pleasantry? People never realised how much of what they said meant nothing.

'I have to be realistic, because how long do I really have? And that's why you're an urgency for me.' He shook his head. 'Just like my mother, the slow slide into the trap, the one that never lets you out.'

Realising this might be the only way he revealed himself, she sat on the sofa. 'Yes, tell me about your family, the one you never mentioned before.'

'Mom was such fun, so beautiful, and then… I can't imagine a worse fate than not remembering you.' He traced an imaginary pattern on the sofa. 'If my father shows up, how will I know he's here? But it's probably best because all I want to do is put a bullet in his head.' He touched the gun tucked into the belt. 'All my life I've loved and hated. Do you know that the line between those two is so blurred, that they feel the same? Reality comes and goes, but if you're not with me, what's the point? Life's unfair, but what would you know about that, you've always had everything you wished for.'

"Including you!" She wanted to say tartly, but told him instead. 'You should discuss this with someone who can help, someone who understands. And you shouldn't drink; it makes you do bizarre things.'

'I don't mean to hurt you but I'm so jealous. Yet, I'd die for you in an instant. I know it sounds trite but you alone have this power over me.' Lifting himself up, he put a hand to her chin. 'You're never going to love me the way you do him, are you? Everything you do tells me this and I hate myself because I'm partly responsible. I know I shouldn't have married Gloria, but I couldn't stop myself.'

'Did you love her?'

'I don't know, maybe in the beginning, but never as I do you. I know my haste caused this disaster, but I'll also admit that I had no feelings when I started dating you. All I wanted then was to hurt your father, not that he realised it. I wanted to turn everything into rubble.'

She frowned; why did he want to hurt her father? He was insane so perhaps there was a maze in his mind that even he was having trouble unravelling.

'I knew you'd never finish law school so I had a plan, to which I should have stuck! Love came later; much later, too late, and it hit me like a jackhammer. And when nothing swayed you… You were supposedly heart-broken!

'The most I expected was for you to ignore me a week, two, perhaps a month. That once I explained my contrition you'd take me back. Instead, you wasted no time in replacing me.' He accused and made an irritated gesture. 'Why not do the same with him, and how long were you married? I hate how you love him.' He was silent for a second. 'If I promise to never hurt him, will you stay with me?'

Then one day, she'd do something he didn't like and he'd kill her by accident or otherwise. Or he'd forget. Worse, changed his mind, and went after Michael or their son. Nothing could be right if she let this continue. She told him softly, 'Edward, we need to talk, but not now. Let's do that in the morning, when you're sober.'

'I want you.' Encircling her waist, he pulled her against his chest. 'This lurking insanity is nothing compared to the madness I feel without your love and I won't rest until I know what it feels like to have you surrender to me.'

'Ed-ward, I can't-'

'And I'm past caring.' Fear always enhanced his sense of condescending superiority, so the look on her face was like a potent aphrodisiac, one that only incited. 'We're alone, Christie. Who will stop me?'

'Me,' a voice announced behind them.

Startled, Edward's grip slackened and pulling the gun from his belt, he turned and fired once.

Christie stared in horror as a red patch spread across the shirt, hands clutching in shock. Rushing towards him, she fell on her knees. 'Oh Stephen-' something hit her temple, a peculiar oblivion filling her. As she sunk to the floor, she heard breaking glass. Odd, someone else had just entered the room. Closing her eyes, she heard a second explosion.

Stirring, she put a hand to her painful head. 'Oww,'

Edward hovered over her on the bed. 'Get whatever you need and let's go.'

'Stephen!' Getting to her feet, she leaned against the wall until the room stopped spinning, then she turned to Edward. 'Don't even entertain the idea of stopping me.' Entering the living room, she saw the traffic officer sprawled in a curious position, staring straight up. Before reaching him, she knew he was dead. 'What have you done?'

'He appeared out of nowhere.' Edward made a nervous gesture. 'Come pack, I want to get out of here.'

'You go.' Falling to her knees, she tore Stephen's shirt open, looking straight into the ugly hole. She had no idea if any major organs had been hit; only that she'd never seen so much blood on one person. That wasn't true, Manoli had looked worse. A hand flew to her mouth to stop the nausea.

'If one came, there might be others.' Edward waved the gun at the lifeless body.

'Do as he says, I'll go for help.' Stephen whispered.

'But you're bleeding. How did you get out?'

'Found the skeleton key.' Stephen squeezed her hand reassuringly then motioned towards the dead man. 'He had to be driving something, buy me ten minutes.'

'It's too risky.' Christie glanced towards the bedroom where Edward was dumping things onto the bed.

Stephen followed her gaze. 'Where does he want to go?'

She shrugged as tears filled her eyes. 'It's just like before, a horrible mess.'

'And you're stronger than this. I know it but he doesn't, and that's your weapon. Go in there and keep him busy.'

'Christie,' Edward bellowed.

She grabbed a cushion, removed the cover, and put it on the wound. 'Promise you'll be careful.'

'I'll be fine. Now do as he says.' He took a painful breath.

'Coming?' Edward asked annoyed from the doorway and glared at her as she helped Stephen to the sofa. 'Leave the damn nuisance, because if you don't get in here in three seconds, he'll be dead instead of comfortable.'

Walking into the bedroom, she began throwing clothes into the suitcase. Then sitting on the bed, she put her hands to her head, seeing out of the corner of her eye Stephen's struggle to get to his feet. 'Do you have to go around hitting people all the time?'

'Let me say this only once. Don't get in my way and everything will run smoothly.'

'Doesn't that just make me feel better? You're too mercurial, the one minute up, the next down,' her hands demonstrated. 'It exhausts me.'

He stared fascinated and took a step closer. 'I love it when you're angry.'

She grabbed a hairbrush. 'I warn you, I will no longer be a pacifist where you're concerned. Come near me and I will fight back.'

'Hallelujah, she has returned! All these days I thought you were acting peculiar, wondering if I had made a mistake, afraid that you'd never surface again.' He grinned. 'I was getting rather bored with that apathetic wimp; this is the Christie I love. Please don't turn back into that insipid soul; it scares me. Come on now, we don't have all night.' He told her cheerfully as he looked into the living room and saw only the blood stain on the sofa. 'Damn, Stephen's gone.' Running to the kitchen, he returned in seconds. 'Can't see where he went.'

Stephen had made a super-human effort to leave the house, feeling dizzy and on the verge of unconsciousness each time he made a wrong move, the pain something unbelievable and definitely unforgettable. At a snail's pace, he reached the sprawled body, bit his lip, bent over it, and checked the pockets for keys. There were none. Then he looked in the holster; empty.

The man had come crashing through the kitchen door after hearing the shot that now sat embedded in Stephen's side and Edward had very neatly put the second bullet in his head. He'd love to put one in Edward's devious mind too.

Wondering where the man had left his vehicle, Stephen leaned against the garage wall and gasped for breath, then gritting his teeth, he turned left. 'Let it be the right direction.' He certainly didn't need that maniac on his trail, and he was sorry he had to leave Christie. But if he made it, then she might be safely home before the night was over.

Glancing at the sky, he noticed that it was overcast. That could be a blessing or a curse. Walking for five minutes felt like an eternity and he was aware that he was bleeding; the drip of his own blood hit the left shoe when he dragged his foot too long. The night became darker as clouds rolled and completely hid the moon from view. He hoped there were no potholes where he could break a leg.

He came upon the vehicle rather abruptly, making contact between his knee and the bumper, a painful gasp escaping him as he half-fell forward. Walking to the side, he opened the door, his hand going to where the keys should be. 'Please be there,' he whispered and let his hand touch the space next to the steering wheel. Then as quickly as he could, he climbed behind the wheel and turned the ignition.

Driving down the gravel road without lights, he was glad that he knew the area well. With a valiant effort, he reached for the radio. 'Hello, anyone out there?' Suddenly, he thought he saw something flicker in the distance. Perhaps he had made a mistake because it wasn't there anymore. He hit a car parked across the road, the absence of a seat belt jerking him forward, knocking his chest against the steering wheel and then back again. Leaning against the backrest, he welcomed the oblivion.

'Sure this is the right way?' Christie tried to peer into the darkness that enveloped them.

'Right way to where? I'm trying to concentrate on this damn sea of sand, but I suppose your artistic nature needed this crap. Give me courtrooms and a good libel suit any day.' He made a gesture. 'I don't expect you to understand, just as you can't grasp the depth of my feelings.'

'Because it's not reciprocated and it's obsessive. Look at the time you wasted in Greece.'

He swerved to avoid a tuft of grass. 'It was the worst time of my life, and for what, to be near you! Ingrate, you still bloody married that damn brother of mine!'

'Heavens Edward, the things you say.'

He turned angrily. 'I'll have you know there are a couple of truths you know nothing about.'

'If they're as absurd as that, you can keep them.'

'Know what's sad?' He told her disdainfully. 'You're so gullible it's pathetic. You're the easiest person to con and I admit; that birth certificate was my best work yet.'

A cold shiver ran through her. 'So you did lie.'

'Feeling guilty you believed it? Rather late, wouldn't you say?' He waved an arm. 'Poor Christie, ran away and wasted her time for nothing.'

'Michael and I are not related?' Her hands became clammy in her lap.

'Knowing righteous Sofia, would she have permitted it?'

'But she said-'

'I was there, she did not, and that was the beauty of my ruse.'

She misled herself if she imagined that she'd be able to control him, because he would simply not allow her to get that close. This was an evil intent on consuming all if he didn't get his way, a fixation that would destroy everyone who dared stand in his way. 'Why are you doing this?'

'Because I love you, because I hate Michael, because I dislike Sofia, because I can.' The vehicle came to a sudden halt. 'Since we're into truths today, pay attention, don't interrupt and you'll never have to ask again.' And for the first time, he unravelled the mystery of his life to another person.

Her head throbbed as things made frightening sense and she agreed with him; she was gullible. She should have stayed and got the explanation Sofia had no doubt tried to give her. She shouldn't have stormed out in flaming hurt and brought everyone so much pain; Sofia had almost died! Her eyes filled with tears of regret. 'You dated me when you believed I was your sister?' She asked horrified. 'But it's not you who's to blame, I let this happen.'

'If it wasn't that I already knew the truth when Gloria came along, that I was free to choose, no one would have stopped us getting married.'

'You're mean, selfish, and destructive, and how stupid of me to believe anything you ever said. I'm such an idiot that I fell straight into your trap.' She hit the dashboard with resentment.

'Something about those Andriottis always drove me up a wall. Then the man I hate most turns out to be my brother? Where's the justice in this world? But I'm getting it today.' He laughed; a high piercing sound close to weeping.

'But I'll never love you. And you can't keep me forever.'

'Is that a threat? If I catch you trying to escape-'

'Then do your worst.' Opening the door, she jumped out and started running over the dunes. As she did, she saw how futile it all was, the escape that would never come. But anger and frustration propelled her. How right he was, she was gullible, stupid, naïve...

'Stop,' he called. 'You'll never make it.'

One hand fell on a shoulder and then on the other. Sobbing, she willed her legs to move, but he was too strong. Falling on the sand, she felt the full force of his body on hers.

'Damn it Christie, don't you understand?' As clouds parted, he turned her over, seeing her chest heave with sobs, no longer tears of fear but of defeat and frustration.

Closing her eyes to blot him out, she turned her face away.

He wiped the tears, then pulling her to a sitting position, kissed the side of her face, his hands gentle on her back as he whispered. 'If only you loved me half of what I do you.' Letting her go, she fell back on the sand in convulsions. 'You did once, but now you torture me.' He pinned her arms down.

'You're hurting me.'

'Then you know how I feel every time you reject me. Why I retaliated in Greece.' He saw her blank expression. 'Chloroform under the bed. It wasn't there when I looked. Who found it?'

'I did.'

'Well done. How many times I almost released it all, but the fear of losing you somehow stopped me. However, the plan wasn't to hurt you but rather to convince everyone that you were going mad, just like me. John would have been the only one who understood, who could comfort you.'

'I beg you, please let me go.'

'Once, I desperately wanted to be somebody, to be important, for people to listen to me, to respect my opinion, to have money and power, to have my rightful name.' He gave a crooked smile. 'Never said I had a short list. Now, as I look at you, none of it is important.' He caressed her cheek. 'I burst with passion for you and nothing else matters.'

Looking up, she saw his face appear and disappear as the clouds moved dreamily across the dark sky, now hiding then revealing the moon. Many had through the ages blamed it for strange deeds. Maybe she was already going crazy, just as he wished.

'Does Michael burn with hunger as I do?' He ran his hands over her body.

'Stop.' She brought her arms across her chest.

'Do you feel nothing when I kiss you?'

'Please,'

Catching both her hands with one of his, he pulled them high above her head, keeping her captive beneath his body.

Writhing frantically, she only succeeded in getting herself immobilised under his strong legs. 'Ed-' she began but didn't finish as his mouth crushed hers. He was finally going to kill her. A shivering panic filled her body. Frantically, she tried to move beneath him but only managed to get her arms mercilessly twisted. Past coherent thought and blinded by fear, she shook her head helplessly.

'Christie, wake up,' he called.

Opening her eyes, she saw him kneeling beside her.

'Do women practice fainting? A convenient means of escape from both pleasure and pain.'

Sitting up with difficulty, she rubbed her arms, and loathed him with every fibre of her being.

'Stop pretending, and admit that it excites you to get men this worked up.' He sneered.

Hugging her knees to her chest, she rocked herself gently.

'Enough said, let's go.'

'Just leave me.'

'Come of your own free will, or I will drag you.' Walking over to the 4x4, he climbed in and drove towards her. 'Get in.'

She wanted to run in the opposite direction but her body told her otherwise, it needed rest or it might pass out again. She hoped Stephen was luckier and had already found help. Glaring at the vehicle, she prayed it would stick in the sand. Climbing into the cab in silence, she banged the door shut and sat as far away from him as possible.

'This brings back memories.'

She ignored him but wondered to what he referred.

'The drive to Plimiri.' He told her.

A tense silence fell between them as each contemplated the present situation; both realising nothing good could come of it, and that neither would give in. Unexpectedly, a bright light appeared in the distance. Perplexed, both stared.

'What the hell,' Edward asked, and then answered himself. 'Helicopter!' Switching the engine and lights off, he reached for her arm. 'Don't even dream that you'd make it.'

Leaning against the backrest, she looked resigned to her plight, but her outwardly appearance hardly mirrored the hope that had suddenly been born in her soul. Before he had time to make a decision, she pushed the door ajar, fell onto the sand in the rush she was in, then scrambling to her feet, she ran towards the light in the sky.

'Here we go again.' Climbing out, he watched her with a mixture of fascination and frustration. He would never be able to hold onto her if she did this at every opportunity. Anger and depression filled him. It was true; he had lost her forever.

'I can't take this anymore.' Michael said as he leaned into the helicopter seat.

They had been flying for the last fifteen minutes, the pilot hovering aimlessly as he tried to guess where Edward would turn up.

Someone - with a bullet wound to his side, and another healing in his thigh - called Stephen Lint, had crashed into one of the roadblocks while driving one of the traffic vehicles. He'd been in deep shock and was barely coherent as he tried to impart information. What everyone knew was this; Edward had shot him, shot a traffic officer dead, and was planning to leave with Christie in a 4x4.

'Did it occur to anyone that Edward might have a different mode of transportation?' Benjamin suggested.

'Such as?' Michael asked tiredly.

'A boat or a hang-glider.'

'A bit much, don't you think?' Michael exchanged a glance with captain Rossow.

'Not from what I heard he's capable of.'

'And this is why you shouldn't even be here. Do you think Edward is merely throwing a tantrum? Don't start trouble you'll regret.'

'All stuff and nonsense.'

'What's that?' Michael queried as he pointed over captain Rossow's shoulder.

The pilot did a semi-circle and listened to the radio for a few seconds. 'Roger that.' He turned to Captain Rossow. 'The house is empty, except for the dead officer. The vehicle hasn't been seen at any roadblock, which makes that flicker down there rather interesting. And what's this?' Turning right, he shone the bright beam on a figure moving across the sand.

'Christie!'

'Finally, results.' Benjamin said. 'So, where's Edward?'

'Right there.' The pilot gestured to another figure.

'Stop him! Do something!' Michael begged as he felt hope and fear sweep over him.

Helplessly, they watched as Christie suddenly came to a halt, slowly went down to her knees, and then collapsed on the sand.

Reaching her quickly, Edward fell beside her. 'Christie,'

Staring upwards, she couldn't answer, an expression of resignation on her face then slowly, her head dropped to the side.

Half lifting her, he realised… but he couldn't remember pulling the trigger. Holding her limp body against his, he found it hard to think; to accept that he'd shot her! If she died… she couldn't, he wouldn't let her. His eyes flew to the hovering craft. Gently dropping her on the sand, he waved to the pilot.

'It doesn't make sense,' Captain Rossow said. 'First he kidnaps her and now he calls us down?'

'Let me talk to him.' Benjamin volunteered.

'Why isn't she moving? What's wrong with her?' Michael persisted.

'This is police business, so I suggest the both of you stay here and let me handle it.' Captain Rossow announced as he climbed out of the helicopter. 'I have to keep him talking until reinforcements get here.'

'Talk all you like but I'm coming along to make sure Christie is all right.' Michael removed the seatbelt and climbed down.

'So am I.' Benjamin declared and followed him.

Edward watched the three silhouettes in the helicopter's bright light. 'My wife had an accident.'

'Your wife?'

'Who is that?'

'Edward, don't you think you've already caused enough misery?'

'Grandfather, what are you doing here? Don't answer, Michael's moral support. Am I then to assume that he's right beside you?'

Captain Rossow threw his hands up in irritation. 'Didn't I ask you to let me handle this? What's wrong with Mrs Andriotti?'

'It was an accident, I didn't mean to. And I don't know how it happened. The gun must have gone off.'

'You shot her? Oh lord!' Michael said, unable to control himself.

Captain Rossow's hand flew out to restrain him. 'Is she still breathing?'

Edward looked down at the immobile figure. 'Yes.'

Feeling Michael's strength move beneath his hand, Captain Rossow gripped harder. 'Then let her go, or you'll regret it if something happens to her.'

'Edward, I'm sorry for not realising that you needed help.' Benjamin said. 'But I promise to get you the best professionals.'

'Which I know all about and don't want.'

'Let us take her.' Benjamin continued to encourage.

'Shut up old man, I know you care nothing for me. Months with you and all I heard was Michael this and Michael that.' He turned his head as he heard approaching sirens.

'Grandfather, he loses his temper very quickly.' Michael warned.

'He's like a child. All he needs is a strong hand.'

'And you're it? This isn't the first time he's hurt someone.' Michael pulled away from Captain Rossow. 'You think you know him? You're just stubborn and I hope you know what you're doing.'

'Don't come any closer.' Grabbing Christie tightly to his chest, Edward waved the gun at the three silhouettes, then, he pulled the trigger. Mesmerised, he watched one of the shadows slump over.

'Grandfather,' Michael rushed to the fallen figure.

Benjamin's chest was already stained. 'Perhaps it's fitting I die this way.'

'Don't talk, the ambulance will soon be here.'

'And I won't need it.' A wistful gaze appeared in Benjamin's eyes. 'You've made me proud... and had your parents... He... wouldn't have existed.'

A semi-circle of bright lights appeared behind Edward.

Benjamin coughed. 'Last time anyone will hear me... and I'm glad... it's you. I hated your mother so long, thought she was... grasping...' He took a painful breath. 'Thirty years ago, things looked different, and I felt nothing. The pain... came later... when I found myself alone. I have many regrets, but only one desire... for both your parents to forgive me. I was a coward... who had no courage to face your mother again.' Tears streamed down Benjamin's face. 'I changed the will last year... before I knew about him.' He made a gesture towards Edward. 'Meant to amend it... but Powells, and the mansion, would have been yours, regardless. Sorry... you have to look after him.' A weak hand pulled Michael closer. Benjamin spoke for about five minutes, something only Michael could hear, and then he closed his eyes.

Dropping him slowly to the ground, Michael looked up to see Captain Rossow. 'I still wanted to know so much. To tell him- Is my wife all right?'

'Edward asked for a blanket and says only you may take it to him. Seemed surprised when I told him he hit his grandfather. Apparently, the bullet was intended for you. And this is why I want you nowhere near him.'

'And I'm past being afraid. Where is it?'

Motioning to a paramedic, Captain Rossow took a blanked from him and held out a bullet-proof-vest to Michael. 'Put this on.'

'It won't be necessary.' Michael stepped into the semi-circle of light.

Edward stared. 'Who would have believed it; you and me, and quite surprisingly, I do have this desire to have you up close, brother! But that's close enough, throw it here.' Waving the gun carelessly, he dropped it.

Never one for wasting opportunities, Michael rushed forward and grabbed Christie out of Edward's grip.

It took Edward two seconds to retrieve the black object from the sand. Spinning the barrel, he pointed it at Michael's chest. 'How about Russian roulette?'

'Don't shoot.' Michael shouted.

'Begging? Only cowards do that.' Edward mocked.

'I'm not asking you; I'm asking them, idiot. Shoot me and you'll be turned into a sieve.'

'My, how very brotherly. Of course, there is another option.' Edward put the gun in his mouth.

Michael felt as if he were paralysed, watching in slow motion. Someone took Christie from him and he rushed forward. Seeing the finger on the trigger, he wished he was closer, then stopped in horror and closed his eyes; feeling the eerie silence preceding the loud explosion.

'Ha ha ha, should see your face.' Edward roared at his own joke, a few police officers already beside him, taking the gun away, cuffing him. 'Oh Michael, did you really believe that I wanted to end my miserable life so easily?'

But Michael was running towards the ambulance.

'Celeste!' Robert greeted half-amused as he watched her disembark. 'Getting used to jungle life, I see.'

'Don't start. I hate every moment of being a meal to a million bugs. Hello, Thomas.'

He hugged her warmly as he tried to avoid having an eye put out by her straw hat. 'Hello. Let me guess, those English people won't leave you alone.'

'Not only that, it's also such a good deal.'

'Didn't I tell you months ago that I'm not interested? I don't want strangers traipsing all over my house, asking questions I don't want to answer, and touching things they have no right to.' Grabbing a fishing net from a pole, he started walking towards the house.

She ran after him. 'You have produced excellent work all your life, people have seen some in the papers, RiverRax, and those posters that other place used to print, why not do something special now?'

'I seem to recall that I already asked this question as well. Do you believe that SMITTEN's pages will do my work justice?' Opening the door, he stood aside for her to enter.

'Thomas!' Celeste exclaimed in delight, her hands flying up to her mouth in astonishment. 'They're exquisite.' She stared at the six-foot black and white prints against the walls. 'I see what you mean; no magazine can ever show their true beauty. But,' she clicked her fingers in the air.

'The price has also gone up. Think what you could do with,' she mentioned a sum.

'Pounds?' He whistled. 'They're mad. And what would I do with it in the jungle? Besides, if I wanted money I'd have stayed in South Africa.'

'Forget the money, think of the exposure. I know you're the best photographer in the world, let the world know it too. And you should have done this years ago, but would you listen?'

'Do you know how disruptive a fashion shoot is? Because that's what this is. They don't work the way I do.' Opening the fridge, he took out some drinks. 'There are cables, lamps, people, and things all over the place.' He pointed to the room. 'I like things the way they are.'

'If this was any other magazine I'd say okay, forget it! But it's SMITTEN and they want to use some of the most famous names in the modelling world.'

'Such as?' He asked without interest.

She pulled a notebook from her bag. 'They'd like three different models to represent the three decade of your work.' She read their names.

'All blondes?'

'They can colour their hair, or wear wigs.' She pointed to one of the prints against the wall. 'Picture them next to that.'

'Good, but no deal. I want peace and quiet, not a carnival in the jungle. Besides, my neighbours would never forgive me.'

'What neighbours?'

He pointed to the window where two spider monkeys sat on a branch outside. 'It would be criminal to bring those people down here, and the junk they'd leave behind could kill off any number of ecosystems. Sorry, I'm not aiding and abetting-'

A hand flew to her head. 'Is that your biggest concern?'

'Isn't it enough? And I don't understand the interest, isn't there anyone else they can bother? What about Helmut Schmidt, Francois du Pont?'

'This is my fault, I didn't explain. They're celebrating twenty years.' She grabbed an old newspaper from her bag and handed it to him. 'Remember?'

'How could I forget, we almost lost our lives chasing this damn Axel Corporation.' He stared at the front-page picture that had become famous around the world. 'I don't see the connection.'

'Same day,' she pointed to the date on an old magazine cover. 'SMITTEN's launch. So they went into the past, to find someone who had done something extraordinary on that day. What could be more outstanding than a handsome photographer who almost single-handedly stopped a multi-million dollar business from dumping mercury into the Amazon River?'

'I didn't do it alone. You were there, so was… what was his name?'

'Ricco, made a bundle in telecommunications.'

'Good. But I still can't see why it has to be me.'

'Because you're smart, talented, handsome, mysterious, and an Englishman.'

'Ugh!' He gave her a crooked grin. 'I can imagine how you elevated my status in my absence. Celeste, I'd go nuts if they came here. Not to mention this small army, they'd never survive it. This is not exactly downtown London or Paris.'

'Then I've just had a brilliant idea.'

'And I can't wait to hear it.'

'Let me exhibit your work in Sao Paulo. You don't want people here, they won't come, they can mess my gallery. This way, SMITTEN gets their shoot and you show the world your genius. What do you think?'

'I don't need this, Celeste.'

'Yes you do, and it will be wonderful.'

He looked thoughtful. 'If I agree, may I make some suggestions?'

'Of course,' she told him excitedly and grabbed a pen. 'In fact, SMITTEN's editor begged you make a few of those. Shoot.'

Sitting down, he looked meditatively at the nearest print, then leaning over, he grabbed one of the magazines Celeste had left behind the last time she'd been there. 'First, I do not want three models and definitely not blonde. I want this one.' He pointed to the smiling face on the page. 'And, they should use a baby in some of the shots; I'll give you a list. If they comply, I agree to both their shoot and your exhibition, as I won't have it here. The money,' he was quiet a moment. 'Find some worthy organisations in Sao Paulo and Xingu I can give it to.'

Not certain if it was day or night, Christie opened her eyes. Almost complete darkness greeted her, making it difficult to see where she was. She had often heard that it was always dark in the beginning, so what kind was she about to embark upon? If Edward was anywhere near then she already felt the gloom his mere presence brought.

As her eyes became accustomed to the darkness, she noticed the blind was a little up, letting the night shadows in. Moving her free hand, she found another. Probing carefully, she wondered if it was Edward's, until her fingers found the ring. He had never worn one, not even his wedding band. Then her heart beat faster, feeling breathless as incredible recognition filtered into her brain. 'Mi-chael,'

Lifting his head, his fingers closed tightly around hers as if he too was afraid this might be a dream and rising quickly, he snapped the light switch above the bed. Leaning over, he kissed her; softly, lovingly, making them both cry. 'Welcome back, sweetheart,' he said with difficulty.

Unable to speak, she threw her arms around him and sobbed.

Later, after many explanations, much apologising, and more tears, they sat gazing at each other.

'How is the baby?' She asked, her eyes filling with tears anew. 'May I see him?'

'Of course, but he's at Sandra's with Gloria.' Smiling, he tucked a lock of dark hair behind her ear. 'He's beautiful, Christie. Just like you.'

'I thought he looked like you.'

'He does, even if blond.' Taking her hand, he held it against his face. 'How I regret not being with you all this time.'

'Are you very angry with me?'

'No, you had no way of knowing.'

'I should've waited for Thea to explain, but I was in such shock.'

'I know. Naturally, the press had a field day. Actually, it was more like months of hell as they hounded, speculated, and guessed.'

'And I'm sorry to have caused it all. Where's Edward?'

'Under observation. As things stand, it's unlikely criminal charges will be brought against him, either here or Greece, and there's quite a list. In the meantime, I've requested they transfer him to Johannesburg. His mother is there, so it might do him good to be near her. Unexpectedly, I have responsibilities... I don't know if you know-'

'That you're brothers?'

'Can you believe it? But we two are definitely not related. Now, all I want to do is sit here looking at you.' Letting his hands go into her hair, he pulled her close.

CHAPTER NINETEEN

'Michael Thomas! How do you do that?' Christie walked over to his playpen and extended a hand. 'Give me those.'

He gurgled as he stuck a paintbrush in his mouth.

Taking the brush away, she wiped his mouth. 'These are mommy's, and those,' she pointed to the discarded toys. 'Are yours.' Picking him up, she walked over to the basin.

'Christie?' Michael called a while later.

'In here.'

Entering the studio, he grinned. She was lying on her back in the middle of the playpen, Michael Thomas sitting on her chest. 'What are you doing?'

'Playing,' getting to her feet, she kissed Michael and put the child in his arms.

Returning the kiss, he dropped another on the small blond head. 'Where's Nichola?'

'The gang appeared,' Christie smiled and started tidying up around the easel. 'And they all went out. You're early.'

'I needed a break. Plus, I got some news. He found him.'

'Him?' Asking blankly, she then put her head around the easel. 'You mean your father, where?'

'Brazil.' He studied Michael Thomas' blue eyes, not exactly like Christie's. Sofia said they were Robert's.

Christie watched Michael. Ever since Benjamin's death he had tried too hard, sometimes giving her cause for concern as she saw this hankering becoming an obsession, this constant exigency to know where he fit. Seeing and feeling his disappointment every time a lead became a dead-end. Now as she saw his face, she was aware of how much it meant to him. 'So?'

Pulling a paper from his pocket, he handed it to her. 'Newa sent me an email.'

Unfolding the paper, she read; '*World-renowned Photographer to hold FIRST EVER exhibition in SAO PAULO.*' She looked at him. 'I can't believe it! This man has been lost almost thirty years and now here he is. But how did Newa get this?' Her eyes opened wide with realisation. 'Of course, if it has anything to do with an exhibition or exposition she collects it. I remember seeing them all over her office.' She looked at him quizzically. 'I didn't know she went to Brazil.'

'A friend of hers did and brought it along.'

'I know you want it to be.' She perused the paper more closely. 'Thomas Robertson!' Her head shot up in recognition. 'What... I don't get it.'

'I didn't either, until this.' He pulled another email. 'An exact copy from Hamilton, and a detailed report that states that Thomas Robertson and Robert Thomas Powell are the same man.'

'But... If it is, how did Newa make the connection?'

'She didn't, merely sent it because she discovered through Gloria that I love his work. I can't believe that a man whose work I've admired all my life turns out to be my father. Hamilton is still trying to get his hands on recent photographs but says he's 99% certain this is he. But he doesn't live in Sao Paulo, stays in the Jungle, so that makes it a little tricky to get an address.'

'I realise Mr Hamilton is a professional, and he did discover that your father emigrated to Brazil, but you have to be prepared that this might not be the right man.'

'If it isn't then what have I lost?'

"More than you're admitting," she thought, her hand going to his face in a caress. 'Do you suppose Thea still loves him?'

'She doesn't say much on the subject, does she?'

'Yes, it's very hard for her to talk about the past.'

Appraising the flat building across the street, Michael thought it an odd mixture of styles. He read the name; GALERIA MODERNA and recalled the elation he'd felt when Ian Hamilton told him that Thomas Robertson and Robert Thomas Powell were definitely the same person.

'Where are the pictures?'

'Here,' Hamilton offered a wildlife magazine. 'First, I looked in the library and came up with this.' He threw a few newspaper copies on the desk. 'It was there that the Librarian pointed me to Mr Robertson's latest commissions. He works for RiverRax. Page twenty three.' He pointed as Michael flicked through the magazine. 'Apart from that dated snapshot, there's nothing else to be found.'

Michael stared at the face. 'Excellent, thank you.'

That very day, he asked Christie to pack so they could be in Sao Paulo before Thomas Robertson's opening night. He wanted to see this man, and soon. There was a huge question mark over what he was going to find or what he'd say, but whatever it took, he was certainly going to try convincing him to go home.

Returning to the present, Michael looked up and down the street, and then strode purposely towards the entrance. The glass doors opened quietly and he was rewarded with a cool interior, as well as two sculpted mermaids standing silent guard. Wandering through the building, he found what he was looking for. Unfortunately, there wasn't much to see, thick ropes cutting the passage in a strange spider-like web. A security guard said something in Portuguese, leaving no doubt that he took his job seriously.

'I apologise, I don't understand.'

'He told you that opening night is tomorrow. Are you interested in this collection?'

Turning, Michael saw a very attractive woman. 'Very much.'

'To buy or to appreciate?' She flashed a beautiful smile.

'Is any of it for sale?' He saw her shake her head. 'I didn't expect it to be. Will Mr Robertson be present at the opening?'

'He does not enjoy crowds but I have made him promise to at least appear for thirty minutes. I am correct to assume that you are not on my guest list?'

'I am not.'

'You know his work well?'

'Since I was a child.'

She regarded him closely. 'Come to Sao Paulo often?'

'My first time.'

'Business or pleasure?'

'Neither, I'm here for personal reasons.'

'Ah, a woman.'

Amusement filled him. 'Do you always ask this many questions of strangers?'

'Only of those who interest me. My name is Celeste,' she offered a hand.

'Pleased to meet you. I'm Michael A-'

'Michael?'

Turning around, he stood in stunned silence.

'As I suspected, a beautiful woman. Hello Evy, you know this gentleman?'

'Yes!' Throwing her arms around Michael's neck, Evy smacked his cheek with pleasure. 'I can't believe it, what are you doing here?'

'I was just about to ask the same thing.' Pushing her a little away, he looked her up and down. 'As beautiful as ever but since you went Down Under and won that model of the year thing, we've hardly seen you.'

'I call.'

'Once a month, but what are you doing here?'

'Trust you to know nothing about the modelling world. Although, I am impressed that you heard I won, so I was in the right place at the right time when SMITTEN came knocking. Would you believe I'm here to be photographed with Thomas Robertson's masterpieces?'

Celeste looked from the one to the other. 'Pity you do not have an invitation. Unfortunately, I have already invited all the people I can without the place looking like a market. But after tomorrow night the exhibition will be open to the public.'

'Don't you know that everyone wants to meet Thomas Robertson?' Evy announced.

'Yes, and it makes him a very unhappy man.'

Evy put her hand on Michael's arm. 'As I have two, I'll give you one.'

Celeste made a face as if Evy had committed sacrilege. 'That invitation was entrusted to you for Mr Neto, SMITTEN's representative in Brazil and I do not think London will be amused if you come with someone else.'

'And of course I want to be on Mr Neto's arm instead of Michael's. And why won't you allow anyone in without a piece of paper? Are you afraid someone might try to destroy the exhibition or is it Thomas Robertson you're afraid for?'

'He has done work many people don't appreciate so it is better to be safe.'

'Has he actually agreed to be here? I'd have thought this isn't his type of thing at all.' Michael said almost to himself. 'RiverRax-'

A look of consternation appeared on Celeste's face. 'You are from RiverRax? Why did you not say? And I promise we read the contract very carefully and are not breaking it by doing this.'

About to correct her, he decided to rely on the confusion. 'Then I may have an invitation?'

'Of course, I have five for absolute emergencies. But you should have said...'

Celeste stuck her head around the silk screen.

'More people trying to get invitations?'

Better not tell him RiverRax had sent someone or he might just disappear. 'In a way, the girl is your model.'

Robert looked at her uncomprehendingly. 'Oh! I don't know why I agreed to this.' He scratched his bearded face.

'Is that why you grew that thing, to hide from prying eyes?'

'Maybe I'm just anti-social.'

'And this is why it is by invitation only, no matter who they say they are.' She glanced around the huge prints. 'I was also careful to only solicit the company of people who will respect your privacy, somewhat. But we'll soon know if living in the jungle has diminished your social skills. Stop worrying, there's no need for apprehension.' Perhaps that wasn't entirely true, with RiverRax in the neighbourhood-

'There was a young man earlier, seems very keen to meet you.' At least later, he couldn't accuse her of never mentioning it. 'He was introducing himself when Evy pounced on him.' A smile passed her dark eyes. 'What I wouldn't give to be twenty years younger.'

'I know the intention was to spend the evening alone, but Evy is here. Do you mind very much?' Michael asked as he kissed Christie's naked shoulder in front of the mirror.

She gave him a wonderful smile. 'Of course not, it's always nice to run into old friends.'

The evening turned out better than either expected. Evy imagined she might hate Christie for catching Michael's heart, instead, she discovered herself free of the girlish crush. And Christie… well, she liked Evy, they were friends, and she could see something had changed in Evy's demeanour towards Michael.

'How long will you be here?' Christie asked curiously.

'We go to the Amazon in three days. SMITTEN tried to strike a deal to have me photographed where Thomas Robertson lives but he wouldn't budge.' Her brows lifted prettily. 'Said that if the Government has no sense and gave us permission to go walk in places we have no business doing; that's their loss, but that he wouldn't help us obliterate any ecosystems. The thing is, his work is excellent, and he knows it, so he basically told SMITTEN they're fortunate he let us near his collection at all. They were desperate so they agreed to everything he demanded.' A beautiful hand made a graceful gesture. 'Listen lovebirds, I see my driver,' she beckoned to someone. 'I have to leave now if I want to get up tomorrow morning looking half-decent.'

Christie smiled, certain the man at the next table had become hypnotised when Evy rose to her full height. 'Have you met Thomas Robertson?'

'Never saw him. And would you believe I have a TV breakfast show to do? They're going to ask me all sorts of things and what do I know; only that his work is great and I wish he'd photograph me. How about lunch, Christie?'

'Sure.'

'I'll check my schedule and call you.' Then with a wave, Evy left the dining room, leaving men gaping as she breezed through the tables.

'Ah Michael,' Celeste looked him up and down, noticing how handsome he was. A simple pair of jeans and a chequered shirt was his attire this morning, but nothing looked simple on him, a strong sensuality emanating from him.

'Morning, I'd like to know if you saw Mr Robertson and mentioned that I wish to speak with him.'

'He will see you tonight.'

'It's not possible I see him privately before then?'

RiverRax was definitely after something. 'He doesn't see people and I usually deal with his affairs. Give me your card?' She didn't want this, whatever it was, erupting into a row and have Thomas disappear.

Perhaps Robert had forgotten the name. Now, Andriotti could mean as much as Smith would, but he couldn't chance losing him after being so close. 'I will explain when I see Mr Robertson.'

'As you wish.' Curiosity filled her as she watched him walk away.

'Ola, Celeste.'

She turned quickly. 'I didn't know you were here. He was.'

'Who?'

'The young man I mentioned yesterday.' She told him dismissively.

'Hope he's not one of those desperados I've encountered so often.' Robert pointed towards the wall. 'I hate that lot, as I knew I would. How much longer are they going to be clicking their cameras?'

'I don't understand you, never have, and how many years have we known each other?'

'It's better this way.'

'For whom?' Then she changed her tone of voice. 'What are you going to do after this, return to the jungle?'

'Funny you should ask, I've been wondering myself. I'm not as young as I used to be and I can't imagine paddling rivers in my old age.'

'Why don't you settle down, get married,' there was a wistful note in her voice.

'No, my time is past.' He gazed at the wall with a distant look.

'I wish I knew the woman who made you this way, she took everything.'

'What's the matter?' Evy queried as a terrible racket broke out both in English and Portuguese.

'The baby model has taken ill, teething!' A cameraman announced and burst out laughing.

'Find another,' she said matter-of-fact.

'That's the problem.' Another cameraman said as he pointed at his watch. 'It's Friday, too late and we have to be out of here by three. Opening night, remember? Where do we find a baby at such short notice?'

'I know where we can find one.' Sitting in the chair, she realised a dozen pair of eyes were staring at her. 'If the parents agree.' She added quickly.

'Call, go there, do something. There's no time to waste.'

'Okay,' she grabbed the phone someone stuck in her face.

Reaching Evy, Christie smiled. 'Lucky you called when you did, I was about to go sightseeing.'

'Where's Michael?'

'At the library, for all we know this is a merry chase.'

'What?'

'Sorry, thinking out loud. So, what are we doing? I thought you were working.'

'I am, and I apologise for getting you here under false pretences. I hope you won't be mad but we desperately need your help. Well, Michael Thomas' really. May we borrow him?'

'Whatever for?'

'The shoot. Our baby fell ill and everyone is going nuts.' Evy pointed to the wall. 'We're on a tight schedule and every minute counts. Please say yes.'

'But he's little and Michael-'

'He doesn't have to do anything but sit on my lap. Just a few shots, perhaps an hour, we have strict rules concerning working children. Please.'

A smile crossed Christie's lips. 'Who knows, he might just succeed where his father fails.'

'What?'

'Thinking out loud again,'

To everyone's surprise, including Christie's, Michael Thomas seemed to have been born for this very purpose.

He smiled when told to, gurgled happily when spoken to, and practically did what the photographer wanted before he asked for it. 'I love this child, he's a natural.' The man threw his arms in the air with pleasure.

Christie sat for a while, wondering how models endured the rigours of work, then realising Michael Thomas didn't need her, she wandered through the rest of the exhibition. Every picture was stunning, but this was something else. Standing in front of Amazonian Indians, she was suddenly aware of a man watching her from behind a giant screen. 'I apologise if I'm intruding.'

He answered in English. 'You're welcome, as long as there isn't a busload of children following you.'

'Only one little boy, and he's back there.' Giving him a quick smile, she returned her gaze to the Indians.

'You like that one,' he waved a hammer.

'It's the most incredible thing. It's as if they're three-dimensional and about to speak to me. They're all beautiful but this one defies description.'

'It's also my favourite,' he smeared the denim pants with dirt.

'You look very busy so let me detain you no further.'

He waved and watched her disappear from sight.

'He's incredible.' Evy announced as she dropped Michael Thomas in Christie's arms.

'Should try it when he's tired or hungry. They're not going to print his name.'

'Not if you don't want them to, and I can already see Michael freaking out,' Evy laughed. 'I'm sorry you can't come tonight. Regrettably, I haven't been out much and now I don't know who to bribe for an extra invitation, as Celeste will have none of it.'

'Stop apologising, it's all right.'

Walking out onto the pavement, Christie tried to hail a taxi, but none seemed to be paying her much attention.

'Sao Paulo's hospitality?' A man asked next to her.

'Hello,' she greeted with recognition. 'Maybe I'm doing it wrong.'

A quick glance down the street assessed the situation. 'We'll have to wait a few minutes. So, this is the little fellow.' He ruffled the child's hair. Turning, Michael Thomas put a small hand to the beard. 'Not afraid of strangers.'

'There comes one.' Christie noticed as a bus stopped a few hundred metres away.

The bus carried on its way and her companion waved at the oncoming taxi. 'Are you coming tonight?'

Her gaze fell as the vehicle stopped in front of them. 'I'm afraid not, which is why I had a sneak peek. But my husband has been fortunate enough to get an invitation.'

'Your husband is coming without you?'

'Oh, it's nothing like that,' she gave him a dazzling smile.

Putting a hand in his pocket, he pulled out an envelope. 'We can't have that. Celeste will probably kill me, but who cares?'

'I couldn't possibly accept.' She told him with consternation.

'*Ola,*' the taxi driver honked. '*Voce quer ir ou que?*'

'He's in a hurry.'

'But I can't accept. How will you get in?'

'Celeste is just being difficult.' Helping her into the vehicle, he waved. 'Besides, it's my exhibition.'

The car was already speeding away. 'What? Driver, stop! Please wait.' Climbing out, she watched Robert get into a Jeep across the street and drive away in the opposite direction. She kicked the pavement in frustration.

'Hello,' Michael greeted as he walked into the bedroom and saw her sitting at the desk. 'Sorry I left you alone so long,' he stopped as he saw the expression of excitement on her face. 'What?'

Picking an envelope from the desk, she waved it at him and then pulled the card from inside. 'And what do you think about this?'

'Where did you get it?'

'A long story and it began when Evy called.'

'You did what?' He sunk into an armchair. 'Michael Thomas modelling,'

'He grows so quickly no one will know it's him by the time the magazine comes out.'

'I don't like this sort of thing for him.'

Rising from the chair, she went to sit on his lap. 'Well, desperate times call for desperate measures.'

'Celeste said the guest list was complete, but I suppose she had to dig out another invitation for services rendered.'

'No, Michael Thomas worked and I snooped around. It's the most fascinating thing and you have to see it even if you don't speak with him. Then, as I waited for a taxi, Mr Robertson himself gave it to me.' She gave him an edited version of their exchange of words. 'Have you thought about what you're going to say?'

'I'm hoping I'll do my Greek ancestors proud and become a great orator. But I've been wondering. He might resent me for intruding in whatever life he's built.'

She caressed his face. 'This is the hard part but try keeping your personal feelings out of it. Just give him the facts and let him make his own decision.'

Pulling her closer, he kissed the side of her face. 'How did you get to be so smart?'

'I made a few mistakes myself.'

From a distance, Celeste watched Christie with immense interest, wondering who she was as Michael was supposed to have come with Evy. Probably another model, though, she looked a little short for it, but that she was beautiful there was no doubt.

To Michael's disappointment, Robert was nowhere to be seen when Celeste made her opening speech, and he smiled with amusement as she gave a concocted excuse about some traffic jam in the city. Then, impatient curiosity took her to him. 'And who is this beautiful lady?'

'Christie, my wife.'

For the first time, she looked at his hand where the gold-band shone brightly. 'But where did you get an extra invitation? I know they are all accounted for.'

'Mr Pow- Mr Robertson gave it to me this afternoon.'

'How very fortunate.' Celeste couldn't imagine how that had happened. Then Evy appeared draped in a magnificent black creation and took them away, soon gathering half the men around herself and Christie. Now she was simply dying to know who they were and what they wanted.

'Hello.'

Turning, Celeste smiled and put a hand to Robert's face. 'I thought you might shave it off.' She watched SMITTEN's editor begin a conversation with Michael, take him towards two Brazilian men, and disappear from sight. 'That persistent young man I told you about is here. And I hear you gave his wife an invitation, yours?'

'What could you do, lock me out? They almost did at the door.' He searched around the room and fixed his gaze on Christie. 'Absolutely stunning.'

'But too young for you.'

'I don't want her, my camera does. Besides, young married women are not my type.'

'Planning to go into the portrait business?'

'Hardly, these would be special. I just had an idea when I saw her earlier.'

'Come to think of it,' Celeste said thoughtfully. 'They don't look like people who pose for public consumption.'

'Their son does, why not her?'

What was it with these people? From the moment they had arrived, they had more or less taken to living here.

'So, what should I do?' He asked and glanced around the room. He knew no one.

She smiled. 'Mingle and listen to people criticising everything.'

'I'm beginning to believe your hermit theory. Have you noticed that everyone we speak to doesn't know what he looks like?' Michael told Evy.

'Some people are funny that way. Why do you want to see him, another wonderful advertising campaign?'

'Evy,' a man interrupted. 'You have to meet these people. They're discussing a new skin range and I immediately thought of you.' He took her away.

Christie glanced at a spotted jaguar. 'Conclusion,'

'Outstanding work, but I was always partial to it. An excellent eye for detail, as if he uses his drawing background to compose the shots. Notice how perfect they are. Probably waits for hours, if not days for just the

right moment, and must have uncommon patience.'
Looking up, Michael saw Evy beckoning to him. 'I'll be right back.'

Christie found herself in front of the Indians again, thinking of what Michael had just said.

'Still analysing this one?'

Turning, she stared at him. Those were definitely Michael Thomas' eyes, but the nose was Michael's. It was odd seeing parts of loved faces on a stranger. Would Michael look like this at fifty? How would Sofia react if she saw him?

'I feel positively stripped after that examination. I also have no doubt that female intuition has revealed all and there is nothing I can hide from you.'

'I beg your pardon; I didn't mean to appear rude. It's just that-' "I see both my son and my husband in your face." 'It's an honour to make your acquaintance, Mr Robertson.' She offered him a hand.

He shook it lightly. 'See, how did you, out of all these people know it's me? I believe your husband would like to have a word with me, may I ask concerning what?'

'As much as I'd like to it's not my place to say. This may seem strange as we don't know each other, but on behalf of my husband, I'm extending you an invitation to visit him at the Marques Towers, suite 502. If you could give him a few hours, it would clear up so much. Here,' she made a circle with her hand. 'Is not the place for discussions of this magnitude.'

'It sounds intriguing.'

'Please Mr Robertson, I know that you seeing Michael would be beneficial, for both of you.'

'Ah, Celeste needs me.' He announced as he saw her beckoning. 'But I admit, you have aroused my curiosity and

I'll see what I can do about making an appointment.' Walking towards Celeste, he wondered what they could possibly be after. Later, he'd quickly hear what the young man had to say, if only with the intention of using her in what he was beginning to perceive as one of his best ideas yet.

Michael came to stand at Christie's side. 'Now I recall why I was never partial to the modelling business.'

'I asked him to see you.'

'He was here? Why don't I ever see this man? Did he agree?'

'I imagine he's wondering what I meant when I never really explained.'

'Andriotti, Mr Michael Robert Andriotti, an urgent phone-call.' A voice announced.

Michael walked over immediately and took the receiver. 'Thank you.' He listened for a few seconds. 'We'll be right there.' Returning the object to the man, he grabbed Christie's hand. 'Let's go.'

As they rushed out of the building, they didn't see Robert in a corner staring after them, looking as if the GALERIA had just exploded. 'Andriotti,' he whispered to himself. His gaze turned automatically to a print half-hidden in a dark corner. The only self-portrait he had ever shot. Except for the colouring, it was almost Michael's young face.

'Why are you hiding?' Celeste asked. 'Thomas, are you all right? You look as if you've just seen a ghost.'

He looked at her strangely. That was exactly it. 'That young man who would like to see me, introduce me to someone who knows him.'

'Of all the people here, you ask for a model. Sure, why not?' It was the first time he requested it and she found it peculiar. This wasn't the man she knew, the man who never let anything bother him, the man who she sometimes thought had no human emotions, he was so panic-stricken she could feel it.

Robert walked the streets of Sao Paulo that night, his mind in turmoil. How was it possible that this young man had travelled across half a world to find him? Because it was no coincidence that he was here. Talking to Evy had been like opening rusty floodgates. Once the sludge of ancient memories had come slowly, the deep raging waters of anger and fury filled him as he heard about things Benjamin had done.

Benjamin had known Michael, while he, his father, had lived in anguish and guilt, day after day going through a destruction of spirit. He had often dreamt of this son, always being filled with bittersweet memories when he met a young man of the same age; when November crept on to remind him that yet another year had passed.

Something puzzled him. How was it possible that Michael carried the Andriotti surname? Had Sofia managed to track him down? If so, he was glad. Who had discovered where he had disappeared? Decades might have passed but the sword of hurt was still deeply plunged as he recalled his father's callousness.

Michael's second name was Robert. He smiled faintly. Had Sofia given it to him? He'd loved her to such an extent that he had never again been able to conduct a successful relationship, not even with Celeste and she had somehow touched his heartstrings, managing to fill some of the emptiness. If they ran into each other again, could they find something in common again?

Stopping in front of a window, he glanced at his shadow, for that was he, lonely and dark. Slowly turning on his heels, he sauntered away. Perhaps if he walked all night things might feel and look differently when the sun rose.

Morning arrived and he wasn't certain where he'd been, but was suddenly aware that he was outside the Marques Towers. Stepping into the coffee shop across the street, he ordered a cup of the brown liquid and sat staring at it for a long time. Eventually, without touching it, he left the establishment, then, glancing towards the heavens as if for reassurance, he crossed the street.

'My baby,' Christie cooed as she picked Michael Thomas out of his bed, eyed the purple bruise, and kissed him. Hugging him to her, she took him back to their bed.

'Umm.' Michael watched the bump critically as he entered from the bathroom wearing a towel.

'He'll be fine. I just detest it when all sense flies out your window.'

Grabbing another towel, he rubbed his wet hair. 'You know how I feel about bumps to the head.'

'And I'm sorry this little mishap might have ruined your chances.'

'I'll go by the gallery and tell Celeste the truth.'

'He's very private.' Christie reminded him.

'I know privacy, this borders on eccentricity. What are you doing?'

'Dressing him to take him down for breakfast and a walk. I'm sure he'll enjoy fresh air after this.'

'Will you be long?' He grabbed her around the waist and pulled her to him. 'You look wonderful.' Dropping his head, he kissed her.

She pushed him away with regret. 'So do you, but I'll see you later.'

After dressing, Michael wondered what he should do. Probably demand Celeste get hold of Robert before he disappeared into the jungle again. He was getting tired of this trying to get an audience with "Mr Thomas Robertson". Opening a drawer, he paged through the papers and magazines Hamilton had accumulated.

Thomas Robertson had been a busy man; there were dozens of front-page articles he had worked on with Celeste Batista. They had covered wars, Indian killings, village murders, forest fires, and land stripping. With his lens and her words, they had made a formidable team. But through it all, no one seemed to know much about him, with perhaps the exception of Celeste.

A knock at the door returned him to the moment. Tidying all papers on top of each other, he threw them back into the drawer and wondered what Sofia would say if she knew what he was doing. Walking over, he opened the door and saw a man in a tuxedo. 'May I help you?'

'Good morning, Michael. May I come in?'

'In connection with what is this?'

The stranger watched him keenly. 'You tell me, since you're the one who's been trying to see me.'

Michael stared a moment. 'You're Thomas Robertson?'

'I was until yesterday. Today, I no longer know. So, what is it you came to say?'

'Celeste?' Michael queried for lack of knowing what else to say.

Robert shook his head. 'Evy.'

Michael motioned to the sofa. 'How much do you know?'

'Probably not everything I should.' Robert watched as Michael passed a hand over his eyes. How could two people who had never seen each other share mannerisms so alike? But he soon forgot about trivialities, feeling numb as Michael began a tale he thought he'd known all the facts to. 'My father had you adopted by your uncle? This is the vilest deed I ever heard of! I hated him back then, but this, it's contemptible, absolutely beyond forgiveness.'

'And yet, that's the only thing he wanted before dying. I too despised him and his methods of manipulation and he knew it. Regardless, he contributed in the search for Christie, and for that, I'll be eternally grateful. Of course, he wasn't to know that his newly acquired grandson was also the very person responsible for all our sorrows.'

'If he hadn't killed him, I'd do it myself. That selfish, pompous, grasping man... How many lives destroyed, and all through underhanded manoeuvring! But why did you feel the need to inform me of this now?' But the words coming out of his mouth hardly expressed what he felt, and leaning back on the sofa, Robert felt a wave of tired melancholy sweep over him.

'Because I believe that you shouldn't end your life in darkness. I tried to find you years ago but as I had no idea where to start, it soon came to naught. After Benjamin died, I hired a private investigator, Hamilton's son, who eventually tracked you down here. As RiverRax is not available in Greece, South Africa, or Britain, I'd never have guessed that you were Thomas Robertson, whose work I have always admired. When I first heard this story, I too was angry, my fury matched only by my contempt for you and my mother. And knowing Benjamin's character, would you have expected him to confess? Yet he did. I don't know if it was for him or me that I came, but I am here, dealing with circumstances the best way I can.'

'Almost thirty years… we can never change that.'

'I know. And I know too that it's near impossible to retrieve what has been lost, but I would like Michael Thomas to have the chance to get to know you. I suppose I'm offering you my son as a substitute as you never had the chance to be a father.'

'What I'll always know is that I should have listened to me! Not let my father bulldoze and demolish. When I finally returned home, it was too late, all intended damage already done. My heart was torn from me and there was no way for it to be mended. Now, I've spent too many years hating to ever do anything else.'

'Benjamin's deeds were inexcusable, but not unpardonable. Look, I didn't come to dig up skeletons but rather to lay them to rest, and perhaps to bring you some sort of peace. Life unfolds through the choices we make and if I had stayed in South Africa, things could have unfolded differently; Edward and I could have been true brothers, the disease might never have become evident, the possibilities are endless.

'Now, this is where we are and I'm satisfied in having done what I set out to do. I can't tell you to return for someone you had no idea existed, as you have your own ghosts to fight and conquer. But you should consider it and not only for Edward's sake.

'No matter what my personal feelings, Powells is a South African giant and I can't simply let it die. Buyers have already approached the attorneys but it feels inappropriate to make deals when I'm not even a true Powell.'

'I walked the entire night speculating over what Evy told me... I didn't choose this path, it was forced upon me. Perhaps it was wrong of me to embrace loneliness, but now I'm so used to it that I don't want to let it go.'

'Only those who love can be hurt, and that's why you're here, because you loved deeply. Why don't you give it another try, in whatever form it will present itself?'

Ever since hearing of this son's existence, he'd watched other fathers and sons enviously, because even amongst the most primitive of tribes, he'd seen this special bond between two men. Would he have loved? And had he not, even if not knowing the face? 'I have to go.' Rising to his feet, Robert extended a hand to this strange part of himself.

Gazing at the hand, Michael shook it half-heartedly. 'Will you at least have dinner with us? We're leaving tomorrow.'

'I'll let you know.'

Robert found himself walking again, this time all the way back to the GALERIA. Unseen, he slipped into Celeste's office to take a shower.

'Is that you, Thomas?' she asked outside the door.

'Yes. Didn't I leave some clothes here once?'

'If it's still around.' She searched in the bottom of a cupboard. 'Here, a shirt and jeans, no shoes.'

'That's fine.' He took them from her.

No matter if absent or present, she would always love him. But he either pretended or was genuinely unaware that she did so she pretended too and simply carried on being his friend. 'Where were you, obviously not home?'

Giving a cursory glance at the discarded tuxedo, she returned to her desk.

'I walked around, thinking.'

'You think too much.'

'What did people say after I left?' Standing in the doorway, he rubbed his hair with a towel.

'I agree, no more exhibitions for you, unless of course you are actually prepared to give something of yourself. Where did you go after interrogating Evy?'

'I told you, I walked.'

She patted a pile of newspapers on the desk. 'Have you seen the reviews? They're very good.'

'I haven't had the chance, I went to see someone.'

'Evy?'

For the first time in years, he realised that she was still jealous. If he'd been able to love her, perhaps life might have been easier, but he hadn't and he knew that she deserved better, for he was unable to give more. Yet, through all they had remained friends, the only other person apart from himself whom he trusted. That in itself was an accomplishment. Never had she complained or made demands, always loyal, even when he did hurt her, and now he was suspicious that he'd probably done it often. He owed her much. 'Not a woman, a man.'

'Mentioning men, did you ever talk to that one who keeps coming around? What should I tell him if he comes again?'

'He won't, he's the one I went to see.'

Her head went up in surprise. 'He's from RiverRax?'

Robert shook his head. 'Is that what he said?'

'He might have implied, or I thought. What did he want?'

'You were right, they don't want anything.' He gazed at her again; she had reminded him of Sofia. Was that why he'd also asked for Evy, because she was Greek, because he wanted to be reminded of the past? 'Or perhaps he expects too much.'

'What does that mean?'

'He's my son.'

Returning his gaze calmly, she asked softly. 'He came looking for you?'

He nodded. 'I still have another son of whom I knew nothing about, and he's not well.'

She had always known that his ties to the past weren't dead. That one day…

'I can't believe any of this.' He sunk onto the leather sofa. 'He asked me to dinner. I don't know what to do'

'You must go.'

'Have you any idea how I'm feeling? I thought I'd left everything behind. Unexpectedly, my past is here, staring me in the face.'

'I can see it's a shock but you must never miss the opportunity to mend things. I have a lot of work to get through, so you would do well to go meet some of your fans.' She announced.

'I'll do that,' he agreed, stood to his feet and kissed her cheek. 'See you later.' Closing the door, he leaned against it, just in time to hear a sob. He reached for the handle but the phone's shrill stopped him from going in.

'*Ola.*' He heard through the closed door. 'Who do you take me for? I said I want him here next week and that's what I meant, so move your comfortable behind off that cushy seat and get going. What do you think I pay you for?' She shouted into the phone.

Smiling, he knew that she would survive.

'It was too much.' Christie announced as she sat at the dressing table. 'He needs to digest the information. A few minutes or hours can't change years of rituals.'

'Somehow, I imagined it would be different.'

'Who's the romantic now? He needs time and space, so let him be alone to get perspective and to adjust to the idea.'

'In the meantime, what am I supposed to do with Edward, pretend I'm my father? You heard what the doctor said one visit from him could do.'

Getting to her feet, she reached for his hand. 'I know it's difficult, but you have to accept whatever happens.'

'Difficult is not the word. It's taken me a while to come to terms that Edward is my brother, my responsibility. I wonder constantly if I'm doing what's right.' They heard a knock. 'Must be the new baby-sitter, she'd better not let him hurt himself.'

Christie opened the door. 'Mr Powell!'

'Is there place for one more? I wasn't going to come, but Celeste-'

'And we're very glad you did.'

Dinner was a strained affair, Christie finding herself in a few tense moments when both men stared at each other as if studying an opponent. Cleverly, she began new topics of conversation and everything went smoothly until one of them made a remark that the other thought was a personal attack. She found herself talking about coffee plantations, piranhas, panthers, and parrots, and then became increasingly irritated with their lack of enthusiasm, and exhausted trying to avoid a public confrontation. This unspoken disagreement was making

Michael rather ridiculous and she wondered if the meal would end peacefully. Her hopes were dashed when Robert announced,

'I'm going back to Xingu in the morning.'

'What's Xingu?' Michael frowned.

'A river, and it's where I was two weeks ago, oblivious to all of this.'

'Why am I such an idiot that I imagined you'd actually do something?'

'Edward is mad, I'm not a pet he can pat for a few hours, and then there'll be a miraculous recovery.'

'Either this damn jungle made you a cynic or you were always one. If that's the case, then I'll never understand why my mother fell in love with you.'

'Michael, thirty years have passed. If I were to see Sofia, we might discover that we no longer have anything in common. We could even hate each other on sight.'

'And when did I ask you to go back for her? She's not even aware that I'm here. I asked for Edward's sake but above all, my son's. I know we can't adapt to a new situation overnight, it takes effort. You think my mother and I fell comfortably into a new relationship?' Michael shook his head. 'But our circumstances are different and I thought it only fair I give you the chance to retrieve something.'

'And I think I'm grateful. But I've never been a father and now I hear I have not one but two adult sons and a grandson. It's extraordinary and I'm utterly bewildered. I need time to think and separate, not get involved in a wave that threatens to sweep me away. In fact, I'll do everyone a favour by staying away.'

'Do whatever you wish; my mission was to inform you about Edward and Powells. I've done that. I hoped that you and my son might get to know one another but that's entirely up to you.' Michael put the serviette down. 'Christie,'

Robert rose to his feet first. 'No. If anyone leaves, it will be me.'

'Typical. When are you going to stop running?'

'Christie, it was delightful meeting you.' Kissing her hand, Robert left without another word.

'Didn't I tell you?'

'And when are you going to learn to keep that temper of yours?' Jumping to her feet, she rushed outside.

'Perhaps I should go home.' Robert said as he saw her.

'I think so too, you look worn out.'

He'd been right about her; she could look into his soul and with a simple sentence tell him something entirely different. 'I've tracked soldiers and wild animals for days and nights, gone without sleep for extended periods of time, but never felt this exhausted.'

'What we're looking for isn't always ahead, sometimes it's behind.'

'Look, all this is new to me. I have no idea what to do, or what to say to Michael.' He got into the taxi. 'Goodbye Christie.'

Shaking her head sadly, she watched the vehicle drive down the road.

Michael stopped beside her. 'He upsets me by being difficult, because the reason for being away no longer exists. It's as if he's cut himself off from the rest of the human race. He's very talented, but that's it. How can anyone merely live for pictures, with no human contact whatsoever?'

'But Michael, all this is new. He hasn't had time to adjust to the idea that you're real and you're already pushing.'

'That I'm real? He's always known about me.'

'And that might be the problem. Before, you only lived in his mind. It's easy to love an idea; you were what he wanted you to be. Now you're real, you voice ideas, and you become angry. Thought you had nothing in common with Edward, look at your temper. But I digress. The image has been shattered and he needs time.'

That night as he stared unseeingly at the wall, she knew he wasn't about to admit to anyone that he missed and desperately wanted to know his father, perhaps imagining that she would think less of him for admitting to such a basic need. She loved him more, for he was human.

He tossed, turned, and then went into Michael Thomas' room, staying there a long time, Christie knowing that he was watching his own son. On returning, he was restless and couldn't close his eyes. Silently, she pulled him towards her, telling him without words what he already knew, that she loved him with all of her heart.

It was early morning when he finally settled down and fell asleep. "Exhausted," she thought and getting out of bed went to check on Michael Thomas. He too was stirring. Waiting until he woke up, she dressed him, took him down to the nursery, and left the hotel.

Thanking the driver, Christie stared at the building before her. Looking up and down the street, she noticed all edifices were similar in character; they had none, except if one considered peeling paint and gaudy colours character.

Standing outside apartment five, she knocked and glanced down the passage. "Nondescript, how can such a talented man live here?"

It didn't take long for the door to open and it was obvious he'd already been up a long time. 'Christie!'

'May I come in?'

'Please,' standing aside, he closed the door.

Her eyes took everything in. The bare walls, one double bed, a fridge, a few chairs, a table with a radio on it, and a sofa in the centre of the room. It was there he led her.

'Sorry about my paltry belongings but this isn't home.' Seeing she could care less if she were standing in Buckingham Palace, he went on. 'How did you find me?'

'Celeste.'

'Does Michael know you came?'

'No. In fact, he didn't have an easy night.'

'Sorry if I upset him, but I don't know what he expects of me. Or perhaps I do, I just don't know if I can give it. Years ago, I'd have been the first to encourage this reunion but now.'

She looked at a few packed bags in the corner. 'So you are leaving.'

'I think it's for the best.'

'For whom, you?' She sat on the edge of the sofa as if about to take flight.

Sitting at the other end, he leaned back and locked his hands behind his head. 'I'm ready to listen.'

'After you left last night, Michael said some things that sounded strange. But as I mulled over them, I realised how true they are. You have cut yourself off the human race, feeling safer in the jungle because there you can't be hurt. But neither can you be happy.'

'I like what I do.' He defended.

'And it's obvious you do. But have you ever wondered why your pictures of people are so beautiful? Your heart cries out for fellowship but you refuse to listen, frightened that it will be broken again. And for that very reason, you won't even take a chance on your grandson, running further, faster, and longer. Once, you took that chance and knew happiness, but today you're terrified, so you refuse to try.

'Michael needs you as much if not more than his son does. He loves his parents dearly but this is different. These are his roots, the family he was robbed of and he desperately needs you to fill the gaps that will make his life complete.' She took a breath. 'Afraid of the unknown, you won't even consider friendship. We all make mistakes, and granted, Benjamin's are so much worse than everybody else's, but no matter how much you punish yourself you couldn't have prevented the heartache he caused. Because you and he ended this way it doesn't mean that you and your son have to.'

Robert stared at her in silence, watching the bright blue eyes that could read a man like a book fill with emotion, the perfect mouth finding it difficult to control itself.

'You may think me presumptuous for coming here uninvited to say these things but I love Michael and when he hurts so do I and he's hurting deeply. He has tried so hard to do something about this situation and now feels as if you're throwing it all back in his face with your dispassionate attitude. I suppose he imagined that you'd be a knot of emotion.

'Don't you remember how it felt thirty years ago? The uncertainty, worry, fear, and finally the pain of discovering that your father caused this grief with his odd intentions? Heaven knows what drove him to it, but at the end he was remorseful.' Her eyes filled with tears, which she quickly wiped away. 'On the way here, I swore I wouldn't become emotional but I can't help myself. For three decades, you needed to know the truth, now that it's here; you no longer want it, dismissing it with a few words.

'All I know is that Sofia will die sad and lonely and you bitter and angry, not even reunited with your son. Please reconsider before you leave here and don't make another mistake you'll regret.'

'That's precisely why I have to go. Clear thought is only possible where one feels comfortable and for me, it's not here, where everything is sentimental, and I'm utterly confused. I never expected this. I had buried it and now I'm supposed to make a decision in a day? Michael isn't giving me any kind of chance.'

She jumped to her feet as if propelled by a motor. 'I too would have liked knowing you, but seeing that's impossible, I hope you'll find the peace you desperately seek in the jungles you obviously love so much.' Reaching in her handbag, she took out a thick envelope. 'Months ago when I went to the mansion for the first time, I found these, so when Michael asked me to come to Brazil, it was the first thing I thought you would need. Photographs can never replace what you've lost, but perhaps,' She wiped away fresh tears. 'I may be young but I too have made mistakes which I've regretted deeply and I can see you're about to do the same.' Then without another word, she ran out the door and down the stairs.

Robert sat in the same position for a few minutes, having had no time to open his mouth again, or to follow her, staring at the open door. Smiling wryly, he threw the envelope into a bag and got to his feet. Gathering the bags from the corner, he walked downstairs and knocked on a door.

'*Quem e?*' A woman's voice queried from within.

'*O senhor Robertson. Quero pagar.*' Mention of payment soon had the door open. 'I don't need the place anymore so you may do with the contents as you wish.'

CHAPTER TWENTY

Seeing Michael's downcast countenance as they walked into their bedroom at home, Christie put her arms around him. 'You did your best. Though, I admit, one would imagine that he'd be glad about finally knowing the truth.'

'Which is why I didn't expect such indifference. It's as if he's given up on life, and no longer cares. It's tragic but obviously I can't do anything about it.' He sat on the bed. 'Where's Michael Thomas?'

'I don't know who was happier to see whom, Martha, or him. Should have heard what she said when she saw the bruise.'

'And I think from now on, she travels with us. I'm not having strangers kill my son.'

'She'll like that.' Sitting beside him, she slipped a hand into his.

'I'm glad I didn't tell mom. But I wonder why Milo says she called a dozen times since yesterday.' The telephone rang, and groaning, he picked it up. 'Hello.'

'Where have you been?' Sofia asked across the miles.

Covering the mouthpiece, he stood up. 'Guess who.'

'No one knew where you were or how I could get hold of you.' Sofia continued.

'We had a short holiday.'

'Why didn't you leave a number? I was going out of my mind.'

'It was only a few days.'

'Do you know what can happen in a few days? World War III could have broken out, Chernobyl might have melted down again, and an oil spill could have wrecked our coastline.'

'That bad, what happened?'

'Edward is bouncing off walls; something is not right with his treatment. All he talks about is Robert. The doctor called me and said so much that I quite lost him.'

'When did this happen?'

'Two days ago.'

'We'll be down as soon as possible.'

Christie sank onto the bed tiredly. 'Do you think Edward knew what was happening with all those tests?'

'He looked calm and in control.' Michael knelt beside her.

'Probably because he's so full of drugs. I know I was afraid of him before but now I feel great pity when I see what he's become. Are you sure they look after him the way they're supposed to?'

'The doctors assure me they've figured it out and he'll be getting the very best treatment from now on.'

'I'm holding them to that because I'd hate for them to hurt him even more.'

He put a hand to her face. 'You have without a doubt the kindest heart I have ever met. With you looking over my shoulder how can I make a mistake?'

Smiling, she kissed his hand. 'Are we going anywhere else until Christmas?'

'I hadn't planned; do you want to go somewhere?'

'The furthest away I want to go is down to the village. I'm going to call Mary and Evy, if I can track her down, and tell them to forget about seeing me for the rest of the year. I think I need to sleep for a week.'

'Should I run you a bath?' He asked and stood up.

'No, I'm too tired to move.' Rolling onto her side, she made a gesture and closed her eyes.

Leaning over her, he saw she was already asleep. A tender smile crossed his lips as he straightened the blonde hair about her face. She was more beautiful now then when he first fell in love with her.

Kneeling on the lawn in front of her beloved rosebushes, Sofia eyed them critically. Something had to be done about this bug if she was to have decent blooms for Christmas. The thought of the holiday brought a smile to her lips. The children were coming from Greece and her heart filled with happiness. After the previous year's frantic search for Christie and Edward's eventual capture, she still thought of it all as a miracle. How odd though, now he too was tied to her. Unexpectedly, she couldn't bring herself to abandon him either. It was true; time and forgiveness were the best medicine.

Snipping a bud with a sharp movement, her thoughts strayed to the children's reaction when she'd jokingly commented,

'It couldn't have been much of a second honeymoon if Michael Thomas went with you.' She'd hoped to lift Michael's spirits, which were in a depression she couldn't associate with Edward's condition.

Something peculiar happened. Christie didn't smile or joke. Instead, her hand slipped into Michael's and held it tightly. 'It wasn't.'

Sofia felt an immense sadness in Michael, something he couldn't share with anyone but Christie. No matter how many years lay ahead, she and Michael would probably never be as close as they had been meant to be. The idea filled her heart with pain. As for Christie, gone were her girlish ways and mindless gossip, she had found her soul mate and with him she shared herself completely.

Then Michael did something that surprised her more. He let go of Christie's hand, stood up, and put his arms around her, somehow telling her something she couldn't understand. Then leaving the room, he went to the garden.

'What was that about?' Sofia asked, her heart constricting curiously.

Also rising, Christie repeated Michael's performance. 'When it no longer hurts, he'll tell you. Did I mention that Michael Thomas fell and had an ugly bruise?'

Sofia had hardly been interested; Michael was suffering. Unfortunately, there was little she could do but wait until he was ready to tell her about it.

Tired of looking at the roses, Sofia got to her feet, removed the gloves, and threw them onto the garden bench. Going inside, she fetched herself an orange juice.

'Mom! You're looking great.'

'Hello darling.' Jane hugged Christie, did the same to Michael, then turned to Michael Thomas. 'My adorable baby, have we got a surprise for you,' and smothered him with kisses.

Michael looked around disbelieving. 'This is the welcoming committee, one?'

'Rob is still at work and your mother went shopping.'

Michael glanced at his watch. 'Almost five o'clock, on a Friday afternoon, in Johannesburg. If it involves this so-called surprise, it must really be something, probably some frivolous toy he doesn't need.'

Jane laughed. 'After that long flight, I suggest you go rest so we may have a wonderful party tonight.'

'Party?'

'Just family,' stopping outside Christie's old room, Jane announced happily. 'I've had it redone as it was totally unsuitable for your needs. Michael Thomas and Martha are down that way.' She pointed further down the passage.

Christie opened the door. 'Thanks mom, it's lovely.'

'I'll see Martha and Michael Thomas to their rooms and I expect you for dinner at seven.'

'Any ideas?' Michael asked as he closed the door behind them.

Christie glanced around the beautifully decorated room in rose, black, and white. 'She always loved a beautiful house and is no doubt thrilled she could throw out all my old junk. As for what's going on, not a clue.' Sitting on the bed, she let her hand run over the bedspread. 'Do you suppose we could go down to Cape Town for a week after Christmas?'

'Is Newa having problems again?'

'Going crazy because Jeffrey hasn't painted anything but babies or close impressions thereof ever since Gloria fell pregnant, must be his baby period. But if she can't get him out of it, how can I?'

Approaching her, he fell down on his knees and put a hand to her face. 'Because he listens to you. Christie, I never asked but I've wondered-'

'What?'

'No, I shouldn't think this way. I did once and made an utter mess of everything.'

Her mouth opened with realisation. 'You're jealous of Jeffrey? Would you still love me if we had ever,' she made a gesture with her hands.

'No matter what.'

She smiled. 'It always thrills me when you give me the right answers. But how could I when all I did was think about you? Don't you know that I could never let anyone else be this close to me?'

'I love you.' He whispered and pulled her down to him.

'Daddy!' Christie hugged him.

Rob looked her up and down. 'You become lovelier by the month and that grandson of mine is delightful. Would your husband consider spending a few months down here at a time? I miss you the minute you walk out the door.'

'Oh, daddy. But what's the occasion; mom won't tell us a thing.'

He chuckled. 'You'll find out soon enough.'

Michael eyed the living room suspiciously, as if knowing something was hiding behind a piece of furniture and it would soon pounce on him. 'How's Edward?'

'Doing very well. Sofia has been to see him regularly over the last few weeks.'

'Really,' Michael began and then stared incredulously at the woman who entered the room. 'Mom! What on earth? You look gorgeous.'

Christie was equally stupefied. "Positively glowing", she thought. 'Thea, you look ten years younger.'

'Sofia, that remote control of yours is on the blink. Why can't people use good old-fashioned manual drawbridges-' the voice stopped. 'Good evening, everyone.'

'As Evy would say, knock me down with a feather.' Christie stared in astonishment.

'What the hell are you doing here?' Michael asked, clearly shaken. 'I thought you went back to that damn river.'

'I did. But Christie's words and photographs,' Robert made an apologetic face. 'Where did you find that pile of my brothers', my mother, even Elizabeth and Edward? The memories were so haunting that I couldn't ignore them.' He stretched out his hands towards her. 'Never take this lady for granted for she knows a thing or two, especially when it comes to making you happy.'

'Stop embarrassing me.'

'If you hadn't come see me and given me sleepless nights, I'd probably not be here today, and what I'd have missed.' Robert turned to Michael. 'May I shake your hand or haven't you forgiven me yet?'

'Of course he has.' Christie encouraged as she saw Michael's face. He was so disconcerted; he didn't know what to do.

The handshake turned into a bear hug and feelings Michael couldn't explain filled him. He was glad, and somehow angry. Relieved that the search was over, that his questions could finally be answered, yet, he felt as if he were about to embark upon unfamiliar seas, devoid of charts. He owed much to Andrea and Sarah, for they had made him the man he was. Or was there something to inheritance? After all, Andrea was his uncle and if there were similarities wasn't it to be expected? Would Robert stay? If he did, would they find common ground to build some kind of relationship, even if not one of father and son? Looking at Sofia, he knew she was their bond. Was she strong enough to keep them together? Only time would tell.

Gazing at Michael Thomas as he ran across the lawn at the Powell mansion in his unsteady steps, Michael closed his eyes and leaned back in the wicker chair, breathing in deeply. Why was it that he suddenly liked these African skies more? Perhaps his father-in-law was right in suggesting he look at some business ventures. After all, what was he supposed to do with Powells? It hardly appealed to him and he'd heard Robert enough times to know that he still wanted none of it.

The mansion however, after tonight's dinner, would go through a restoration. He'd asked Robert if he saw the possibility of getting the dining room into some decent shape for a grand Christmas celebration as Christie had invited just about everyone she considered important in their lives.

Robert looked at him. 'Son, it's your house-'

'Not really, it's still yours. So it's all right to do a bit of fixing?'

'Just tell me what you want done.' Then Robert did the only thing he knew, turned to Sofia, and asked her to help him because he wasn't sure about anything in Johannesburg anymore.

Days had passed since that first evening and Michael was finding it increasingly easier to talk to the man who had lived in his mind for so long. Christie had been right about the reality of people who existed in another's thoughts, but not concerning Robert, he'd been the one with the shattered dreams. Years ago, he'd formulated an image around a face he'd discovered; now he had to remind himself to give others a chance to prove themselves.

So far, Robert seemed to be doing extremely well, treating Elizabeth, but especially Edward with a tenderness few imagined possible in such a rugged man, although, nothing seemed to surprise Sofia. Perhaps he had rushed ahead of himself again and made too many assumptions. He'd done that once before and almost lived to regret it.

'Michael,' Sofia called. 'What are you dreaming of?' She smoothed his hair, feeling the thrill of being able to touch him without fear.

He glanced around. 'Where's Michael Thomas?'

'That's what I was telling you as you travelled in the clouds. Over there.' She pointed to the end of the hyacinths.

Rising from the chair, he peered over the flowers. Michael Thomas sat on the grass, his hands full of rose petals, Robert clicking his camera in deep concentration as if he were about to win a prize for the shots. 'What are they doing?'

'Getting to know one another. He would have been a wonderful father, as you are.'

'I'm certainly trying. Come sit with me.' He reached for her hand. 'You still haven't told me about your reunion.'

Ah yes, that meeting weeks ago.

She had come in from the garden and was drinking an orange juice when the doorbell rang. She swung the door open. 'Jane-' the words died on her lips. 'I apologise, I thought you were a friend.'

The man looked at her curiously. 'Hello, Sofia, how have you been?'

'Have we met?'

'A lifetime ago.'

Everything happened at once. Her mind went blank, she couldn't speak, the juice all over the floor, and the glass in shards. Shaking uncontrollably, she leaned against the wall, thinking she was hallucinating. She had imagined what it would be like if the moment came, but nothing had warned her that it would be so vivid and shocking.

'Are you at least glad to see me?' He asked with concern as he watched the drowning eyes.

'Robert, where have you been?'

'Lost,' he wiped the tears away.

'But… how… when…'

'Our son found me, and Christie gave me the address.'

'How is that possible?'

'I know a little, so you'll have to ask them for details.'

Her eyes filled with tears again. 'They never told me.'

'Oh Sofia,' he sighed and wrapped his arms around her.

Sofia smiled with remembrance. 'It's crazy, but it was as if we'd been in contact with each other. So how did Mr Hamilton find him?'

He explained.

'Do you sometimes think about it all?'

'Not anymore, especially concerning Christie. I realise we haven't been married long but I can't imagine another woman knowing me the way she does,' the corners of his mouth turned up a little.

'Edward was right in that respect; she was raised for you, just not by me. I had never considered it until I noticed your interest. How old was she?'

'Sixteen. I was captivated as soon as I saw that smile and amazing blue eyes.'

The huge dining room was splendidly set in its Christmas finery, and Robert nodded approval at what the people had done in so short a time. Overall, the entire house needed serious renovations but for one night, one room would do.

Obviously, he didn't know most of the people who were coming to dinner, but they were all family and friends of Sofia, Michael's, and Christie's. The ones he had already met, he already liked. Christie had been right, he did need fellowship. He believed he was going to enjoy meeting every one of them.

When everyone eventually sat down, Robert felt a knot in his stomach. Elaine, his mother, had always dreamt of filling this house with happiness. How badly Benjamin had messed up. Chasing some senseless pursuit, he had destroyed his own empire. Now, Michael, his grandson, had managed to resurrect it.

Christie was ecstatic when she saw Mary and Evy. She'd been worried both would excuse themselves as they stayed so far away. Mary would be in the US another three months before returning to Rhodes and Evy would go to Japan in February.

And then she became happier when she saw Stephen do a funny double take when he saw Evy in all her regal height trying to re-attach mistletoe that had come loose. He was beside her in three seconds flat, offered to help, and put an arm around her waist so he could lift her up. She watched the sweet scene as Evy blushed when Stephen whispered something. Christie guessed he'd said, "it's mistletoe, I have to kiss you". And there, a gentle brushing of lips that wanted to be so much more. Only, how was this going to work with one in Cape Town and the other all over the planet? Why was she concerned, if they wanted to be together they would find a way and make it work.

Sandra, Donald, Emmett, Brenda, and Newa, the friends she would treasure forever.

Stephanie and Jaqueline, the beautiful girls, raced around the room with Theo, Andrew and Georgia's son, and Michael Thomas; both giggling uncontrollably out of their little heads. Brian chased, and Ricky, the teenager, pretended he wasn't enjoying himself.

Poor Gloria had eaten a little too much of something, and being pregnant, she couldn't quite move now. Christie watched Jeffrey warmly, glad he'd finally found his true love. Both deserved the happiness she saw was coming to them.

Uncle Peter and aunt Patricia couldn't stop looking at their daughter, both fretting about how she felt. "It's probably only indigestion," Christie thought and smiled.

Andrew and Georgia, Daniel and Cathy, Christie didn't know well at all but she would make the effort, and perhaps build new friendships.

She had wondered how Andrea and Sarah would deal with Robert's presence, if resentment would grip them when they saw Michael's unashamed interest in his biological father. But they seemed to be handling it well and knowing the truth was almost always salve to hurt feelings.

Her own parents were at peace.

Paul and Mary sat talking excitedly. Christie tried to imagine what it could possibly be as neither knew much about the other's field. Paul and psychology, what kind of question was that? He was a happy-go-lucky guy, who did not break his head about serious stuff. Mary, goodness, she ran miles from dresses, and she such an attractive girl, but don't tell her that because she won't believe it. Those two had been close for so long, she wondered when they'd eventually see each other.

Christie glanced at Sofia. Finally, that look was gone from her face. Christie had known it ever since she could see, that sad yeaning that tore at her own heart because she had always known that although Sofia loved her, there was someone else missing. But he was here now, actually, both of them.

Robert, she was going to enjoy herself discovering things about Michael through him.

'Sweetheart,' Michael called. She'd been quite lost for the past ten minutes, just studying everyone around the table.

'Sorry, did you say something?'

'I asked if you'd like to go for a walk. It's a little hot.'

'I'd love to.'

Holding her hand, he took her outside, and then started walking down the garden path. 'Do you think my parents will marry?'

She made a cute face. 'Maybe, but what I do know for certain is that you're happy.'

'Thanks to you,'

Stopping, she put a gentle hand to his face. 'I only helped him make the right decision. Now, he'll keep doing that on his own. You just have to believe in him as much as I'm willing to, then, let him forgive the past and move on. I realise there will be times when you won't know what to do, when you'll feel more like strangers than father and son, but no matter how hard or crazy everything seems, you have to give it a chance.'

'Every morning, as I open my eyes, I see how blessed I am to have you lying next to me, knowing that I love you deeper than yesterday. Then, I think it's impossible I'll ever love you more. But tomorrow, I always do.'

"Love is strange," she thought. All had dreamt, searched and it seemed, finally found it. At least for now, because who knew what tomorrow brought? Perhaps more heartache, or even sorrow. Now too, she believed Edward; there was madness in love. She knew it with certainty because she felt it every time she looked at the man who now stood before her.

A little sadness crossed her eyes. One that took her into the darkness she never wanted to revisit. Love could also exist in madness and that somehow exonerated Edward and the past, making it more forgivable, forgettable, and bearable. Yet, nowhere was it written that the future would be painless or perfect.

 Athina Paris lives in South Africa but spent her formative years in Mozambique, where she was born. Years in convents and boarding schools prompted a deep curiosity, which quickly developed into an avid interest in reading and storytelling and led to a lifelong obsession with the written word and books. By fifteen, she had discovered ancient civilizations and became fascinated with various mythologies; a love she has kept to this day.

She studied Interior Design then turned to Creative Writing and followed that with Scriptwriting.

She became a spectator of human nature, quiet and shy, she preferred recording conduct and so built a treasure-trove of observations from which she drew the plots and settings for her romantic novels.

Set in faraway and exotic places, Athina's romantic works take her characters on voyages of self-discovery while dealing with catastrophic love lives in an imperfect world.

A stint as a high school English teacher polished her skills, a position she has vacated to concentrate on her professional goals of writing, editing, and proofreading.

If you enjoyed reading this book, please leave a review and let Athina know.

Here are more titles by Athina:

 Knight Kisses

 When Dani Smiled

 All I Ever Wanted: Jessie

RockHill Publishing LLC

There are some lessons that only time can teach, but you do not learn talent, you only perfect it over time.

www.rockhillpublishing.com

www.ingramcontent.com/pod-product-compliance
Lightning Source LLC
Chambersburg PA
CBHW060756210726
48292CB00013B/201